D1601484

Investigating Dickens' Style

Investigating Dickens' Style

A Collocational Analysis

Masahiro Hori

First published 2004 by
PALGRAVE MACMILLAN
Houndmills, Basingstoke, Hampshire RG21 6XS and
175 Fifth Avenue,
New York, N.Y. 10010
Companies and representatives throughout the world

PALGRAVE MACMILLAN is the global academic imprint of the Palgrave Macmillan division of St. Martin's Press, LLC and of Palgrave Macmillan Ltd. Macmillan® is a registered trademark in the United States, United Kingdom and other countries. Palgrave is a registered trademark in the European Union and other countries.

ISBN 1–4039–2051–6

This book is printed on paper suitable for recycling and made from fully managed and sustained forest sources.

A catalogue record for this book is available from the British Library.

Library of Congress Cataloging-in-Publication Data
Hori, Masahiro.
    Investigating Dickens' style : a collocational analysis / Masahiro Hori.
        p.   cm.
    Includes bibliographical references and index.
    ISBN 1–4039–2051–6
    1. Dickens, Charles, 1812–1870 – Literary style.   2. English language –
19th century – style.   I. Title.

PR4594.H67   2004
823'.9–dc22

                                                            2003064650

10   9   8   7   6   5   4   3   2   1
13 12 11 10 09 08 07 06 05 04

Printed and bound in Great Britain by
Antony Rowe Ltd, Chippenham and Eastbourne

For my wife, Yoko Hori

Contents

List of Figures

List of Tables

Foreword

I had the good fortune to host Professor Masahiro Hori in the Department of Theoretical and Applied Linguistics of the University of Edinburgh during the 2001–2002 academic year, when he was 'breaking the back' of the book you now hold. Our weekly meetings were like a master class in the problems and potentialities of a stylistics grounded in corpus linguistic analysis, with Professor Hori as master and I his intensely interested and mildly combative pupil. The pupil learned a staggering amount. As for the master, he benefited mostly from the discipline of preparing for our weekly meetings, moderately from my insights as a reasonably well-read native speaker of English, and occasionally from a hard question of mine that he had to formulate an answer to. I say 'had to', but the truth is that most scholars have learned to duck really hard questions. Part of my great admiration for Professor Hori is that he never took the easy way out, no matter how much time and effort it took to satisfy his sparring partner.

What I learned over the course of the year, and what readers of this book will learn, falls into three main areas. The first is spelled out in the book's main title, *Investigating Dickens' Style* – though *styles* would have been no less appropriate, since at least two distinct styles are employed in the book which serves as the main study example, *Bleak House*. On the other hand, one might argue that Dickens' genius lies precisely in his ability to merge such distinct stylistic strands into a synthetic whole. Professor Hori has been working on Dickensian stylistics for many years, and has been the person primarily responsible for the marvellous Japanese corpus apparatus that is now at our disposal. So I would have stood to learn a lot about Dickens' style from him even prior to his latest research. But his new findings cranked up the level of excitement all the more.

There have of course been countless attempts to describe the features that make Dickens' prose so immediately recognizable. In the case of *Bleak House*, it has become a 'received idea' that what distinguishes the chapters written as third-person narrative from those written in the first-person voice of Mrs Allan Woodcourt (*née* Esther Hawdon, *alias* Esther Summerson) is the simplicity, candour and naivety of the heroine's account. The evidence cited for this is usually lexical: overt expressions of emotion (always more common in first than in third-person narrative), but also an absence of the verbal creativity and tendency to neo-logize that Dickens is prone to in his unmediated authorial voice. Yet by examining the language of *Bleak House* not word-by-word or sentence-by-sentence, but as *collocations* – word-groups that form a closely joined unit – Hori shows us how Esther's voice quickly grows in confidence and maturity from the early chapters onwards, so that, for most of the book, her own language is no less original in the way it joins words together than the third-person narrator's is. This insight has enormous potential for shaping new interpretations, not just of *Bleak House*, but of Dickens' entire oeuvre.

The second area in which Hori has made a substantial contribution is in refining a methodology for bringing together corpus data, linguistic analysis and stylistic interpretation. His work addresses a wide range of fundamental questions concerning the nature of linguistic and literary originality and creativity, and how corpus data can be used and misused in assessing a particular author or text in this regard. Even text analysts who have no particular interest in Dickens can learn a great deal from the approach Hori has developed and his explanations of why it has taken this particular shape rather than other conceivable ones. The robustness of his findings adds strongly, in my view, to the overall case for taking the collocation as the basic unit of language analysis, as British linguists and applied linguists have been arguing for more than half a century, with a rapidly increasing number of people taking heed of their arguments in the last decade.

The third area in which Hori's work marks a significant step forward involves what is sometimes referred to as *voice*, though there is wide variation in what that term is taken to mean among those who use it. What I mean by it is the conglomeration of features that makes the output of a particular speaker or writer identifiable as belonging to him or her. Had you asked me in the autumn of 2001 what were the most important such features, I would have pointed to such categories as lexical choice, lexical variety, lexical density, sentence length and intricacy, presence or absence of colloquialism, ellipsis, ambiguity, irony, metaphor and other figurative language, as well as any idiosyncrasies of grammar and syntax. By the spring of 2002 Masahiro Hori had convinced me irrevocably that what gives individual character to a writer's voice is, more than anything else, how he or she combines words, not into propositions or sentences, but into collocations. Something very fundamental is clearly happening at that level. Linguistics has largely neglected it up to now, and a serious shift in the research agenda is needed so that we can understand what it is with greater precision.

This way of looking at texts from the perspective of voice grounded in collocation has already greatly enriched my own teaching and research, and I am certain that it will continue to do so for many years to come. I expect that it will do the same for others as well. It is difficult to imagine how a work in stylistics might make a more profound or a more welcome contribution.

These comments have merely scratched the surface of this book's riches. I have tried to emphasize that, while its appeal to Dickens specialists will be evident, it should in fact be much more widely shared – something I am in a good position to emphasize, not being a Dickens specialist myself. This is not to imply however that Dickens studies on their own do not provide sufficient justification for this book. In fact, I had been much looking forward to sending a copy of this book to my old undergraduate professor of English literature, Herbert Barrows, who convinced me nearly thirty years ago that Dickens is the greatest writer of at least the last 200 years and *Bleak House* the greatest novel in the English language. I know he would have found the book enlightening and stimulating. Sadly, Professor Barrows died in August 2002, just weeks after Professor Hori and I completed our colloquy, during which I often thought of him, recalling how his teaching enriched my youth, every bit as much as Masahiro Hori's wonderful research has enriched my thinking today.

JOHN E. JOSEPH
Professor of Applied Linguistics
University of Edinburgh

Acknowledgements

Thich Nhat Hanh, a Vietnamese Zen Buddhist, has said, 'If you are a poet, you will see clearly that there is a cloud floating in this sheet of paper. Without a cloud, there will be no rain; without rain, the trees cannot grow; and without trees, we cannot make paper.'

Though I am no poet, I can see clearly many faces smiling in every page of this book. Without the aid of several people, this book would not exist. I credit three respected teachers for leading me on my odyssey of English Philology and Stylistics. Hiroyuki Ito introduced me to the study of the language and style of Charles Dickens, and has continued to provide a healthy amount of advice and guidance. At the reading circle under his leadership, Bunshichi Miyauchi first initiated me into the intriguing and profound language and style of Shakespeare. The late Gerald Sullivan stimulated me to become more involved in the study of word stories, and we later co-authored a series of books, *My Word!*, as a result. These three teachers repeatedly encouraged me to publish this present work.

Without Richard Gilbert's professional friendship and laborious editing, this book might not have come to be. As a careful reader of this script he provided invaluable comments and many helpful suggestions. During my one-year sabbatical at the University of Edinburgh I had the opportunity, each Tuesday afternoon, to meet with John Joseph, who listened to my presentations and afforded excellent insights. Norman Macleod, at the same university, also kindly found the time to discuss my ideas and read my papers concerning Dickens' style. Knud Sørensen's opinions regarding my project convinced me of the significance of research into Dickens' language in terms of collocational analysis. Yutaka Tsutsumi contributed to the creation of 'Picking-up Dialogue and Non-dialogue' for this research. Tatsuaki Tomioka patiently read through the draft of this book and provided many helpful comments. Joseph Tomei gave me appropriate advice when I was in trouble.

In addition to those who have directly helped me accomplish this research project, many others have indirectly contributed. Some are senior professors and friends at my alma mater who have looked forward to the publication of this book, but more, provided relaxation with their good humour and bonhomie: Shoshichiro Adachi, Michitaka Iki, Yoshinori Watanabe, Takashi Kaijima, Sadahiro Kumamoto, Shiro

Ikeda, and Mitsuru Orita. As a member of the Kumamoto English Stylistics and Philology circle, I had many chances to discuss ideas concerning Dickens' language and style with Yoshiya Kojyo, Yuko Ikeda, Osamu Ueda, Keisuke Koguchi, Jun'ichi Kamo, Tomoji Tabata, Kazuho Murata, Hirotoshi Takeshita, and Noriko Murata. I am also grateful to Masanori Toyota for his continuous encouragement regarding my research of English stylistics, from my university days to the present.

This book is funded by the Kumamoto Gakuen University Press Grant-in-Aid for publication, 2004.

M. H.

Abbreviations

COBUILD	*COBUILD English Collocations on CD-ROM* (1995) London: Harper Collins Publishers.
COD	*Concise Oxford English Dictionary of Current English* (1995).
ECF	*Eighteenth-Century Fiction on CD-ROM* (1996). This database comprises the works of 30 of the most influential writers of the British Isles in the eighteenth century. It contains 77 collected works or 96 discrete items.
EP	Eric Partridge's *A Dictionary of Slang and Unconventional English* (8th edn, 1983).
LGSWE	*Longman Grammar of Spoken and Written English* (1999).
NCF	*Nineteenth-Century Fiction on CD-ROM* (2000). This database contains 250 complete works of prose fiction by 109 authors from the period 1781 to 1901.
NCFWD	A nineteenth-century corpus of fiction (approximately 2.2 million words) excluding Dickens' texts.
OED	*The Oxford English Dictionary* and its Supplement.
OED2	*The Oxford English Dictionary on Compact Disc, 2nd edn, Macintosh Version* (1993).
(OMF II, 5)	This means (*Our Mutual Friend* Book the Second, Chapter 5).

The following is a list of the texts compiled in the Dickens Corpus:

SB	*Sketches by Boz* (1833–36)
PP	*The Pickwick Papers* (1836–37)
OT	*Oliver Twist* (1837–39)
NN	*Nicholas Nickleby* (1838–39)
OCS	*The Old Curiosity Shop* (1840–41)
BR	*Barnaby Rudge* (1841)
AN	*American Notes* (1842)
MC	*Martin Chuzzlewit* (1843–44)
CC	*A Christmas Carol* (1843)
Chimes	*The Chimes* (1844)
CH	*The Cricket on the Hearth* (1845)
BL	*The Battle of Life* (1846)
HM	*The Haunted Man* (1848)

DS	*Dombey and Son* (1846–48)
DC	*David Copperfield* (1849–50)
BH	*Bleak House* (1852–53)
HT	*Hard Times* (1854)
LD	*Little Dorrit* (1855–57)
TTC	*A Tale of Two Cities* (1859)
UT	*The Uncommercial Traveller* (1860)
GE	*Great Expectations* (1860–61)
OMF	*Our Mutual Friend* (1864–65)
ED	*The Mystery of Edwin Drood* (1869–70)

Part I
Introduction

1
Theoretical Background

1.1 A short history of the study of collocation

In 'Modes of Meaning' (1957) J.R. Firth advocated the importance of the study of collocation as a means of investigating semantic statements of meaning in descriptive linguistics. Consequent to this article, the study of collocation may be chronologically classified into three periods: (1) the 1960s, when collocation was deepened theoretically and various topics and problems relating to collocation were discussed; (2) the 1970s, when the methodology of the study of collocation was suggested and some tentative approaches were made; and (3) from the 1980s onwards, when the results and achievements of the study of collocation began to appear. What now follows is a more in-depth study of each of these periods.

In the 1960s the most important event concerning the study of collocation was a staff seminar held at the School (now Department) of Applied Linguistics, Edinburgh University, in 1961. Among the participants would have been M.A.K. Halliday, John Sinclair, Angus McIntosh, J.C. Catford and Ronald Mackin, all of whom were then on the Edinburgh University staff. (J.R. Firth himself was a visiting professor in the Department of English Language and General Linguistics from 1958, following his retirement from the University of London, until his death in 1960.) One of the topics discussed at the seminar was collocation, and in 1966 Halliday, Sinclair and McIntosh published articles on collocation that were partly based upon these discussions. I would now like to consider these papers and briefly point out their main characteristics and importance in terms of the study of collocation.

Recognizing the importance of lexical studies in descriptive linguistics – as repeatedly stressed by Firth – Halliday, in 'Lexis as a linguistic level' (1966), deepened the theoretical study of collocation and pointed out various problems relating to collocation, for instance a need 'to devise methods appropriate to the description of these patterns in the light of a lexical theory that will be complementary to, but not part of, grammatical theory' (p. 148). Thus he developed the tentative theoretical outline which he had earlier presented in 'Categories of the Theory of Grammar' (1961). According to Halliday, this view was already implicit in Firth's recognition of a collocational level of language. However, since in Halliday's view collocations of an item were not limited to immediately adjacent items, his main interest turned to cohesion, a more lexicogrammatical topic within the more extensive environment of language as observed in the term 'collocational cohesion' (Halliday and Hasan, 1976: 287) and described as follows: 'this is simply a cover term for the cohesion that results from the co-occurrence of lexical items that are in some way or other typically associated with one another, because they tend to occur in similar environments'.

John Sinclair's paper, 'Beginning the Study of Lexis' (1966) is a preliminary article that presents both a theoretical background and practical problems regarding the computer-assisted study of collocation. Nearly all of the technical terms which are today used in the study of collocation are defined and treated in this paper: node, span, collocate, cluster, formal meaning, casual collocation, significant collocation, range and lexical sets. In addition to these key terms, Sinclair discusses aspects of language – polymorphemic lexical terms, homograph, polysemy – and identifies the problem of language varieties that may create practical difficulties in the use of computers in handling the data involved in studies of collocation. Paul van Buren's paper, titled 'Preliminary aspects of mechanisation in lexis' (1967), helped to clarify and modify Sinclair's ideas for the computer-assisted study of collocation. Van Buren discussed in more detail 'the three problems that are of central importance in the study of lexis, i.e., definitions of the concepts "*cluster*" (and by implication "collocation" and "lexical item"), "*homograph*", and "*multiverbality*"' (p. 89), which had been only partially treated by Halliday and Sinclair.

Halliday and Sinclair's central interest was focused on usual collocations of common words in current English, but Angus McIntosh chose to deal with unusual collocations in his paper, 'Patterns and ranges' (1966). McIntosh proposed that the notion of *range* 'has to do with the specific collocations we make in a series of particular instances' in connection with lexis, which is distinguished from *pattern*, which 'has to do with the structures of the sentences we make' on the grammatical side (p. 199). McIntosh's paper also differs from those of Halliday and Sinclair in that, while Halliday and Sinclair dealt with usual collocation in non-literary language, McIntosh considered the importance of unusual collocation in literature.

What unites these three papers is that they each in different ways emphasize that the study of collocation is the study of lexis as an independent part of language. The three also have complementary arguments for the study of collocation in that Halliday presented the collocational approach in the study of lexis, Sinclair promoted this approach by discussing its implementation by means of computer-based research, and McIntosh extended the approach by his work on unusual collocation, an area which was not adequately dealt with by Halliday and Sinclair.

The 1970s, the second period in the study of collocation, may be said to be the period of pilot or experimental studies in the area of collocation. Two representative researchers of the period were John Sinclair and Sydney Greenbaum.

Sinclair and his group, basing their work on the theoretical outline provided by Halliday (1966), Sinclair (1966) and McIntosh (1966), started the linguistic computational project for the study of 'meaning by collocation' advocated by Firth, and published *English Lexical Studies* in 1970. The theoretical background in this book (Sinclair et al. 1970) followed Sinclair (1966), but the definitions of technical terms were more precise in this later work. For example, the definition of 'collocation' in *English Lexical Studies* was 'the co-occurrence of two items in a text within [a] specified environment' (p. 15), but in fact 'collocation' was limited to 'significant collocation', which was defined as 'regular collocation between two items, such that they co-occur more often than their respective frequencies and the length of text in which they appear would predict' (p. 15). The degree of significance of the collocational frequencies is statistically tested, and collocation that is not acknowledged as significant is treated as 'casual collocation', and therefore is not examined. In addition, in 1966 Sinclair defined the term 'span' as three lexical items before and after each node, whereas in 1970 he defined it as four items on either side of a node.

In *English Lexical Studies*, the first computer-assisted study of collocation, Sinclair and his group of researchers knew from the beginning the problems of the text size and the limitations on computer performance. Concerning text size, they stated, 'in order to describe fully the collocational behaviour of even the 3000 most common words in the language a text of several million words would be required' (p. 23). The small size of Sinclair et al.'s texts – 135,000 words of British spoken English, 50,000 words of British written English, and approximately one million words of American written English from the 'Brown, University text' (known later as the Brown Corpus) – limited the validity of their study. The value of *English Lexical Studies*, however, lies in the fact that it helped to establish some basic research methods and principles and provided a firm base for future research on collocation.

Greenbaum's *Verb-Intensifier Collocations in English: an Experimental Approach* (1970: 10) begins by criticizing Sinclair's corpus study of collocation as an item-oriented approach: 'Unfortunately, the study, as envisaged in his [Sinclair's] article, would be based exclusively on linear co-occurrence of items, and would not include the syntactic and semantic statements that are often essential in a treatment of collocations.' Instead of basing an investigation on a corpus either written or spoken, Greenbaum proposed a method of 'native informant' tests that include the syntactic and semantic aspects of collocation of an item. From his informant experiments Greenbaum gave the example of the collocation of *much* (the asterisk signifies an ungrammatical sentence):

> *Much* collocates with a preceding verb *like* in negative sentences but not in affirmative sentences. We can therefore say:
> I don't *like* him *much*.
> but not
> *I *like* him *much*.
> However, this last sentence becomes perfectly acceptable if *much* is premodified, for example:
> I *like* him *very/too/so much*. (pp. 11–12)

Greenbaum's result is interesting and valuable, but there are some problems with his approach. For example, according to Greebaum's informants in completion tests, '*agree* appeared in 82 per cent of the responses after *I entirely*' (p. 80). However, it appears that Greenbaum did not sufficiently consider the responses from the remaining 18 per cent of his informants nor did he make clear his definition of 'native informants'. In addition, this approach is limited to the study of present-day English – for the simple reason that it is impossible to find native informants from past centuries – and cannot be applied to the historical study of collocation.

From the 1980s onward, the rapid development of computers and corpus linguistics greatly advanced Sinclair's project, which developed to become what is now known as the COBUILD project. The huge COBUILD corpus, otherwise known as the 'Bank of English', has not only contributed to the study of collocation but also the compilation of dictionaries. With respect to the contribution of the corpus to the study of collocation, we also have Sinclair's book, *Corpus, Concordance, Collocation* (1991). This book is chiefly composed of papers Sinclair wrote in the 1980s and includes not only a comprehensive overview of the theoretical and methodological background to the study of collocation but also presents the results of studies on the collocations of words such as 'yield', 'set', 'of' and 'back'. Then, in 1994, Kjellmer's *A Dictionary of English Collocations: Based on the Brown Corpus* was published in three volumes. This publication, however, had serious disadvantages in text size, methodology and user-friendliness, and was based on a corpus of only one million words. The greatest achievement for the study of collocation was to come a year later with the *COBUILD English Collocations on CD-ROM* (1985). *COBUILD English Collocations* was produced from a corpus of 200 million words and not only compiles the 10,000 headwords regarded as the core vocabulary of English, but also presents 2,600,000 authentic examples, taken from The Bank of English, showing collocations in their actual use. (There is an important dictionary, Senkichiro Katsumata's *New Dictionary of English Collocations*, which does not follow Firthian theory. It was published in Japan in 1939, eighteen years earlier than Firth's advocacy of the study of collocation in 1957, and revised in 1958. In terms of his dictionary's functional characteristics Katsumata stated in his preface that he collected 'carefully and widely' units of expression formed by a habitual association of words and compiled the collocations according to the grammatical structures or combinations of them (my translation). This is certainly a lexicogrammatical dictionary.)

Above, I have attempted a short historical survey of the study of collocation, using as starting point the 1966 papers of Halliday, Sinclair and McIntosh, influenced by Firth's paper 'Modes of Meaning' (1957). Halliday and Sinclair's papers have shown results in both the study of lexis and the area of methodology. However, McIntosh's attempt at a stylistic study of collocation, which Firth wanted especially to advocate in his paper 'Modes of Meaning', has not seen such satisfactory development. This topic will be discussed further in the following sections.

1.2 Collocations in literary language

As observed above, the main focus of collocational study has been directed toward a computer-assisted approach to habitual collocations in contemporary English, as a study of lexis in descriptive linguistics, promoted mainly by John Sinclair. The project he began at Edinburgh

University in 1963 and continued at the University of Birmingham in 1967, after 'a fallow period from September 1965 until January 1967' (Sinclair 1970: 15), is now called the University of Birmingham/COBUILD project. As of its latest release in January 2002 'the corpus [amounts] to 450 million words and it continues to grow with the constant addition of new material' (Bank of English 2002). The COBUILD corpus has contributed greatly not only to the linguistic analysis of present-day English but also to pedagogical aspects, such as the compilation of dictionaries. However, with respect to a stylistic study of collocation in literary language, neither the COBUILD project nor any other projects have as yet produced satisfactory results, although their corpora include fictional texts. Particularly regarding the study of collocations of writers and their literary texts before the twentieth century, there are very few papers other than tentative articles written about Anglo-Saxon poetry, Chaucer and Shakespeare (see, for example, Yamamoto (1950); Daunt (1966); Masui (1967); Oizumi (1971)).

When Firth advocated the importance of the study of collocation in 'Modes of Meaning' (1957), his overall interest was in providing statements of meaning in descriptive linguistics in general; his specific focus was the way in which linguistic collocational analysis could be applied to the stylistic study of collocation:

> The present essay is an attempt to sketch the framework of a language of description in English about English for those who use English, to illustrate what I understand by linguistic analysis, and especially to show the dangers of an over-facile superficial use of the word *stylistics*, without an adequate logical syntax or even without considering the essential prerequisites of linguistics. (p. 190)

His definition of collocation was wider than Sinclair's 'collocation is the occurrence of two or more words within a short space of each other in a text' (Sinclair 1991: 170), which has led to the study of significant collocations or usual collocations. In other words, from the beginning, Firth's study of collocations included not only usual collocations but also unique or, in some cases, unusual collocations, whereas Sinclair's computer-assisted research has, to date, only focused on usual collocations.

As for usual collocations, Firth assumed that not only general collocational patterns of common words but also particular collocational patterns reflecting given texts or registers, and personal styles were important objects of study: 'This kind of study of the distribution of common words may be classified into general or usual collocations and more restricted technical or personal collocations' (Firth 1957: 195). His interest in usual collocations was focused on more specified texts:

> Just as phonetic, phonological, and grammatical forms well established and habitual in any close social group provide a basis for the mutual expectancies of words and sentences at those levels, and also the sharing of these common features, so also the study of the usual collocations of a particular literary form or genre or of a particular author makes possible a clearly defined and precisely stated contribution to what I have termed the spectrum of descriptive linguistics, which handles and states meaning by dispersing it in a range of techniques working at a series of levels. (Ibid.)

It seems that in Firth's mind the study of collocation was primarily to make clear collocational patterns in the languages of fiction and poetry, and the authors of those literary texts. In actual fact, the texts that he referred to or took examples from were mostly literary texts: Edward Lear's limericks, *Gorboduc*, Blake's *King Edward the Third* and Swinburne's poems.

I do not mean to imply that scholars who have studied collocations in present-day English have ignored the necessity of the study of collocations in literary language. For example, M.A.K. Halliday stated in 'Lexis as a linguistic level' (1966) that: 'These [collocations] include studies of register and of literary style, of children's language, the language of aphasics and many others. In literary studies in particular such concepts as the ability of a lexical item to "predict" its own environment, and the cohesive power of lexical relations, are of great potential interest' (p. 160). In like manner, Sidney Greenbaum declared that: 'In the stylistic analysis of literary works, a study of collocations may reveal the predilection of individual writers or genres for particular collocations, their avoidance of collocations that are frequent elsewhere, and their selection of collocations that are rare or unique' (1970: 81).

What can be pointed out here is that while the necessity for the stylistic study of collocations in literary texts has been sufficiently recognized we have not yet had adequate or particularly fruitful results from previous studies. However, Alan Partington's article 'Kicking the habit: the exploitation of collocation in literature and humour' (1995), deals partly with creative language use in literature, and is quite valuable and useful for the study of collocations in literary texts. He pursued 'unusuality' or 'an imaginative reworking of the usual' (Partington 1998: 121) by investigating approximately 2500 headlines from the CD-ROM of the *Independent* newspaper in *Patterns and Meanings* (1998). He suggests four mechanisms of change of collocation – substitution, expansion, abbreviation and rephrasing – which provide an important clue for analysing creative collocations in literary language.

Firth also proposed a historical or chronological approach to collocation (although the COBUILD project does not engage with these approaches):

> There are many more of the same kind throughout this work [Blake's *King Edward the Third*], and of course a large number of collocations which have been common property for long periods and are still current even in everyday colloquial. This method of approach makes two branches of stylistics stand out more clearly: (a) the stylistics of what persists in and through change, and (b) the stylistics of personal idiosyncrasies. (Firth 1957: 196)

As an example of historical or chronological approach analysis, Firth attempted to observe a continuity of collocations as seen from the eighteenth through the twentieth century:

> A cursory examination of certain letters of the eighteenth and early nineteenth centuries clearly shows collocations which will be recognized as current for at least two hundred years – that is, as part of the common stock of what we may call recent modern English. In studying the extracts we note that many collocations are still generally current. In setting them out I have enclosed in brackets 'pieces' which to me seem glaringly obsolete. (Ibid., pp. 203–4)

Firth suggested the historical study of collocation, which I will also deal with, by showing the chronological change of collocations of *utterly, infinitely, terribly* in Section 1.3. In addition, Firth declared the study of a writer's collocational style seen on the basis of the findings of 'the common property for long periods', that is, chronologically unchanging usual collocations.

With respect to unique or unusual collocations, it should be mentioned that Firth understood language as a creative activity: 'To begin with, we must apprehend language events in their contexts as shaped by the creative acts of speaking persons' (ibid., p. 193). From such a viewpoint Firth's examination of constructions of collocations in Swinburne attempted to make 'Swinburnese' collocations clear:

At the level of meaning by word collocation there is the interesting point that, both as a whole and in phrases, the collocations are unique and personal, that is to say, a-normal. In the wider context of the whole poem, even within the context of the six exclamatory units, similar collocations accumulate which must be referred to the personal stylistics of the poet, to what may, indeed, be called Swinburnese. (Ibid., p. 198)

Firth's research and analysis of unique and personal collocations which are a-normal is another important aspect of his study, and is indispensable for the study of collocations in literary language. Such unique and personal collocations could be called creative if they are not found in other writers' texts or if a writer used the collocations in his or her own unique manner. Concerning creativity of unusual collocations Angus McIntosh states in his paper 'Patterns and Ranges' (1966: 197) that:

These [unusual collocations] are the kind which tend to be of such importance in literature, and especially in poetry. They are part of the machinery whereby the prose writer or the poet strives, over a larger or smaller stretch of text, to convey something which he cannot achieve by normal means, and he thereby sets us a problem in which we can lean on no experience of directly relevant instances. It may be of course that in a given case we are in the presence of the very birth of something which thereafter passes into general use and from then on forms part of the normal inventory of collocations involving the words in question; so with various phrases adopted into the language from Shakespeare and the Bible. It would be an interesting study to attempt to determine what there was about them that led to their adoption on this scale while others often no less striking, passed virtually unnoticed.

As observed so far, the statistical or quantitative study of collocation, which is now the major current of collocational research, is but one aspect of the study of collocation proposed by Firth in 'Modes of Meaning'; there is also a necessity to pursue the other side of the study, that is, the stylistic or qualitative study of collocation, particularly through an examination of literary texts. Furthermore, such studies of collocation in literary language need to include researches into not only usual collocations but also unique or unusual collocations, and discussions about what is used in the novelist or poet's peculiar or creative manner (for example, 'Swinburnese'), against the background of what is perceived as 'usual collocation', in both a synchronic and diachronic sense.

Next I would like to consider creativity of collocations in literary language in more detail and then discuss this topic according to the following framework, which Angus McIntosh offered in 'Patterns and ranges' (1966: 193):

> To put the matter with considerable crudity, we can already say on this basis that there is the possibility of four obviously distinct stylistic modes: (1) normal collocations and normal grammar, (2) unusual collocations and normal grammar, (3) normal collocations and unusual grammar, (4) unusual collocations and unusual grammar.

As McIntosh himself admits 'to put the matter with considerable crudity', this framework is rather simplistic and the argument is not presented with enough examples of each collocational type. However, this framework seems to be useful for a discussion of creative collocations in literature.

First, I would like to present the 'normal collocations and normal grammar' (type 1, above). This type is a 'usual' or 'normal' collocation while the other three are what can be called unusual collocations. The study of usual collocations with high frequencies in the corpus of writers' whole texts may reveal their predilection for particular collocations; and repeated usual collocations in their works could be considered the characters' idiolects and be susceptible to interpretations in the larger context. At any rate, usual collocations with high frequencies are significant. However, usual collocations with low frequencies can also be significant in literary language. For example, the collocation 'blue eyes' is a usual collocation with a low frequency but has common semantic features seen among the characters with *blue eyes* in Dickens. The semantic features are *innocent* and *favoured*. The characters with blue eyes possessing such semantic features are Nell in *The Old Curiosity Shop*, Emily and Dora in *David Copperfield*, Ada and Prince Turveydrop in *Bleak House*, Joe in *Great Expectations* and Lucie Manett in *A Tale of Two Cities*. (Interestingly, the *OED* records an example from 1924 as the earliest of 'blue-eyed' in the meaning 'innocent, ingenuous; favoured, especially, in the phrase, blue-eyed boy', but Dickens had previously used 'blue eyes' with a similar connotation.)

McIntosh's second distinct stylistic mode is 'unusual collocations and normal grammar'. This type of collocation has many examples, typical of which is the oxymoron. This type of collocation is also called 'collocational clash' or 'collocational deviation': *loving hate, anything of nothing, heavy lightness* and *serious vanity*. These examples are certainly unusual collocations, but there often arises the problem of whether they are, more definitively, unusual, unique or unfamiliar. That is to say, there is the problem of collocational acceptability. There seem to be two aspects involved in this problem of acceptability, especially in literary texts before the twentieth century: a lack of native informants for informant tests (which are often used for present-day English), and the lack of a machine-readable corpus. For example, if we have a test of acceptability concerning the collocation *snobbishly mean*, most native speakers of English in the twenty-first century may determine that this collocation is acceptable. However, would native speakers of English in the eighteenth and nineteenth centuries have determined these collocations in a similar manner, given that Thackeray coined the word *snobbishly* in his work in 1848 according to the *OED*? Informant analysis by native speakers of English in the twenty-first century may work for collocational patterns that chronologically persist and are unchanging but carries a risk on new collocations before the twentieth century. Another aspect of the problem of collocational acceptability concerns the shortage of historical corpora for judging whether a collocation is new or common. Fortunately, for eighteenth and nineteenth-century fiction, *Eighteenth-Century Fiction* (*ECF*) and *Nineteenth-Century Fiction* (*NCF*) (on CD-ROM, Chadwick-Healy), 1996 and 2000, respectively, covering almost all the fiction in these centuries, are now available.

McIntosh's third distinct stylistic mode is 'normal collocations and unusual grammar'. As an example of this type of collocation there are many appropriate examples from fiction utilizing a stream of consciousness, free direct or indirect speech or thought presentation. The following is from Joyce's *Ulysses* (1922):

> Yes because he never did a thing like that before as ask to get his breakfast in bed with a couple of eggs since the *City Arms* hotel when he used to be pretending to be laid up with a sick voice doing his highness to make himself . . .

This quotation is normal in collocation but very unusual orthographically and grammatically.

English haiku may also be full of these types of collocations. They often lack determiners, articles, pronouns or prepositions: this from

Jim Kacian, *Six Directions: Haiku & Field Notes* (La Alameda Press, Albuquerque, New Mexico, 1997: 54):

>   cupped hands
>   some of the stream
>   runs through

Rather than:

>   [my/these] cupped hands
>   [through which] some of the stream
>   runs through

It can also be said that most English haiku use the simple present, tending to avoid either the continuous-present, past or future tenses. So the above poem uses 'runs through' not 'is running' or 'is running through'.

The last distinct stylistic mode is 'unusual collocations and unusual grammar'. This type of collocation is difficult to find in literary texts. Even the poems of e.e. cummings or the prose of *Finnegans Wake*, considered near to this type, seem to be consistent or usual in terms of collocation. But it is easy to create such an indecipherable and nonsense sentence as 'colourless ideas the green furiously and sleep'. This expression has discursive syntax and words belonging to different registers.

The first two of these four types of collocations provide the background for my study of collocation in Dickens. Within these parameters, if a collocation is significant quantitatively, qualitatively, synchronically or diachronically, in the context of Dickens' entire oeuvre or in relation to a larger context or the range or nineteenth-century fiction, the collocation can be considered creative, regardless of whether it is a usual or unusual collocation.

1.3 Chronological change of collocation

'Semantic prosody' has appeared as a recent term in the study of collocation. This term was first used by Bill Louw (1993), though Louw acknowledges that John Sinclair had used the term in personal communication with him beginning in 1988, 'applying the term "prosody" in the same sense that Firth ... used the word to refer to phonological colouring which was capable of transcending segmental boundaries' (p. 158). For example, as Sinclair (1991) points out, the phrasal verb *set in* commonly collocates with unpleasant states of affairs, and this tendency is called 'bad, unpleasant or negative semantic prosodies'; *bad weather sets in, decay sets in, despair sets in.* There are many similar examples. To borrow Michael Stubbs's words (1995b: 246):

> Similarly, things which *break out* are usually unpleasant, and include *disagreements, riots, sweat, violence,* and *war* . . . It is easy to find other examples of words with unpleasant or negative prosodies. People COMMIT *adultery, crimes, murder, offences, sins, suicide.* Things can UNDERGO *changes, transformations,* and *modifications,* which can be *considerable, extensive, radical,* or *rapid*; people often undergo *crises, difficulties, ordeals,* and *risks,* or *medical treatments* or *tests* and *surgical procedures* which can be *traumatic.*

Another example of such unpleasant or negative semantic prosodies is *utterly.* Louw cites collocations of *utterly* from the original 18 million word corpus of *COBUILD*: *utterly against, utterly confused, utterly demolished* and *utterly meaningless.* He concludes (1993: 160): 'The concordance shows that *utterly* has an overwhelmingly "bad" prosody: there are few "good" right-collocates.'

However, there are in fact a few collocates of *utterly* that have 'good' prosody. In the *COBUILD English Collocations on CD-ROM* (1995), which was based on a much larger corpus (200 million words) than that of Louw, there are instances of *utterly* collocating with adjectives having good prosodies, most notably *utterly beautiful* (14 instances out of the 2689 collocations of *utterly*) and *utterly convinced* (17 instances). The following example is taken from an article in the *Independent* (4 October 2001) on the superstar UK footballer Steven Gerrard: 'Gerrard plainly believes in himself now and in a way, which is *utterly fundamental* to the confidence of any athlete.'

Such examples demonstrate that an unpleasant or negative semantic prosody on *utterly* is not absolute in present-day English. Another point that can be made is that the semantic prosody of *utterly* has changed through time. Evidence for this can be found in that among the 945 instances of *utterly* in the *OED2*, there are no citations of *utterly convinced, utterly beautiful* or *utterly fundamental.* Further evidence may be found by an examination of the *ECF* that comprises the works of 77 of the most influential writers of the British Isles in the eighteenth century, as well as the *NCF* which contains 250 complete works of prose fiction by 109 authors from the period 1781 to 1901. There are no collocations of *utterly beautiful* or *utterly fundamental* in either database, and only one example of *utterly convinced* (in Barry, 1887). A comparison of this finding with the higher frequency of occurrence of *utterly* with positive prosody in recent publications clearly indicates that the semantic prosodies of *utterly* do change chronologically.

This chronological change in collocation happens not only in semantic prosodies but also in grammatical collocation or colligation: 'the term given to the specifically grammatical relations along the syntagm' (Carter 1998: 59). According to *COBUILD English Collocations*, the word *infinitely* quite often (about 50 per cent of the time) collocates with comparative forms (for example, *infinitely better*, not *infinitely good*) in contemporary English. However, when *infinitely* entered English from French in the fifteenth century, it tended to collocate mainly with verbs (for example, *passeth infynytely*) until the first half of the seventeenth century. Later, *infinitely* developed the tendency to collocate with an adjective or adverb and its comparative form as seen in present-day English. Table 1.1, compiled from the *OED2*, gives a chronological survey of the collocational pattern of *infinitely*.

As the table indicates, the tendency of *infinitely* to collocate with verbs is observed until the first half of the seventeenth century. However, in the latter half of the seventeenth century, verbs collocating with *infinitely* were replaced by adjectives or adverbs. It is only since the latter half of the eighteenth century that the collocation of *infinitely* with adjectives or adverbs has become the norm.

Table 1.1: The number and ratio of word classes collocating with *infinitely* in the *OED2*

Period	Adjective/adverb	Verb	Others	Total
–1500	0 (0.0%)	2 (100.0%)	0 (0.0%)	2 (100%)
1501–1550	1 (100.0%)	0 (0.0%)	0 (0.0%)	1 (100%)
1551–1600	3 (23.1%)	10 (76.9%)	0 (0.0%)	13 (100%)
1601–1650	6 (25.0%)	17 (70.8%)	1 (4.2%)	24 (100%)
1651–1700	29 (51.8%)	27 (48.2%)	0 (0.0%)	56 (100%)
1701–1750	29 (55.8%)	19 (36.5%)	4 (7.7%)	52 (100%)
1751–1800	28 (77.8%)	7 (19.4%)	1 (2.8%)	36 (100%)
1801–1850	39 (70.9%)	13 (23.6%)	3 (5.5%)	55 (100%)
1851–1900	61 (77.2%)	16 (20.3%)	2 (2.5%)	79 (100%)
1901–1950	39 (88.6%)	5 (11.4%)	0 (0.0%)	44 (100%)
1951–	30 (88.2%)	3 (8.8%)	1 (2.9%)	34 (100%)
Total	265	119	12	396

Note: Percentages indicate the ratio of each word class for each period.

Table 1.2: The number and ratio of comparative
adjectives and adverbs which are modified by *infinitely*
in the OED2

Period	Comparative adjective/adverb	Words*	(%)
–1500	0	2	0.0
1501–1550	1	1	100.0
1551–1600	0	13	0.0
1601–1650	2	24	8.3
1651–1700	9	56	16.1
1701–1750	6	52	16.1
1751–1800	9	36	25.0
1801–1850	26	55	47.3
1851–1900	29	79	36.7
1901–1950	16	44	36.4
1951–1980	15	34	44.1
Total	113	396	28.5

Notes: Percentages indicate the ratio of comparative forms of
adjectives and adverbs which are modified by *infinitely* for
each period.
* The number of words that are modified by *infinitely*.

Another chronological feature of *infinitely* is a marked tendency
toward collocation with a comparative adjective or adverb (Table 1.2).

Since the nineteenth century, *infinitely* has shown a strong tendency
to collocate with comparative adjectives or adverbs, and the ratio of collocates of the comparative form reaches approximately 40 per cent, on
average, from the nineteenth to the twentieth century.

This brief survey of the collocation of *infinitely* provides a general basis
in order to examine the tendency of its grammatical collocation or colligation. Based upon this survey, when, in a nineteenth-century author's
collocation of *infinitely* the word does not collocate with any comparative form at all, his or her collocation of *infinitely* is considered unique
or characteristic in collocation. However, if we do not know the tendency of its grammatical collocation, we are able to describe the fact of
the author's collocation of the item but are not able to comment on his
or her stylistic characteristic of collocation. In the case of Dickens, for
example, the collocations of *infinitely* with the comparative forms of
adjectives or adverbs comprise 62 (77.5 per cent) of the 80 instances in
the Dickens corpus. This figure shows the high percentage of a grammatical tendency or colligation of *infinitely* to collocate with compara-

tive forms in Dickens, as this result can be compared with the statistics showing the overall nineteenth-century use of the corresponding grammatical collocation (approximately 40 per cent as shown in Table 1.2). Therefore, it could be said that there is a high probability that the collocation of *infinitely* with a comparative adjective or adverb is a characteristic of Dickens' style.

A more distinctive chronological change in collocation is the collocation of *terribly*. According to *COBUILD English Collocations* the most frequent collocate with *terribly* is *important*. However, there is no collocation of *terribly important* in either the *ECF* or the *NCF*. The *OED2* cites two examples of the collocation, one of them from 1865 and the other from 1930. This indicates a rapid chronological change of the collocation *terribly* from an adverb retaining its literal meaning to an intensive adverb losing its literal meaning in twentieth-century English. (Another interesting chronological change is shown by McBride (1998: 5) who pointed out that 'the word *worship*, which in Late Middle English named an obligation-related social value, had by early modern times been largely replaced with *honour*'.)

From the above, we can conclude that in discussing an author's stylistic collocations we have to keep in mind that semantic prosodies, colligations (grammatical collocation), and collocates of a word may change chronologically. This means that, just as grammar and phonology are discussed in relation to the historical development of English, so must an author's patterns of collocation or collocational style be considered within the context of collocational change.

1.4 Collocations in Dickens

Bearing in mind what has been outlined in the previous sections I would like to make clear various features of collocations in Dickens, which will be discussed in Parts II and III. Before launching into an exhaustive or comprehensive study of collocation in Dickens' whole works, a brief survey of characteristics of collocations in Dickens may be useful for understanding Dickens' predilections, structures, uniqueness, and idiosyncrasies of collocations.

In the context of the movement of the language of English fiction, Dickens' collocations (and his structural or symbolic use of them) show not only a greater variety but also far more unique patterns than those of authors of eighteenth-century English fiction. As an example, in Defoe's *Robinson Crusoe*, we find only two instances of the collocation 'adjective + *eyes*': *the same eyes* and *shining eyes*. The rarity of collocations of adjectives with the word *eyes* may indicate that 'Defoe's empha-sis is all . . . on the difficulty of exact, objective description, on the problem of getting the shade just right, not on the author's momentary feelings toward the subject' (Adolph 1968: 280–1).

Smollett's *Roderick Random* does not have many instances of colloca-tions of the word *eyes* either. We find the following instances (all taken from the *ECF*): *little grey eyes* (3 times, chs. 7, 11, 18), *lively blue eyes* (ch. 22), *aged eyes* (chs. 38, 67), *fierce eyes* (ch. 52), and *owlish eyes* (ch. 46). The adjectives *little, grey, blue, owlish* refer to the physical appearance of eyes while the adjectives *lively* and *fierce* imply the characters' feeling and states of mind, but these collocations are familiar collocations. Dickens is seen 'as essentially a disciple of Smollett, greater than his master' (Allen 1958: 163) in terms of his method of character creation, but as for the collocation 'adjective + *eyes*', Dickens' unusual or deviant collocations of *eyes*, which may be regarded as one of his significant methods of char-acter creation, do not seem to have been inherited from Smollett.

In Fielding's *Tom Jones* there are not many instances of this type either (from *ECF*):

> *black eyes* (3 times, IV, 2, V, 12, XIII, 5), *fiery eyes* (V, 11), *languid eyes* (XIV, 7), *prettiest eyes* (XII, 7), *pure eyes* (I, 3), *sloe-black eyes* (I, 11), *sparkling eyes* (2 times, IV, 2, XIII, 8), *strongest eyes* (V, 4), and *swollen eyes* (XI, 5)

The collocations *sloe-black* and *sparkling eyes* may be unfamiliar but they are not unusual.

Richardson's collocations are far richer than those of other eighteenth-century English fiction authors, in terms of this type of col-location. He gives a variety of depictions of feelings through his char-acters' eyes in *Pamela* (from *ECF*):

> *different eyes* (Letter 23), *speaking eyes* (2 times, Letter 23, Journal 24), *red eyes* (Journal 2), *an hundred eyes* (Journal 4), *fiery saucer eyes* (Journal 11), *great staring eyes* (Journal 17), *charming eyes* (2 times, Journal 29, Letter 33), *favourable eyes* (Journal 9), *fiery eyes* (2 times, Journal 25, Letter 34), *dear eyes* (Journal 29), *half-affrighted eyes* (Letter 23), *sweet eyes* (Letter 25), *worthy eyes* (Letter 25), *tearful eyes* (2 times, Letters 27, 35), *surrounding eyes* (Letter 32), *foolish eyes* (Letter 33), *weak eyes* (Letter 35), *black eyes* (Letter 38), *fine eyes* (2 times, Letters 63, 64), *pleased eyes* (Letter 64), *delighted ones* (*eyes*) (Letter 64), *little watchful eyes* (Letter 64), *pretty eyes* (Letter 64)

In *Pamela* we come across many collocations of *eyes* that express the characters' feelings and states of mind. Some of these collocations, such as *speaking eyes* and *sweet eyes*, are unusual or deviant collocations. Such unusual collocations are more frequently used in Richardson's later novel *Clarissa Harlowe*. Dickens might be said to develop Richardson's techniques of collocations in terms of unusual collocations of *eyes*.

We have so far made a brief survey of the representative works of the four originators of the English novel for the collocation of 'adjective + *eyes*'. Next, I would like to examine this type of collocation in Dickens' *Hard Times*:

> (Mr Gradgrind) *cavernous eyes, deep-set eyes* (I, 4); (Mrs Sparsit) *black eyes* (2 times) (II, 10, 11), *dark eyes* (4 times) (I, 11, II, 9, 11, 11), *classical eyes, distracted eyes* (II, 9); (Bitzer) *cold eyes* (I, 2), *blinking eyes* (III, 2); (Sissy) *trusting eyes* (II, 9), *confiding eyes* (III, 2); (Rachael) *gentle eyes* (I, 10), *pleasant eyes* (I, 10), *moistened eyes* (I, 13), *woeful eyes* (I, 13), *bold eyes* (in Mrs Sparsit's dialogue) (II, 1); (Tom) *not too sober eyes* (II, 3); (Mrs Gradgrind) *fine dark thinking eyes* (in Stephen's dialogue) (II, 6); (Stephen) *winking eyes* (II, 6); (Louisa) *searching eyes* (III, 1); (others) *both eyes* (I, 2), *eager eyes* (III, 4), *practised eyes* (III, 6), *all eyes* (III, 6), *many eyes* (III, 6)

These collocations are used not only to individualize each character but also to imply their feelings. Some of them are unusual collocations: *cavernous eyes, classical eyes, cold eyes, confiding eyes, deep-set eyes, practised eyes, trusting eyes, woeful eyes*. These unusual collocations have various types and structures (as discussed in Part II). One of them – *cavernous eyes* – is a metaphorical collocation.

This rich variety of the collocation 'adjective + *eyes*' is not only seen in *Hard Times* but also in Dickens' other works, and a similar sort of analysis can also be applied to the collocations of other nouns and verbs, such as *hand, face, head* (expressing parts of a body), verbs of perception, and reporting verbs. This richness of collocation in Dickens' works may be considered his contribution to the development of the language of English fiction.

Next, I would like to point out that Dickens' use of collocations also has general characteristics regarded as unique in Dickens' language. Randolph Quirk's (1974: 7) statement regarding Dickens' language is also applicable to Dickens' collocations: 'We may come nearer to a sympathetic appreciation of Dickens' language if we consider it under four heads: his use of language for individualization; for typification; his use of it structurally; and his use of it experimentally.'

We will also use the collocations of *eye* as an example, that is, the collocation 'adjective + *eye* or *eyes*'. First, concerning individualization little need be said; particular collocations used to identify Dickens' characters are so striking that we can easily identify individual characters, as observed in the instances from *Hard Times*.

Secondly, Quirk states, on typification, that 'More important to Dickens than individualizing, however, was the urge to express a regional, social, occupational, or philosophical typification by language' (p. 8) Indeed, there are a few instances of expressions of an occupational typification by collocations of *eye* or *eyes*. We have:

> Mr Lorry's *business eye* (TT III, 8); (Mrs Tradle) *her household eyes* (DC 59); *the eyes of the laity* (BH 22); (Sleary) *the riding-master eye* (HT I, 6); (Joe) *a smith's eye* (GE 16)

What seems peculiar to Dickens' typification of collocation is a tendency to create personality traits common to two or more characters for whom he uses the same collocation of the word *eye*. For example, the collocation *blue eyes*, as pointed out in Section 1.2, has common semantic features among the characters with *blue eyes* in Dickens: *innocent*, *ingenuous* and *favoured*. It is interesting to note that Christopher Casby, a ruthless landlord in *Little Dorrit* also has blue eyes. He has some of the characteristics of a boy; 'There was the same smooth face and forehead, the same calm *blue eye*, the same placid air' (LD I, 13). In fact however, he is a crafty imposter and conceals his rapaciousness under a benevolent 'patriarchal' exterior. Casby's deceptive characterization is attributed partly to his *blue eyes* which typify an innocent, ingenuous and favoured person in Dickens.

An emphasized or repeated brightness of characters' eyes may hint at their discontent, or at emotions hidden beneath the surface. Edith in *Dombey and Son* was married at the age of eighteen and became a widow two years later. She later became Mr Dombey's well-connected wife to grace his house. The brightness of her eyes is often emphasized:

> *its bright eyes* (Ch. 30), *brightened eyes* (Ch. 46), *her brilliant eyes* (Ch. 30), *her full bright flashing eye* (Ch. 45), *her kindling eyes* (Ch. 52), *the Bride, whose sparkling eye* (Ch. 36)

Such a repeated brightness of eyes is also applied to Mrs Sparsit in *Hard Times*, who is Mr Bounderby's housekeeper, a stately widow with a 'Coriolanian style of nose' implying aristocratic connection, and to Miss Havisham in *Great Expectations*, the eccentric old lady who was jilted on her wedding morning. They share 'pride' and 'haughtiness' as common semantic features, but also, in the structure of each plot, express pent-up fury in the blockaded situation on matrimony, and an abnormality of mind demonstrated in aberrant actions. (As an example of the attachment of semantic features to a character, Fowler (1977: 36) discussed Tom Buchanan in *The Great Gatsby*, stating that 'Among the semantic features which constitute him are: restlessness, physical strength, virility, athleticism (both competitive and social), dandyism, wealth, materialism, extravagance, vulgarity . . .')

Thirdly I would like to discuss Dickens' structural language use. A typical example of this is the contrasting use of the collocations of the word *eye* applied to Dora, David's first and childish wife, and Agnes, his second and ideal one, in *David Copperfield*. Let us look at the following:

> **Dora:** *the blue eyes* (Chs. 50, 53), *her delighted bright eyes* (Ch. 48), *my childish eyes* (Ch. 50), *her glittering eyes* (Ch. 44)
> **Agnes:** *her beaming eyes* (Ch. 39), *her mild clear eyes* (Ch. 62), *her cordial eyes* (Chs. 42, 60), *a mysterious eye* (Ch. 27), *her quiet eyes* (Ch. 62), *her calm seraphic eyes* (Ch. 35), *those beautiful soft eyes of hers* (Chs. 25, 39), *her sweet eyes* (Ch. 62), *her tender eyes* (Ch. 25), *thy true eyes* (Ch. 62)

Adjectives that describe Dora's eyes concern their outward appearance, or physical beauty, such as *blue*, *bright* and *glittering*. In regard to Agnes, on the other hand, the word *eyes* occurs with the adjectives *mild*, *cordial*, *quiet*, *calm*, *soft* and *tender*, which relate to the psychological depiction of her, and with the adjectives *seraphic* and *true* which are tinged with a religious colouring. This contrast in the collocations between David's first and second wives may have a close thematic relation to David's mental growth.

The fourth heading formulated by Quirk is Dickens' experimental use of language. The experimental use of collocations may be called unusual or deviant collocations. For example, such collocations as '*the knowing eyes*' (BH 54) and '*choking eyes*' (BH 8) are not in mutual expectancy and may be regarded as his experimental and innovative use. We come across many collocations of this type in Dickens' works. The following are the collocations of the word *eye* or *eyes* in which a character's eyes are compared to an animal's:

> (Misses Lavinia and Clarissa) *little bright round twinkling eyes, like birds' eyes* (DC 41); (Miss Murdstone) *this Dragon's eye* (DC 38); (Rob the Grinder) *the ferret eyes* (DS 52); (Miss Tox) *the fishy eye* (DS 7, 59); (Pumblechook) *his fishy eyes* (GE 9); (Mrs Sparsit) *her hawk's eyes* (HT II, 10); (Bagstock) *his lobster eyes* (DS 7, 20, 40, 59); (Mr Carker) *his lynx-eyed vigilance* (DS 46)

Such unusual collocations, which are considered creative language use, are discussed in more detail below (Chapter 3).

In this introductory section, Dickens' richness, variety, and uniqueness of collocations have been briefly surveyed as a preparation for a comprehensive study of collocations in Dickens. In Part II, Dickens' collocations will be analysed exhaustively from the following two viewpoints: usual collocations and unique or creative collocations. Dickens' collocations will also be examined quantitatively and discussed qualitatively and/or stylistically (as seen through his complete oeuvre), not only in terms of his unique collocations but also his predilection for and avoidance of certain usual collocations. Based on the discussions in Part II, this study of collocation will next focus on *Bleak House* as a case in point: collocations in *Bleak House* will be discussed in closer relation to Dickens' literary themes, topics, contexts, characters and narrative strategies.

1.5. Definition of collocation

The definition of collocation used throughout this book will be taken to mean a relationship of habitual co-occurrence between words. 'Words in collocation' do not mean lemmas. (These are used conventionally as the base form of a word in dictionaries of English: for example, 'the lemma TAKE is realized in text by the word-forms *take, takes, took, taking* and *taken*. Similarly, the lemma of the noun RABBIT is realized by the word-forms *rabbit, rabbits, rabbit's* and *rabbits'*; and the lemma of the adjective BIG is realized by *big, bigger* and *biggest*' (Stubbs 2001: 25)). Rather, word forms that differ in number, tense or aspect are treated as different words. The reason for this is that the singular form of a word can act differently in collocate from its plural, as will be discussed in the collocations of *gentleman* and *gentlemen* (Chapter 2). Such types of different collocations are also observed in the differences of tense and aspect (for example, *say*, *said* and *saying*), and in comparative or superlative forms (for example, *good*, *better* and *best*).

Generally, collocates of a word are regarded as composed of the four or five lexical items to either side of a node. This concept of collocates can be problematic, in that there are at least two different types of collocates, as observed in the collocation of *little* and *so* given below:

(a) to reconcile, having *so little* experience or practical knowledge
(b) the suffering, quiet, pretty *little* thing! I am *so* sorry for it

In (a), *little* is modified by *so*, while in (b) there is no relationship of modification between *little* and *so*. We can say that in the relationship of collocation of *little* with *so*, (a) is grammatical while (b) has semantic coherence between *little* and *so*, in context. However, a computer cannot distinguish a collocational difference in relationship between type (a) and type (b) but counts *so* twice as a collocate of *little*. Here is an example from COBUILD. The list of collocates of *utterly* in COBUILD illustrates collocates with *beautiful*. The following shows all the examples of these collocations:

(1) olescence. When she bloomed into an **utterly beautiful** creature. It was a compet

(2) ow.⟨S⟩ Yeah.⟨S⟩ Do you think I look **utterly beautiful** with this lipstick on?⟨S⟩

(3) fferent kind of body, 'utterly new, **utterly beautiful** – Of course there were da

(4) Angela recalls: 'I thought she was **utterly beautiful** in a very profound way. S

(5) peace, in other words, and utterly, **utterly beautiful** According to Michael Str

(6) ir of vanished splendour about this **utterly beautiful** area of the Coin valley.

(7) l, cathartic, shockingly stupid and **utterly beautiful** modern art. PHOTOS WITH

(8) e been chosen 'because they look so **utterly beautiful** against the grey plaster

(9) t, it's a must if you possibly can. **Utterly beautiful** in South Pacific style, i

(10) new sense of tactile feeling. **utterly beautiful'**,
'He's   she breathed. He gave a

(11) ion of an 'other body,   **utterly beautiful'**.
utterly new,   In the first volume of

(12) r hand up for his inspection. **utterly beautiful**.
'It's   Thea said she had not im

(13) They were perfect and   **utterly** cold, and he
beautiful and   suddenly remembered Ha

(14) **eautiful** woman, beautifully **utterly** enviable in any
dressed,   stranger's eyes. Sh

(15) blistering that it's **beautiful**; so **utterly** gone in its
                                  desperation and yet nea

(16) any such vision of an   **utterly** new, utterly
'other body,   **beautiful'**. In the fir

(17) **beautiful** – I agree.   **utterly** predictable. Boring',
Beautiful and   was Chris's v

(18) Sophia she is **beautiful**,   **utterly** self-possessed: one of
cool and   the biggest

(19) kind of peace, in other   **utterly**, utterly **beautiful**
words, and   According to Mi

(20) eedback throbbing in the   **utterly** wild and eerily
form of an   **beautiful** beast cal

Among the 20 examples of *utterly* indicated above, there are 13 examples of a grammatical relationship of modification between *utterly* and *beautiful* (for example 'she was **utterly beautiful** in a very profound way' in (4). The list of collocates of *utterly* also has seven examples of another type of collocation in which *beautiful* appears within four words before or after *utterly* but is not modified by it (for example, 'that it's **beautiful**; so **utterly** gone in its desperation' in (15)). However, when discussing the collocational tendency, semantic prosody, and colligation of *utterly*, we cannot proceed with the analysis of these two types of collocations in the same way. Therefore, throughout this book, not only collocates, words which occur 'in close proximity to a word under investigation' (Sinclair 1991: 170), but also the syntactic relationship between a word and its collocates will be examined in the following manner: adjective + noun, adverb + adjective, verb + adverb, noun + verb, verb + noun and preposition + noun (cf. Leisi 1985: Ch. 11).

1.6 Methods, corpus data and software

This book aims to provide new and profound insights into Dickens' language and style through the study of collocation. My approach to the study of the language and style of Dickens follows Tadao Yamamoto (1950), G.L. Brook (1970), Randolph Quirk (1974), Knud Sørensen (1985) and Robert Golding (1985), all of whom based their work on a close and sensitive reading of Dickens, and I am indebted to them. However, by taking advantage of a computer-assisted approach, it has been possible to present complete datasets which were not previously available and which allow the analysis of new aspects of Dickens' language through the study of collocation. My approach, however, takes a different line to that of statistical stylistics as presented by John Burrows (1987) and David Hoover (2001), considered as representative achievements of the field (specifically as regards the cluster analysis of high-frequency words). Such works have suggested new ways to study the language of fiction, but at the same time they have convinced me that statistical approaches are not sufficient, in particular as a means of demonstrating the significant usage of writers' creative literary language. In other words, as Firth proposed in 'Modes of Meaning', the statistical or quantitative study of collocation is only one side of the coin: it is also necessary to pursue the qualitative study of collocations of low-frequency words. Such studies of collocation in literary language need to include researches not only into usual collocations but also into unique or creative collocations, and furthermore, such studies need to discuss in some detail exactly how collocations are used in the novelist's or poet's creative and idiosyncratic manner. Therefore, the most important thing in this approach is to consider and interpret carefully both Dickens' usual and unique collocations, obtained by a corpus-driven approach, in the context of individual texts or in the larger context of his complete oeuvre.

With regard to the unusual or creative collocations dealt with in Chapter 3, I used two methods of confirming whether they were in fact common or uncommon. One of them utilized native informant tests; whenever a collocation that seemed to be strange or unique was found, I queried it with a few British and American researchers of English literature and language. More systematic native informant tests were conducted to determine whether or not specific collocational differences between the two different narratives of *Bleak House* are comprehended by native speakers. These informant tests revealed that native speakers of present-day English still find many strange and unusual collocations in Dickens' texts, written more than 100 years ago. However, these informant tests are not absolutely reliable, in that though this kind of test is effective in studies of contemporary English, it may be problematic regarding nineteenth-century English. In order to compensate for this weakness I also used the database of electronic texts of eighteenth and nineteenth-century fiction to make further comparisons. For example, in the collocation *comfortable wickedness* (Chimes 2), each word (*comfortable* or *wickedness*) is common; however the combination (*comfortable wickedness*) is uncommon, and this type of collocation can be considered a semantic deviation or deviational collocation. Until recently it has been impossible to determine whether or not this collocation is Dickens' own innovation, though we may be able to point to such a collocation as 'Dickensian'. Only if no other eighteenth to nineteenth-century novelists have used this collocation, can we confidently claim that Dickens' use was innovative. In fact, the collocation *comfortable wickedness* is found only once, in Dickens' *The Chimes*, according to the *NCF* and the *ECF*. Of course, the fact that a collocation is not found in a corpus spanning a hundred years does not prove that it did not exist at that time, rather it demonstrates that it is not frequent in the text types present in that corpus (Partington 1996: 146). However, the fact that the *NCF* and the *ECF* contain almost all of the fictional texts (327 complete works) of a wide range of authors of the eighteenth and nineteenth centuries provides proof enough to claim, at the present time, that Dickens is the first novelist in eighteenth and nineteenth-century fiction to use this collocation. Such unusual collocations in Dickens indicate his innovation or creativity in language use, revealing new modes of identification of his style or language.

The Dickens Corpus accessed for this volume contains approximately 4.6 million words. The full list of texts compiled in the Dickens Corpus, together with the abbreviations used, is given in the preliminary pages.

In addition, in order to compare the collocations of Dickens with those of other nineteenth-century authors, a corpus of nineteenth-century fiction (NCFWD; approximately 2.2 million words, excluding Dickens' texts) has been consulted. This corpus is a compilation of fiction written between 1830, when Dickens began writing, and 1870, the date of his death. One text is chosen for each author. The following is a list of the texts compiled:

The Last Days of Pompeii (1834) by Edward George Bulwer-Lytton (1803–1873)
Sybil (1845) by Earl of Beaconfield Benjamin Disraeli (1804–1881)

Agnes Grey (1847) by Ann Brontë (1820–1849)
Wuthering Heights (1847) by Emily Brontë (1818–1848)
Jane Eyre (1847) by Charlotte Brontë (1816–1855)
Vanity Fair (1848) by William Makepeace Thackeray (1811–1863)
Cranford (1853) by Elizabeth Cleghorn Gaskell (1810–1865)
The Ordeal of Richard Feverel (1859) by George Meredith (1828–1909)
The Mill on the Floss (1860) by George Eliot (1819–1880)
The Woman in White (1860) by Wilkie Collins (1824–1889)
Alice's Adventures in Wonderland (1866) by Lewis Carroll (1832–1898)
The Last Chronicle of Barset (1867) by Anthony Trollope (1815–1882)
Erewhon (1872) by Samuel Butler (1835–1902)

As a concordance software of these self-made corpora of Dickens and other nineteenth-century writers, I used CONC 1.76 (a text retrieval tool for the Macintosh which 'generates concordances and indexes, displaying the original text, concordance, and index in separate windows). Selecting a word in any of the three windows causes the display of entries for that word in the other two windows. The sort order can be defined and the concordance can be limited to words matching a search expression. Letter concordances can also be generated. Results can either be printed or saved as text files' (CONC 1994). Whenever unique collocations in Dickens' works were found, the *ECF* and *NCF* databases were consulted. If the collocation was found, its occurrences and by whom it was used were recorded. All quotations throughout the book are taken from the *Oxford Illustrated Dickens* (Oxford: Oxford University Press, 1947–58).

1.7 Outline of the book

The book is divided into three main parts as follows.

Part I is intended to provide a theoretical background to the collocational analysis of literary texts. A historical survey of the study of collocation reveals that a corpus-based study of present-day English collocation has attained fruitful developments but a stylistic study of collocation in English literature has not yet seen satisfactory developments. Moreover, it is argued that just as phonology, vocabulary, and grammar are subject to change over time, the collocation of a word may change chronologically, and that Charles Dickens' collocational style, including his innovation or creativity of collocation, should be discussed in terms of the chronological change of collocation.

Part II consists of three main chapters. Chapters 2 and 3 are an investigation into both familiar or usual collocations and creative collocations in Dickens. Usual collocations of each word class, particularly nouns, adjectives and adverbs, which illustrate Dickensian collocational features, are dealt with. Based on the findings of these typical collocations, some usual collocations are discussed in terms of semantic prosodies and colligation. Creative collocations are divided into eight types: metaphorical, transferred, oxymoronic, disparate, unconventional, modified idiomatic, parodied and relexicalized collocations. In each type of creative collocation attention is given to the structure of Dickens' creative use of collocation. Chapter 4 is an examination of collocations and first citations from Dickens found in the *OED2*. After the observation of several characteristics of the first citations in the *OED2*, a relationship between collocations and neologisms is discussed. The discussion provides evidence that Dickens' coinages can rightfully be considered aspects of his literary creativity.

Part III provides a case study of collocations in *Bleak House*. Collocational analysis of this text indicates that the language or style of *Bleak House* differs from that of any other work of Dickens in terms of collocation rather than vocabulary. In the comparison of collocations between the third-person narrative and Esther's narrative, attention is devoted to usual collocations peculiar to each narrator's non-dialogue, and then to the differences of unusual collocations of each narrator's non-dialogue. Unusual collocations in both non-dialogues are examined using native informant tests. Collocations and characters in this text are discussed in terms of collocations and collocational patterns peculiar to characters in non-dialogues as well as in speeches. Part III also contains discussion of different mind styles of the first person narrators, that is, Esther in *Bleak House*, David in *David Copperfield* and Pip in *Great Expectations*, from the viewpoint of collocations. In the final section an attempt is made to explain new compound words as collocation.

Collocation has grown to become a main pillar in applied linguistics. It is hoped that collocation will also attract the attention of people who are interested in the language and style of literary texts as an important component in the stylistic analysis of literature. Moreover, it is hoped that the present book may be useful for those people who are trying to analyse the language and style of a novelist's or poet's texts in terms of collocation.

Part II
Collocation in Dickens

2
Familiar Collocations

As discussed in Part I, J.R. Firth (1957: 195) suggested that the study of collocations of common words was a necessity in stylistics, and that 'this kind of study of the distribution of common words may be classified into general or usual collocations and more restricted technical or personal collocations'. Greenbaum (1970: 81) also endorsed the study of collocations of common words, as well as unique or peculiar collocations of literary works: 'In the stylistic analysis of literary works, a study of collocations may reveal the predilection of individual writers or genres for particular collocations, their avoidance of collocations that are frequent elsewhere, and their selection of collocations that are rare or unique.'

In this chapter, therefore, familiar collocations of highly frequent nouns, adjectives and adverbs will be dealt with. Before discussing collocations of highly-frequent words, I would like to observe the 100 highest-frequency content-words in Dickens. The total number of words in Dickens' works as a whole (the Dickens Corpus) is approximately 4.6 million words. In order to create a corpus of content-words the following types of words have been removed from the database: function words (pronouns, articles, prepositions, conjunctions, auxiliaries and relatives), proper nouns, and titles such as *Mr*, *Mrs*, *Miss* and *Sir*. In addition to these removals, words having different parts of speech, such as *have*, *had* (auxiliary and verb), *so* (conjunction, adverb and pronoun) and *do* (verb and auxiliary) are also omitted. Other words removed are *be*-verbs, *all* (adjective, pronoun, adverb and noun), *one* (adjective, noun and pronoun) and *there* (adverb, pronoun and interjection). In addition *not* is also taken off the list because the adverb is usually shortened to *n't* with *is*, *are*, *was*, *were*, *has*, *have*, *had*, *do*, *does* and so on. These words are very frequent in all Dickens' texts and thus, like function words, show no distinctive features among particular texts.

The NCFWD, which was made from texts compiled from other nineteenth-century authors (see Section 1.6 above), is used for comparison. The list given below in Table 2.1 contains the 100 highest-frequency content-words and their occurrences per million words which allows for a better comparison between the two corpora with their different word totals. This list has been tabulated by means of 'word-forms' rather than 'lemmas'. That is to say, *say*, *said* and *saying* are treated as different collocates and counted separately.

Table 2.1 illustrates many peculiar and interesting features of and differences between the Dickens Corpus and NCFWD, but some distinctive features might be summarized according to the classification of parts of speech (although some words may be used as other parts of speech). First, most notable among nouns is the high frequency of the word *gentleman*, which is ranked 45 in the 100 highest-frequency content-words and ranked 13 in respect of the highest-frequency nouns in the Dickens Corpus, while it is not found at all in the 100 highest-

Table 2.1: The 100 highest-frequency content-words in the Dickens Corpus and NCFWD

The Dickens Corpus			NCFWD		
Rank	Lexical form	Occurrence per million words	Rank	Lexical form	Occurrence per million words
1	said	6518	1	said	5549
2	no	3598	2	no	3417
3	very	2898	3	very	2325
4	little	2476	4	now	2145
5	man	2037	5	more	2007
6	more	2021	6	little	1895
7	old	1973	7	some	1671
8	now	1945	8	know	1603
9	know	1884	9	man	1587
10	some	1851	10	see	1533
11	time	1833	11	any	1532
12	any	1689	12	never	1520
13	say	1572	13	well	1504
14	good	1551	14	only	1502
15	again	1531	15	like	1495
16	never	1525	16	time	1490
17	like	1518	17	say	1459
18	much	1496	18	come	1440

Table 2.1: Continued

The Dickens Corpus			NCFWD		
Rank	Lexical form	Occurrence per million words	Rank	Lexical form	Occurrence per million words
19	such	1491	19	think	1406
20	here	1487	20	own	1379
21	come	1439	21	good	1384
22	well	1407	22	such	1351
23	other	1352	23	go	1349
24	great	1324	24	old	1335
25	see	1310	25	much	1334
26	hand	1289	26	lady	1284
27	dear	1284	27	made	1225
28	made	1240	28	thought	1191
29	head	1222	29	house	1180
30	young	1211	30	other	1177
31	way	1193	31	day	1157
32	two	1162	32	again	1110
33	think	1134	33	great	1096
34	own	1093	34	too	1092
35	day	1086	35	two	1060
36	night	1079	36	first	1008
37	face	1075	37	room	981
38	too	1064	38	way	968
39	house	1027	39	came	965
40	back	1026	40	here	962
41	go	991	41	young	940
42	door	986	42	make	898
43	eyes	985	43	back	876
44	only	978	44	hand	871
45	gentleman	968	45	last	870
46	long	963	46	yet	864
47	looked	960	47	life	854
48	room	954	48	went	846
49	away	950	49	tell	834
50	quite	936	50	still	833
51	first	911	51	away	824
52	looking	910	52	take	824
53	look	904	53	long	820
54	came	890	54	eyes	816
55	ever	885	55	even	817
56	take	864	56	father	817
57	went	851	57	ever	811
58	returned	846	58	poor	809
59	lady	834	59	dear	790

Table 2.1:   Continued

The Dickens Corpus			NCFWD		
Rank	*Lexical form*	*Occurrence per million words*	*Rank*	*Lexical form*	*Occurrence per million words*
60	another	829	60	love	775
61	replied	823	61	most	773
62	many	820	62	face	765
63	last	806	63	mind	759
64	thought	801	64	quite	733
65	make	801	65	let	726
66	mind	798	66	looked	726
67	most	792	67	left	722
68	every	773	68	look	719
69	same	772	69	heart	708
70	place	765	70	always	700
71	going	744	71	woman	689
72	even	737	72	just	684
73	better	735	73	heard	680
74	put	732	74	wife	678
75	took	723	75	every	669
76	round	718	76	people	668
77	life	711	77	give	665
78	always	707	78	told	652
79	cried	698	79	night	649
80	still	686	80	better	645
81	friend	673	81	got	639
82	once	665	82	moment	635
83	tell	661	83	saw	633
84	hands	658	84	knew	628
85	let	656	85	took	625
86	done	656	86	head	616
87	got	639	86	place	616
88	left	622	86	put	616
89	half	618	89	many	615
90	home	612	90	door	614
91	people	592	91	get	612
92	yet	590	92	friend	607
93	poor	584	93	found	596
94	saw	574	94	done	587
95	right	566	95	half	580
96	boy	563	96	felt	572
97	name	561	97	words	569
98	manner	547	98	seemed	569
99	child	538	99	going	568
100	seemed	535	100	another	566

frequency content words in NCFWD. There are 4454 examples of *gentleman* in the Dickens Corpus (4.6 million words), 825 in the NCFWD (2.2 million words) and 2777 examples in *COBUILD* (200 million words). Therefore, the tokens per million words of *gentleman* are 968 words in Dickens and 375 words in NCFWD, and 13.9 words in *COBUILD*. This sharp decrease of frequency of *gentleman* from the nineteenth century to the twentieth century may reflect the change of the word's meaning and usage. What is clear is that the frequency of *gentleman* in Dickens amounts to 2.6 times that of the NCFWD. The collocation of *gentleman* in Dickens may also show a different tendency from that of other nineteenth-century writers. The fact that the high frequency of *gentleman* is observed throughout Dickens' texts may be a clue or key to literary topics or themes underlying his whole works. Another writer who uses *gentleman* much more frequently than other nineteenth-century writers is William Thackeray. In *Vanity Fair* there are 269 examples of *gentleman*. It is interesting to note that, generally speaking, woman writers tend to use the word *gentleman* less frequently. For example, Jane Austen has 36 examples in *Emma* and 33 examples in *Mansfield Park*. The Brontë sisters offer 39 examples in *Jane Eyre*, 13 examples in *Wuthering Heights*, and 22 examples in *Agnes Grey*. We can find 332 and 715 examples respectively in Dickens' *Oliver Twist* and *Pickwick Papers*.

The second notable feature is the high frequency of nouns referring to body parts such as *hand* (ranked 26), *head* (29), *face* (37), *eyes* (43), and *hands* (84). The Dickens Corpus exceeds the NCFWD by a range of 1.2–2.0 times the tokens per million of these words: *hand* (1.5 times: 1289 vs. 871), *head* (2.0 times: 1222 vs. 616), *face* (1.4 times: 1075 vs. 765), *eyes* (1.2 times: 985 vs. 816), *hands* (1.5 times: 658 vs. 447). The recurrent use of words referring to body parts may also imply particular co-occurrences different from those of the NCFWD.

Other nouns occurring at remarkably higher-frequency in the Dickens Corpus are *night* (36), *door* (42), *boy* (96), *manner* (98) and *child* (99). The ratios of these tokens per million words for the Dickens Corpus and the NCFWD stand as follows: *night* (1.7 times: 1079 vs. 649), *door* (1.6 times: 986 vs. 614), *boy* (1.7 times: 563 vs. 333), *manner* (1.9 times: 547 vs. 285) and *child* (1.6 times: 538 vs. 338). These particularly frequent nouns may imply recurrent motifs through Dickens' texts. For example, the high frequency of *boy* and *child* among these nouns seems to relate to the fact that in some of Dickens' texts boys and children are heroes and heroines: the word *boy* most frequently appears in *Oliver Twist* while the word *child* is used most frequently in *The Old Curiosity Shop*.

One of the nouns which has a much lower frequency in the Dickens Corpus than in the NCFWD is *love*. In the Dickens Corpus the tokens of *love* per million words are 420 words while the NCFWD contains 775 words. Certain differences of collocational tendency of *love* may also be found in comparing these corpora.

With respect to high-frequency adjectives: *little, old, young, many* and *same* in the Dickens Corpus are found 1.3 times more frequently than in the NCFWD. Above all, in the use of *old* (1.5 times) and *same* (1.5 times) Dickens far exceeds other nineteenth-century writers.

Dickens uses a variety of reporting verbs, although *said* is the highest of the 100 highest-frequency content-words in both corpora. In the Dickens Corpus (in tokens per million words) the verbs *returned* (846), *replied* (823) and *cried* (698) appear 3.2 times, 2.8 times and 2.4 times as often as in the NCFWD. (By the same measure, in the NCFWD they are 264, 299 and 290 respectively.) The main reason why these verbs are much more frequently used by Dickens than by other nineteenth-century writers is that most of them play the role of reporting verbs.

Adverbs such as *very, again* and *never* (in the 100 highest-frequency content words) are so common in both corpora that they tend to collocate with a very large number of words and show no distinctive features. Concerning the usual collocations of adverbs, therefore, I would like to examine -*ly* manner adverbs, showing certain features of fiction which are regarded as distinct from other registers such as conversation, newspapers and academic papers (Biber et al. 1999: 541), though no -*ly* manner adverb, except for *only* (ranked 44), is within the 100 highest-frequency words.

In relation to the highly-frequent words mentioned above, I would like to examine and discuss the familiar or usual collocations of common nouns, adjectives and adverbs. In the following sections the *NCF*, which compiles all the representative fiction texts published in the nineteenth century, will be used in order to discern particular characteristics of Dickens' collocations.

2.1 Nouns

In discussing the usual collocations of common nouns a list of the top ten collocates of each noun in the Dickens corpus will be presented, then, for comparison, examined in relation to those found in the NCFWD corpus. As before, in the lists of collocates the following types of words have been removed from the database: function words (pronouns, articles, prepositions, conjunctions, auxiliaries and relatives), proper nouns and titles such as *Mr, Mrs, Miss* and *Sir*. In addition to these removals, words having different parts of speech, such as *have*, *had* (auxiliary and verb), *so* (conjunction, adverb and pronoun) and *do* (verb and auxiliary) are also omitted. The following discussions, therefore, are based on the findings of familiar or usual collocations in both corpora. The top ten collocates of each word in the Dickens Corpus are first listed in order of frequency.

gentleman: *old, said, young, very, single, no, lady, little, replied, good.*
Approximately one-third of the examples of the word *gentleman* are modified with the adjective *old* or *young*. The collocation *single gentleman* is used only once in the NCFWD but is found 137 times in the Dickens Corpus. Most of the collocations (121 of 137) appear in *The Old Curiosity Shop* and are almost all used for Little Nell's great-uncle, the narrator of the story. The narrator refers to himself as if *the single gentleman* were a proper name. The collocation of *gentleman* and *very* (140 examples) is also distinctive in Dickens, while there are only 16 examples of the collocation in the NCFWD, although *very* is ranked 3 in the 100 highest-frequency content-words in both corpora. This means that Dickens tends to exaggerate the appearance and character of a gentleman such as 'one *very* stout *gentleman*, whose body and legs', 'another *gentleman* in *very* shabby black', and 'one young *gentleman* was *very* anxious to hang'. The word *faced* is not within the top 20 collocates of *gentleman* but all of the 43 examples of *faced* with *gentleman* show the same grammatical collocation. That is to say, *faced* functions as the second (head) element of the compound word 'adjective + faced' and all these compound adjectives with *faced* are attributive, such as *the pink-faced gentleman* and *the mottled-faced gentleman*. According to the *NCF* this type of collocation 'adjective + *faced gentleman*' is found only nine times among other nineteenth-century writers. This collocation most frequently appears in *Pickwick Papers* (17 times). The collocation of *gentleman* and *little* which is found 91 times in the Dickens Corpus but only seven times in the NCFWD, is also one of Dickens' favourites. For example, according to the *NCF*, of the 31 examples of the phrase *little old gentleman* in nineteenth-century fiction, 23 are found in Dickens.

gentlemen: *young, all, said, ladies, two, other, very, old, three, no.*
The noun *gentlemen* (the plural form of *gentleman*) has a collocational tendency different from that of its singular form. The singular form *gentleman* shows a stronger collocational tendency with *old* than *young* but the plural form *gentlemen* much more frequently (three times in tokens)

occurs with *young* than *old*. Another difference in collocation between *gentlemen* and *gentleman* is that there are very frequent collocations with the words expressive of such numbers as *two* and *three* (which come within the top ten collocates of *gentlemen*), and *both* (which is the eleventh).

eyes: *face, fixed, tears, said, all, little, again, turned, no, very.*
The top collocate of *eyes* in Dickens is *face* while *face* is the ninth in the NCFWD. This fact means that in Dickens the description of *eyes* has a much stronger tendency to be accompanied with that of *face*. The collocates of the singular form *eye*, as often pointed out (Carter 1998: 63), show a different tendency. The top ten collocates of *eye* are: *glass, said, up, all, bright, man, out, very, caught, no.*

hand: *out, right, put, said, other, little, left, laid, laying, held.*
Right is the second collocate of *hand* and almost all the collocations of *hand* and *right* are *right hand* (269 examples). The tokens of the collocation *left hand* are 126, and approximately half of that of *right hand*. In the NCFWD *right* and *left* are the seventh and eighth collocates respectively. The verbs *put, laid* and *laying* are found within the top ten collocates in Dickens but not in the NCFWD.

business: *no, said, man, like, all, any, little, up, very, way.*
The top collocate of *business* is *no* and approximately half of the collocations of *business* and *no* are *no business* (87 examples). On the other hand, in the NCFWD *no* is the fourth collocate and the collocation *no business* provides 16 examples. Another characteristic of *business* in Dickens is a collocation with *like*. In this context, *business like* is Dickens' favourite collocation and Dickens uses this collocation most frequently among writers in the nineteenth century: that is to say, 65 of the 155 examples of this collocation in nineteenth-century fiction are from Dickens (*NCF*).

manner: *most, very, all, said, same, like, no, more, old, usual.*
The adjective *same* is the fourth collocate and the collocation *same* (+ adjective) *manner* is a frequent collocation (69 out of the 82 examples), while in the NCFWD, there are only four examples of this type of collocation. The adjective *usual* is the tenth collocate and 42 out of the 49 examples of the collocation of *manner* and *usual* are the type of the collocation *usual* (+ adjective) *manner*, while in the NCFWD this type of collocation is found three times.

door: *opened, open, out, room, shut, said, street, house, up, little.*
The collocation *street door* meaning 'the chief external door of a house or other building, giving immediate access to the street' (*OED*) is frequently used in Dickens. According to the NCF Dickens is the most frequent user of this collocation among nineteenth-century writers; and 110 examples, half of the total number, appear in Dickens' fiction.

love: *said, all, no, dear, know, never, much, more, little, very.*
The tokens of *love* per million words in Dickens are approximately half that of the NCFWD but the tokens of the collocation *my love* per million words in Dickens occur 2.5 times more frequently than in the NCFWD. The co-occurrence of *love* with *my* amounts to one-third of the 1932 examples of *love* in Dickens. What is interesting about the collocation *love* is the contrasting use of the collocation between David's love for Dora and for Agnes in *David Copperfield*. David, an I-narrator, expresses his love for Dora by the collocation *love and beauty* such as 'I was sensible of a mist of *love and beauty* about Dora, but of nothing else' (Ch. 33) and 'Oh, my child-wife, there is a figure in the moving crowd before my memory, quiet and still, saying in its innocent *love and* childish *beauty* . . .' (Ch. 53). On the other hand, his love for Agnes is narrated by the collocation *love and truth* such as 'how strong she was, indeed, in simple *love and truth*' (Ch. 35) and 'I pray Heaven that I never may forget the dear girl in her *love and truth*, at that time of my life' (Ch. 35). This contrasting collocational usage may suggest that his love for Dora is represented in terms of her physical beauty but the locus of his love for Agnes is her mental beauty.

dear: *said, oh, no, old, friend, all, very, good, boy, know.*
The word *dear*, which is an adjective but is treated as a noun when used as a term of endearment, is highly frequent (ranked 27) and represents 25 per cent of all the examples of *dear* collocated with *my*. The ratio of tokens of *my dear* per million words is double that of the NCFWD. The collocation *my dear* is found most frequently in *Bleak House*, especially in Esther's narrative.

2.2 Adjectives

As with the usual collocations of common nouns in the last section, the top ten collocates of common adjectives from the Dickens Corpus are given first, with discussions based on the findings of usual collocations in both the Dickens Corpus and the NCFWD.

old: *man, said, gentleman, lady, woman, up, no, very, all, little.*
The adjective *old* has a very strong tendency of co-occurrence with the top collocate *man*, with 14.3 per cent of all the examples of *old* collocating with *man* in Dickens, and 7.5 per cent in the NCFWD. The collocation *little old* as observed in the phrases 'the *little old* gentleman' and 'the *little old* lady' appears 112 times in the Dickens Corpus and only six times in the NCFWD. According to the *NCF,* Dickens most frequently uses the collocation *little old* among writers of nineteenth-century fiction, and 84 out of the 225 examples of the collocation in the nineteenth century are from Dickens.

good: *said, very, night, all, deal, no, dear, man, time, fellow.*
The top collocates of *good* are overwhelmingly used in fixed collocations: *very good, good night, a good deal of, good time* and *no good.* Approximately 80 per cent of the examples of the collocation *good time* are accompanied with *in* (that is, *in good time*). The collocation of *good* and *man* is found more than twice as often as that of *good* and *woman,* but the collocation of *good* and *gentleman* is only half as frequent as that of *good* and *lady.* The collocation of *good* and *natured* is always found in the collocation *good natured.* Dickens uses this collocation less frequently than other writers in the nineteenth century and the token ratio of *good natured* in Dickens is a third of that in the NCFWD.

great: *deal, many, no, said, very, all, man, out, made, like.*
The top ten collocates of *great* show a weaker tendency of fixed collocations than those of *good* but a few high-frequent fixed collocations are found: *a great deal (of)* and *great many.* More than 80 per cent of the examples of the second collocate *many* appear in the collocation *great many* and the token ratio of *great many* in the Dickens Corpus is five times that of the NCFWD. Collocations of *great* show a collocational difference in gender, which might be called 'collocational gender'. The number of collocations of *great* and *man* such as 'the *great man*', 'the old *man* with *great* curiosity' and 'a portly *man* in a *great*-coat' is 125, but that of *great* and *woman* is only 12. If limited to the collocations *great man* and *great woman, great man* is found 44 times but *great woman* only once in the Dickens Corpus. The collocation *great woman* is used for Madam Defarge, an eccentric woman, in *A Tale of Two Cities*: 'Her husband smoked at his door, looking after her with admiration. "A *great woman*," said he, "a strong woman, a grand woman, a frightfully grand woman!"' (II, 16). (The collocation *grand woman* is also used only for Madame Defarge and in no other Dickens' texts.)

Approximately half the collocations of *great* and *no*, the third most usual collocate, are a type of collocation '*no great* + noun' (127 times). The most frequent collocation among them is *no great distance* (25 times).

poor: *said, little, dear, fellow, old, girl, no, child, all, very.*
In the NCFWD, *lady* is the fifth most usual collocate of *poor* but it is not even within the top 50 in the Dickens Corpus. For example, the collocation *poor* (+ adjective) *lady* is found only 17 times in the Dickens Corpus and the token ratio of this collocation is a seventh of that in the NCFWD.

black: *hair, eyes, man, white, face, little, velvet, long, all, large.*
The third most usual collocate of *black* is *man*, though this is not within the top ten in the NCFWD. The adjective *black* usually functions as a part of an adverbial phrase following *man* such as 'the *man* with the *black* eye' and 'little old *man* in *black*' rather than as an attributive adjective of *man* such as 'a *black man*'. In the collocation of *black* and *face* the adjective rarely functions as an attributive and the collocation *black face* appears only twice in the Dickens Corpus. Approximately 33 per cent of the examples of the collocation *black* and *face* are *black in the face* (18 occurrences). On the other hand, in the collocation of *black* and *velvet* 47 out of the 49 examples are *black velvet* and 33 per cent of the examples of this collocation in the *NCF* are from Dickens.

red: *very, man, face, eyes, faced, hot, brick, white, all, little.*
The top collocate of *red* in the NCFWD is *nose* but in the Dickens Corpus the collocation of *red* and *nose* is not within the top ten. Fifty-five out of the 61 examples of the collocation of *red* and *faced* are *red-faced*. One-third of the examples of this collocation in the *NCF* are from Dickens. Similarly, in the collocation of *red* and *hot* almost all the examples (55 out of the 61 examples) are *red-hot* and one-third of the examples in the *NCF* are from Dickens.

blue: *coat, eyes, sky, bright, out, gentleman, up, bag, dragon, white.*
Ten per cent of the examples of *blue* (63 out of 699 examples) appear in the collocation *blue* (*dress* or *great*) *coat*. Concerning the colours of various types of coats in Dickens' works, more than a third of them are *blue* (therefore *blue* is the most common coat colour). Other colours of coats are black, green, brown, white, grey, and red in order of collocation frequency. As noted before, what is characteristic in the collocation of *blue* and *eyes*, the second most frequent collocate, is that characters

with *blue eyes* have certain common personality traits, that is, 'an innocent, favoured character'. Blue-eyed characters are Nell in *The Old Curiosity Shop*, Emily, Dora in *David Copperfield*, Ada, Mr Prince Turveydrop in *Bleak House*, Joe in *Great Expectations* and Lucie Manett in *A Tale of Two Cities*. Mr Casby in *Little Dorrit* also has blue eyes. In appearance, he acquires some of the innocent, favoured characteristics of a boy: 'There was the same smooth face and forehead, the same calm *blue eye*, the same placid air' (I, 13). In reality, he is 'a crafty imposter' and 'a heavy, selfish, drifting Booby'. Therefore, the 'innocent and favoured' connotation of *blue eyes* which is observed in other characters is used ironically in his case. In addition, *blue eyes* tends to co-occur with words having good connotations in appearance and with character: 'her *blue eyes* sparkling like jewels', 'the sweet *blue eyes* of Little Emily', 'the cloudless *blue eyes*' (Emily in *David Copperfield*), 'her tender *blue eyes*', 'such soft *blue eyes*' (Ada in *Bleak House*), 'her mild *blue eyes*' (Nell in *The Old Curiosity Shop*) and 'the soft *blue eyes*' (Lucie in *A Tale of Two Cities*). (All the collocations of *blue* and *dragon* appear as 'the *Blue Dragon*', the name of an inn. This collocation is not used except in Dickens' *Martin Chuzzlewit*.)

2.3 Adverbs

Among the 4.6 million words of the Dickens Corpus there are approximately 60,000 tokens of some 1900 different *-ly* adverbs. Table 2.2 illustrates the tokens of the 30 highest-frequency *-ly* adverbs in Dickens.

According to the semantic classification of Quirk et al. (1985: 8.2–8.10), among the 30 most frequent *-ly* adverbs in Table 2.2 there are various semantic types: adverbs expressive of modality – such as *really* and *certainly*; time – such as *immediately* and *suddenly*; degree – such as *highly* and *extremely*; and manner – such as *softly* and *easily* (although semantic roles and affinities partly overlap). More than 25 per cent (16,305) of the *-ly* adverb tokens (about 60,000) in Dickens are represented by the above 30 most-frequent *-ly* adverbs, although these adverbs constitute less than 2 per cent of the 1900 different *-ly* adverbs used by Dickens. In fact, many such adverbs occur just once or twice: about 500 *-ly* adverbs are used only once among the 4.6 million words in the corpus (representing nearly 30 per cent of the *-ly* adverbs overall).

In addition, 80 per cent (more than 400) of the one-time-use *-ly* adverbs are manner adverbs. Concerning the frequency of *-ly* manner adverbs in fiction, Biber et al. (1999: 541) observe that certain features

Table 2.2: The 30 highest-frequency *-ly* adverbs in Dickens

Rank	Type	Tokens	Rank	Type	Tokens
1	really	1458	16	gradually	431
2	certainly	1021	17	merely	427
3	immediately	844	18	quickly	423
4	slowly	821	19	generally	419
5	suddenly	723	20	highly	413
6	hardly	704	21	hastily	395
7	perfectly	703	22	possibly	395
8	scarcely	670	23	usually	392
9	nearly	614	24	gently	376
10	exactly	543	25	greatly	370
11	directly	528	26	surely	368
12	particularly	502	27	extremely	362
13	presently	468	28	quietly	350
14	softly	466	29	naturally	333
15	easily	459	30	evidently	327

Note: *-ly* adverbs which have identical forms in both adjective and adverb functions, such as *only*, *early* and *likely*, are excluded.

of fiction are distinct from other registers of usage (conversation, newspapers, and academic papers):

> It is interesting to note that, overall, fiction also uses many different descriptive *-ly* adverbs, although few of these are notably common (occurring over 50 times per million words). Rather, fiction shows great diversity in its use of *-ly* adverbs. In describing fictional events and the actions of fictional characters, writers often use adverbs with specific descriptive meanings.

Similarly, the Dickens Corpus also shows a great diversity in the use of *-ly* manner adverbs which 'express information about how an action is performed' (Biber et al. 1999: 553). Therefore, the quantitative and qualitative investigation of the collocations of *-ly* manner adverbs in the language of Dickens should provide us with a deeper understanding of his fictive language.

The list given below (Table 2.3) contains the 35 highest-frequency *-ly* manner adverbs, showing their occurrences per million words in the Dickens Corpus (totalling 4.6 million words); *-ly* manner adverbs in the NCFWD are examined for comparison.

Table 2.3: Occurrence per million words in the Dickens Corpus versus the NCFWD: *-ly* manner adverbs

-ly manner adverbs	Dickens Corpus	NCFWD
slowly	178.4	116.8
softly	101.3	36.3
easily	99.7	78.6
gradually	93.6	48.6
quickly	92.1	69.5
hastily	86.9	45.4
gently	83.2	59.0
quietly	78.4	85.4
carefully	65.2	56.3
heartily	54.3	25.9
steadily	46.7	19.0
frequently	41.9	51.8
gravely	40.9	24.1
earnestly	40.0	38.1
thoughtfully	39.3	4.5
hurriedly	37.6	14.5
eagerly	36.5	49.0
freely	34.8	24.0
firmly	34.3	29.5
happily	32.4	27.2
solemnly	32.4	32.3
cheerfully	31.5	18.1
sharply	31.0	25.0
lightly	30.6	26.3
anxiously	30.4	34.0
silently	30.4	29.5
rapidly	29.5	53.1
tenderly	29.3	25.9
impatiently	28.4	24.0
coolly	28.2	11.8
attentively	27.8	16.8
seriously	27.1	45.0
angrily	26.3	29.5
sternly	26.3	11.8
timidly	26.3	19.0

In 28 *-ly* manner adverbs out of the above list of 35, the Dickens Corpus surpasses the NCFWD in frequency. Notably, *softly, heartily, steadily, thoughtfully, hurriedly, coolly* and *sternly* in the Dickens Corpus occur at roughly twice the average frequency of the NCFWD. Remarkably, *thoughtfully* in the Dickens Corpus occurs almost nine times as often as in the NCFWD, and may thus be considered as Dickens' favourite manner adverb. It is interesting to note that there are 525 examples of *thoughtfully* in nineteenth-century fiction but only two examples of *thoughtfully* – in T. Amory's *Jun Buncle* and F. Burney's *Evelina* – in eighteenth-century fiction according to the *NCF* and the *ECF*. This fact may reflect a marked increase of the use of *thoughtfully* from the eighteenth century and throughout the nineteenth century.

The list of usual collocations of *-ly* manner adverbs in Appendix 1 illustrates many peculiar and interesting collocations. In Appendix 1 the top row in the second column presents those collocates which an *-ly* manner adverb modifies. The second row presents collocates which modify the *-ly* manner adverb and the third row presents those collocates of an *-ly* manner adverb which have no grammatical relationship of modification but do show distinctive characteristics. In the second row, the occurrences of *very* and *so* as *-ly* manner adverb modifiers have been shown in order to compare their differing usages, although there were very few occurrences found; occurrences of *more* and *most* have also been counted. Concerning the first row of collocates some characteristics of note can be summarized as follows:

(1) On the whole, *-ly* manner adverbs show a general tendency toward collocations with the reporting verb *said*, which is directly related to dialogue. The following *-ly* manner adverbs collocate with *said* (each exceeding 10 per cent of total occurrences): *impatiently* (25.2 per cent), *sternly* (19.8 per cent), *cheerfully* (19.3 per cent), *thoughtfully* (17.7 per cent), *timidly* (17.4 per cent), *solemnly* (16.1 per cent), *hurriedly* (15.6 per cent), *eagerly* (14.9 per cent), *coolly* (14.6 per cent), *sharply* (14.0 per cent), *earnestly* (13.6 per cent), *angrily* (13.0 per cent) and *gravely* (12.8 per cent). Research into collocations of *said* used by I-narrators reveals an avoidance of collocations with *-ly* manner adverbs. For example, in Esther's *Bleak House* narrative, collocations of *I said* with *-ly* manner adverbs appear only three times among more than 300 examples. These three adverbs are: *freely*, *timidly* and *lightly*. In *Great Expectations* only seven of the approximately 300 examples (of either *I said* or *said I*) show collocations with *-ly* manner adverbs: *snappishly*, *decidedly*, *confusedly*, *boldly*, *timidly*, *shortly* and *scornfully*. David in *David Copperfield* uses more *-ly* manner adverbs for his reporting clause (*I said* or *said I*) than the other two I-narrators: *exultingly*, *drily*, *tenderly*, *cheerfully* (twice), *civilly*, *gaily*, *indignantly* (twice), *hurriedly*, *bashfully*, *briskly*,

condescendingly, thickly, loftily and *respectfully*. It is notable that these three I-narrators use very few collocations of *I said* or *said I* with *-ly* manner adverbs, compared with other Dickens characters. Esther seems rigidly to avoid these collocations when compared with the other two I-narrators.

(2) Some *-ly* manner adverbs tend to modify *looked* and *looking*. For example, *steadily* collocating with either *looked* or *looking* amounts to over 30 per cent of its total tokens. On the other hand, the NCFWD shows only four out of the 42 examples of *steadily* collocating with *looked* or *looking*. The marked tendency of this collocation in Dickens shows a difference in the collocability of *steadily* from other nineteenth-century writers.

Dickens' other *-ly* manner adverbs which exclusively collocate with *looked* or *looking* are: *anxiously* (27.9 per cent), *attentively* (26.6 per cent), *earnestly* (20.1 per cent), *thoughtfully* (17.1 per cent), *eagerly* (15.5 per cent) and *sternly* (14.9 per cent). The collocations of *looked* or *looking* with *-ly* manner adverbs can often be used to reveal or contrast individual traits of personality or character. For example, in *Hard Times* Louisa's manner of looking at her father is described with the repeated collocation of *looking* and *fixedly*, as exemplified in the following: 'From the beginning, she had sat *looking* at him *fixedly*' (I, 15), 'she, with a hand upon his shoulder, *looking fixedly* in his face' (II, 12), and 'she . . . still *looking fixedly* in his face, went on' (II, 12). Her act of looking fixedly at her father has a symbolic implication revealing her superficially strong mind but also, in reality, her craving for a father's true love. On the other hand, *looked* as used for her brother Tom, nicknamed 'the Whelp' by Harthouse, collocates with other various *-ly* manner adverbs, as observed in the following: 'He [Tom] *looked* at his companion [Harthouse] *sneakingly*, he *looked* at him *admiringly*, he *looked* at him *boldly*, and put up one leg on the sofa' (II, 3). The delineation of Tom's act of viewing also co-occurs with *-ly* manner adverbs expressive of his mental state: 'and from time to time, he *turned the whites of his eyes restlessly* and *impatiently* towards his father' (III, 7). Such a contrastive use of usual collocations of *looked* or *looking* with *-ly* manner adverbs for characterization could be considered Dickensian. This is because in Dickens the act of viewing can often be as significant as the depiction of the physical appearance of a character's eyes, which is one of Dickens' indispensable devices regarding characterization. Above all, the very high-frequency perception verb *look*, which is accompanied with adverbs or adverbial phrases and used contrasted with other perception verbs such as *see*, contributes not only to characterization but also conveys symbolic meanings which closely relate to the themes of the texts. For example, in *Dombey and Son* Mr Dombey's eyes which are always attracted to little Paul show that his son becomes the centre of his life; Florence's looking at Mr Dombey is indicative of the love she offers timidly to her father; Paul's gaze at Florence implies a continuous sense of confidence in her.

(3) *Heartily* tends to collocate closely with *laughed* or *laughing* and the ratio of the collocation of *heartily* with either *laughed* or *laughing* amounts to over one-third of the examples of *heartily*. By contrast, the NCFWD shows that only seven of 56 examples of *heartily* collocate with *laughed* or *laughing*. Dickens' earlier texts present a predominant tendency of co-occurrence of *laughed* or *laughing* with *heartily*: 15 of 27 instances in *Pickwick Papers*, and nine of 10 instances in *Oliver Twist*. Such a tendency in the use of fixed collocations in Dickens' earlier texts can be observed in additional collocations as well.

In eighteenth-century fiction, *heartily* often collocates with verbs not only expressing positive connotations but also expressions of negative emotion or the implication of distaste toward other people, such as *despise, dislike, hate* and *detest*. Of the 75 occurrences of *heartily* in the first edition of *Clarissa Harlowe*, 16 are collocates of *despise, hate* and *detest*. Moreover, we find many examples of *heartily* collocating with words of negative or unpleasant states of affairs in eighteenth-century fiction, such as, *heartily swear, heartily quarrel, heartily vexed* and *heartily plague*. This collocational tendency was gradually decreasing throughout the nineteenth century but can still be observed among nineteenth-century writers: 'which I *heartily despise*' (Collins' *The Woman in White*), 'had *heartily mistrusted* her' (Thackeray's *Vanity Fair*), 'having *scolded* her *heartily*' (Brontë's *Wuthering Heights*) and so on.

On the prevailing collocational trend with positive terms, *heartily* in Dickens illustrates a strong tendency of collocation with verbs expressing positive connotations such as *laugh, shake hands* and *thank*. Among the 250 examples of *heartily* in Dickens there is only one example of *heartily* with a verb expressing negative emotion, in *David Copperfield*. David holds an intense hatred for Uriah Heep, the hypocrite: 'I . . . *disliked* him [Uriah Heep] so *heartily*' (Ch. 52). Such a nuanced contrast of collocability trends may allow us to infer creative authorial significance, although this sort of avenue has been largely overlooked. The contrast of collocational pattern of *heartily* between Dickens and other eighteenth and nineteenth-century fiction writers serves as an excellent example of the patterns that can be discerned using a collocational approach.

(4) Some of the less highly-frequent *-ly* manner adverbs (which do not appear in Table 2.3) also show distinctive collocational tendencies. For example, the following manner adverbs illustrate a marked tendency to collocate with *looked* or *looking: fixedly* (43 out of 53: 79.2 per cent), *wistfully* (35 out of 56: 62.5 per cent) and *vacantly* (29 out of 51: 56.9 per cent). Moreover, 35 (39.3 per cent) of the 89 collocations of *busily* are collocated with *engaged*, especially in Dickens' early works. In *Sketches by Boz* all seven instances of *busily* are found in the collocation *busily engaged*. This tendency toward the use of more fixed collocations in Dickens' early works, as observed in the collocation of *busily* with *engaged* and the collocation of *heartily* with *laughed* or *laughing*, is also found in the usual collocations of other words and may lead us to an awareness of the change or development of his collocational style throughout his later works.

(5) All of the distinctive collocates which the 35 highest-frequency *-ly* manner adverbs in Appendix 1 modify are verbs; there are no adjectives found in the list.

With respect to the middle row (Appendix 1) of collocates by which *-ly* manner adverbs are modified, the following characteristics are worth pointing out:

(6) The manner adverbs which tend to be modified by *so, very, more* and so on are: *freely* (34.4 per cent), *heartily* (32.4 per cent), *earnestly* (30.4 per cent), *easily* (26.1 per cent), *attentively* (21.1 per cent), *seriously* (18.4 per cent), *lightly* (16.3 per cent), *frequently* (17.6 per cent), *happily* (14.1 per cent), *quickly* (13.4 per cent), and *quietly* (11.1 per cent). On the other hand, those *-ly* manner adverbs which tend to be unmodified by other adverbs are: *impatiently* (none out of 131), *gradually* (0.7 per cent: three out of 431), *timidly* (0.8 per cent: one out of 121), *hurriedly* (1.7 per cent: three out of 173), *thoughtfully* (2.2 per cent: four out of 181), *angrily* (2.4 per cent: three out of 123) and *hastily* (2.5 per cent: 10 out of 400).

(7) Some *-ly* manner adverbs show a differing tendency of usage between the adverbial modifiers *very* and *so*. For example, *carefully*,

slowly and *heartily* have a tendency to collocate with *very* while *lightly, freely, happily, rapidly* and *tenderly* are predominantly modified by *so*.

Collocates in the third row of Appendix 1 do not have any grammatical relationship of modification with -*ly* manner adverbs but do show some distinctive characteristics as summarized in the following:

(8) The manner adverbs *lightly* (12: 8.5 per cent), *timidly* (9: 7.4 per cent), *gently* (28: 7.3 per cent), *tenderly* (9: 6.7 per cent), *heartily* (15: 6 per cent) and *softly* (16: 3.4 per cent) co-occur with *hand*: for example, 'the man passed his *hand lightly* over the poor fellow's face', 'laying his *hand timidly* on that of Nicholas' (NN 22), 'laying his *hand gently* on her head' (OCS 24), 'Flora put her *hand tenderly* on his' (LD I, 23), '*heartily* shaking (or shook) *hands*' (DC 51) and 'He laid his *hand softly* upon the latch' (OCS 70). In the NCFWD the co-occurrences of *lightly, gently, tenderly* and *softly* with *hand* are as follows, respectively: two out of 58 (3.4 per cent), zero out of 42, 11 out of 139 (7.9 per cent), one out of 57 (1.8 per cent), and one out of 84 (1.2 per cent).

(9) Some -*ly* manner adverbs occur with *head*. For example, *gravely* co-occurs with *head* (27: 14.4 per cent) and almost all of its collocations are found in the phrase '(*gravely*) shaking or shook one's head *gravely*' (21 times) while only one example of the co-occurrence of *gravely* and *head* (one out of the 53 examples: 1.9 per cent) can be found in the NCFWD. The six collocations of *seriously* and *head* all appear in the phrase 'shake one's head *seriously*'. The co-occurrence of *firmly* and *head* as observed in the phrase 'secured it *firmly* on his head' appears six times in Dickens, but before Dickens, such a co-occurrence is not found, according to the *NCF* and the *ECF*.

(10) The -*ly* manner adverb *steadily* tends to occur in the phrase 'looking *steadily* in one's *face*' (nine times). It is noticeable that 23 (12.7 per cent) of the 181 examples of *thoughtfully* co-occur with words expressive of body parts, as observed in the phrases 'drawing his *hand thoughtfully* down his *face*' and 'nodding his *head thoughtfully*'. In the NCFWD however, such collocations of *thoughtfully* are very rare: and only 10 examples (2.8 per cent) of the 355 collocations of *thoughtfully* (excluding Dickens' examples) in the *NCF* collocate with words relating to body parts. Limiting a search to examples of nineteenth-century fiction written before Dickens, only a few examples of such collocations are found. Therefore, the

collocations of *thoughtfully* with words expressive of body parts can be considered Dickensian.

(11) Dickens appears to like the collocation of *softly* or *carefully* with *door* much more than other nineteenth-century writers; approximately one-third of the co-occurrences of *softly* or *carefully* with *door* (in nineteenth-century fiction) are Dickens' examples, according to the *NCF*. The collocation of *softly* with *door* appears 40 times (8.6 per cent). In Dickens the collocation of *carefully* and *door* occurs 18 times. In contrast, in eighteenth-century fiction the example of the collocation of *carefully* and *door* is found only once, in the phrase 'kept the *door carefully*' in Mary Manley's *Memoirs of Europe* (1710) according to the *ECF*.

(12) *Thoughtfully*, which is a much more frequent adverb in Dickens than in the work of other nineteenth-century novelists and which occurs only twice in eighteenth-century fiction (*ECF*), co-occurs with *fire* 11 times (6.1 per cent): for example, in 'looking *thoughtfully* at the *fire*'. According to the *NCF* and the *ECF* there are 17 examples of the collocation of *thoughtfully* and *fire* but most (11 examples) are from Dickens.

(13) *Easily* shows a marked tendency to occur with auxiliary verbs: *could* (45: 9.8 per cent), *have* (40: 8.7 per cent), *might* (36: 7.8 per cent), *may* (26: 5.7 per cent) and *can* (21: 4.8 per cent). The ratio of the collocation *easily* with auxiliary verbs amounts to 36.6 per cent and displays the highest frequency among the 35 highest-frequency *-ly* manner adverbs in Dickens. Another approach would be needed to explain the reason why *easily* is predominantly accompanied with auxiliary verbs.

(14) An interesting collocate concerning the collocations of *firmly* is *but*. *Firmly* appears right after *but* 14 times (8.9 per cent) as observed in 'said Darnay, modestly *but firmly*' (TT II, 10). *Poorly*, which is not contained in the above list, also co-occurs with *but*, 13 times (22.0 per cent) out of 59 examples.

(15) *Mournfully* (which Table 3.2 does not contain) also shows a distinctive collocational tendency. Fourteen of the 72 examples of *mournfully* co-occur with *head* in 'shaking (or shook) one's head *mournfully*' (19.4 per cent).

(16) *Exactly* has a tendency to collocate with *same*. Most of the collocations of *exactly* and *same* (59 out of 66 examples) appear in the phrase *exactly the same*. The token-ratio of this collocation is approximately four times that of the NCFWD. According to the *NCF* one-third of the examples of the collocation *exactly the same*

(49 out of 161 examples) in nineteenth-century fiction are from Dickens.

(17) The co-occurrence of *-ly* manner adverbs with certain characters illustrate obvious collocational ties. For example, 12 out of the 30 examples of *impatiently* in *Nicholas Nickleby* are used for Ralf Nicholas, and *timidly* in *Dombey and Son* co-occurs with Florence (16 out of 21 occurrences). This issue of the collocational tie of a particular word with a particular character will be discussed in detail in 'Collocations and Characters' (Chapter 6).

2.4 Semantic prosodies

As argued in Section 1.3 (Chronological change of collocation), the recent concept of semantic prosodies for studies of collocation is not only interesting but is also very useful in determining an author's collocational style. This section will be devoted to Dickens' collocational style in terms of his semantic prosodies.

The term 'semantic prosody' is first mentioned by Louw (1993), though strictly speaking, according to Louw, this term was first used in a private conversation between Sinclair and himself. The term is used to indicate that some words not only have particular collocates but also that these connect more broadly across certain semantic groups. For example, as a negative semantic prosody Stubbs (1995: 246) gives an example of *break out* which collocates with unpleasant words such as *disagreements, riots, sweat, violence* and *war*. The verb *provide* is given as the example of a positive prosody because its collocates are *food, help, relief* and *support*.

Such semantic prosodies of certain specific words are often different among different authors. For example, the adverb *heartily* in Dickens, as shown in Section 2.3, has a strong tendency to collocate with verbs expressing positive connotations such as *laugh, shake hands* and *thank*, while other nineteenth-century writers do not show such a clear tendency regarding collocations of *heartily* and indeed may link *heartily* with negative emotions, such as *despise* and *hate*. Dickens' strong tendency of collocation of *heartily* with verbs expressing positive connotations could be said to be a Dickensian semantic prosody of *heartily*, in that it is possible to differentiate Dickens' prosodic application from that of other writers. Examples of specific authorial semantic prosodies are not easily discernable and may not be frequently found, nevertheless this prosodic aspect is definitely a new perspective of collocational style, attainable from the viewpoint of a collocational analysis. The following examples may be considered to be Dickensian semantic prosodies.

The collocation *blue eyes* in Dickens, as mentioned above co-occurs with words having a positive connotation such as *sweet* and *tender*. The collocation *blue eyes* leads us to an awareness of a group of characters (mainly women) yielding positive images, such as Nell, Little Emily, and Ada. *Great* and *wise* illustrates a stronger tendency of collocation with masculine words in Dickens than other contemporary writers, and collocations with *woman* are almost completely avoided by Dickens. For example, *great woman* and *wise woman* are only once used; *wise lady* is not found in the Dickens Corpus, although *great woman*, *wise woman* and *wise lady* are found 10 times, 40 times, and six times respectively among other nineteenth-century writers, according to the *NCF*.

In Dickens, *lovely* is only collocated with a group of words referring to the feminine gender. You cannot find *lovely boy* or *lovely gentleman*, to say nothing of *lovely man* in Dickens. These collocations are also quite rare among other nineteenth-century writers: no example of *lovely man*; 11 examples of *lovely boy*; *lovely gentleman* is used only once according to the *NCF*, although *man* is the thirteenth most-frequent collocate of *lovely* in the *COBUILD English Collocations on CD-ROM* in present-day English.

2.5 Colligations

Stubbs (2001: 65) describes colligation as 'the relation between a pair of grammatical categories or, in a slightly wider sense, a pairing of lexis and grammar'. Stubbs goes on to give the example of the word-form *cases* and its tendency to co-occur with the grammatical category of quantifier, in phrases such as *in some cases* or *in many cases*. Hoey defines colligation more directly as 'the grammatical company a word keeps and the positions it prefers; in other words, a word's colligations describe what it typically does grammatically' (2001: 234). I would like to further classify colligation into two types. The first is taken from the viewpoint of grammatical context and the second involves a classification in terms of word order. That is to say, a lexical item may have a strong tendency to occur in a certain position in a relation with another item or in a text. For example, in the collocation of *busily* and *engaged* you will find *busily engaged* but not *engaged busily*.

Such colligations of certain words can also show authorial differences among writers. As with semantic prosodies, we cannot easily determine such colligations as particular to a writer. Nevertheless, when found, such colligations can be regarded as giving us an insight to the writer's collocational style. The following paragraphs present two types of colligation specific to Dickens.

The intensive adverb *infinitely* (as pointed out in Section 1.3) as used by Dickens has a remarkably strong tendency of collocation with the comparative form of adjectives and adverbs (approximately 80 per cent) in comparison to other nineteenth-century writers (approximately 40 per cent). Such a strong tendency of the colligation of *infinitely* in Dickens can be considered Dickensian.

The tendency of *heartily* to be modified by intensive adverbs such as *very* and *so* is also quite strong in Dickens, amounting to approximately 30 per cent, but only 5 per cent in the NCFWD. This tendency of *heartily* is stronger in Dickens' early texts.

As an example of another type of colligation the word order of the collocation of *steadily* and 'look' (*look, looks, looking* and *looked*) will be taken up. In Dickens *steadily* always functions as a postmodifier of *looking*, for example, '*looking steadily* in her face' and '*looking* at him *steadily*', but not as a premodifier of *looking*, such as in 'Still *steadily looking* at her, he set himself to fix the language' in Collins' *Amadale*. In the *NCF* there are four example of *steadily* premodifying *looking*. This feature of word order is also true of the collocation of *steadily* and *looks* or *look*. Concerning the collocation of *steadily* and *looked*, in 39 out of the 40 examples *steadily* follows *looked*, as in 'he *looked* long and *steadily* at her' and 'she *looks* at him so *steadily* and coldly'. This post-modification of *steadily* for 'look' is a colligational feature which is rigidly maintained through the eighteenth and nineteenth centuries, and there are no examples of premodification of *steadily* to *looked* in other authors in the eighteenth and nineteenth centuries according to the *ECF* and the *NCF*. In *Great Expectations* Dickens breaks this colligation once:

> He emptied his glass, got up, and stood at the side of the fire, with his heavy brown hand on the mantelshelf. He put a foot up to the bars, to dry and warm it, and the wet boot began to steam; but, he neither looked at it, nor at the fire, but *steadily looked* at me. It was only now that I began to tremble. (GE 39)

In this scene Pip is horrified by gradually realizing that this man is the escaped convict, Magwitch, and his benefactor. This violation of post-modification of *steadily* to *looked* may reflect or partly represent Pip's horror at a shocking revelation.

2.6 Conclusion

As observed in the foregoing discussions, familiar or usual collocations of common words can be considered in three ways: as collocates, semantic prosodies and colligation. The usual collocations of some words may reflect strong tendencies towards particular collocates, particular sets of meanings, and particular grammatical features of collocates, but other words may not demonstrate the same features. In any case, however, 'words acquire colligations and semantic prosodies, as well as collocations, by being repeated in similar contexts' (Hoey, 2001: 238). This also applies to authorial style. Not all the usual collocations of words investigated in the Dickens Corpus always illustrate the clear tendencies of collocations in terms of these three aspects. However, the important thing to note is that Dickens has a unique collocational style, which is best revealed through the analysis of usual collocations of common words. The collocational tendencies of some words indicate obvious predilections or avoidance in Dickens, which proves to be characteristic. In addition, some collocations peculiar to Dickens are structurally or creatively used in the context of an individual text or in the larger context of his whole oeuvre. Therefore, what might be called 'Dickensian' has been observed definitively through the analysis of the usual collocations in the Dickens Corpus.

3
Creative Collocations

Chapter 2 looked at Dickens' familiar collocations of common words and indicated certain distinctive collocational tendencies, Dickens' characteristic predilection for particular collocations, and his avoidance of collocations frequently found among other nineteenth-century writers through a quantitative survey of his works. As well, some familiar collocations used structurally or rhetorically were (through the analysis of collocations in relation to characters, themes and contexts) shown to be evidence of Dickens' 'creative' language use. However, a more definitive treatment of what may be considered 'Dickensian' will be presented in the following sections, which examine unique or unusual collocations, known as 'creative collocations'. These will be examined under eight categories: (1) metaphorical collocations, (2) transferred collocations, (3) oxymoronic collocations, (4) disparate collocations, (5) unconventional collocations, (6) modified idiomatic collocations, (7) parodied collocations and (8) relexicalized collocations.

3.1 Metaphorical collocations

Metaphor can be thought of as a matter of lexical collocation, in that the degree of metaphorical effect is dependent upon the mutual unexpectedness or unusualness of two or more co-occurring words, that is, the constituent elements of the collocation. In other words, creative metaphor is an interaction of words which are not conventionally associated.

In this section, the following syntactic constructions will be discussed: 'adjective + noun', 'adverb + adjective/verb', 'noun + verb' and 'verb + noun'.

3.1.1 Adjective + noun

In metaphorical collocations of 'adjective + noun' there are three cases: either the (1) noun or (2) adjective can be a metaphorical word, or (3) both can be metaphorical words. Examples are given below:

(1) 'Raising his [Heep's] great hands until they touched his chin, he rubbed them softly, and softly chuckled; looking as like a *malevolent baboon*, I thought, as anything human could look.' (DC 39)
(2) 'Toodle being the family name of *the apple-faced family.*' (DS 2)
(3) (In Mr Mantalini's dialogue) 'She [Madame Mantalini], who coils her fascinations round me like a pure and *angelic rattlesnake!*' (NN 34)

In the first example the adjective *malevolent* implies Heep's character and the noun *baboon* is used to allude to his behaviour. The adjective *apple-faced* in the second example is a metaphorical expression for these family members' identical plump, rosy-cheeked faces. The third example has two figurative expressions, 'angel' and 'rattlesnake', both of which are used for the same person, Madam Mantalini. In any narrative, a collocational clash or discrepancy of associations between different metaphors may convey a sense of a character's curious personality, but the fact that the collocation *angelic rattlesnake* in (3) is used in Mr Mantalini's dialogue implies Mr Mantalini's strange personality. Such a use of two different metaphorical words within a single instance or phrase to describe a person is called 'a mixed metaphorical collocation'. Of these three cases of metaphorical collocation, the second example (adjectival) is the type found most frequently in Dickens.

Collocations in which a noun is metaphorical, as observed in the first and third examples, are very often accompanied with markers or indicators such as *like*, *as* and *as if*. These may be called simile in a generic sense; in this section not only simile, but also metonymy and synecdoche are treated as literary metaphor. Some collocations of the metaphorical noun are given below:

(1) 'Has the *sly old fox* made his fortune then, and gone to live in a tranquil cot in a pleasant spot with a distant view of the changing sea?' (OCS 13)
(2) 'he had been a *sad dog* in his time.' (SB 7)
(3) 'From my Lord Boodle, through the Duke of Foodle, down to Noodle, Sir Leicester, like a *glorious spider*, stretches his threads of relationship.' (BH 28)

(4) 'So might an *industrious fox*, or *bear*, make up his account of chickens or stray travellers with an eye to his cubs; . . .' (BH 39)

According to Andrew Goatly's *The Language of Metaphors* (1997: 99–100), the most productive suffix among denominal adjective suffixes for metaphor is -*like*; all adjectives collocated with -*like* are considered metaphorical. As such, one finds that in Dickens' language the suffix -*like* is very productive for metaphorical collocations:

> There was a smell of black dye in the airless room, which the fire had been drawing out of the crape and stuff of the widow's [Mrs Clennam's] dress for fifteen months, and out of the *bier-like sofa* for fifteen years. (LD I, 3)

The collocation *bier-like sofa* seems to refer literally to the shape of a sofa. However, considering that Mrs Clennam 'hasn't been out of it fifteen times in as many years' and has been staying home since her husband died, the collocation *bier-like sofa* connotes the symbolic meaning that she is alive but leads life as though she were a corpse lying on a bier. *Bier-like sofa* is used four time in *Little Dorrit* but is not found in other writers of the *NCF*. This metaphorical collocation of -*like* tacked onto a noun to form a hyphenated adjective not only yields a visual image for a thing or a character but also, through various associations of the concrete noun, contributes to the character related to or referred to by the collocation. Therefore, collocations of '-*like* (stemming from a concrete noun) + noun' are overwhelmingly more frequent than those of '-*like* (stemming from abstract noun) + noun'. Let us consider these instances of collocations of animals, fish and insects as 'animate' metaphors:

> fish-like eyes (BR 1), the cricket-like chirrup of little Solomon Daisy (BR 3), spider-like embrace (BR 51), with a cow-like lightness (BH 19), fish-like manner (BH 45), bee-like industry (BH 32), her [Volumnia's] bird-like hopping about and pecking at papers (BH 66), any cat-like quality (DS 46), dog-like manner (GE 5), mouse-like feet (NN 28), kitten-like playfulness (NN 34), cat-like obsequiousness (NN 47), crab-like way with him (LD I, 3), crab-like old man, (LD I, 3), rook-like aspect (ED 2), the dog-like smile (OCS 4), eel-like crawlings (OCS 33), this lynx-like scrutiny (DC 29), his [Uriah Heep] fish-like hand (DC 42), a bird-like fondness (DC 42), of the two little bird-like ladies (DC 43), eel-like position (OT 7), bird-like

habit (PP 22), un-swan-like manner (PP 29), lamb-like manner (PP 45)

The metaphorical collocations applied to various people or occupations are striking:

the epicure-like feeling (BH 4), alderman-like form (BR 7), Gorgon-like mind (DS 23), skipper-like state (DS 4), lady-like amateur manner (GE 18), her [Miss Havisham's] witch-like eagerness (GE 19), child-like vivacity (MC 2), the workman-like manner (MC 35), a connoisseur-like air (NN 44), undertaker-like Cupid (LD I, 5), ghost-like manner (OCS 63), a saint-like and holy character (OCS 66), cannibal-like manner (OCS 67), his ancient scribe-like finger intent upon the work (OMF III, 3), sailor-like turn on his cravat (OMF IV, 14), spinster-aunt-like envy (PP 4), ghost-like air (PP 24), gong-like clash and clatter (BH 21), ghost-like punctuality (NN 4), apothecary-like manner (PP 37)

The following collocations are inanimate metaphors referring to such things as objects and buildings:

prison-like yard (BH 48), the hearse-like panel of the door (BH 51), his hammer-like hand upon the table (BH 57), statue-like manner (DS 29), the siren-like delusion of art (MC 4), a toga-like simplicity of nature (MC 7), gauze-like mist (MC 36), dungeon-like opposite tenements (LD II, 5), His [Pancks'] steam-like breathings (LD II, 26), a jail-like upper rim of iron and spikes (OMF I, 15), dungeon-like black out-door (OMF II, 6), the bell-like notes of that gifted amateur (DC 63), an automaton-like rapidity (PP 22), cork-like manner (PP 32).

As for the collocations of '-*like* stemming from abstract noun + noun' we have few examples:

death-like silence (BR 48), A death-like stillness (MC 17), death-like faces (OCS 29), the death-like stillness (OT 50), whist-like appearance (PP 34)

Goatly (1997: 100) states that 'the suffix -*like* has no restrictions on its productivity' for 'marking active metaphor' but in metaphorical collocations of '-*like* adjective + noun' in Dickens, the -*like* adjectives are most frequently formed from concrete nouns giving physical, visual or perceptive images, while *-like* adjectives formed from abstract nouns are very few, except for the examples of *business-like*, as shown below. A distinctive use of *-like* adjectives formed from abstract nouns is noted in the high frequency of *business-like*. The word *business-like* appears 64 times throughout Dickens' oeuvre and is found at least once in nearly all of his works. Dickens' predilection for collocations of *business-like* is seen clearly in the collocations of *business-like manner* or *way*; this type of collocation is used sixteen times throughout his works. Some of the collocations of *'business-like* + noun' are unique or unusual:

> *business-like* Old England (TTC II, 24), a *business-like* delight (LD I, 13), his *business-like* 'Get on, my lad!' (BH 57), cool, *business-like*, gentlemanly, self-possessed regret (DS 1), a *business-like* sedateness (NN 50), a sufficiently *business-like* appearance (LD I, 30), a *business-like* face at parting (LD I, 30), an equable *business-like* possession of the deceased (LD II, 25), *business-like* usage in his steady gaze (OMF I, 1), these practical and *business-like* details (DC 28)

Goatly's (1997) list of productive denominal adjective suffixes for active metaphor indicates decreasing productivity in the following order: *-y, -ish, -oid, -ous, -ic (-iac, -an, -ian), -al (-ial, -ine), -en (-ed)*. However, in Dickens a distinctive suffix next to *-like* among these adjective suffixes, productive of adjectives for active metaphors, is *-ed*. It will be demonstrated in Chapter 4 that the suffix *-ed* is very productive of new compound words used as premodifiers in Dickens. Some striking examples are:

> lynx-eyed vigilance (DS 27), a little white-headed apple-faced tipstaff (PP 42), the identical rosy-cheeked apple-faced Polly (DS 56), the peachy-cheeked charmers (BH 66), bulbous-shoed old benchers (BH 1), my little cherry-cheeked, red-lipped wife (OCS 6), a knock-knee'd mind (OMF III, 4)

In cases where the noun in the collocation 'adjective + noun' is expressive of a part of a body, we often find metaphorical collocations:

> (*eyes* or *eye*) the fish eye (DS 7), his fishy eyes (GE 9), with glazed and fishy eyes (MC 22), the frosty eye (DS 11), his [Mr. Gradgrind's] cavernous eyes (HT I, 4), Major's lobster eyes (DS 20), his lobster-eyes (DS 40), the ferret eyes (DS 52), hazel eyes (DS 53), seraphic eyes (DC

35), her lightning eyes (DC 56), demon eyes (LD I, 14), the eagle eye
(PP 4), its death-cold eyes (CC Stave 1)
(*fingers*) his [Heep's] fishy fingers (DC 39), ghostly fingers (DS 23),
aquiline fingers (OMF I, 10)
(*head*) his [Jerry's] spiky head (TTC II, 14), the burning head (MC 25
& 28)
(*cheeks*) peachy cheeks (BH 56)
(*hair*) his sandy hair (GE 9)

Some other interesting metaphorical collocations are given below:

aristocratic slowness (DC 52), the aristocratic pavements of Belgrave
Square (NN 21), the eminently aristocratic door (OMF I, 17), the
pertinacious oil lamps (BH 58), a wrathful sunset (BR 56), her [Miss
Flight's cat's] tigerish claws (BH 5)

3.1.2 Adverb + verb/adjective

In this type of collocation, a manner adverb modifies an adjective or
verb grammatically but functions in a figurative way. The instance given
below is typical:

The carriages in the streets are few, and other late sounds in that
neighbourhood there are none, unless a man so very *nomadically
drunk* as to stray into the frigid zone goes brawling and bellowing
along the pavement. (BH 58)

Since the *man* being described as *nomadically drunk* is not a nomad, there
is no doubt that the manner adverb *nomadically* modifies *drunk* figuratively. This example, from *Bleak House* (1852–53), is an earlier example
than that recorded in the *OED2*, dated 1862. Moreover, this manner
adverb is used just once in Dickens. Therefore, the collocation *nomadically drunk* may be called a deviant or abnormal collocation.

The following collocation might be considered even more deviant:

'The Commandments say, no murder. NO murder, sir!' proceeded
Mr. Honeythunder, *platformally pausing* as if he took Mr. Crisparkle
to task for having distinctly asserted that they said: You may do a
little murder, and then leave off. (ED 17)

The hypocritical philanthropist Honeythunder strikes an affected pose
as if standing on the speaker's platform. The adverb *platformally* which
figuratively modifies *pausing* includes the two derivational suffixes -*al*

and -*ly* added to the noun *platform*. However, the adjective *platformal* is not included in the *OED2*, which records this example of *platformally* as the earliest usage. This collocation *platformally pausing* also appears only once in the Dickens Corpus. Such very low frequency of use is distinctive of this type of figurative collocation and is expressive of Dickens' creativity.

Some similar instances are taken up below:

(1) 'Young Sparkler hovering about the rooms, *monomaniacally seeking* any sufficiently ineligible young lady with no nonsense about her . . .' (LD I, 21)
    (The adverb *monomaniacally* in this work is treated as the earliest example in the *OED2*.)
(2) 'Here Bazzard awoke himself by his own snoring; and, as is usual in such cases, sat *apoplectically staring* at vacancy, as defying vacancy to accuse him of having been asleep.' (ED 11)
    (The adverb *apoplectically* in this work is an earlier example than that of the *OED2* first citation of 1881.)
(3) 'Poor Noggs literally gasped for breath as this flood of questions rushed upon him, and *moved spasmodically* in his chair at every fresh inquiry, staring at Nicholas meanwhile with a most ludicrous expression of perplexity.' (NN 40)
    (The adverb *spasmodically* in this work is treated as the earliest example in the meaning 'in a jerky or sudden manner' in the *OED2*.)
(4) 'For aught I know, it may be a reference to Pickwick himself, who has most unquestionably been a *criminally slow* coach during the whole of this transaction . . .' (PP 34)
(5) 'Mr. Brass would then set the office-door wide open, hum his old tune with great gaiety of heart, and *smile seraphically* as before.' (OCS 57)
(6) 'Then it was that I began, if I may so *Shakespearianly express myself*, to dwindle, peak, and pine.' (DC 52)
    (The adverb *Shakespearianly* in this work is an earlier example than that of the *OED2* first citation of 1890.)
(7) 'She *cherubically escorted*, like some severe saint in a painting, or merely human matron allegorically treated.' (OMF 4)

In the above examples, contemporary readers may find Dickens' use of *monomaniacally seeking*, *apoplectically staring*, *criminally slow* and *smile seraphically* to be normal/familiar, while *Shakespearianly express* may seem unfamiliar and *cherubically escorted* may seem unusual. However, none of these collocations of -*ly* manner adverbs were found among other eighteenth and nineteenth-century writers and thus represented abnormal usage in the Victorian age.

3.1.3 Noun + verb/verb + noun

Verbs used metaphorically will often be those easily evoking imagery or those referring to physical acts and events. When considering such verbs in metaphorical clauses M.A.K. Halliday's model of verbal processes is very useful. (Both Goatly (1997: 87–8) and Moon (1998: 207–11) use Halliday's model for analysing the metaphorical phrase, metaphorical fixed expression and metaphorical idiom.) With respect to the types of processes in the English transitivity system, Halliday (1994: Ch. 5) classifies them into the following three main types:

(1) Material processes	event	the lion sprang
	action	the lion caught the tourist
(2) Mental processes	affection	Mary liked the gift / the gift pleased Mary
	cognition	I know / I believe you / the quiet puzzles me
	perception	it hurts my ears
(3) Relational processes	attributive	Sara is wise / the fair is on a Tuesday / Peter has a piano
	identifying	Tom is the leader / the piano is Peter's

In Halliday's classification, material processes refer to external phenomena, that is, the processes of the external world, while mental processes constitute inner experience, that is, processes of consciousness. Processes of classifying and identifying are considered to be relational processes.

In addition to these three principal types of process in the English clause, Halliday recognizes three subsidiary types: behavioural processes (sharing characteristics of material and mental processes), verbal processes (sharing characteristics of mental and relational processes) and existential processes (sharing characteristics of relational and material processes). In other words, behavioural processes are 'processes of (typically human) physiological and psychological behaviour, like breathing, coughing, smiling, dreaming and staring' (Halliday 1994: 139), verbal processes are 'processes of saying, as in *What did you say? – I said it's noisy in here*' (p. 140), and existential processes 'represent that something exists or happens, as in *there was a little guinea-pig, there seems to be a problem, has there been a phone call?, there isn't enough time'* (p. 142). According to Goatly (1997: 87) the process verbs used as metaphors are material process verbs, and above all 'the general tendency is to use Material metaphors for Mental processes', but in fact various and complex metaphoric usages are found in Dickens. This first example is a material metaphor:

(1) *The cold within him froze his old features, nipped his pointed nose, shrivelled his cheek, stiffened his gait; made his eyes red, his thin lips blue*; and spoke out shrewdly in his grating voice. A frosty rime was on his head, and on his eyebrows, and his wiry chin. He carried his own low temperature always about with him; (2) *he [Scrooge] iced his office in the dog-days; and didn't thaw it one degree at Christmas.* (CC 1)

In the above passage, sentence (1) expresses a metaphorical material process because material processes are processes of 'doing' something. In (1) the 'actor' of the process is *the cold within him*. The 'goals' of the processes: *froze, nipped, shrivelled, stiffened* and *made* are: *his old features, his pointed nose, his cheek, his gait* and *his eyes* (and *his thin lips*), respectively. These material metaphors are used for a relational process because we can say that the conceptual meaning of sentence (1) is 'Scrooge is a very cold-hearted man'. It is interesting to note that both the actor and the goal of sentence (1) are Scrooge and that in fact or as a physical phenomenon there is no process of 'doing'.

The material metaphor of sentence (2) may be more complex. As analysed in (1), the metaphorical process of (2) is also used for the relational process 'Scrooge is a very cold-hearted man' or 'Scrooge is misanthropic'. However, there is a difference of goal between (1) and (2); Scrooge's body parts are the goal in sentence (1) and his office is the goal in sentence (2). When considering the processes of *'iced his office in the dog-days; and didn't thaw it one degree at Christmas'* we also may take into account a mental process and a behavioural process in addition to the relational process: 'Scrooge is a very cold-hearted man' or, 'Scrooge is misanthropic'. In considering Scrooge's mental process we may add 'he dislikes having or maintaining friendly relationships with other people' or 'he dislikes people'. His behavioural process, which is represented through the material process of making his office cold, might be paraphrased without any metaphorical collocations in the following manner:

He [Scrooge] did not have a warm personality; he lived or behaved as though his office had become colder due to his presence even during the dog-days of summer and his personality did not change even at Christmas, a time of warmth and celebration.

Therefore, in sentence (2) there are at least three possibilities for interpretation of the underlying process of the material metaphor. As a fourth possibility, the author may also be implying all of the above metaphoric types. This suggests that it is difficult to specify which process the material metaphor of (2) is used for. In other words, functions of metaphorical process may be equivocal in some usages and metaphors often function multi-dimensionally. Furthermore, with respect to the above paraphrase of (2), this contains about three times as many words as the original sentence using metaphorical collocations. The use of metaphorical collocations with material-process verbs has the benefit of economy of expression. However, what is more important in the use of metaphor is that vivid images of metaphorical collocations created through material-process verbs are often impossible to express as concisely and eloquently through other expressive means.

The following is an example of a metaphorical collocation with a verbal process verb:

> *The system which had addressed him* [Richard] in exactly the same manner as *it had addressed hundreds of other boys*, all varying in character and capacity, *had enabled him to dash through his tasks* . . . (BH 17)

Here, *the system* plays the role of an agent and Richard occupies the passive role of a person who has something done to him, or the affected participant (cf. Halliday 1994: 110). The metaphorical expression with the verbal process of 'saying' *the system had addressed him* does not refer to an actual process of saying (verbal speech) but metaphorically to Richard's mental process 'that he likes a new occupation'. In addition, the metaphorical clause with a material process, *the system had enabled him to dash through his tasks* implies that in his behavioural process he tends to be easily absorbed in new occupations.

The following is more complex:

> Mr. Vholes . . . takes off his close black gloves as if he were *skinning his hands* . . . (BH 39)

Vholes's behavioural process of taking off his gloves is described through the metaphorical behavioural process of *skinning his hands* implying a mental process of consciousness rather than a form of behaviour. Therefore, the unusualness of the behavioural process of *skinning his hands* suggests his unusual mental and behavioural processes, that is, Vholes's strange, curious personality or behaviour.

The following example is a material metaphor for a material process:

The pavement smoked as if *its stones were cooking* too. (CC 3)

The material process of the smoking pavement is metaphorically represented by the material process of cooking.

The best-known behavioural metaphor used for a material process in Dickens may be a fog coming in from all quarters, at the beginning of *Bleak House*:

Fog creeping into the cabooses of collier-brigs; *fog lying out* on the yards, and *hovering* in the rigging of great ships; *fog drooping* on the gunwales of barges and small boats. (BH 1)

The material process of fog coming in is displayed by means of the behavioural metaphor of an animate movement, a sense of aliveness, as though the fog were an animal.

Here is a case where a mental metaphor is used for a mental process:

And he laid her down there, *saw the pride of his heart and the triumph of his system, lying, an insensible heap*, at his feet. (HT II, 12)

This sentence contains different types or layers of various metaphorical collocations. These collocations – *the pride of his heart, the triumph of his system* and *an insensible heap* – stand for Louisa, metaphorically, from the viewpoints of Mr Gradgrind, her father – and the narrator. In addition, the order of the metaphorical collocations expressive of Louisa implies Mr Gradgrind's changing state of mind toward Louisa, as well as the narrator's changing empathy toward Mr Gradgrind (as *an insensible heap* is taken from the viewpoint of the narrator). We might explicate the various metaphorical collocations expressive of Louisa as follows:

Louisa was the pride of his heart as a father when she was born.
Louisa was the triumph of his system, that is, an honour student in his utilitarian education where only facts were taught.

Louisa, who was devastated by his system, now looks like an insensible heap to him as a result of the failure of his utilitarian programme, seeing both sides of her, that is, the pride of his heart and the triumph of his system simultaneously.

Moreover, the mental-process verb *saw* (cf. Halliday 1994: 115) and the metaphorical collocations referring to Louisa also make additional metaphorical collocations of 'verb + noun' in that the verb of perception *see* takes a physical object in general, but its objects here, *the pride of his heart* and *the triumph of his system* are abstract nouns. Mr Gradgrind remembered how he was pleased when Louisa was born, what a good student she was, and recognized the failure of his system, through seeing (that is, witnessing) a devastated Louisa. Therefore, the above example indicates Mr Gradgrind's rapid shift of mental process from confidence to despair, as well as the narrator's shift of empathy toward him.

Mental process can often be described through the use of metonymy, where a word is used for something related to that which it usually refers to; for example, *eye, skirt, breathe*, in 'Keep your eye on the ball [watch]'; 'He's always chasing skirt [girls]'; 'It won't happen while I still breathe [live]' (cf. Halliday, 1994: 340–41). For example:

It was well that soft touch came upon her [Louisa's] neck, and that she understood herself to be supposed to have fallen asleep. *The sympathetic hand did not claim her resentment.* Let it lie there, let it lie. (HT III, 1)

Here, the synecdoche with the verbal process as behaviour *claim* is used for Sissy's behavioural process of softly touching Louisa, who is lying with a wounded heart. Body parts such as *hand, head, eye* and so on are favorite sources of synecdoche in Dickens:

(1) 'Good gracious bless me how *my poor head is vexed and worried* by that girl Jupe's so perseveringly asking, over and over again, about her tiresome letters!' (HT I, 9)
(2) 'Even to this honour, *Mrs. Rouncewell's calm hands lose their composure* when she speaks of him, and unfolding themselves from her stomacher . . .' (BH 7)
(3) '*His [Carton's] practised eye saw* it, and made the most of it.' (TTC III, 8)
(4) '*the curiously roughened forehead was very intent upon him*' (TTC I, 4)

The application of Halliday's model of verbal processes for the metaphorical collocations of the type 'noun + verb' or 'verb + noun' leads us to an awareness of how variously and equivocally Dickens uses metaphorical collocations.

3.2 Transferred collocations

Consider the following transferred collocation:

> The ploughman homeward plods his *weary way*.

This is known as a transferred epithet. That is to say, the adjective *weary* grammatically qualifies the noun *way* but literally or semantically applies to the noun *the ploughman*. In this section, this collocation is treated as a transferred or dislocated collocation. The types of syntactic construction which are discussed here are 'adjective + noun', 'adverb + verb' and 'adverb + adjective'.

3.2.1 Adjective + noun

Some of the metaphorical collocations in Section 3.1 have certain features in common with the subject-oriented collocations to be examined in this section. The first example concerns a subject-oriented collocation:

> She [Peggotty] rubs everything that can be rubbed, until it shines, like her own *honest forehead*, with perpetual friction. (DC 43)

The adjective *honest* grammatically qualifies the noun *forehead* but literarily or semantically refers to the subject of the sentence: Peggotty. The usual collocates of *honest* are human beings but not body parts. Therefore, *honest forehead* is an unusual collocation. An alternative expression might be as follows:

> like the forehead of honest Peggotty / like honest Peggotty's own forehead

At any rate, the original collocation *her own honest forehead* is a more economical and condensed expression. This transferred adjective *honest* is used not only to indicate the body parts of Clara Peggotty, David's loving nurse, and Mr Peggotty, such as *her honest face* (Ch. 4), *his honest brow* (Ch. 51), but also to indicate their laughter and joy, for example in: *an honest laugh* (Ch. 3) and *their honest joy* (Ch. 21). Moreover, the collocation *an honest home* (Ch. 32) functions as a synecdoche, representing the Peggotty family. (A synecdoche is 'A figure of speech by which a part is put for the whole' (*Webster's Collegiate Dictionary*, 2002), for example, *string, roof, bite* as in: 'At this point the strings take over [stringed instruments]'; 'They all live under one roof [in one house]'; 'Let's go and have a bite [have a meal]' (Halliday, 1994: p. 341).) It is also interesting to note that the same kind of collocation functioning as synecdoche, *our poor but honest roof* (ch. 25), is spoken by Uriah Heep. However, Heep's *honest roof* may indicate the opposite of the narrator's intended meaning, yielding a certain tinge of hypocrisy, in contrast to the collocation *an honest home* referring to the Peggotty family as used by David, the narrator. The collocations *honest home, honest roof, honest brow* and *honest forehead* were not used by other novelists in the eighteenth and nineteenth centuries according to the *ECF* and the *NCF*.

This type of collocation is seen often throughout Dickens' works. Mostly they comprise a combination of an adjective delineating character or state of mind and a part of a character's body, such as in 'her *honest forehead*' or *the restless hand* (TTC II, 15). For example:

(1) '"That's true," Mr. Lorry acknowledged, with *his troubled hand* at his chin, and *his troubled eyes* on Carton.' (TTC III, 8)

(2) 'Whereat Mr. Twemlow leaned *his innocent head* upon his hand, and moaned a little moan of distress and disgrace.' (OMF III, 13)

(3) 'she sunk into a chair . . . drawing the coverlet with her, half to hide *her shamed head* and wet hair in it, and half, as it seemed, to embrace it, rather than have nothing to take to *her repentant breast.*' (LD I, 2)

(4) 'Such a picture, too, he makes, with his dear little peepy eyes, and *his benevolent chin!*' (DS 27)

(5) 'He is a tall, thin, bony man, with *an interrogative nose*, and little *restless perking eyes . . .*' (SB Our Parish 4)

(6) '"Beautiful indeed," echoed a red-haired man with *an inquisitive nose* and blue spectacles . . .' (PP 22)

(7) 'Another, and another with your head up, your eyes flashing, and *your vexed mouth* worrying itself . . .' (DS 22)

(8) 'who listened with *admiring ears* to the accounts of Abel Cottage' (OCS 38)

(9) 'The dear little fellow . . . was standing upon *her most tender foot* . . .' (SB Tales 3)

(10) '"Don't you think any more," returns Mr. Bucket with *admonitory finger*, "of throwing yourself out of window . . ."' (BH 54)
(11) 'She had large *unfeeling handsome eyes*, and dark *unfeeling handsome hair*, and a broad *unfeeling handsome bosom*, and was made the most of in every particular.' (DS 20)
(12) '"And now," said Mr. Stryver, shaking his *forensic forefinger* at the Temple in general . . .' (TT II, 12)

The following examples are transferred collocations of a behaviour or gesture:

> a *haughty inclination* of the head (MC 9), a *languid inclination* of the head (OMF I, 8), a *despondent gesture* with both hands (*Chimes* 2), a *ferocious gesture* of his head (DS 54), a *waggish shake* of her head (OMF II, 1), one *bewildered glance* (OT 50), a *preparatory cough* (PP 25), [Snagsby's cough] *deferential cough* (BH 10), *explanatory cough* (BH 10), *apologetic cough* (BH 11), *forlornest cough* (BH 19), *admiring cough* (BH 22), *confirmatory cough* (BH 32), a *penitential poke* in the side (OMF III, 9)

'Despondent gesture' in *Chimes* 2 is given by the *OED2* as the earliest example of 'despondent' having the meaning 'of or belonging to despondency'.

The next type of collocation may be considered a possessor-oriented collocation, as in the following:

> (In Peggotty's dialogue with David.) The day may come when she'll [David's mother will] be glad to lay *her poor head*. On her stupid, cross, old Peggotty's arm again. (DC 4)

Here Peggotty shows her sympathy with David's mother, feeling that David's mother is unfortunate. Therefore, the transferred adjective *poor* is subject-oriented or possessor-oriented, indicating the empathy of Peggotty, the speaker. But in the following, since the narrator is David in (1) and the third-person narrator in (2), *this terrible verb passive* and *the genteelest slang* may be narrator-oriented collocations:

(1) 'Nobody had the least idea of the etymology of *this terrible verb passive* to be gormed' (DC 3). (The *OED2* defines 'gorm' as 'a vulgar substitute for "(God) damn"' and quotes from *David Copperfield* as the earliest use.)

(2) 'She is discussed by her dear friends with all *the genteelest slang* in vogue'. (BH 58)

This type of collocation may be considered a possessor-oriented collocation as in:

> Mrs. Prig seized the patient by the chin, and began to rasp *his [the patient's] unhappy head* with a hair-brush. (MC 29)

The transferred adjective *unhappy* in the above example refers to the possessor of the head but is not represented from Mrs Prig's point of view, because she does not feel that the patient is unhappy or unfortunate.

The following example may be a controversial collocation if treated as a subject-oriented collocation:

> Scrooge took *his melancholy dinner* in *his usual melancholy tavern*; and having read all the newspapers, and beguiled the rest of the evening with his banker's-book, went home to bed. (CC 1)

As an interpretation of *melancholy* in *melancholy dinner* and *melancholy tavern*, there is a possibility of a subject-oriented collocation. We may paraphrase the original as follows:

> Melancholy Scrooge took his dinner in his usual tavern.

Scrooge, who is 'hard and sharp as flint . . . secret, and self-contained, and solitary as an oyster' (Stave 1) is not likely to feel melancholy at dinner in the tavern. Given this fact, who is or feels melancholy? A second interpretation is that the adjective *melancholy* is taken from the viewpoint of the narrator. We might rearrange the sentence to create a literal exemplification:

> Scrooge took his plain dinner that makes us feel melancholy or sad, in his usual plain tavern that makes us feel melancholy or sad.

However, the narrator-oriented collocations *melancholy dinner* and *melancholy tavern* seem to leave room for a Scrooge-oriented adjective, considering how he is converted into a generous man afterwards. The following may be another possible paraphrase:

Scrooge who feels unconsciously melancholy took his dinner that makes us feel melancholy, in his usual tavern that makes us feel melancholy.

Most of the transferred collocations are subject or possessor-oriented collocations, but there are some collocations whose meanings are equivocal, as observed in *melancholy dinner* and *melancholy tavern*, given that there are often different interpretations depending on whose viewpoints the adjectives in transferred collocations are perceived to be taken from. Another example is the adjective *poor*.

> (In the context where Doctor Manette's eloquent courtroom testimony saves Darney, Luci's husband's life.)
> When she [Lucie] was again in his [Doctor Manette's] arms, he said to her: 'And now speak to your father, dearest. No other man in all this France could have done what he has done for me.'
> She laid her head upon her father's breast, as she had laid *his poor head* on her own breast, long, long ago. He was happy in the return he had made her, he was recompensed for his suffering, he was proud of his strength. (TTC III, 6)

This adjective *poor* is the possessor-oriented adjective but the problem is who feels *poor* for Doctor Manette. There are at least two interpretations of the collocation *his poor head*:

(1) Lucie shows pity for the past Doctor Manette.
(2) The narrator describes the *poor* situation of the past Doctor Manette.

If we accept the interpretation of (1), Lucie is laying her head upon his breast and at the same time remembering her father's unfortunate past while in the throes of extreme joy, in that her husband's life has been saved. The second interpretation reminds us of his past *poor* situation: he had been imprisoned in the Bastille for eighteen years. Additionally, there may be the further possibility of the narrator's empathy with the father and his daughter. The same can also be applied to the following:

> But a word from Florence, who was always at his [Paul, her brother's] side, restored himself; and leaning *his poor head* upon her breast, he told Floy of his dream, and smiled. (DS 16)

As argued above, the transferred collocation of 'adjective + noun' has the benefit of economical expression but is inclined to be equivocal and susceptible to diverse and variously subtle levels of interpretation. This collocational technique may be called Dickensian.

3.2.2 Adverb + verb

Before discussing transferred collocations of adverbs, something needs to be said concerning neologisms of *-ly* adverbs in Dickens, which are closely related to this type of collocation, that is, the transferred collocation of 'adverb + verb'. Sørensen (1985: 44) states that 'most of Dickens' adverbial neologisms are forms in *-ly*; there are more than thirty of them', but according to this present research there are at least 74 coined or quasi-coined *-ly* adverbs, most of which are manner adverbs. They can be divided into three types.

(1) *-ly* adverbs that are recorded as first citations in the *OED2* (40).
   abstractedly (NN 8), acutely (NN 12), buzzingly (GE 10), changingly (TTC II, 6), cherubically (OMF I, 4), confusingly (Letter 1863), constitutionally (PP 36), ding-dong-doggedly (Letter 1870), disconcertedly (HM 1), distractingly (AN 7), emetically (UT 18), emotionally (OMF I, 2), engrossedly (OMF III, 5), exasperatingly (Letter 1851), fadedly (BH 51), fearfully (Letter 1835), inflammatorily (Letter 1840), locomotively (GE 14), melodramatically (PP 13), metropolitaneously (Letter 1852), monomaniacally (LD I, 21), mouldily (Letter 1869), phosphorescently (DS 1), platformally (ED 17), polygamically (UT 22), potentially (GE 43), predictively (OCS 31), rakishly (OT 37), roundaboutedly (ED 9), skirmishingly (DS 35), slily (PP 31), spaciously (OMF I, 11), spasmodically (NN 40), spectacularly (TTC II, 1), surely (PP 6), unpromisingly (DS 13), unsympathetically (GE 7), uproariously (OT 9), uvularly (UT 3), viciously (BR 9)
(2) *-ly* adverbs that are earlier or in the same year as the first citation in the *OED2* (22).
   apoplectically (ED 11), banteringly (LD I, 21), blinkingly (HT II, 1), buoyantly (SB), caustically (OT), chivalrously (BH), connubially (SB Our Parish 5), cringingly (BH 33), detrimentally (LD I, 34), gloweringly (TTC I, 5), grandiloquently (LD II, 3), inanely (LD I, 23), lugubriously (SB Tales 11), nomadically (BH 58), reassuringly (OMF IV, 4), repellantly (HT II, 1), Shakespearianly (DC 52), smoothingly (BH 65), unadmiringly (LD I, 19), uncomplainingly (LD II, 5), unmistakably (DC 52), unmistakingly (OMF I, 10)
(3) *-ly* adverbs that are not recorded in the *OED2* (12).

aperiently (BR 51), assassinatingly (UT 19), colloquially (BH 11) (cf. Sørensen 1985: 44), evil-adverbiously (TTC II, 2), patientissamentally (LD II, 28), pipingly (LD I, 31), repeatually (BH 11), teedlely (OMF I, 4), toodlely (OMF I, 4), temperedly (MC 6), undauntingly (DS 44), unwholly (GE 15)

It is interesting to note that most of these -*ly* manner adverbs are used only once in Dickens. Therefore, these -*ly* manner adverbs are likely to form unfamiliar collocations. Manner adverbs are particularly inclined to form subject-oriented collocations:

> Subject-orientation thus effects a characterization of the referent of the subject with respect to the process or state denoted by the verb. Most of the subjuncts concerned are manner adverbials, and all are either adverbs or prepositional phrases. (Quirk et al. 1985: 574)

Thus, a subject-oriented collocation refers to a manner adverb that literally or semantically qualifies the subject rather than, or as well as, the process or state denoted by the verb which it grammatically modifies. Such collocations are very often found in Dickens:

> I felt a liking for him, and a compassion for him, as he put his little kit in his pocket – and with it his desire to stay a little while with Caddy – and *went away good-humouredly* to his cold mutton and his school at Kensington, that made me scarcely less irate with his father than the censorious old lady. (BH 14)

The manner adverb *good-humouredly* grammatically modifies the phrasal verb *went away* and at the same time, semantically qualifies the character, rather than the process, expressed by the verb. The same can be said of the following instances:

(1) ' "Well!" said the pale young gentleman, *reaching out his hand good-humouredly*, "it's all over now, I hope, and it will be magnanimous in you if you'll forgive me for having knocked you about so".' (GE 22)
(2) ' "No, Wegg," said Mr Boffin, *shaking his head good-humouredly*. "Not at my peril, and not on any other terms".' (OMF IV, 14)
(3) ' "It's a thing to laugh at, Martha, not to care for," whispered the locksmith, as he followed his wife to the window, and *good-humouredly dried her eyes* . . .' (BR 80)

Here, the manner adverb *good-humouredly* qualifies not only the ways of reaching out a hand and of shaking a head and of drying eyes but also describes the *good-humoured* character and the 'cheerful' state of mind of the subject.

Notably, subject-oriented collocations of manner adverbs are often singularly applied to particular characters. To take a few examples, the manner adverb *majestically* (for example, 'Sir Leicester is *majestically wroth*') occurs five times with different collocates, all with reference to Sir Leicester in *Bleak House*. The figurative manner adverb *cherubically* which the *OED2* cited as a first-citation from Dickens is found five times in characterizations of Reginald Wilfer in *Our Mutual Friend* (for example, 'he *cherubically added*'). This kind of co-occurrence of manner adverbs and subjects expressive of particular characters has a kind of coherence or a resounding relationship rather than a grammatical connection. This can be considered a characteristic of Dickens' language.

Examples of subject-oriented collocations are abundant:

(4) '"Oh!" said Pancks, watching him as he *benevolently gulped* down a good draught of his mixture. "Anything more?"' (LD II, 32)

(5) '"Ah! You will know the friend of your family better, Tootleums," says Mr. Veneering, *nodding emotionally* at that new article, "when you begin to take notice".' (OMF I, 2)

(6) 'He *told her, good-naturedly*, that she was young and ought to be amused and entertained, and must not allow herself to be made dull by a dull old fellow.' (DC 36)

(7) 'Joe *apologetically drew* the back of his hand across and across his nose . . .' (GE 7)

(8) 'At last the various cleansing processes are *triumphantly completed*.' (BH 49)

3.2.3 Adverb + adjective

Subject-oriented collocations of 'adverb + adjective' are often expressed as a single complex idea by modifying an adjective with an adverb instead of as two ideas (and words) connected by *but*. Let us take a typical example:

> In a little restless flutter of happiness, which made her [Dolly Varden] do everything wrong, and yet so *charmingly wrong* that it was much better than right! (BR 80)

The adverb *charmingly* modifies the adjective *wrong*, and the collocation *charmingly wrong* seems to be one idea, but in fact two ideas are present.

Dolly Varden is *charming* in her behaviour or appearance but she does everything 'wrong', in reality. The subject-oriented collocation *charmingly wrong* in the structure of modification is interpreted more ambiguously than *charming but wrong* or *wrong but charming*. This synthesized collocation of two ideas *charmingly wrong* is not found in other writers in the eighteenth and nineteenth centuries, according to the *ECF* and the *NCF*. The same can be said of the following example:

> Mr. Nupkins looked *calmly terrible*, and commanded that the lady should be shown in . . . (PP 24)

The adverb *calmly* in the collocation *calmly terrible* qualifies the adjective *terrible* and moderates the meaning of the adjective but in fact there are two different descriptions, regarding appearance and reality. That is to say, Mr Nupkins looks *calm* in his appearance but looks *terrible* in reality or in his feeling. The collocation *calmly terrible* in the structure of modification renders Mr Nupkins's external appearance more ambiguously than *calm but terrible*. Similar examples are given below:

(1) 'They . . . being perhaps a little *innocently jealous of her* [Lady Dedlock] too, sir.' (BH 58)
(2) 'It [the world] was an *innocently credulous*, and a much ill used world.' (DS 58)
(3) 'That *charmingly horrible* person is a perfect Blue Chamber' (BH 53)
(4) 'She became *charmingly confused* . . .' (NN 23)
(5) 'It was one of those *delightfully irregular* houses . . .' (BH 6)
(6) 'Rosa could only look *apologetically sensible* of being very much in her own way, and in everybody else's.' (ED 22)

None of the above usages is found in other eighteenth and nineteenth century writers according to the *ECF* and the *NCF*. This type of collocation can reasonably be considered a Dickensian creative collocation.

3.3 Oxymoronic collocations

By using component analysis and the concept of the semantic scale to investigate oxymora with an attempt to distinguish between poetic and non-poetic types, Shen (1987) classifies oxymora into two main types: the direct (for example, *a feminine man* and *living death*) and the indirect (for example, *silent whistle* and *sweet sorrow*). In the direct oxymoron the structure 'consists of two terms which are antonyms, namely, whose only difference consists of a change in the "+/−" sign of their lowest, distinctive, feature, all others being identical' (p. 109). Of the indirect oxymoron, in which 'one of its two terms is not the direct antonym of the other, but rather the *hyponym of its antonym*' (ibid.), Shen concludes that it 'may be characterized as the poetic [oxymoron] structure' (p. 107) because this type of indirect oxymoron is 'the most frequent on our poetic corpus' (ibid.).

In Dickens there are many oxymoronic collocations but all of these examples are of the second type, that is, the indirect oxymoron (inclusive of those collocations so far discovered in this research), following Shen's classification. In this respect Dickens' oxymoronic collocations may be said to be poetic oxymora. Furthermore, these oxymoronic collocations are divided into two main types: a contradiction of the literal meanings, and a discrepancy of the connotative meanings. The syntactic constructions examined in this section are 'adjective + noun' and 'adverb + adjective/verb'.

3.3.1   Adjective + noun

As an oxymoronic collocation caused by a contradiction of the literal meanings, the following is a typical example:

He had been to call upon the dear *old infant* [Skimpole]. (BH 37)

In the combination *old infant* it is the incompatibility between the semantic feature (+ matured) for *old* and the semantic feature (– matured) for *infant* that produces the anomaly. This oxymoronic collocation is an appropriate and condensed description of an anomalous character, Skimpole. That is to say, he is *old* in the sense that he is a grown-up man having a wife and several children, including three daughters, but *infant* in the sense that he is apparently innocent of worldly concerns.

To take a similar example:

Or supposing that you [Daniel a judge] strayed from your five wits – it's not so far to go, but that it might be – and laid hands upon that throat of yours, warning your fellows (if you have a fellow) how they [the poor] croak *their comfortable wickedness* to raving heads and stricken hearts. What then? (Chimes 3)

The combination *comfortable wickedness* is a mismatch of literal meanings between *comfortable* and *wickedness* in terms of the semantic feature (+ comfort). However, when considering the context of the narrator's satirical commentary on the judge from the viewpoint of the poor, the contradictory collocation *their comfortable wickedness* makes sense, as it implies that the wickedness or crimes themselves are more comfortable to the poor than the routine hardships of their lives lived in poverty.

The examples examined above show clear collocational clashes but the following collocation may be less clear in its degree of collocational clash:

> 'You are very pleasantly situated here!' said Mrs. Pardiggle.
> We were glad to change the subject; and, going to the window, pointed out the beauties of the prospect, on which the spectacles appeared to me to rest with *curious indifference*. (BH 8)

In the combination *curious indifference* there is a contradiction of literal meanings between *curious* and *indifference* in terms of the semantic feature (+ interest). This oxymoronic collocation may have two feasible interpretations. One interpretation is that Mrs Pardiggle shows her curiosity to the 'beauties of the prospect' in her appearance when she looks out of the window, saying 'You are very pleasantly situated here!' but in reality she is not interested in them at all. The other interpretation is that Mrs Pardiggle's indifference to the beauties of the prospect is *curious* to *me* (the narrator, Esther).

The following is a similar example of an oxymoronic collocation which is also less clashing:

> Arthur assented, and said once more with new expression, 'If you will be so good as to give me the address.'
> 'Dear, dear, dear!' exclaimed the Patriarch [Mr. Casby] in *sweet regret*. 'Tut, tut, tut! What a pity, what a pity! I have no address, sir.' (LD II, 9)

The term *regret* in the combination *sweet regret* meaning 'sorrow or disappointment due to some external circumstance or event' (*OED2*) has the semantic feature (– agreeable) or (– delightful), but the term *sweet* meaning 'yielding pleasure or enjoyment to the senses; especially to the sight' (*OED2*) has the opposite semantic feature (+ agreeable) or (+ delightful). Mr Casby expresses his regret but tries to give an agreeable or delightful impression to Arthur in appearance. This oxymoronic collocation of *sweet regret* may partly contribute to the characterization of Mr Casby, a crafty imposter. (Neither *curious indifference* nor *sweet regret* are used by any other novelists in the nineteenth century according to the *NCF.*)

The following example shows a discrepancy of the connotative meanings of two words:

> (In Mr Mantalini's dialogue.) She [Madame Mantalini], who coils her fascinations round me like a pure and *angelic rattlesnake*! (NN 34)

The combination *angelic rattlesnake* is not literally but, rather, connotatively contradictory, because *angelic* has the semantic feature (+ favourable) while *rattlesnake* has the semantic feature (– favourable). *Angelic rattlesnake* is one of the expressions of flattery lavished upon Mrs Mantalini by Mr Mantalini. Mr Mantalini also applies *the cunning, rummest, superlative old fox* (Ch. 34) to Ralph Nickleby. In this collocation there is a discrepancy of the associative meanings between *cunning, rummest* and *old fox* having the semantic feature (– favourable) and *superlative* having (+ favourable). The same can also be said of the collocation *a demd [damned] savage lamb* (Ch. 64) used for Mr Mantalini's new wife (a laundress), where *savage* and *lamb* are clashing connotative meanings. Mr Mantalini's favourite word *demd* (for *damned*) forms many collocations used profanely as a strong expression of reprehension or dislike, such as *a demd devil of a time, like a demd native* (Ch. 10), and *a demnition egg* (Ch. 17), and is also used as a mere intensive such as *demd handsome* (Ch. 10), *a pretty bewitching little demd countenance, a demd fine husband, two demd fine women, the demdest little fascinator* (Ch. 17) and *a demd enchanting, bewitching, engrossing, captivating little Venus* (Ch. 21).

These oxymoronic collocations cause collocational clashes in the literal meanings or connotative meanings between two words in conjunction but make contextual sense or are capable of contextual or reasonable interpretations.

3.3.2 Adverb + adjective/verb

The oxymoronic collocations observed in the syntactic construction 'adjective + noun' are also found in the collocations of manner adverbs, as in this first example, where there exists a clashing collocation of differing viewpoints or perspectives:

> 'My Lady is looking charmingly well,' says Mrs. Rouncewell, with another curtsey. My Lady signifies, without profuse expenditure of words, that she is as *wearily well* as she can hope to be. (BH 12)

When she had greeted Lady Dedlock with an idiomatic expression *charmingly well*, Mrs Rouncewell would have expected any of the conventional greetings *quite well, pretty well* or *very well*. However, Lady Dedlock combines the contradictory words of *wearily* connoting (– favourable) and *well* connoting (+ favourable) with respect to the semantic feature.

Next comes an example of a collocation which is literally contradictory between appearance and reality:

'Eh?' The Father of the Marshalsea always lifted up his eyebrows at this point, and became *amiably distraught* and *smilingly absent* in mind. (LD 18)

William Dorrit, called the Father of the Marshalsea, is represented by combinations of semantically opposed words, referring to his expression and his internal thought. This type of hybridized collocation contributes to producing humour, irony and characterization.

The following example contains two more utterances or points of view within a collocation in a single speaker:

[In the context where Wopsle has been reading of the tragedy of a man coaxed by his mistress into murdering his uncle, and compares the story to Pip's situation.] Even after *I was happily hanged* and Wopsle had closed the book, Pumblechook sat staring at me, and shaking his head, and saying, 'Take warning, boy, take warning!' (GE 15)

The literally conflicting collocation *I was happily hanged* can be described from various viewpoints. The verb *hanged* in the expression does not refer to Pip's actual death by hanging, but rather the death of the main character George Barnwell in the book which Wopsle had been reading to Pumblechook and Pip. From the viewpoint of Pip, he was *happily hanged* in the dual sense that he was both bored by the story and happy that it was over. Moreover, from the viewpoint of Wopsle and Pumblechook, who consider Barnwell and Pip as one and the same, *I was happily hanged* implies that the main character (who killed his uncle in the conclusion of his love affair with a prostitute) was hanged as a deserved punishment, in the ending of the story, which satisfies Wopsle and Pumblechook. Therefore, *I was happily hanged* shows a fused construction of mixed points of view. Such oxymoronic collocations seem to allow for divergent interpretations.

Two more examples are given below:

(1) 'Edith was toasted again. Mr. Dombey was again *agreeably embarrassed.* And Mr. Carker was full of interest and praise.' (DS 27)
(2) ' "She is perfectly exquisite. Besides which, she is so *charmingly ugly,"* relapsing into languor.' (DC 36)

3.4 Disparate collocations

The oxymoronic collocations examined in the last section were of the 'collocational clash' type as defined by the contradiction of literal or connotative meanings of two items in conjunction. The collocational clash to be discussed in this section is caused by the incongruous combination of two items taken from different semantic fields or registers. Such a mismatching combination is treated as a disparate collocation in this section. Let us look at the first example:

That when Miss Murdstone took her into custody and led her away, she [Dora] smiled and gave me her *delicious hand.* (DC 26)

If you are asked to complete the following sentence:

She gave me a/some *delicious* (   ).

you are likely to consider items such as 'cake', 'dinner', 'drink' and some may choose 'jokes'. But it is unlikely that 'hand' would be considered. In fact, *delicious* belongs to a group of words in the semantic field relating to food, whereas *hand* is not edible and pragmatically does not belong to the same semantic field as *delicious*. This semantically incongruous combination of *delicious* yields further intriguing clashes:

(1) 'He [Skimpole] was charmed to see me; said he had been shedding *delicious tears* of joy and sympathy, at intervals for six weeks, on my account.' (BH 37)
(2) ' "Gad, Nickleby," said Mr. Mantalini, retreating towards his wife, "... You're enough to frighten my life and soul out of her little *delicious wits* ..." ' (NN 34)
(3) ' "You never tasted this," said Arthur. "Its *eau-d'or* – golden water. I like it on account of its name. It's a *delicious name"*.' (NN 51)

This type of disparate collocation is also often found in the syntactic construction 'noun + noun'. The following example may be typical:

As if he contemplated putting in something very weighty: and now and then bursting into a short *cough of inexpressible grandeur.* (PP 7)

The word *cough* occurs with a group of words relating to the condition of health, especially bad health (for example, *an asthmatic cough*) and uncomfortable or bad feelings (for example, *a nervous cough*) but not with a group of words relating to greatness or lofty dignity. As for this type of collocation of *cough* the coughs of Snagsby in *Bleak House*, a man of few words, are famous for expressing his various emotions:

(1) '"And how do you find yourself, my poor lad?" inquires the stationer, with his *cough of sympathy.*' (BH 47)
(2) 'after consulting his *cough of consideration* behind his hand . . .' (BH 11)
(3) 'coughing his *cough of deference* behind his hand . . .' (BH 19)
(4) 'returns the stationer, with his *cough of modesty* . . .' (BH 22)

Similar examples of the collocation of 'noun + noun' with semantic incongruity are collocations of *ghost.* Dickens combines *ghost* with words taken from diverse semantic fields: *the ghost of his old smile* (DS 55), *the ghost of an intention* (HT II 9), *the ghost of a cry* (ED 12), *the ghost of a departed Time* (OMF III 15), *the ghost of water* (OMF IV 7) and so on. The following may be most amazing in its abundant use of *ghost* collocations:

Charles Darnay seemed to stand in a company of the dead. Ghosts all! *The ghost of beauty, the ghost of stateliness, the ghost of elegance, the ghost of pride, the ghost of frivolity, the ghost of wit, the ghost of youth, the ghost of age* . . . (TT III, 1)

3.5 Unconventional collocations

The collocations treated in this section are not a type of collocation caused by semantic incompatibility (as observed in Sections 3.3 and 3.4) but a type of unnatural collocation. For example, *raw* means 'of the weather: damp and chilly' (*OED*); there is such a collocation as *raw evening.* However, *raw afternoon* as used in the following citation is unusual:

My first most vivid and broad impression of the identity of things, seems to me to have been gained on a memorable *raw afternoon* towards evening. (GE 1)

The word *afternoon* often occurs with adjectives concerning weather, such as *a chilly afternoon, misty afternoon* and *rainy afternoon*. The following is a similar example:

> We were to stay a month at Mr. Boythorn's. My pet [Ada] had scarcely been there a *bright week*, as I recollect the time . . . (BH 37)

Some usual collocations of *bright* are with words having to do with time: *a bright day, a bright night, bright summer*. The word *week* does sometimes collocate with words concerning weather; we can say *a rainy week* and *a snowy week*. For example, the *OED2* offers the following example of *a fine week*:

> Peacock wound up *a fine week* in Scotland, where Nevett landed a treble for him on Saturday. (*Daily Express*, 21 September 1931)

According to an informant test of *a bright week* (see Section 5.3) a majority of undergraduate students considered it an unusual collocation but 13 out of 78 respondents considered it to be a usual collocation. The following example may be more striking:

> Miss Charity deposited her *housekeeping keys* with much ceremony upon the parlour table . . . (MC 30)

Forty-two students out of 78 (54 per cent) in the informant test of *housekeeping keys* answered with 'not usual'; other students considered it 'usual'. Some usual collocations of *housekeeping* are *housekeeping rooms, housekeeping facilities* and *a housekeeping book*. This collocation may become more familiar in the future as the collocation *housekeeping book*, a neologism in the Victorian age, is now common. In this sense, *housekeeping keys* can be said to be an unconventional collocation.

The *OED2* records *housekeeping keys* from *Bleak House* (1853) as the earliest use of the collocation, although the example above, from *Martin Chuzzlewit* (1844), pre-dates it; the earliest example given of *housekeeping book* is cited from *David Copperfield* (1850).

3.6 Modified idiomatic collocations

Idioms are 'restricted collocations which cannot normally be understood from the literal meaning of the words which make them up. Thus, *to have/get/give cold feet* (= to be/to make afraid) cannot be modified to "frozen feet" or "chilly feet" without changing the meaning' (Carter 1998: 65). However, Dickens often modifies idioms, replacing the constituents of idioms with other words and abbreviating the idioms in unique ways. These collocations are discussed as modified idiomatic collocations in this section.

In *Growth and System of the Language of Dickens* (1950) Tadao Yamamoto has collected and analysed a huge mass of idioms in Dickens' works on the basis of Yamamoto's belief that Dickens' language is essentially idiomatic. Yamamoto also compiled and pointed out many modified idioms in Dickens, although the modified idiomatic collocations discussed in this section are examples not compiled by Yamamoto. In this regard, they may serve as a supplement or complement to Yamamoto's book. Dickens makes interesting creative language-use of modified idioms, and it seems helpful to classify a creative use of modified idiomatic collocations, that is, 'an imaginative reworking of the usual' (Partington 1996: 121, ch. 8) into four types, applying Partington's mechanisms of change of collocation: 'substitution, expansion, abbreviation and rephrasing'. (Partington (1996) investigated approximately 2500 headlines from the CD-ROM of the *Independent* newspaper using these mechanisms.) Modified idiomatic collocations examined in this section prove (using the *NCF* and *ECF*) to be unique to Dickens, among eighteenth and nineteenth-century novelists. Therefore, the modified collocations treated in this section will be regarded as Dickens' creative language use.

3.6.1 Substitution

The first of four categories of phraseological alteration is substitution, in which 'one of the items of the original collocation is replaced by another, but the replacement must not change the phrase so drastically as to make the original unrecognizable to the text receiver' (Partington 1996: 126). In this example:

> little and big, young and old: yet growing up, or already *growing down* again – there are not, I say, many people who would care to sleep in a church. (*Chimes* 1)

The first part of the above quotation, meaning 'everybody' *young and old*, is paraphrased as *growing up* and *growing down*. *Growing up* is a very common idiom for 'a development from childhood to adulthood' but *growing down* is an unusual collocation coined for the meaning 'a "person" becoming less in height or in size because of an advanced age'.

This is a kind of word-play of the antonym of *up* and *down*, derived from the antonyms of *little and big* and *young and old*.

The following may be a similar example:

> The fact is, when – was it you that *tumbled up* stairs, Copperfield? (DC 59)

The usual collocates of *tumble* are with *down*, *over* and *backwards*; however, David Copperfield tumbled up stairs as if he had tumbled down stairs. The following example of *tumble up* may be a kind of word-play:

> 'Why, just as you may suppose,' said Mr. Jarndyce: his countenance suddenly falling. 'It is said that the children of the very poor are not brought up, but dragged up. Harold Skimpole's children have *tumbled up* somehow or other. – The wind's getting round again, I am afraid. I feel it rather!' (BH 6)

Here there are three verb phrases with *up*: *bring up* meaning 'to educate and care for a child until it is grown up' is a very common idiom, and *drag up*, which is used in the sense of 'to rear roughly or without delicacy', is also an idiom, though not as common as *bring up*. The third verb phrase *tumble up* also has the adverb *up* but this verb phrase is unusual and is a coined idiomatic expression. Skimpole's children (who are not looked after by their father) might have been corrupted as if they had 'tumbled down' stairs but they have grown up well so far on their own, each in their own way, as if they had 'tumbled up' stairs. Based on the fixed expression *tumble down*, Jarndyce coined *tumble up* by making the verb phrase agree with the previous two verb phrases using *up*.

In the next example, the narrator humorously substitutes *bad* for *good* and intends to mean 'any time' by the phrase *in good time, or in bad time*:

> In good time, or *in bad time*, as the reader likes to take it, for Mrs. Nickleby's impatience went a great deal faster than the clocks at that end of the town . . . (NN 19)

Joe replaces *on* with *off* to mean 'to calm down', that is, to imply the opposite meaning of *on the rampage*:

> '*On the Rampage*, Pip, and *off the Rampage*, Pip – such is Life!' (GE 15)

One of the techniques in Sam Weller's speech – known as 'Wellerisms' – is a replacement of familiar idioms:

'it's reg'lar holiday to them   *all porter and skettles* [skittles].' (PP 40)

The idiom *beer and skittles* meaning 'amusement' is changed to *porter and skettles*.

In the idiom *as dead as a door-nail* meaning 'completely or certainly dead', *door-nail* is often replaced, with *a herring, the* (or *a*) *dodo* and *mutton*. In addition to these items, in Dickens the following items are used:

(1) ' "Faith, dear ladies!" said Rigaud, smiling and shrugging his shoulders, "somebody has poisoned that noble dog. He is *as dead as the Doges!*" ' (LD II 6)
(2) 'It is beyond a doubt that he is indeed *as dead as Pharaoh* . . .' (BH 11)
(3) 'Now, Nimrod being *as dead as the mighty hunter* . . .' (BH 25)

The Doges in (1) refers to 'the title of the chief magistrate in the formerly existing republics of Venice and Genoa' (*OED2*) and is used as a pun on *dog*.

The fixed expression *self-made* to mean 'made by oneself, one's own action or efforts' (*OED2*) is combined with *un* to express the opposite meaning:

'There was I, a dragoon, roving, unsettled, not self-made like him, but *self-unmade* . . .' (BH 55)

3.6.2 Expansion

The second mechanism of collocational change is expansion, where 'an element has been added to the original quotation' (Partington 1996: 127). According to the *OED2* the earliest example of the idiom *by degrees* in the meaning 'by successive steps or stages, by little and little, gradually' occurs in 1563. The *OED2* also records several variations of this idiom: *by certain degrees* (1588), *by continual degrees* (1597), *by easy degrees* (1611), *by small degrees* (1614), *by unappearing degrees* (1640), *by insensible degrees* (1641), *by indifferent degrees* (1673) and so on. In contemporary English, *by slow degrees* and *by imperceptible degrees* may be acceptable but the others may not be so familiar. The following examples are from Dickens:

(1) 'To awaken it, to gratify it *by slight degrees*, and yet leave something always in suspense . . .' (BR 37)

(2) '. . . said Mrs. Blinder getting her heavy breath *by painful degrees*.' (BH 15)

(3) '*By corresponding degrees* she sunk into a chair . . .' (LD I, 2)

(4) '. . . said Noah, getting his legs *by gradual degrees* abroad again.' (OT 41)

(5) '*By slow but sure degrees*, the terrors of that hateful corner swell . . .' (AN 7)

According to the *ECF* and *NCF*, these idioms with added adjectives are found in no other eighteenth and nineteenth-century novelists. Therefore, we can consider these collocations to be Dickens' creative language use.

The examples given below are also found only in Dickens.

In reality

(1) ' "And I am, *in plain reality*. The truth is, my dear Charles," Mr. Lorry glanced at the distant House . . .' (TTC II, 24)

(2) 'the figure which *in grim reality* is substituted for the patient boy's on the same theatre . . .' (DS 41)

(3) 'though her sister did all that *in quiet reality*.' (LD I, 20)

To some extent

(1) 'but once moved, she is susceptible and sensitive *to the last extent*.' (DS 26)

(2) 'In a preposterous coat, like a beadle's, with cuffs and flaps exaggerated *to an unspeakable extent* . . .' (HT III, 7)

(3) 'their rocking-chairs developed *to a distracting extent*.' (MC 17)

(4) 'All the three children enjoyed this *to a delightful extent* . . .' (OMF I 16)

(5) '. . . said Mr. Micawber, "and my friend Mr. Thomas Traddles . . . would weigh upon my mind *to an insupportable extent*".' (DC 36)

For the behoof of

(1) ' "Girl number twenty unable to define a horse!" said Mr. Gradgrind, *for the general behoof of* all the littel pitchers [his pupils].' (HT I, 2)

(2) ' "Yes, of course you did," said Mrs. Raddle . . . raising her voice its loudest pitch, *for the special behoof of* Mr. Raddle in the kitchen.' (PP 31)

(3) 'Vholes ... employs himself in carrying sundry little matters out of his Diary into his draft bill book, *for the ultimate behoof of* his three daughters.' (BH 39)

All the world and his wife

'*All the world and his wife and daughter* leave cards. Sometimes *the world's wife has so many daughters*, that her card reads rather like a Miscellaneous Lot at an Auction ...' (OMF I, 17)

As a special case there is a kind of 'blending', where two idioms are mixed:

(In Guppy's dialogue) That party [Mr. Tulkinghorn] ... did make it, *at every turn and point* ... (BH 55)

This is a blending of *at every turn* in the meaning 'at every change of circumstance' and *at every point* in the meaning 'in every particular'.

3.6.3 Abbreviation

The third mechanism of collocational change is that of truncation or abbreviation. The following may be typical:

'... as it's rather late, I'll try and get a wink or two of *the balmy*.'
'*The balmy*' came almost as soon as it was courted. In a very few minutes Mr. Swiveller was fast asleep ... (OCS 8)

Here, *the balmy* implies 'sleep'. The meaning of 'sleep' for *the balmy* is based on 'To have their balmy slumbers wak'd with strife' in Shakespeare's *Othello* (II iii, 260). In Shakespeare, the word 'balmy' itself means 'figuratively deliciously soft and soothing' (*OED2*) but Dickens cuts off the second word of *balmy slumbers* and uses *balmy* alone to indicate 'sleep' (the *OED* records this example of *balmy* in Dickens as the earliest).

The following may be more striking:

Durdles becomes so very uncertain, both of foot and speech, that he half drops, half throws himself down, by one of the heavy pillars, scarcely less heavy than itself [one of the heavy pillars], and indistinctly appeals to his companion for *forty winks* of a second each.

'If you will *have it* so, or must *have it* so,' replies Jasper, 'I'll not leave you here. *Take them*, while I walk to and fro.' Durdles is asleep at once; and in his sleep he dreams a dream. (ED 12)

The collocation *forty winks* in 'indistinctly appeals to his companion for forty winks of a second each' does not mean literally that he desire to wink forty times in a second, but that he looks sleepy. *Forty winks* cannot be replaced with *thirty winks* or *fifty winks* because the choice of *forty winks* depends upon the idiom *have/take forty winks* (meaning 'have a short sleep' or 'take a nap'). Therefore, in Jasper's reply the pronoun *it* in *have it* means 'a short sleep', although there is no anaphoral noun or antecedent to which the pronoun *it* refers. Similarly, the pronoun *them* in *Take them* also implies *forty winks*. Dickens achieves a humorous effect based on both the literal meaning of *forty winks* and the idiomatic meaning of *have/take forty winks*.

The following is a similar example of the abbreviated collocation where the original idiom is *cry over spilled milk.*

'If we could have packed the brute off with Georgiana; – but however, that's *spilled milk.*' (OMF III, 12)

3.6.4 Rephrasing

The last mechanism of transformation is rephrasing or reformulation in which the reader can recognize the original idioms. The following example seems to be rephrased from the idiom *last but not least*:

'*Lastly, and most of all,*' pursued the Bell. (*Chimes* 3)

The meaning of *lastly, and most of all*, meaning 'last but most important' in this context, enables the reader to recognize *last but not least*.
Based on the idiom *to go the whole hog*:

opposing all half-measures, and preferring *to go the extreme animal.* (NN 2)

The *OED2* cites this as the earliest example of the alternative slang phrase of *go the whole hog*, meaning 'to do the thing thoroughly or completely (*slang*)'.

3.7 Parodied collocations

It has frequently been pointed out that Dickens' works are full of quotations from and allusions to the Bible (Larson 1985), Shakespeare's plays (Gager 1996), various literary sources, proverbs, sayings and so on. For example, Larson (1985) demonstrated that Dickens' use of Biblical allusion and quotation was as sophisticated and multi-faceted as his use of character, narrative, description and plot. Among quotations from the Bible collected in Larson's work there are also many modified Biblical collocations. These will later be classified into several categories in terms of creative use. In this section I would like to discuss Dickens' use of nursery rhymes from the viewpoint of modified collocations which might also be called parodied collocations. These are treated under the following three headings: substitution, analogy and rephrasing.

It should be noted at the outset that Dickens alludes frequently to nursery rhymes. Fujino (1987: 90–134) stated that Dickens quoted more nursery rhymes than any other English novelist and that his works contained at least 26 instances. However, it seems that the number of nursery rhymes quoted in his works is not less than 100, of which I have discovered over 80 instances. In addition, Yamamoto (1950: 36–82) picked out 26 examples of nursery rhymes and according to Sylvère Monod (1968: 30–2), S. Stevens listed 35 nursery rhymes in *Quotations and References in Charles Dickens* published in Boston (1929). *The Dickens Index* (1988) gathers 33 examples of nursery rhymes, and compare Hori (1993).

3.7.1 Substitution

Humpty Dumpty signifies an egg in the riddle and is 'allusive, used of persons or things which when once overthrown or shattered cannot be restored' (*OED*). The reason why all the king's horses and all the king's men couldn't put Humpty together again is commonly known. Accordingly, readers easily understand the significance of 'all the queen's horses and all the queen's men' even though 'the king' is substituted with 'the queen's' for the Victorian age.

> My lords and gentlemen and honourable boards ... you must off with your honourable coats for the removal of it, and fall to the work with the power of *all the queen's horses and all the queen's men*, or it will come rushing down and bury us alive. (OMF III, 8)

Miss Mowcher, a dwarf and dealer in cosmetics in *David Copperfield*, summons Steerforth as if calling to ducks, as in the following:

> 'Well then,' cried Miss Mowcher, 'I'll consent to live. Now, *ducky, ducky, ducky, come to Mrs. Bond and be killed.*'

This was an invocation to Steerforth to place himself under her hands
... (DC 22)

The first stanza of the nursery rhyme is as follows:

> Oh, what have you got for dinner, Mrs. Bond?
> There's beef in the larder, and ducks in the pond;
> *Dilly, dilly, dilly, dilly, come to be killed,*
> For you must be stuffed and my customers filled!

The word *dilly* is 'a call to ducks' and 'a nursery name for duck' (*OED*, the nursery rhyme is cited as the first example). Miss Mowcher substitutes *dilly* with *ducky*, a term of endearment.

3.7.2 Analogy

Next I would like to shift the focus of attention to an analogical quotation based upon a nursery rhyme. This type of parodied collocation is likely to be overlooked and though it is difficult to determine, from a single instance, the original use of a given nursery rhyme, a close reading may help us discover such an analogical collocation. For example:

> Whosoever has observed *that sedate and clerical bird, the rook*, may perhaps have noticed ... (ED 2)

The image of the clerical rook reminds us of part of the nursery rhyme 'Who killed Cock Robin?' as in the following:

> Who'll be the parson?
> I, said the Rook,
> With my little book,
> I'll be the parson.

This may not be definitive proof of a nursery rhyme quotation, because a rook is usually 'applied to a person as an abusive or disparaging term' (*OED*). However, the fact that Dickens' manuscript shows a revision from 'crow' to 'rook' (Jacobson 1986: 32) may mean that the phrase 'that sedate and clerical bird, the rook' refers to the rook who plays the role of parson in the nursery rhyme.

'Up-stairs, down-stairs and in my lady's chamber' is a quotation from a nursery rhyme beginning, 'Goosey, goosey gander' and means 'everywhere in the house'. This phrase is modified to 'uphill and downhill and round crooked corners' in the following:

> The letter, which was scrawled in pencil *uphill and downhill and round crooked corners*, ran thus . . . (OMF IV, 9)

Here it seems to be used as the figurative meaning of 'every letter is deformed'.

A similar example can be found in the following passage:

> Miss Wren was in the act of handing it to him over her bench, when she paused. 'But you had better see me use it,' she said, sharply. *'This is the way. Hoppetty, Kichetty, Peg-peg-peg. No pretty*; is it?' (OMF IV, 16)

This is the way seems to be a modified jingle from the following rhyme:

> *This is the way* the ladies ride
> Nimble, nimble, nimble, nimble;
> *This is the way* the gentlemen ride,
> A gallop a trot, a gallop a trot;

3.7.3 Rephrasing

Dickens sometimes rephrases nursery rhymes, while imitating the words, rhythm, jingle and syntax. For example, a satirical parody of the famous tongue twister 'Peter Piper' is used for Mr Gradgrind's obsession with the doctrine of facts:

> to paraphrase the idle legend of Peter Piper, who had never found his way into their nursery, *If the greedy little Gradgrinds grasped at more than this, what was it for good gracious goodness' sake, that the greedy little Gradgrinds grasped at?* (HT I, 3)

Here an uncomfortable sound 'g' in alliteration may be symbolic of his unnatural philosophy, a limited, fact-obsessed formal education, parodied as constant repetition of which the end result is meaningless, as in the original tongue-twister.

In his speech, Skimpole in *Bleak House*, who possesses a childlike gaiety and simplicity but who is really a shameless sponger, composes a parody of the familiar cumulative nursery rhyme, 'This is the house that Jack built':

The boy being in bed, man arrives – like *the house that Jack built. Here is the man who demands the boy who is received into the house and put to bed in a state that I strongly object to. Here is a bank-note produced by the man who demands the boy who is received into the house and put to bed in a state that I strongly object to. Here is the Skimpole who accepts the bank-note* . . . (BH 61)

3.8 Relexicalized collocations

It has been observed that some of the examples from sections 3.6 and 3.7 contain word strings in which Dickens disregards the original meaning and, in his unique way, uses them figuratively or symbolically. That is to say, Dickens implies a second meaning without any modification to the fixed, conventional, or well-known expressions or quotations and thus reinterprets them in his own way. This collocation I treat here as a 'relexicalized collocation' (cf. Partington (1996: 133–5); Moon (1998: chs 9 and 10) uses the relexicalization with a looser definition for analysing fixed expressions and idioms). For example, Captain Cuttle in *Dombey and Son* uses many nautical terms in everyday language:

> 'If I answer in that tune, you *sheer off*, my lad, and come back four-and-twenty hours arterwards . . .' (DS 32)

Captain Cuttle, a retired seafarer, uses the nautical term *sheer off* to mean 'change your way of thinking'. This technique of borrowing a term from a different register may be called 'deviation of register', following G.N. Leech's definition (Leech 1969: 42–52). To explain further, the collocation *sheer off* typically means 'alter the ship's direction'. This typical meaning is first delexicalized in this context and then revitalized with the new meaning of 'change your way of thinking'.

There is also relexicalization accomplished through the 'specialization' of a meaning. *London particular* (BH 3) is a fixed expression, which means 'a particular thing in London' but when Dickens does not change the collocation of *London particular*, and yet specifies the meaning of *London particular* to London fog, we can say that it is relexicalized; the *OED2* records *London particular* in *Bleak House* as the earliest example for 'London fog'. Dickens also delexicalizes the literal meaning of *London ivy* and in a metaphorical manner refers anew to 'the smoke of London, which clings to buildings and blackens them' by the same collocation *London ivy* (BH 10) (the *OED2* also records this as the earliest example of this sense).

In *Little Dorrit*, Mr Meagles's *I ask you* is an exclamatory phrase indicating his disgust or asseveration rather than an expression to begin a question. After saying this phrase *I ask you*, Mr Meagles does not ask for any additional information but expresses his objections and states his complaints by using a rhetorical question, even within a question. In other words, in Mr Meagles's speech *I ask you* loses the literal meaning but acquires the second meaning and consequently becomes a habitual expression of introduction for his objections:

> 'Now, *I ask you*,' said Mr Meagles in the blandest confidence, falling back a step himself, and handing his daughter a step forward to illustrate his question: '*I ask you* simply, as between man and man, you know, DID you ever hear of such damned nonsense as putting Pet in quarantine?' (LD I, 2)

Mr Meagles's *if you ask me* has a similar meaning. This phrase is used to indicate the new meaning: *in my opinion* (the *OED2* cites both these examples – *I ask you* and *if you ask me* – as earliest usages). Such an implication of a second meaning to the phrase is dependent on the context in which it is used and on the characterization of the individual that uses it. And when those phrases are repeated, they imply literary idiolects, that is, linguistic identifiers peculiar to the characters concerned.

In *Bleak House* Mr Snagsby's phrase *not to put too fine a point* is relexicalized as an idiomatic expression of the meaning 'to state bluntly or in plain terms' and associated with his emotional make-up in the use of the phrase as follows:

> '. . . he was in want of copying work to do, and was – *not to put too fine a point upon it –*' a favourite apology for plain-speaking with Mr. Snagsby, which he always offers with a sort of argumentative frankness, 'hard up!' . . . (BH 11)

The phrase *not to put too fine a point upon it* is used fifteen times by Mr Snagsby but does not appear in Dickens' other works.

The following example is from Esther's narrative in *Bleak House*:

> Stunned as I was, as weak and helpless at first as I had ever been in my sick chamber, the necessity of guarding against the danger of discovery, or even of the remotest suspicion, did me service. I took such

precautions as I could to hide from Charley that I had been crying; and I constrained myself to think of every *sacred obligation* that there was upon me to be careful and collected. It was not a little while before I could succeed or could even restrain bursts of grief; but after an hour or so, I was better, and felt that I might return. (BH 36)

The expression *sacred obligation* is used in a religious context, or at least has some association with religion. However, Esther does not use this expression with a religious meaning. Of course, there may be a tinge of religious meaning, but *sacred obligation* in this passage is not used in the general or common sense, because Esther thinks of *sacred obligation* as 'an obligation as a child who loves her mother' in Esther's own creative interpretation.

4
Collocations and First-Citations from Dickens in the *OED2* on CD-ROM

In his painstaking work *Charles Dickens: Linguistic Innovator* (1985), Knud Sørensen pointed out an innovative aspect of Dickens' prose by focusing on neologisms, syntactic and stylistic oddities. He found 1059 neologisms (used in a broad sense) in Dickens' fiction, including periodical essays, basing his work on a close and sensitive reading of the texts, utilizing the *OED* and its Supplement. The majority (732) of these are recorded in the *OED*. Consequently, he concluded that Charles Dickens was 'linguistically ahead of his time', that is to say, a linguistic innovator (Sørensen 1984: 238). Sørensen also states that such a study of writers' neologisms is intended not only to identify stylistic character and form part of an assessment of literary achievement, but may also serve as a contribution to language history (p. 247).

A writer's use of neologism has much to do with collocation; the fact that a writer coins many neologisms indicates that they tend to create many unfamiliar collocations, as Angus McIntosh (1966: 198) observes:

> If, contrary to normal practice, two words X and Y are collocated, there is a common tendency to assume that the resultant phrase exemplifies a rare use of X only or of Y only, i.e. that the oddity belongs somehow to one of the forms and not to both.

Generally speaking, the combination of two words leads to a familiar collocation (for example, *dark night*), or an unfamiliar but not unusual collocation (for example, *delicious sleep*), or an unusual collocation (for example, *a knock-knee'd mind*). These differences of collocation depend upon the degree of 'mutual expectancies' (Firth 1957: 195) and collocational restrictions of the meanings of the words in question. Thus, a neologism or a word which is endowed with a new meaning is likely to create a new collocational meaning.

As Sørensen's research on Dickens' neologisms is based on first-citations in the *OED*, I have also relied on the *OED* and analysed Dickens' neologisms from the point of view of collocation. When discussing first-citations from Dickens in the *OED* as neologisms, it is necessary to classify them into several groups, because some of them are not regarded as Dickens' own neologisms. Therefore, considering the significance of a first-citation in the *OED*, I would like first to point out several characteristics of Dickens as seen through first-citations not mentioned by Sørensen, and I will also discuss the relationship between collocation and Dickens' neologisms.

In order to make clearer Dickens' role as a linguistic innovator, an exhaustive list of first-citations from Dickens will be provided, making use of the *OED2*. According to the results of this investigation, several findings will be discussed: the difference of frequency among first-citations in Dickens' works, the high frequency of first-citations in his non-fiction, and lexical items that are thought to have existed before Dickens published them. As well, I will discuss those Dickens' neologisms having a close relation with collocation.

4.1 Findings of the investigation utilizing the *OED2* on CD-ROM

Prior to providing quantitative results of a computer-assisted study of the first-quotations from Dickens in the *OED*, I would like to comment on the validity of the *OED* for this kind of study. A first *OED* citation does not mean that Dickens necessarily coined all of the words cited. Schäfer (1980) has discussed the reliability of the *OED*'s first-citations, and critics such as Brewer (1993) and Jucker (1994) have pointed out the shortcomings of the *OED*. Nevertheless, despite such problems, they acknowledge that the *OED* is the most comprehensive available record of the historical development of the English language, and as Jucker and Arai (1998) demonstrate there exists some potential for the use of the *OED*.

4.1.1 Total number of Dickens first-citations in the *OED*

When we use the 'quotation search' function for 'Dickens' in the *OED2* on CD-ROM, we find 8536 words and quotations. However, when using the 'test search' function for 'C. Dickens' we find only 27 entries. This inconsistent notation is one of the *OED*'s shortcomings. Through a close

Table 4.1: The numbers of first-citations from Dickens' main fictional works in the OED

Title of work	Year	Approximate word-tokens	Total no. accepted: Sørensen	Total no. accepted: OED2
Pickwick Papers	1837	303,000	93	215
Oliver Twist	1839	159,000	32	109
Nicholas Nickleby	1839	325,000	54	107
The Old Curiosity Shop	1841	220,000	31	81
Barnaby Rudge	1841	256,000	20	66
Martin Chuzzlewit	1844	340,000	22	61
Dombey and Son	1848	345,000	41	119
David Copperfield	1850	359,000	9	29
Bleak House	1853	357,000	45	89
Hard Times	1854	104,000	21	33
Little Dorrit	1857	341,000	27	67
A Tale of Two Cities	1859	137,000	11	29
Great Expectations	1861	186,000	25	52
Our Mutual Friend	1865	329,000	40	127
The Mystery of Edwin Drood	1870	95,000	7	15
Total		3,856,000	478	1199

examination of each quotation, it can be discovered that there are some quotations from writers other than Dickens; such citations were excluded. It is also sometimes difficult to say whether certain quotations are first-citations or not. In such cases Sørensen's reading and judgement were relied upon. Table 4.1 presents the comparative results of Sørensen's and my investigations of first-citations from Dickens' fiction.

As Table 4.1 shows, Sørensen's examination yields 478 citations from Dickens' main fictional works, while the computer-assisted investigation yields 1199 citations: two-and-a-half times that of Sørensen's. This demonstrates one of the major advantages of computer-assisted investigation in quantitative research.

According to Table 4.1, the number of first-citations within each text varies from work to work. However, it can be seen that the early works have more citations; the number in *Pickwick Papers* is noticeably high. Among the later texts, *Our Mutual Friend* stands out as having a much higher frequency of first-citations than the other works. It is also interesting to note that *David Copperfield* shows the smallest number. It seems important to consider the topics and themes of the works in comparison with the varying number of the citations in the *OED*: Monod's

Table 4.2:   The number of first-citations in Dickens' non-fiction

	Letters (1832–70)	Sketches by Boz (1836)	American Notes (1842)	Uncommercial Traveller (1860–69)	Total non-fiction first-citations
Approximate word tokens		189,000	102,000	143,000	
Non-fiction citation (%) of total no. of citations	136 (31.5%)	215 (49.8%)	39 (9.0%)	42 (9.7%)	432 (100.0%)

keywords in his analysis of *David Copperfield*'s language in *Dickens the Novelist* (1968) (for example, 'spontaneous', 'sentimental', 'emotional') may hint at the reason why *David Copperfield* has significantly fewer first-citations than Dickens' other texts.

4.1.2 First-citations from Dickens' non-fiction

Table 4.2 shows the number and percentage of first-citations from Dickens' non-fiction in the *OED* (Letters, *Sketches by Boz*, *American Notes* and *Uncommercial Traveller*).

The total number of first-citations from the Letters, *Sketches by Boz*, *American Notes* and *Uncommercial Traveller* yields 432. This is 24.3 per cent of the total number of first-citations in Dickens' complete published works. Approximately 30 per cent of the first-citations from his non-fiction are from his letters. This figure appears to be very high. In addition, the Letters containing *OED* first-citations span the years 1832 (Dickens at age 20) to 1870 (the year of his death). This evidences Dickens' acute sense of innovative language throughout his career, even in everyday correspondence.

Below are two examples of first-citations from Dickens' letters, one from 1832 and the other from 1870:

(1) 'I give you this early notice not because there is anything formal or *party like* in the arrangements.' ('party like' as adjective) (30 July 1832)
(2) I have been most perservingly and *ding-dong-doggedly* at work.' ('ding-dong-doggedly' as an adverb or 'nonce-word' with the meaning 'vigorous and dogged repetition of effort' and 'perservingly' for 'perseveringly') (1870)

4.2 Lexical items not regarded as neologisms

Sørensen discussed first-citations from Dickens in the *OED* from the viewpoint of linguistic innovation, but here another aspect of Dickens' first-citations not mentioned by Sørensen can be pointed out, the aspect of Dickens' 'linguistic recording or discovery' of his era.

Among the 1779 words and phrases discovered here as first-citations from Dickens in the *OED*, there are many lexical terms which cannot be considered to be neologisms. These are words and phrases which were already in use at the time of Dickens, but that had not been used in other writers' works until Dickens used them. Some of these words and phrases are treated as regional dialect and slang, while others are illustrative of various commodities, such as food and tools. Based on the description of the *OED*, regional dialect words and phrases will be discussed first, followed by a discussion of slang, and finally, words and phrases relating to various commodities.

4.2.1 Regional dialect

The *OED* describes seventeen first-citations of Dickens as dialectical (see Appendix 2). Some of these words are used in present-day English: *anyways* for 'in any case', *flummox* for 'bewilder, dumbfound' and *ginger* for 'of a ginger colour'. In the chapter 'Regional Dialect', G.L. Brook (1970) divided Dickens' usage of dialect into three regions: East Anglia, Yorkshire and Lancashire. It may be of interest to note that six of the seventeen examples are from characters in London: Jo, Pleasant Riderhood, Tony Weller, Bumble and Sampson Brass, and two of the examples are from Mr Peggoty in Great Yarmouth, East Anglia, which Dickens visited, although he never lived there.

4.2.2 Slang

Sixty-five of Dickens' first-citations in the *OED* are described as slang (Appendix 3). Two of these, 'ikey' and 'ginger', are also described as dialect.

Eric Partridge's *A Dictionary of Slang and Unconventional English* refers to nearly all of the slang expressions from Dickens as assigned by the *OED*, and in most instances he follows the *OED*'s assignments. However, with respect to the year of first use, Partridge adds the word 'about' to the year of first publication. Partridge (1983: xxi) offers this rationale:

The words and phrases that are dealt with in this Dictionary are by their very nature unlikely to be found in print until, in many instances, long after their introduction into the (usually lower strata of the) spoken language. Datings must therefore be treated with caution, and with careful regard to the sources given.

Even when Partridge's dictionary mentions earlier examples of slang than those cited as Dickens', the dating is declared conservatively. For example, concerning 'gonoph' which the *OED* cited as a first example from *Bleak House* in 1853: Partridge defines the word as 'a thief; especially a skilful pickpocket from *about 1835*'. In other words, first quotations dealt with as slang in the *OED* are not regarded as neologisms, but rather as words and phrases which had been in use or had begun to be used at that time in spoken language. Therefore, the writers from whom the *OED* assigned first-citations are considered to be earlier recorders or 'discoverers' of these words and phrases.

With respect to Dickens' contribution to the spread of slang, Partridge states in *Slang Today and Yesterday* (1933: 87):

> Throughout his career, Dickens was to use much slang in his novels and stories, and his influence on the slang of 1840 to 1880 would be very difficult to assess: but one may declare that it was certainly farther-reaching than that of any other author, or of any dictionary; and it would probably be no exaggeration to add that the same remark would apply to the whole century.

Moreover, concerning the common use of slang in the nineteenth century, Partridge explains (p. 88) that:

> Usually less obtrusively and therefore more effectually, Dickens – the most read British author of the century – garnered a very large proportion of the slang current during the forty years ending in 1870, endowed much of it with a far longer life than it would otherwise have had, so popularized certain slang terms that they gained admittance to standard speech, and so imposed on the public certain slangy innovations of his own that they became general slang and then, in a few instances, were passed into the common stock.

4.2.3 Various commodities, such as food and tools

In Dickens' first-citations there are many lexical items relating to commodities, such as food, tools and occupational articles. For example, the word 'Guinness', as is well known, is the proprietary name of a brand of stout manufactured by the Guinness firm, founded in Dublin in 1759. Arthur Guinness II first produced this beer in 1824, and it sold well both in Ireland and Britain. Dickens wrote 'a large hamper of Guinness's stout' in *Sketches by Boz* in 1836, which seems to have been the first published reference. However, even though Dickens was the first writer to use the word 'Guinness' in literature (an *OED* first-citation), we cannot conclude that the word *Guinness* is Dickens' neologism (additional examples are listed in Appendix 4).

Some of these items are now quite commonly used in contemporary English: *birdseed, boa, butter-knife, first-floor* and *saveloy* (in British English). It may be surprising to learn that *business hours, cattle-market, door-key, door-chain, door-knocker* and *kidney-pie* are recorded as Dickens' first-citations in the *OED*.

The lexical items for various commodities mentioned in this section tend to be seen in the early works of Dickens, especially *Sketches by Boz, Pickwick Papers* and *Oliver Twist*, all written in the 1830s. If these items were used for figurative meanings we could consider them creative uses. Again, we cannot say that these items provide evidence of Dickens' innovative use of lexical words or neologisms, though the *OED* cites them from Dickens as first-citations. The above examples demonstrate some of the various words and phrases (impressively, from widely different registers) that Dickens collected and 'discovered'; they also provide an insight into Dickens' 'ear' for colloquial language (his excellent linguistic recording ability).

4.3 Collocations and neologisms

The lexical words and phrases treated as first-citations in the *OED* reflect Dickens' acute consciousness of English but are not said to be his neologisms. The following sub-sections will continue the discussion of neologisms or words endowed with new meanings that may be considered a creatively idiosyncratic use of language. The focus will be on Dickens' unfamiliar, new and unusual collocations. The following collocational forms will be analysed: 'adjective + noun', 'adverb + adjective/verb' and compound words.

4.3.1 Adjective + noun

The sentence below provides a first example of *angry-eyed* and *inflammatory-faced* according to the *OED2*:

he put his open hand to the side of his hat, in a military manner which that *angry-eyed buttoned-up inflammatory-faced old gentleman* appeared but imperfectly to appreciate. (OMF I, 5)

It can be said that the phrase 'that angry-eyed, buttoned-up, inflammatory-faced old gentleman' is unusual or unfamiliar. The *OED* takes its first-citations of 'angry-eyed' and 'inflammatory-faced' from this quotation (although the earliest quotation of 'buttoned-up' is 1826; before Dickens). These compound adjectives in '-ed' are, therefore, unfamiliar or new collocations in themselves, and in addition their attributive use is also unfamiliar. The same information could be conveyed as follows:

> that old gentleman who had an angry look in his eyes, was buttoned up, and had an inflammatory look on his face.

But this gives us a wordy impression, which may not be appropriate for the old man, who behaves briskly and in a military manner. The repeated words, 'had', 'in' and 'his', are grammatically necessary, but lead to a verbose explanation. By inventing a new word or collocation, Dickens achieved more compact and integrated adjectival compounds, reflective of the character being described.

Such economical or compact figurative compound adjectives may carry a vivid image of the modified person. The expression 'half a dozen blossom-faced men' (OMF IV, 9), in which the first-citation of the compound adjective *blossom-faced* is from Dickens (*OED*) could be rewritten in a postmodified construction without the use of the compound adjective:

> half a dozen men who had red bloated faces as if their faces were in bloom.

Sørensen (1985: 39) advances two reasons why premodified constructions are more striking than corresponding postmodified ones: 'In the first place a construction with qualifiers preceding the head noun is often felt to be heavy, and in the second place premodification tends to imply the idea of a permanent state of things.' Sørensen emphasizes that there is a clear difference between predicative and attributive modification, that is, that the premodified phrase expresses permanence while the corresponding postmodified form expresses relative impermanence (1980: 77–84). At any rate, when these new compound adjectives are used as attributive, they make unfamiliar collocations. There are many collocations of compound adjectives in '-ed' in Dickens. The following list gives examples of premodified construction of compound adjectives in '-ed' collocating with nouns expressive of 'person':

a *baby-faced* chit of a girl (NN 54)

I only know two sorts of boys, – mealy boys, and *beef-faced* boys (OT 14)

a couple of large-headed, *circular-visaged* males (PP 5)

never was such ingenious posturing, as his *fancy-dressed* friends exhibited (PP 15)

the *first-named* young gentleman (OT 18)

a snub-nosed, *flat-browed* . . . boy (OT 8)

such a *full-whiskered* dashing young man (NN 17)

a *good-tempered-faced* man-cook (OT 39)

many *hunger-worn* outcasts close their eyes in our bare streets (OT 23)

a kind, excellent, *independent-spirited* . . . man (PP 28)

here the *leather-legginged* boy laughed very heartily (PP 19)

one of those *long-limbed* . . . people, to whom it is difficult to assign any precise age (OT 42)

he was a brown-whiskered, *white-hatted*, *no-coated* cabman (SB Scenes 17)

one of the *peachy-cheeked* charmers (BH 58)

a little hard-headed, Ripstone *pippin-faced* man, was conversing with a fat old gentleman in one corner (PP 6)

a little fat *placid-faced* old gentleman (OCS 14)

proud-stomached teachers (NN 13)

some *rat-ridden* doorkeeper (ED 1)

as the *room-ridden* invalid settled for the night (LD I, 15)

in conversation with a *rustily-clad*, miserable-looking man (PP 30)

to wit a *wooden-featured*, blue-faced, Major, with his eyes starting out of his head (DS 7)

Of these 22 examples, 'first-named' in the fifth does not work as an inherent adjective as in the other examples but rather as a non-inherent adjective; it does not characterize the young gentleman directly (cf. Quirk et al. 1985: 7.43). About 80 per cent of the 22 examples are from the early works of Dickens, that is, before 1841: seven come from *Pickwick Papers* and six from *Oliver Twist.* All of these are OED first-citations, but if other compound adjectives are included, such research data may provide a basis for a separate comparative study of premodified and postmodified constructions of compound adjectives for characterization between the early and later works of Dickens.

The list below gives premodified constructions of compound adjectives in '-ed' collocating with other nouns:

a little white-headed *apple-faced* tipstaff (PP 42)
a *black-bordered* letter to inform him how his uncle . . . was dead (NN 1)
blue-nosed, *bulbous-shoed* old benchers (BH 1)
the time and *damp-worn* monuments (BH 18)
dressed in a dusty *drabbish-coloured* suit (AN 10)
one of the chateau's four *extinguisher-topped* towers (TT II, 9)
he found himself in a little *floor-clothed* room (NN 16)
a *full-sized* wine-bottle carefully corked (OT 39)
Mrs. Bloss . . . was dressed in a *geranium-coloured* muslin gown (SB Tales 1)
[Sydney] stood waving the *gold-banded* cap (Letter 1860)
a small, *green-baized*, brass-headed-nailed door (SB Scenes 8)
it was constitutionally a *knock-knee'd* mind (OMF III, 4)
the now *lamp-lighted* streets (MC 5)
the *last-named* apartment (OT 42)
I had been leading a romantic life for ages to a brawling, splashing, *link-lighted* . . . miserable world (DC 19)
towards the *mist-enshrouded* city (DS 33)
rows of *mud-bespattered* cows (DS 55)
along the *night-enshrouded* roads (TT II, 23)
a certain *oak-panelled* room with a deep bay window (BR 1)
an *oilcake-fed* style of business-gentleman (OMF I, 10)
men of a red-nosed, *pimpled-faced*, convivial look (OCS 49)
a small *rat-infested* dreary yard (OCS 4)
he turned into a *red-curtained* tavern (MF I, 3)
it was as heavy on him in his scanty sleep, as in his *red-eyed* waking hours (OMF IV, 15)
a gross or two of *shark-headed* screws for general use (GE 15)
travellers jogging past on little *short-stepped* horses (OCS 46)
one beaming smile, from his nut-brown face down to the *slack-baked* buckles in his shoes (BR 41)
in stiff-necked *solemn-visaged* piety (AN 15)

if the Pickwick has been the means of putting a few shillings in the *vermin-eaten* pockets of so miserable a creature . . . (Letter 1837)

About 40 per cent of these 29 examples are from early works of Dickens, that is, before 1841, although no particular work contains a large number of them.

These compound adjectives are often dealt with as nonce-words in the *OED*. In Dickens there are many other compound adjectives in nonce-use which the *OED* does not contain and therefore they also form unfamiliar or occasionally unusual collocations.

4.3.2 Adverb + adjective/verb

Sørensen (1985: 44) states that 'most of Dickens' adverbial neologisms are forms in -*ly*; there are more than thirty of them', but according to this present research, there are at least 74 coined or quasi-coined -*ly* adverbs, most of which are manner adverbs. Of the 74 -*ly* adverbs found, only 40 are recorded as first-citations in the *OED*; 22 are found to be earlier or in the same year as the first-citation in the *OED*, and there are 12 -*ly* adverbs which are not compiled by the *OED* (see Section 3.2.2 above). These -*ly* adverbs are very infrequently used, most occurring only a few times in the Dickens Corpus of 4.6 million words. Thus, they naturally form very rare collocations, not otherwise found in eighteenth and nineteenth-century fiction. These are typed as creative collocations rather than as unfamiliar or unusual collocations. The first and second examples given below are humorous collocations for characterization; the third is known as a subject-oriented collocation – the use of an adverb as a kind of a transferred epithet; the fourth is a figurative collocation, and the last is an oxymoronic collocation:

(1) 'Every morning, the regular water-drinkers took their quarter of a pint, and *walked constitutionally*.' (PP 36)
(2) 'Poor Noggs . . . *moved spasmodically* in his chair.' (NN 40)
(3) 'The people . . . croaked over their scanty measures of thin wine and beer, and were *gloweringly confidential* together.' (TT I, 5)
(4) 'young Sparkler hovering about the rooms, *monomaniacally seeking* any sufficiently ineligible young lady with no nonsense about her . . .' (LD I, 21)
(5) 'It is a handsome city, but *distractingly regular*.' (AN 7)

All of the -*ly* adverbs shown above are recorded as first-citations in the *OED*. In Chapter 3, collocations including common -*ly* adverbs were divided into a variety of types, based on effects of use, and discussed in detail. What is important concerning *-ly* adverbs taken as first-citations from Dickens in the *OED* is that they always construct unfamiliar collocations.

4.3.3 Compound words as collocations

Although a compound word is a word made up of two or more lexical words, this alone may not qualify it as a collocation (which is defined as a relation of a particular word with another particular word or words). However, when considering the fact that more than a quarter of 1779 lexical terms from Dickens treated as first-citations in the *OED2* are compound words, one cannot help but recognize Dickens' power of expression, through which two or more words may be seemingly combined or juxtaposed at will. I would next like to discuss such combinations or juxtapositions of words as a type of collocation.

With respect to the notation of a compound word there are three possible representations: (1) as a single word: *schoolboy*; (2) with a hyphen: *school-boy*; and (3) as two words: *school boy*. This current research includes all three representations, as the *OED* does not seem to draw a clear dividing line between compound and combination words. Neither does Dickens make consistent use of compounds, for example: *birdseed* (OCS Ch. 13), *beer-boy* (OCS 34) and *crush hat* (NN 19). The same compound words may be notated differently in various texts: *new-laid* (BH 19) in *The Illustrated Dickens* but *new laid* in Bradbury and Evans (1853). Table 4.3 shows the number of lexemes of each part of speech of compound words treated as first-citations from Dickens in the *OED*.

Within Dickens' first-citations there are four different types of compound words and compound nouns are by far the most frequent. However, there are very few unfamiliar compound nouns; most are lexical terms relating to various commodities, as observed in Section

Table 4.3: Classification of the compound words from Dickens treated as first-citations in the *OED*

Part of speech	Number of lexemes
Compound noun	354 (75.5%)
Compound adjective	95 (20.3%)
Compound verb	13 (2.8%)
Compound adverb	7 (1.5%)
Total (compound word)	469 (100.0%)

4.2.3. On the other hand, almost all of the compound adjectives present uncommon formations, while all of the compound verbs and adverbs are unusual. Next, each part of speech relating to compound words will be treated separately.

Compound nouns

In English, noun compounding is said to be highly productive of various patterns or formations, which will be discussed below. Table 4.4 shows a classification of the compound nouns based on Biber et al. (1999: 327).

As Table 4.4 shows, 75 per cent of the total number of compound nouns are of the type: 'noun + noun'. The four types: 'noun + noun', 'adjective + noun', 'verb-*ing* + noun', and 'noun + verb-*ing*' occupy 94.6 per cent; the remaining types have very few occurrences. There are no types such as: 'verb + particle' (*go-between*) and 'particle + verb' (*bypass*), which are said to be productive. As observed above, most compound nouns relate to commodities: 'noun + noun' examples are nearly all 'commodity' compounds. However, regarding 'adjective + noun' and 'verb-*ing* + noun', there are several compound nouns in these groups which can be regarded as Dickens' own:

(1) ' "Now, young un!" said Sikes surlily . . . "hard upon seven! You must step out. Come, don't lag behind already, *Lazy-legs!*" ' (OT 21)
(2) ' "He must be a *first-rater*," said Sam.' (PP 41)

Table 4.4: Classification of compound nouns from Dickens assigned as first-citations in the *OED*

Type	Example	Number of lexemes
Noun + noun	allotment-garden, bowie-knife	266 (75.1%)
Adjective + noun	lazy-legs, flat candle	31 (8.8%)
Verb-*ing* + noun	baking-dish, copying-clerk	23 (6.5%)
Noun + verb-*ing*	boot-cleaning, coffee-imbibing	15 (4.2%)
Verb/noun* + noun	pass-door, pay-box	5 (1.4%)
Noun + verb-*er*	concert giver, crossing-sweeper	3 (0.8%)
Reduplicative	quack-quack, bon-bon	3 (0.8%)
Others	catch-em-alive-o', Jack-in-the-box	8 (2.3%)
Total		354 (100.0%)

Note: * This means that the first element of the compound could be either a verb base or a noun.

(3) 'preparing a *baking-dish* of beef and pudding for the dining room.' (LD I, 39)

(4) 'I keep a *Minding-School*: I can take only three . . .' (MF I, 16)

(5) '"I'm in a *working humour* now," said Miss Sally, "so don't disturb me, if you please".' (OCS 35)

Because these compound nouns were the only examples given in the *OED 2*, these word-combination neologisms may be attributed to Dickens.

Compound adjectives

Table 4.5 shows a classification into thirteen types of combination according to Biber et al. (1999: 534).

There are fewer compound adjectives than compound nouns, but their types are more various. What is distinctively characteristic is the number of compound adjectives with an *ed*-participle. There are four different varieties with *ed*-participles and, in all, 64 compound adjectives to which -*ed* is suffixed. These are 61 per cent of the whole. Another type with a participle, a compound adjective with *ing*-participle, has three different varieties and a total of 14 (13 per cent) different lexical items. Therefore, it can be said that Dickens tends to coin participial-

Table 4.5: Classification of the compound adjectives from Dickens treated as first-citations in the *OED*

Type	Example	Number of lexemes
Noun + *ed*-participle	apple-faced, beef-faced	33 (34.7%)
Adjective + *ed*-participle	angry-eyed, bulbous-shoed	25 (26.3%)
Noun + *ing*-participle	business-looking, life-thirsting	8 (8.4%)
Noun + adjective	ginger-beery, self-devotional	5 (5.3%)
Adverb + *ed*-participle	first-named, slack-baked	5 (5.3%)
Noun + noun (attributive)	dog's-meat, cherry stick	5 (5.3%)
Adjective + *ing*-participle	blithe-looking, responsible-looking	4 (4.2%)
Adjective + noun (attributive)	half-quartern, half-price	2 (2.1%)
Adverb + *ing*-participle	out-speaking, over-swinging	2 (2.1%)
Adjective + adjective	politico diplomatico	1 (1.1%)
Adverb + adjective	over-particular	1 (1.1%)
Verb + *ed*-participle	draggle-haired	1 (1.1%)
Others (attributive)	devil-may-care, matter-of-course	3 (3.2%)
Total		95 (100.0%)

ized compound adjectives, because the element in such adjectival compounds that is suffixed with -*ed* or -*ing* is usually a verb. However,
'solemn-visaged', is originally an example of an adjective–noun compound: 'solemn-visage', to which -*ed* is suffixed and so is therefore a
conversion of a noun into a verb. The following examples are similar
types of compound adjectives:

coppice-topped, draggle-haired, circular-visaged, dressing-gowned,
flat-browed, full-whiskered, green-hearted, leather-legginged, long
limbed, peachy-cheeked, proud-stomached, yellow-legginged

There are no examples of conversion of compound adjectives with -*ing*.
Another characteristic concerning compound adjectives is an attributive usage. There are not many examples but they are striking in terms
of unfamiliarity:

'That's what I call a self-evident proposition, as the *dog's-meat* man
said, when the house-maid told him he warn't a gentleman.' (PP 22)

This attributive use might have something to do with Dickens' predilection for a premodified construction (as discussed in Section 4.3.1).

Lastly, strictly speaking, *like* is treated as a suffix but retains the
meaning of *like* as a separate word, and therefore is near the boundary between affixation and compounding. 'The suffix -*like* is particularly versatile in its ability to derive new adjectives from nouns'
(Biber et al. 1999: 533). Seven examples from Dickens are given as
first-citations in the OED – *jail-like* (OMF I, 15), *kitten-like* (NN 34),
mouse-like (NN 28), *rook-like* (ED 2), *skipper-like* (DS 4), *undertaker-like*
(LD I, 5) and *whist-like* (PP 34) – although he uses -*like* on many other
occasions.

apothecary-like (PP 37), *bassoon-like* (BH 27), *bier-like* (LD I, 3), *cast-
away-like* (OMF IV, 13), *children-like* (BH 38), *connoisseur-like* (NN 44),
courting-like (MC 5), *dull-like* (DS 59), *elfin-like* (BR III, 25), *faint-
hearted-like* (MC 17), *frightened-like* (DC 9), *habit-like* (OMF II, 9),
Macbeth-like (DC 22), *most-like* (DC 51), *passage-like* (BH 40), *peevish-
like* (DC 51), *rattle-like* (OMF II, 9), *retainer-like* (BH 2), *revenge-like*
(OMF I, 3), *scribe-like* (OMF III, 2), *secret-like* (DS 39), *spinster-aunt-like*
(PP 4).

The following are found earlier in Dickens than in the citations in the
OED2: *dungeon-like* (LD II, 5), *girl-like* (PP 53), *gong-like* (BH 21), *tigress-
like* (BH 54) and *toga-like* (MC 7).

Compound verbs and adverbs

Looking at compound verbs, there are 13 examples and all are quite unique. Their constructions are various and of eight types: 'adverb + verb' (*counter-pray*), 'adjective + verb' (*French-polish*), 'noun + verb' (*opium-smoke*), 'verb/noun + noun' (*drawbridge*), 'noun + adjective' (*rose-pink*), 'noun + preposition + noun' (*mother-in-law*), 'noun + noun' (*soap-and-water*) and 'reduplicative' (*moddley-coddley*). In use, although some of them may also belong to other types, they may be classified into the following four groups: (1) a nonce-word, *counter-prayed*, *mother-in-lawed*, *opium-smoked*, *out-pushed*; (2) conversion, *drawbridged* (as an adjective), *mother-in-lawed* (as a verb), *rose-pinking* (as a verb), *soap-and-water* (as a verb); (3) transference of meaning, *French-polish*, *half-baptize*, *rough-dried*, *soap-and-water*; and (4) reduplicative.

(1) (nonce-word): 'I will not ... submit to be *mother-in-lawed* by Mrs. General.' (LD II, 14)
(2) (conversion): 'Mrs. Miff says, by-the-bye she'll *soap-and-water* that 'ere tablet presently, against the company arrive.' (DS 31)
(3) (transference): 'You could ... *French-polish* yourself on any one of the chairs.' (SB Tales 1)
(4) (reduplicative): 'there's a good fellow. I like anything better than being *moddley-coddleyed*.' (ED 2)

There are only seven examples of compound adverbs and each has a different construction. They also all form unusual collocations:

(1) 'I have been most perservingly and *ding-dong-doggedly* at work.' (Letter 1870)
(2) 'The landlord ... applied himself to warm the same in a small tin-vessel shaped *funnel-wise* ...' (OCS 18)
(3) 'He takes me *half-price* to the play ...' (MC 32)
(4) 'As the boy ... lays a hand on Jasper's shoulder, Jasper cordially and gaily lays a hand on his shoulder, and so *Marseillaise-wise* they go in to dinner.' (ED 2)
(5) 'The spoon is not generally used *over-hand*, but under.' (GE 22)
(6) 'Places of distrust, and cruelty, and restraint, they would have left *quadruple-locked* for ever.' (BR 41)
(7) 'A *self-assertingly* temporary and nomadic air.' (OMF II, 16)

4.4 Conclusion

Sørensen's research (1985), based on Dickens' first-citations in the *OED*, in which he discusses collocations, is not only an important reference but also a starting-point for my own study of collocation in Dickens. However, Sørensen's base-data is limited; additionally, he seems to have overlooked certain important characteristics in Dickens, in work based upon a limited selection of first-citations in the *OED*. In this research, after investigating a complete listing of *OED2* first-citations (utilizing a CD-ROM version of the *OED*) and pointing out Dickens' acute consciousness of English as an excellent linguistic recorder or discoverer of the Victorian age, new issues concerned with neologism and collocation were raised and discussed. Most of the word and phrase examples presented here demonstrate that Dickens' coinages tend to form unusual or unfamiliar collocations.

Although contemporary readers may not find all of the collocational coinages of Dickens to be unusual or abnormal, they are all *OED2* first-citations, and therefore unfamiliar collocations during the Victorian age. The neologisms presented here have been brought about partly through Dickens' own collocational creativity, and therefore we may conclude that words and phrases constituting examples of this type demonstrate that Dickens' coinages can rightfully be considered aspects of his literary creativity.

Part III
Case Study: Collocations in *Bleak House*

5
Collocations and Narratives

5.1 Highest-frequency content-words: their collocations in *Bleak House* and the Dickens Corpus

The final part of this book is devoted to an exploration of how collocation can be connected with literary themes, topics, contexts, characters and narratives. As a case study for a close examination of collocations in a literary text, I selected *Bleak House* for two particular reasons. One is Dickens' use of the unusual strategy of dual narration in the text. The story is narrated by two quite different narrators: a third-person narrator, who seems to be a mature and experienced male adult, and a first-person narrator who is a young woman. The two distinct voices can be easily discerned from the viewpoints of subjectivity, gender, theme, characters and style. However, a collocational approach can bring into relief another distinction between the narrators' points of view and the tone of language and style that each uses, throwing a new and notable light upon the study of style of *Bleak House*. The second reason for choosing *Bleak House* is that in this work, as Miller (1991: 12) points out, 'each character, scene, or situation stands for innumerable other examples of a given type'. The various characters and scenes deserving to be regarded as 'an imitation in words of the culture of a city' and 'a model of English society' (ibid.) are represented through collocations appropriate or peculiar to them, in idiosyncratic ways. Thus, a collocational approach can yield rich dividends.

Before discussing the collocations in *Bleak House* (1852–53), I would like to observe the 100 highest-frequency content-words in *Bleak House* (Table 5.1). The total number of words in Dickens' works as a whole (the Dickens Corpus) is approximately 4.6 million, while *Bleak House* has approximately 357,000 words. In order to create a corpus of content-

Table 5.1: The 100 highest-frequency content-words in *Bleak House* and the Dickens Corpus

Bleak House (Approximately 357,000 words)			Dickens Corpus (Approximately 4.6 million words)		
Rank	Lexical form	Tokens	Rank	Lexical form	Tokens
1	said	1744	1	said	29985
2	no	1254	2	no	16553
3	little	1152	3	very	13331
4	very	1080	4	little	11389
5	now	908	5	man	9372
6	know	886	6	more	9298
7	says	876	7	old	9074
8	old	764	8	now	8949
9	more	717	9	know	8667
10	dear	709	10	some	8514
11	say	694	11	time	8433
12	lady	676	12	any	7771
12	never	676	13	say	7230
14	time	660	14	good	7135
15	good	647	15	again	7042
16	like	637	16	never	7013
17	much	617	17	like	6982
18	man	600	18	much	6881
19	come	596	19	such	6860
20	here	593	20	here	6842
21	some	571	21	come	6620
21	such	571	22	well	6473
23	again	539	23	other	6218
24	see	529	24	great	6089
25	think	499	25	see	6026
26	great	470	26	hand	5930
27	way	469	27	dear	5905
28	day	438	28	made	5702
29	hand	434	29	head	5622
29	head	434	30	young	5571
31	house	428	31	way	5488
32	go	427	32	two	5347
32	young	427	33	think	5218
34	quite	422	34	own	5028
35	too	417	35	day	4997
36	well	410	36	night	4965
37	made	398	37	face	4943
38	guardian	396	38	too	4896
39	two	394	39	house	4724
40	only	393	40	back	4718
41	night	386	41	go	4559

Table 5.1: Continued

Bleak House (Approximately 357,000 words)			Dickens Corpus (Approximately 4.6 million words)		
Rank	Lexical form	Tokens	Rank	Lexical form	Tokens
42	other	379	42	door	4534
43	face	375	43	eyes	4529
44	room	373	44	only	4497
45	nothing	369	45	gentleman	4454
46	look	368	46	long	4431
47	looking	362	47	looked	4416
48	thought	345	48	room	4387
49	ever	336	49	away	4368
49	long	336	50	quite	4307
51	away	333	51	first	4189
52	back	325	52	looking	4185
53	take	324	53	look	4160
54	came	318	54	came	4093
54	make	318	55	ever	4072
56	first	316	56	take	3976
57	went	314	57	went	3914
58	own	312	58	returned	3891
59	mind	310	59	lady	3836
60	still	309	60	another	3814
61	better	308	61	replied	3788
62	even	301	62	many	3772
63	door	297	63	last	3708
64	woman	296	64	thought	3685
65	place	295	65	make	3683
66	going	294	66	mind	3671
66	last	294	67	most	3641
68	eyes	293	68	every	3555
69	friend	291	69	same	3549
70	always	284	70	place	3518
71	put	283	71	going	3424
72	another	280	72	even	3388
73	many	280	73	better	3381
74	yet	275	74	put	3368
75	anything	274	75	took	3328
76	same	270	76	round	3304
77	life	258	77	life	3271
78	something	254	78	always	3250
79	manner	249	79	cried	3213
80	tell	248	80	still	3157
81	every	246	81	friend	3095
82	got	246	82	once	3058
83	name	245	83	tell	3042

Table 5.1: Continued

Bleak House (Approximately 357,000 words)			Dickens Corpus (Approximately 4.6 million words)		
Rank	*Lexical form*	*Tokens*	*Rank*	*Lexical form*	*Tokens*
84	home	240	84	hands	3029
85	found	238	85	let	3019
85	returned	238	86	done	3018
85	right	238	87	got	2938
85	told	238	88	left	2862
89	looked	237	89	half	2842
90	done	231	90	home	2817
91	poor	230	91	people	2725
92	girl	226	92	yet	2715
93	saw	220	93	poor	2685
94	round	218	94	saw	2640
95	most	215	95	right	2602
96	present	214	96	boy	2588
97	child	213	97	name	2579
98	half	211	98	manner	2517
99	hands	210	99	child	2474
100	sure	208	100	seemed	2459

words the following types of words have been removed from the database: function words (pronouns, articles, prepositions, conjunctions, auxiliaries and relatives) and proper nouns. In addition to these removals, words having different parts of speech, such as *have*, *had* (auxiliary and verb), *so* (conjunction, adverb, pronoun) and *do* (verb and auxiliary) are also omitted as they are highly frequent in numerous texts and registers and thus, similar to function words, show no distinctive features among particular texts or registers. (*COBUILD English Collocations on CD-ROM* also omits these words (*have*, *had*, *so*, *do*, *did* and so on) as well as function words from the main list of 10,000 nodes.)

Ninety-one of these are common between *Bleak House* and the Dickens Corpus. The following are the nine highest-frequency words that appear in *Bleak House* but are not among the 100 highest-frequency content-words in the Dickens Corpus:

says (Rank 7), guardian (Rank 38), woman (Rank 64), anything (Rank 75), told (Rank 85), girl (Rank 92), saw (Rank 93), present (Rank 96), sure (Rank 100)

Says is Rank 7 in *Bleak House* and Rank 101 in the Dickens Corpus. The higher rank of *says* depends upon the fact that one of two different narratives in *Bleak House* is written in the present tense. The word *guardian* in Rank 38 refers to Jarndyce, one of the main characters. As for the top 20 in *Bleak House*, seventeen words (except *says*, *dear* and *lady*) appear in the Dickens Corpus as well. *Lady* is Rank 12 in *Bleak House* and Rank 59 in the Dickens Corpus. The reason for the higher rank of *lady* in *Bleak House* is that Lady Dedlock is one of the main characters. Importantly, with respect to the 100 highest-frequency content-words in *Bleak House* and the Dickens Corpus, we find nearly the same tendencies (although some characteristic words reflect the themes and topics of *Bleak House*).

Next, I would like to examine whether or not these most-frequent lexical words in both corpora show the same collocational tendencies as they already have regarding the aspect of lexeme. *Conc (1.76)* Software was used to create a concordance for the purpose of examining the collocates of keywords, and the collocates produced range from four to six words on either side of each keyword. The following lists are of the top ten collocates of Rank 1 *said* in *Bleak House* and the Dickens Corpus:

Bleak House: said (1,744)
no (135), dear (122), well (76), yes (75), sir (73), know (71), now (68), very (66), oh (62), good (55)

Dickens Corpus: said (29,985)
sir (1,450), no (1375), well (968), dear (956), man (916), now (834), old (819), know (796), very (638), oh (573)

Eight collocates (*no, dear, well, sir, know, now, very, oh*) appear in both corpora and all of them seem to indicate dialogic features, because *said* is used, for the most part, as a reporting verb. The same tendencies are also observed in the top ten collocates of the other 19 most-frequent content-words. Based upon these results, we can conclude that the highest-frequency content-words in *Bleak House* tend to have almost the same features of collocability as those of the Dickens Corpus.

It is interesting that comparing the top ten collocates in both corpora with the *COBUILD* corpus, there are only three collocates (*no, know* and *very*) common to all three. The *COBUILD* top ten collocates for *said* (557,665) are:

spokesman (13416), no (13279), yesterday (131110), last (8146), government (7666), also (6586), people (6315), police (5808), know (5525), very (5484)

This difference between collocates of *said* among the three corpora may demonstrate variance between the different texts used. For example, the higher frequencies of *spokesman*, *government* and *police*, and the collocates of *said* in *COBUILD* appear to reflect the characteristics of a journalism-oriented corpus. Stubbs (2001: 67) observes 'The raw first-order data for the Cobuild (1995b) collocations CD-ROM consisted of a corpus of 200 million running words of general English: about 70 per cent British, 25 per cent American, and 5 per cent other native varieties. About 65 per cent of the text samples are from the mass media, written and spoken: newspapers and magazines, but also radio (especially BBC World Service). About 7 per cent is transcribed spoken language: over half of this is spontaneous conversation, the rest is from scripted radio broadcasts. The corpus did not contain highly technical and scientific books and articles, though there is a lot of specialized vocabulary in relatively popular academic books and the like.'

5.2 Collocations found in *Bleak House* only

As shown in the last section, the highest-frequency collocates of the highest-frequency content-words do not present collocations peculiar to *Bleak House*. The more unique collocational characteristics of *Bleak House* are found in low-frequency collocations. The following is a list of collocations of body parts, found in *Bleak House* though not in Dickens' other works.

eye: ancient eye (Ch. 20), confiding eye (Ch. 39), discoloured eye (Ch. 8), distrustful eye (Ch. 39), encouraging eye (Ch. 46), fresh eye (Ch. 34), over-shadowed eye (Ch. 26), sudden eye (Ch. 9), troubled eye (Ch. 62), uncommon eye (Ch. 28), venerable eye (Ch. 20)
eyes: accustomed eyes (Ch. 26), choking eyes (Ch. 8), compassionate eyes (Ch. 5), envious eyes (Ch. 48), fashionable eyes (Ch. 29), grateful eyes (Ch. 67), kind eyes (Ch. 8), knowing eyes (Ch. 54), languishing eyes (Ch. 13), motherly eyes (Ch. 55), ravenous eyes (Ch. 21), spectacled eyes (Ch. 14), sprightly eyes (Ch. 43), surprised eyes (Ch. 13), too-eager eyes (Ch. 23)
hand: anxious hand (Ch. 46), disdainful hand (Ch. 41), gracious hand (Ch. 31), hammer-like hand (Ch. 57), unwholesome hand (Ch. 1), wary hand (Ch. 4)
hands: angry hands (Ch. 26), calm hands (Ch. 7), fluttering hands (Ch. 55), troubled hands (Ch. 38)
head: care-worn head (Ch. 15), fat head (Ch. 25), gracious head (Ch.

12), relentless head (Ch. 54), sulky jerk of his head (Ch. 57), unconscious head (Ch. 41)

heads: warded heads (Ch. 1)

face: busy face (Ch. 46), darkened face (Ch. 3), disdainful face (Ch. 30), flung-back face (Ch. 41), quick face (Ch. 6), resolute face (Ch. 44), shaded face (Ch. 48), tight face (Ch. 54), trusting face (Ch. 3), trusty face (Ch. 8), well-filled face (Ch. 56)

finger: admonitory finger (Ch. 54), well-remembered finger (Ch. 62)

fingers: so-genteel fingers (Ch. 12)

legs: martial legs (Ch. 26), rusty legs (Ch. 39), untidy legs (Ch. 38)

foot: maternal foot (Ch. 10), unaccustomed foot (Ch. 16)

breast: peaceful breast (Ch. 8), stately breast (Ch. 12)

mouth: feline mouth (Ch. 12)

eyebrows: pleasant eyebrows (Ch. 61)

forehead: sprightly forehead (Ch. 43)

chin: persecuted chin (Ch. 19)

According to the *ECF* and *NCF*, the collocations listed above are unique to Dickens as they are not used by other eighteenth and nineteenth-century writers. Therefore, we can say further that these collocations are peculiar to *Bleak House* and that they can be considered to be Dickens' creative collocations. Because the constituent words of these collocations are very common – for example, *choking* and *eyes* – and become rare and unusual collocations only with Dickens' first use (and unique use, among eighteenth and nineteenth-century writers), we can also say that the characteristics of language and style peculiar to *Bleak House* are found in collocations or combinations of words rather than in the vocabulary of the novel, per se. There are more than 700 of these unique collocations in *Bleak House*.

However, some constituent words of the unusual collocations in *Bleak House* are considered to be Dickens' neologisms. The italicized words or phrases shown below are treated as first-citations in the *OED2*:

Antipodean lumber room (Ch. 66), the *best-groomed* woman (Ch. 2), chronic malady of *boredom* (Ch. 28), *bulbous-shoed* old benchers (Ch. 1), *Chadband* style of oratory (Ch. 19), *Chancery Judge* (Preface), *damp-worn* monuments (Ch. 18), A *dolly* sort of beauty (Ch. 28), *fadedly* furnished (Ch. 51), *gingery* complexion (Ch. 19), *housekeeping keys* (Ch. 6), *London ivy* (that is, the smoke of London) (Ch. 10), *London particular* (that is, a London fog) (Ch. 3), an *Ogreish* kind of jocularity (Ch. 34), *peachy-cheeked* charmers (Ch. 58), *quick-march* time (Ch.

34), *sidewise* look (Ch. 12), *slangular* direction (Ch. 11), *unpensioning* country (Ch. 40), their goat-hair and horse-hair *warded* heads (Ch. 1), a *watered* pavement (Ch. 19), a *weak* chance (Ch. 10), a *weather-tanned* woman (Ch. 52)

5.3 Comparison of collocations between the third-person narrative and Esther's narrative

The major peculiarity of Dickens' *Bleak House* is that the story is narrated by two distinct voices, the third-person narrator who is 'anonymous, objective, and presumably masculine and stands outside the action' and the first-person narrator, Esther Summerson (later Esther Woodcourt) who is 'subjective, feminine, and a major character in the story' (Page 1990: 55). Dickens hoped to achieve by means of such a technique 'the possibility of our seeing the story from radically different angles of objectivity and subjectivity' (Smith 1974: 8). Accordingly, differences of style between the third-person narrative and Esther's narrative can be discerned easily from the viewpoints of vocabulary, sentence structure, sentence length, symbolism and metaphor, as well as of person and tense. The aim of this section is to show that there is, additionally, a difference of lexical collocation between the two different narratives in terms of usual collocations, and that there are many linguistically experimental unusual collocations in Esther's narrative as well as in the third-person narrative.

5.3.1 Discourse structure of *Bleak House*

Before discussing usual and unusual collocations in the two different narratives and in order to make a clear distinction in discourse between Esther's narrative and the third-person narrative, and to demonstrate contrasts between the narrators' interferences in the dialogues and non-dialogues, I would like to outline the discourse structure of *Bleak House*, applying the idea of 'the rhetoric of discourse' from Leech and Short's *Style in Fiction* (1981: 257).

Language is a vehicle of communication whereby one person conveys messages to another for a range of different purposes, *eg* informing, ordering, persuading, reassuring. The way the message is used to achieve such ends may, in ordinary speech situations, be called 'the rhetoric of discourse'. But in a novel or short story, the rhetoric of discourse has a rather different implication.

It is important to note that a novel is considered a message (as is ordinary speech), but with the difference that a novel, as a message from an author to a reader, has a structure different from ordinary speech situations in terms of rhetorical structure.

Authors of novels can assume that they, along with readers, have a certain amount of shared knowledge and experience. For example, when Fielding wrote *Shamela* he was able to assume that his readers would be well acquainted with Richardson's *Pamela*. If modern readers have not read *Pamela* they would have to read it in order to discover the position of Fielding's assumed reader, in order fully to appreciate the satirical dimension of the novel (p. 259). This means that there is an assumed reader existing between the (actual) reader and the work. Such an assumed reader is termed 'the implied reader' (Booth 1961: 138–9), and was earlier known as the 'mock reader'. Just as there is an implied reader between the reader (addressee) and the work (message), so there is 'an implied author' between the author (addresser) and the work (message). To give a specific application of this concept: the author of both *David Copperfield* and *Great Expectations* is Dickens but the assumed author of *David Copperfield* (that is, David Copperfield) is quite different from the assumed author of *Great Expectations* (that is, Philip Pirrip). The discourse structure of *Bleak House* can thus be illustrated as follows (Figure 5.1).

Bleak House, or Dickens' (Addresser 1) message to his reader (Addressee 1), is also considered the message of the assumed or implied author (Addresser 2) to the assumed or implied reader (Addressee 2). When there is only a single omnipotent narrator in a novel, there may not be a practical need for us to distinguish between the real author and the implied author. In *Bleak House*, however, the implied author creates two different narrators, the third-person narrator, and Esther, the first-person narrator. In other words, the implied author is neither the third-person narrator nor Esther, and another level of description must be added under the 'message' between the implied author and the implied reader, as illustrated in Figure 5.2.

Each message to the implied reader is divided into dialogue, that is, the parts put in quotations, and non-dialogue. This division is ascribed to the existence of quotation marks but is also closely connected with the matter of the narrators' involvement or control of their narratives. What must be noted in the language of Victorian novels is that, according to I.A. Gordon (1966: 162), there are 'four prose "systems": dialogue, narrative, description, and commentary', which took shape in the previous century. In Gordon's terminology, 'dialogue' is the characters'

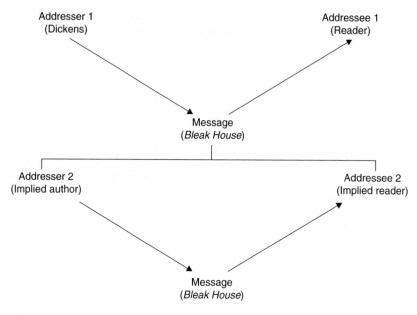

Figure 5.1: The discourse structure of *Bleak House* (1)

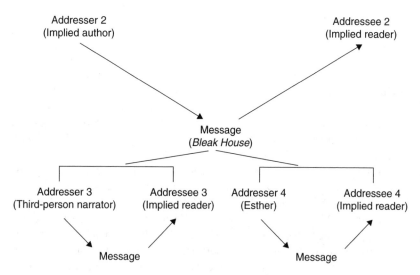

Figure 5.2: The discourse structure of *Bleak House* (2)

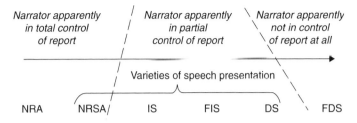

Figure 5.3: Cline of 'interference' in report

speechifying, while 'narrative' is the narration of events. Moreover, 'description' is the portrayal of characters and objective scenery, while 'commentary' indicates the narrator's comments. Narrators can be in control of narrative, description, and commentary but not of dialogue. Gordon (ibid.) states that 'the four systems are separate, and each could be written in a separate manner', but in *Bleak House*, the three prose systems (excepting dialogue) are not always separate. For example, we cannot often distinguish commentary from narrative in descriptions tinged with Esther's emotions.

With respect to narrational interference in the reporting of the occurrence of some act or speech act, Leech and Short (1981: 318–51) classify the modes of report into six types: narrative report of action (NRA), narrative report of speech acts (NRSA: for example, He promised to visit her again), indirect speech (IS: for example, He said that he would return there to see her the following day), free indirect speech (FIS: for example, He would return there to see her again tomorrow), direct speech (DS: for example, He said 'I'll come back here to see you again tomorrow'), and free direct speech (FDS: for example, without an introductory reporting clause: 'I'll come back here to see you again tomorrow'). According to Leech and Short, from NRA towards FDS, a narrator's interference becomes 'less and less noticeable, until, in the most extreme version of FDS, he apparently leaves the characters to talk entirely on their own' (p. 324). Figure 5.3 is from Leech and Short (1981: 324).

Dialogue is considered 'free direct speech' in Leech and Short's terms and is not under the control of a narrator. This means that division into dialogue and non-dialogue provides an indication as to whether or not there is narrational interference. There is another type of free direct speech, lacking quotation marks. For instance, in *Bleak House* the coroner converses with Mr Tulkinghorn at the inquest on Nemo who died an accidental death:

O! Here's the boy, gentlemen!
Here he is, very muddy, very hoarse, very ragged. Now, boy! – But
stop a minute. Caution. This boy must be put through a few preliminary paces. (Ch. 11)

This does not have reporting clauses or quotation marks but conveys
the coroner's words without interventions. In this study, such free,
direct speeches are added to dialogue as speechifying not under the
control of the narrator.

Several pages have been so far devoted to the explanation of the discourse structure of *Bleak House*. There are two main reasons for this.
First, the difference of discourse between the third-person narrative and
Esther's narrative in *Bleak House* has been illustrated from the viewpoint
of discourse rhetoric. Second, the significance of the division of dialogue
and non-dialogue has been justified by making clear the difference of
the narrators' involvement or interference between dialogue and non-
dialogue. This provides a theoretical background for discussion of the
difference of narrative style in the non-dialogues written by the third-
person narrator and Esther (the first-person narrator), in terms of usual
and unusual collocations.

5.3.2 The 100 highest-frequency words and collocations of some high-frequency words in Esther's narrative and the third-person narrative

Before discussing usual collocations I would like to examine the frequent content-words in both narratives. Table 5.2 gives a list of the 100
most frequent words in Esther's narrative and in the third-person narrative, from which function words and proper names have been
removed. The left side of the table presents frequent words in Esther's
narrative; the right side of the table shows frequent words in the third-
person narrative.

Among the 100 most-frequent words, 79 words are common between
Esther's narrative (EN) and the third-person narrative (TN). Some
present tense verbs, for example: *says*, *returns*, *looks* and *comes*, show
high frequencies – dependent upon the fact that the third-person narrative is written in the present tense.

John Jarndyce, one of the main characters, is referred to as a *guardian*
(Rank 14) 395 times in EN but only once in TN. In contrast the word
trooper, usually referring to George Rouncewell, appears 145 times in the
third-person narrative but only nine times in Esther's narrative. Some

Table 5.2: The 100 highest-frequency words in Esther's narrative and the third-person narrative

Esther's narrative (192,474 words; 10,036 different words)			Third-person narrative (164,425 words; 11,985 different words)		
Rank	*Item*	*Tokens*	*Rank*	*Item*	*Tokens*
1	said	1668	1	Mr.	1759
2	Mr.	1332	2	says	838
3	so	1287	3	sir	781
4	all	860	4	so	726
5	little	732	5	all	636
6	very	703	6	no	602
7	no	650	7	lady	482
8	dear	539	8	old	433
9	know	513	9	little	420
10	now	504	10	now	402
11	miss	478	11	Mrs.	386
12	never	420	12	know	376
13	more	418	13	very	374
14	guardian	395	14	man	338
15	much	390	15	like	316
16	time	387	15	say	316
17	say	377	17	any	312
18	good	373	18	here	310
19	any	360	19	more	299
19	such	360	20	come	285
21	well	341	21	good	277
22	then	340	22	time	275
23	old	332	23	never	256
24	some	328	24	well	246
25	like	321	25	hand	244
26	think	319	26	some	240
27	come	312	27	again	235
28	again	304	28	much	229
29	see	303	29	see	227
30	quite	302	29	young	227
31	Mrs.	290	31	head	220
32	here	284	32	two	216
33	great	280	33	such	211
34	went	276	34	then	209
35	made	270	35	night	207
35	thought	270	36	too	202
35	way	270	37	way	200
38	came	268	38	returns	193
39	house	264	39	great	190
40	man	263	40	other	185
41	day	260	41	think	183

Table 5.2: Continued

Esther's narrative (192,474 words; 10,036 different words)			Third-person narrative (164,425 words; 11,985 different words)		
Rank	Item	Tokens	Rank	Item	Tokens
42	sir	252	42	looking	180
43	go	250	43	day	178
44	only	246	44	go	177
45	face	241	44	look	177
46	returned	232	46	friend	176
47	too	217	47	dear	170
48	head	216	47	looks	170
49	nothing	215	49	house	168
50	ever	213	50	long	162
50	room	213	51	room	160
52	first	206	52	woman	155
53	young	200	53	nothing	155
54	hand	195	54	own	152
55	lady	194	55	place	150
55	other	194	56	last	149
57	look	191	57	only	148
58	seemed	185	58	door	145
59	better	183	58	eyes	145
60	going	182	58	make	145
60	looking	182	58	trooper	145
60	take	182	62	take	142
63	told	181	63	still	138
64	night	180	64	even	137
65	always	178	64	mind	137
66	saw	176	66	name	136
67	long	174	67	face	134
68	make	173	68	comes	132
68	mind	173	69	yet	130
68	poor	173	70	done	129
68	still	173	71	another	128
68	two	173	72	made	127
73	even	169	72	many	127
74	knew	167	74	court	126
75	put	164	75	better	125
76	own	161	76	ever	123
77	child	157	77	anything	122
77	home	157	77	hands	122
79	same	156	79	present	121
79	tell	156	80	put	120
81	door	153	81	quite	119
81	many	153	82	right	117
83	another	152	83	half	116
83	anything	152	83	same	116

Table 5.2: Continued

Esther's narrative (192,474 words; 10,036 different words)			Third-person narrative (164,425 words; 11,985 different words)		
Rank	Item	Tokens	Rank	Item	Tokens
85	took	152	85	round	115
86	eyes	148	86	family	114
86	manner	148	86	yes	114
88	place	147	88	going	112
89	life	146	88	life	112
89	yes	146	90	every	111
91	felt	145	91	first	110
91	last	145	91	got	110
91	yet	145	93	always	107
94	woman	141	94	give	106
95	love	139	95	taking	104
96	most	137	96	business	103
97	got	136	96	eye	103
98	every	135	96	gentleman	103
99	asked	134	99	goes	102
99	girl	134	100	ladyship	101
			100	manner	101

words, such as *seemed* (185 times in EN, though 10 times in TN) and *poor* (173 times in EN, though 57 times in TN) may reflect Esther's personal style. In this way the differences between the two narratives can be discerned on the level of vocabulary, as well as of person and tense.

There is also a difference between the narratives in the collocations of frequent words, although collocational differences are not recognized as easily as are vocabulary, person and tense. For example, let us consider the collocations of *little* and *so*, which are frequently used in both narratives.

Little shows a very high frequency in both narratives (Rank 5 in EN and Rank 9 in TN). The following is a list of the top ten collocates of *little* in each narrative:

Esther's narrative: *little* (732)
so (59), said (55), very (39), old (26), all (25), now (22), such (21), poor (20), dear (19), some (19)

The third-person narrative: *little* (420)
woman (41), Mr. (26), so (17), more (16), says (16), man (15), way (15), very (13), like (12), time (12)

For example:

> (a) 'to reconcile, having so *little* experience or practical knowledge.'
> (b) 'the suffering, quiet, pretty *little* thing! I am so sorry for it.'

I will briefly explain the meaning of the collocates of *little*. For example, the most-frequent collocate of *little* in Esther's narrative is *so*, but there are two types of collocates. In one of them, *little* is modified by *so*, as observed in (a), and in the other there is no relation of modification between *little* and *so*, as observed in (b). Therefore, not all of the 59 examples of *so* co-occurring with *little* modify *little*. (The collocates are four or five lexical items before and after each node in my concordance. Sinclair (1966) defined the term 'span' as three lexical items before and after each node, whereas in 1970 Sinclair et al. defined it as four items on either side of a node.)

What is interesting in the collocates of *little* is the combination with *poor*. This collocation *poor little* (such as *the poor little things* for Mrs Jellyby's children and *the poor little creature* for Miss Flite) appears 14 times in Esther's narrative, and all these instances of the collocations of *poor little* except one example in Mr Snagsby's dialogue are used in Esther's narration. This reveals Esther's pity or sympathy for Mrs Jellyby's children and Miss Flite. On the other hand, among the four instances of *poor little* in the third-person narrative, three instances occur in the characters' dialogues rather than in the third-person narration. The collocational differences of *little*, as observed in *poor little* in Esther's narrative and *little woman* in the third-person narrative, reveal each narrator's mental attitude toward the characters, while at the same time implying differences in the meaning of *little*; that is, Esther's *little*, as 'an implication of endearment or of tender feeling on the part of the speaker' (*OED*), the third-person narrator's *little*, as: 'a small body'.

The frequency of *so* is also very high in both narratives (Rank 3 in EN and Rank 4 in TN). The following is a list of the top ten collocates of *so* in each narrative:

Esther's narrative: *so* (1287)
much (150), said (123), Mr. (65), very (56), all (55), little (51), good (50), say (47), no (46), now (44)

The third-person narrative: *so* (726)
much (67), Mr. (64), many (34), sir (33), all (27), long (26), man (25), far (23), say (23), see (23)

The word *so* co-occurs frequently with a variety of words, therefore the difference in the use of *so* between both narratives is not easily discerned. However, the collocation *so very* is distinctive in both narratives. Among the 32 instances of *so very* in Esther's narrative, 24 instances are used by Esther (22 times in her narration and twice in her dialogue), while in the third-person narrative there are 12 instances (seven in the narration and five in the dialogues). The use of *so very* by male characters occurs only in Prince Turveydrop's dialogue in Esther's narrative, and in Smallweed's and Guppy's dialogues in the third-person narrative. The fact that the collocation of similar intensives of *so very* are never used by other male characters (such as Jarndyce, Woodcourt and Bucket) may imply that Dickens dealt with *so very* as a style of diction to which only women are inclined. The following is a list of collocates of *so very* in Esther's narration and the third-person narration (non-dialogues):

> Esther's narrative: *so very* (22)
> good, cold, clear, military, embarrassing, ridiculous, anxious, pretty, gallant, often, watchful, much, chatty and happy, likely, earnest, sorry (twice), solicitous, ill, long, far, indignant

> The third-person narrative: *so very* (7)
> bad, remarkable (twice), large, trying, disagreeable, nomadically

The collocates of *so very* are tinged with emotional colouring in Esther's narration, as observed in adjectives such as 'embarrassing, anxious, sorry, solicitous and indignant'. *So very much* in the following quotation seems to be tinged with a strong emotion:

> Afterwards, when Mr. Woodcourt came to reflect on what had passed, he was *so very much impressed* by the strength of Richard's anxiety on this point . . . (Ch. 51)

The collocations that have been treated in this section are usual and familiar, but we are able to realize differences in the use of usual collocations between Esther's narrative and the third-person narrative.

5.3.3 Comparison of usual collocations between Esther's and the third-person non-dialogues

In this section we will first examine usual collocations in non-dialogues, that is, narratives written by the third-person narrator and Esther, the first-person narrator. Non-dialogues narrated by two different narrators

Table 5.3:   The total number of words and different words in dialogue and non-dialogue of the two narratives

---

Bleak House: 356,931 words, 15,412 different words
(Dialogue 140,591 words; Narrative 216,340 words)

Third-person narrative *(164,455 words, 11,985 different words)*		*Esther's narrative* *(192,476 words, 10,036 different words)*	
Dialogue	*Non-dialogue*	*Dialogue*	*Non-dialogue*
63,320 words (5579 different words)	101,135 words (10,982 different words)	77,271 words (6543 different words)	115,205 words (8183 different words)

---

were extracted by 'Picking-up dialogue and non-dialogue' software. Table 5.3 gives word-totals, as well as the total number of different words, that is, morphologically distinct words such as *say, says, saying* and *said* are each counted as different words, in the dialogue and non-dialogue of the two narratives.

As Table 5.3 shows, the third-person narrative has fewer words in total than Esther's narrative, but a greater number of different words. The ratio of different words per 10,000 words in the third-person narrative is 1.4 times as many as those of Esther's narrative (723 different words in the third-person narrative and 521 different words in Esther's narrative). The ratio between dialogue and non-dialogue in both narratives is almost the same (1:1.6 in the third-person narrative and 1:1.5 in Esther's narrative). The different words per 10,000 in both dialogue and non-dialogue in the third-person narrative are: (in dialogue) 881 words, (in non-dialogue) 1086 words; in Esther's narrative: (in dialogue) 847 words, (in non-dialogue) 710 words.

There is little difference in the dialogues of the two narratives but an obvious difference can be recognized in different words contained in the non-dialogues of the two narratives. We can conclude that Esther's phraseology is more dependent upon repetition than that of the third-person narrator.

Taking this into consideration, we will first examine usual collocations of adverbs in non-dialogues in the two narratives.

The highest-frequency adverb among modifiers of adjectives, adverbs or verbs in the non-dialogues of both narratives is *so* (660 times in Esther's non-dialogue and 274 times in the third-person non-dialogue).

The following is a list of highly-frequent collocates of *so* in both non-dialogues:

The third-person non-dialogue: *so* (274)
much (19, 6.9%), many (13, 4.7%), long (12, 4.4%), far (8, 2.9%), very (8, 2.9%), close (4, 1.5%), well (4, 1.5%), interesting (3, 1.1%), near (3, 1.1%), quite (3, 1.1%)

Esther's non-dialogue: *so* (660)
much (74, 11.2%), very (23, 3.5%), many (18, 2.7%), good (16, 2.4%), far (14, 2.1%), happy (12, 1.8%), full (10, 1.5%), glad (9, 1.4%), little (9, 1.4%), long* (9, 1.4%), beautiful (7, 1.1%), well (7, 1.1%) (**so long* is not used in Dickens to mean 'goodbye'; the earliest such usage recorded by the *OED* is 1865)

The examples of the adverbial modifier *so* are collected only in the case of '*so* + adjective/adverb/verb'. Regarding the total count of this adverbial modifier, Esther's non-dialogue has almost twice as many examples as the third-person non-dialogue. This is also true of the counts of the adverb *very* and other adverbs. This difference of frequency of common adverbs between the two different non-dialogues shows a distinct contrast in language-use between the third-person narrator and the first-person narrator, Esther.

A marked characteristic among the collocates of *so* in both narratives is the highest frequency of *much* (11.2 per cent) in Esther's non-dialogue. Also of note is that *interesting*, an adjective expressing the narrator's subjective evaluation, is only present in the third-person non-dialogue, although Esther's non-dialogue contains additional evaluative adjectives: *good*, *happy*, *glad* and *beautiful*.

The next most-frequent of the adverb-modifying adjectives and adverbs is *very* (196 times in the third-person non-dialogue and 401 times in Esther's non-dialogue). Here are the collocations of *very* in both non-dialogues:

The third-person non-dialogue: *very* (196)
little (8, 4.1%), much (8, 4.1%), so (8, 4.1%) (in fact, *very* is modified by *so*, as in *so very*), ill (4, 2.0%), long (3, 1.5%), near (3, 1.5%), well (3, 1.5%)

Esther's non-dialogue: *very* (401)
much (34, 8.5%), so (22, 5.5%), little (19, 4.7%), well (18, 4.5%), fond (12, 3.0%), good (11, 2.7%), slowly (6, 1.5%), glad (5, 1.2%), difficult

(5, 1.2%), happy (5, 1.2%), same (5, 1.2%), short (5, 1.2%), soon (5, 1.2%), sorry (5, 1.2%)

Generally, *very* in Esther's non-dialogue shows a stronger tendency to collocate with particular words than those of the third-person non-dialogue. With respect to adjectives collocating with *very*, *little* is the most frequent collocate in both non-dialogues, although there is a difference of the kinds of nouns that *very little* modifies: all the examples of *very little* in the third-person non-dialogue are inanimate (for example, *a very little counsel* and *a very little fire*) but six of the 19 examples of *very little* in Esther's non-dialogue are animate (for example, *a very little child* and *a very little canary*). The second most-frequent adjective, *fond*, in Esther's non-dialogue always appears in the phrase *very fond of* while *very* does not collocate with *fond* in the third-person non-dialogue.

What is interesting in the collocates of *very* is that the collocation *very good*, which is used 11 times in Esther's non-dialogue, never appears in the third-person non-dialogue.

With respect to other modifiers of adverbs, *much better* is used five times in Esther's non-dialogue though not at all in the third-person non-dialogue. *Very often* appears nine times in Esther's non-dialogue but only once in the third-person non-dialogue. *Pretty well* is used eight times in the third-person dialogues and six times in the dialogues in Esther's narrative, but in the non-dialogues Esther uses the collocation only once. *Much more* occurs ten times in Esther's non-dialogue, though it does not appear in the third-person non-dialogue. *So fast* occurs three times in the whole text of *Bleak House* and all these collocations appear in Esther's non-dialogue.

Next, I would like to turn to the collocations of *-ly* adverbs. In the third-person non-dialogue there are 504 different *-ly* adverbs while in Esther's non-dialogue there are 460 different *-ly* adverbs. As for the number of *-ly* adverbs per 10,000, the third-person non-dialogue has some 50 different *-ly* adverbs and Esther's non-dialogue has around 40. Table 5.4 lists the 20 highest-frequency *-ly* adverbs in the non-dialogues of both narratives.

As shown in Table 5.4, 13 of the 20 highest-frequency *-ly* adverbs in the non-dialogues are common to both lists. The most-frequent word in both non-dialogues is *only*. A common characteristic in both non-dialogues is the high frequency of the collocation *not only*. In the third-person non-dialogue there are 13 (16 per cent) of 80 examples, and in Esther's non-dialogue there are 14 (11 per cent) out of 123 examples.

Table 5.4: The 20 highest-frequency *-ly* adverbs in the non-dialogues of both narratives

Third-person non-dialogue (101,135 words)				Esther's non-dialogue (115,205 words)			
Rank	Type	Tokens	Per 10,000 words	Rank	Type	Tokens	Per 10,000 words
1	only	80	7.9	1	only	123	10.7
2	slowly	34	3.4	2	really	65	5.6
3	particularly	24	2.4	3	presently	31	2.7
4	merely	22	2.2	4	quietly	30	2.6
5	really	21	2.1	5	scarcely	29	2.5
6	quietly	20	2.0	6	certainly	28	2.4
6	suddenly	20	2.0	7	slowly	24	2.1
8	perfectly	19	1.9	8	immediately	21	1.8
8	softly	19	1.9	9	perfectly	20	1.7
10	immediately	18	1.8	9	hardly	20	1.7
10	occasionally	18	1.8	9	naturally	20	1.7
12	generally	17	1.7	9	softly	20	1.7
13	presently	16	1.6	13	early	19	1.6
14	stately	15	1.5	14	directly	18	1.6
15	highly	13	1.3	14	nearly	18	1.6
15	nearly	13	1.3	14	particularly	18	1.6
17	gradually	12	1.2	14	quickly	18	1.6
17	scarcely	12	1.2	18	gently	16	1.4
19	quickly	11	1.1	19	suddenly	14	1.2
20	entirely	10	1.0	20	frequently	13	1.1
20	easily	10	1.0				
20	ghostly	10	1.0				
20	heavily	10	1.0				
20	rarely	10	1.0				
20	sufficiently	10	1.0				

The second most-frequent collocate of *only* in the third-person non-dialogue is *one* (9 times, 11 per cent) though there is only one example in Esther's non-dialogue.

5.3.4 Usual collocations peculiar to Esther's non-dialogue

Section 5.3.3 examined usual collocations in both narratives. This section will focus on the personal style of Esther as a narrator, as seen from the viewpoint of usual collocations, while the usual collocations of the third-person non-dialogue will be discussed in the following section. In order to discuss the narrative styles of Esther and the third-person narrator, we can also use Roger Fowler's term 'mind-style', defined as 'any distinctive linguistic presentation of an individual mental self' (Fowler 1977: 103). This analysis of usual collocations in Esther's narrative, which tend to be overlooked because of very common expressions, will reveal her mental attitude about her narration and characters.

An obvious characteristic in Esther's non-dialogue, which provides a contrast with the third-person non-dialogue, is the use of the first-person pronoun *I*. In the third-person non-dialogue there are 26 examples of *I*, but none of them refers to the narrator himself: 13 appear in George's letter to Esther, and seven, four and two examples are used in the free direct thought of Jo, one of the Dedlock family, and Sir Leicester respectively. The most notable feature in the collocations of *I* is that it tends to collocate with verbs of inert cognition or mental process, such as *think, thought, feel, felt, know, knew, hope, hoped, believe* and *believed*.

> I thought (115), I think (34), I don't think (9), I did not think (4), I know (21), I knew (74), I felt (93), I feel (2), I hope (17), I hoped (7), I believe (10), I believed (6)

These cognitive verbs are used to present the narrator's personal attitude or epistemic stance on information. In other words, 'they can mark certainty (or doubt), actuality, precision, or limitation; or they can indicate the source of knowledge or the perspective from which the information is given' (Biber et al. 1999: 972). Esther seems to avoid a decisive narrational form by the use of these collocations. For instance:

> *I believe* that nothing belonging to the family, which it had been possible to break, was unbroken at the time of those preparations for Caddy's marriage; that nothing which it had been possible to spoil in any way, was unspoilt; and that no domestic object which was capable of collecting dirt, from a dear child's knee to the door-plate, was without as much dirt as could well accumulate upon it. (Ch. 30)

Esther is describing the Jellybys' lodgings where, to paraphrase, 'nothing is unbroken and unspoilt any more'. By means of the addition of *I believe*, indicative of Esther's personal attitude, with the use of elaborate double negatives, she tries to escape giving the impression of unfairness or a direct way of speaking, and consequently maintains her stance as a careful and unobtrusive narrator.

> *I believe* – at least *I know* – that he was not rich . . . He [Woodcourt] was seven years older than I. Not that I need mention it, for it hardly seems to belong to anything. *I think* – *I mean*, he told us – that he had been in practice three or four years, and that if he could have hoped to contend through three or four more, he would not have made the voyage on which he was bound. (Ch. 17)

Here, *I believe* implies a personal uncertain understanding but the expression *I know* shows a firmer belief. Similarly, *I think* expresses uncertainty but the restatement *I mean* conveys a tone of giving more precise information. The use of these fixed collocations makes us feel her hesitation in giving this kind of information about her future husband, Woodcourt.

The use of *I hope* appears with a self-critical circumlocution:

> *I hope* it is not unkind in me to say that she certainly did make, in this, as in everything else, a show that was not conciliatory, of doing charity by wholesale, and of dealing in it to a large extent. (Ch. 8)

Esther judges that Mrs Pardiggle approaches her philanthropic charity work in a manner similar to that of a wholesaler, selling items in large quantities at low prices (mechanistically). However, she tries to avoid censuring Mrs Pardiggle directly and refrains from making an unguarded assertion by means of the use of *I hope*, which is 'often used in weakened sense' (*OED*), in addition to the double negative, *not unkind*. The same is true of the following:

> *I hope* it was not a poor thing in me to wish to be a little more used to my altered self, before I met the eyes of the dear girl I longed so ardently to see; but it is the truth. (Ch. 35)

> *I hope* it may not appear very unnatural or bad in me, that I then became heavily sorrowful to think I had ever been reared. (Ch. 36)

Such uses of '*I* + a verb of inert cognition' ('which is passive in meaning'; Leech 1971: 21) prove to be aspects of Esther's subjective personal style and, as well, a means of her providing an understated narrative.

Esther's stylistic mental attitude in narration is also found through the usage of her reporting clauses. These are composed of very simple collocations. Nearly all the reporting clauses in Esther's speeches are *said I* (approximately 260 times) or *I said* (approximately 80 times, including the clauses in indirect speech) without any modifier expressive of her emotion, throughout her narrative. Let us compare Esther's reporting clauses with those of Richard and Skimpole. The following are their reporting clauses in Chapter 37.

Esther (16)
(1) Reporting clauses without any modifier (14): said I (11) / I returned / I asked / I said
(2) Reporting clauses which contain words expressive of some emotion (2): I remonstrated / said, timidly enough

Richard (32)
(1) Reporting clauses without any modifier (16): said Richard (13), Richard resumed / acknowledged Richard / he said
(2) Reporting clauses which contain words expressive of some emotion (16): said Richard, just as heartily as before / cried Richard, gaily / said Richard, forcing a careless laugh / Richard spoke with the same shade crossing his face as before / said Richard, impatiently / retorted Richard / said Richard, a little more gaily / replied Richard, in his vivacious way / replied Richard, softening / pursued Richard, impetuously / returned Richard with a fierceness kindling in him / he returned, affectionately / said he, laughing / said Richard, astonished at my simplicity / said Richard, quite amused with me / said Richard, flushed, and triumphantly at Ada and me

Skimpole (11)
(1) Reporting clauses without any modifier (6): said Mr. Skimpole (3) / he resumed / returned Mr. Skimpole (2)
(2) Reporting clauses which contain words expressive of some emotion (5): said Mr. Skimpole, looking beamingly at us over a glass of wine-and-water / he repeated . . . with the pleasantest smile / said Mr. Skimpole, receiving the new light with a most agreeable jocularity of surprise / he retorted / he looked inquiringly at us with his frankest smile (in this last example there is seemingly no reporting verb but *looked inquiringly* carries out its function)

As can be seen, the reporting clauses of the direct speech of Richard and Skimpole very often include verbs or adverbs expressive of emotion. On the other hand, in the case of Esther, fourteen of the sixteen reporting clauses have no emotional verbs or modifiers. Esther's eleven reporting clauses are *said I*. This is the case not only in Chapter 37 but throughout her narrative. Such a customary and consistent use of the reporting clause *said I* in Esther's speech may reflect her maintenance of impartiality or modesty as a narrator, as well as the tenor of a soft-spoken person.

Esther's unpretentious narrative style (as a soft-spoken narrator) can also be observed through the distribution or position of reporting clauses in the presentation of direct speech. The position of a reporting clause is divided into initial position, medial position, final position and ø-stage or no reporting clause. Bonheim (1982: 75) gives the distribution of inquits or reporting clauses historical and stylistic consideration and from a broad and adequate survey concludes as follows: 'In modern prose the inquit tends to come in final position. Second in popularity is the medial position. The intial position was dominant in narratives of the renaissance, but today's writers, by and large, avoid it. In the early narrative almost every speech was accompanied by some kind of inquit, whereas the modern tendency is to let speech follow speech, if possible without interruption. An inquit in medial position is one way of allowing speech to follow on speech. The more radical tendency is to do without the inquit altogether.'

(1) Initial position: He said, smiling, 'Aye, it's you, little woman, is it?'
(2) Medial position: 'Not at all,' said I, 'I take it as compliment.'
(3) Final position: 'I think it is ready,' said I.
(4) ø-stage: 'It never can be forgotten.'

As Table 5.5 shows, the reporting clauses of Richard, Skimpole and Jarndyce occupy mainly the medial position; more than 80 per cent in

Table 5.5: Ratios of the position of reporting clauses of Esther, Richard, Skimpole and Jarndyce

	Initial	Medial	Final	ø-stage	Total
Esther	5 (2.6%)	74 (38.5%)	61 (31.8%)	52 (27.1%)	192 (100%)
Richard	2 (1.9%)	75 (72.1%)	17 (16.3%)	10 (9.6%)	104 (100%)
Skimpole	6 (7.9%)	62 (81.6%)	2 (2.6%)	6 (7.9%)	76 (100%)
Jarndyce	0 (0.0%)	32 (58.2%)	15 (27.3%)	8 (14.5%)	55 (100%)

Note: Esther: chapters 13, 14, 17, 23, 30, 37, 44, 51, 59; Richard: chapters 13, 14, 23, 37, 43, 51; Skimpole: chapters 18, 37, 43, 44; Jarndyce: chapters 14, 17, 18, 44.

the case of Skimpole. On the other hand, the final position and ø-stage position are much more frequent in Esther than in Richard, Skimpole and Jarndyce (although it should be noted that Esther's reporting clause is liable to occupy a final position because of her short speech). This dominance of the final position and ø-stage in Esther's reporting clauses, as Bonheim (1982: 76) points out, may reflect the intention of narrating without intervention as much as possible. Leech and Short (1981: 324) also deal with speech lacking reporting clauses (that is, ø-stage speech) as free direct speech, stating that the narrator is apparently not in control of the reporting of speech acts.

Next we will turn to conversational collocations in Esther's non-dialogue. Table 5.6 lists idiomatic collocations found in Esther's non-dialogue but not found in the third-person non-dialogue.

Table 5.6:   Conversational collocations used in Esther's non-dialogue

Type	Tokens	Esther's narrative		Third-person narrative	
		Non-dialogue	Dialogue	Non-dialogue	Dialogue
God bless them[a]	10	1	6	0	3
good time	8	5	1	0	2
I dare say	51	10	33[b]	0	11
Mercy upon us	1	1	0	0	0
much better	16	7[c]	6	0	3
much more	17	10	3	0	4
my goodness	1	1	0	0	0
no time	7	4	2	0	1
pretty well	15	1	6	0	8
quite so much	3	2	0	0	1
quite soon	1	1	0	0	0
so fast	3	3	0	0	0
so fond of	7	4	2	0	1
so often	5	3	1	0	1
too often	2	2	0	0	0
very fond of	15	12	3	0	0
very good	51	11	18	0	22[d]
very likely	6	1	5	0	0
very soon	9	5	3	0	1

Notes: [a] *Good bless her* (or *you*) is also included.
[b] In the dialogue of Esther's narrative, all 33 examples of *dare* are used in the idiomatic collocation *I dare say* while in the dialogue of the third-person narrative only two of the 13 examples of *dare* collocate with other words.
[c] One of them is used in Ada's letter to Richard.
[d] Jo's *wery good* (9 times) is also included.

God bless them, I dare say, Mercy upon us and *my goodness* in Table 5.6 are idiomatic collocations used in conversation. Biber et al. (1999: 546–7) describe *much better, much more, very good, very likely, pretty well* and *so fast*, as the most common collocations among 'adverb + adverb' combinations in present-day British and American English. The other collocations are also used very commonly in conversations. Therefore, we can say that Esther's non-dialogue utilizes more colloquial collocations than that of the third-person non-dialogue.

One notable feature among *-ly* adverbs in Esther's non-dialogue is the high frequency of *really*. In Esther's non-dialogue the frequency of *really* (see Table 5.4) is approximately three times that of the third-person non-dialogue. As *really* is very common in conversation according to Biber et al. (1999: 870), the more frequent use of *really* in Esther's non-dialogue may reflect her more conversational style, compared with the third-person non-dialogue. A characteristic of collocations of *really* in Esther's non-dialogue is that they tend to co-occur with words expressing Esther's emotions:

(1) I began to be *really afraid* of him now, looked at him with the greatest astonishment. (Ch. 3)

(2) I am *really vexed* and say, 'Dear, dear, you tiresome little creature, I wish you wouldn't!' but it is all of no use. (Ch. 9)

(3) and as I *really enjoyed* that refreshment, it made some recompense. (Ch. 57)

The higher frequency of negative adverbs in Esther's non-dialogue is also remarkable: *never* occurs 222 times – double the number of occurrences in the third-person non-dialogue (111). Another negative adverb, *not*, in Esther's non-dialogue also shows a higher frequency (694) than that of the third-person non-dialogue (430). Similarly, negative adverbs such as *scarcely* and *hardly* are also used more frequently in Esther's non-dialogue than in the third-person non-dialogue. This is because Esther's non-dialogue is narrated in a more conversational style, and 'negative forms are many times more common in conversation than in writing' (Biber et al. 1999: 159). In addition, this frequent use of negative adverbs by Esther is attributed to her use of 'meiosis', that is, 'a figure of speech which contains an understatement for emphasis: often used ironically, and also for dramatic effect, in the attainment of simplicity' (Cuddon 1982: 386–7) and 'litotes' in which 'an affirmative is expressed by the negative of the contrary' (*OED*). For instance:

And as our utmost endeavours could only elicit from Richard himself sweeping assurances that everything was going on capitally, and that it really was all right at last, *our anxiety was not much relieved by him*. (Ch. 24)

In this context, Richard, who quit studying medicine with Mr Badger and law at Kenge's office, is going to get a commission in the army this time. Although Esther describes her anxiety as 'not much relieved by him', in reality, her apprehensive solicitude concerning Richard's future has deepened. To put it another way, Esther's comment is different from the literal or logical meaning as in the following:

	our anxiety was not much relieved by him
(Literal meaning):	our anxiety was a little relieved by him
(Contextual meaning):	our anxiety was deepened by him

The following instances present litotes:

He [Jarndyce] did *not* seem *at all disappointed*: quite the contrary. (Ch. 8)

I was *not without* misgivings that he had gone to Newgate market in search of me. (Ch. 5)

Another example of litotes is shown by the collocation of *scarcely less*, which appears five times in the text of *Bleak House*; all instances are from Esther's non-dialogue:

(1) 'Ada's colour had entirely left her, and Richard was *scarcely less* pale.' (Ch. 5)
(2) 'I am sure that I was *scarcely less* enchanted than they were, and *scarcely less* pleased with the pretty dream.' (Ch. 9)
(3) 'I felt a liking for him [Prince Turveydrop], and a compassion for him, as he put his little kit in his pocket – and with it his desire to stay a little while with Caddy – and went away good-humouredly to his cold mutton and his school at Kensington, that made me *scarcely less* irate with his father [Mr. Turveydrop, a model of Deportment] than the censorious old lady.' (Ch. 14)

5.3.5 Usual collocations peculiar to the third-person non-dialogue

The third-person non-dialogue has fewer colloquial collocations than Esther's non-dialogue, although it is difficult to point out collocations peculiar to it. The following collocations in the third-person non-dialogue are not found in Esther's non-dialogue:

behoof of, in bygone times, no thoroughfare (twice), be applied to, to occur in, be known as

Be applied to, to occur in and *be known as* are described as the most common prepositional verbs in written registers (news reports and academic prose) according to Biber et al. (1999: 416–18). Of course, common prepositional verbs in written registers are also used in Esther's non-dialogue. For example, *to refer to, to consist of, be associated with* and *be composed of*, which are used six times, twice, three times, and three times, respectively, in the third-person non-dialogue, also appear twice, twice, four times, and once in Esther's non-dialogue.

The distinctive formal style of collocation in the third-person non-dialogue (which does not occur in Esther's non-dialogue) is the collocation of '*the* + adjective + proper name'. This type of collocation is classified into three heads according to the semantic meaning of adjectives in context: a relatively long-term, stable aspect of character or situation, a temporal emotion or situation, and 'others'. Within this collocational type referring to the characters' personality or situation, we find the following collocations:

the hapless Jo (Ch. 19), the eloquent Chadband (Ch. 19), the sagacious Smallweed (twice) (Ch. 20), the active Smallweed (Ch. 20), the susceptible Smallweed (Ch. 20), the trusty (used ironically) Smallweed (Ch. 20), the venerable (used ironically) Mr. Smallweed (Chs 21, 26, 33), the eminent Smallweed (Ch. 20), the Elfin Smallweed (Ch. 21), the unoffending Mrs. Smallweed (Ch. 21), the snappish Judy (Ch. 21), the blooming Judy (Ch. 26), the perennial Judy (Ch. 34), the fair Judy (Ch. 26), the grim Judy (Ch. 26), the imperturbable Judy (Ch. 27), the sportive Judy (Ch. 34), the virtuous Judy (Ch. 39), the Honourable (used ironically) William Guppy (Ch. 32), the audacious Boythorn (Ch. 66), the innocent Mr. Snagsby (Ch. 25), the devoted Mr. Snagsby (Ch. 33), the unfortunate George (Ch. 34), the sanguine George (Ch. 34), the fair Dedlock (twice) (Ch. 40), the great old Dedlock family (Ch. 58), the handsome Lady Dedlock (Ch. 66), the Honourable Mr. Bob Stables (four times) (Chs 2, 28, 40), the Right Honourable William Buffy, M.P. (Ch. 12), the parent Vholes (Ch. 39), the chaste Volumnia (Ch. 41), the fair Volumnia (Chs 53, 58), the giddy Volumnia (Ch. 58), the worthy Lignum (the nickname of Matthew Bagnet) (Ch. 49), the charitable Guster (Ch. 25)

The following collocations express the temporal emotions or situations of characters:

the injured Guppy (Ch. 33), the afflicted Mr. Guppy (Ch. 7), the disconsolate Mr. Guppy (Ch. 33), the admiring Mrs. Snagsby (Ch. 19), the watchful Mrs. Snagsby (Ch. 25), the sprightly Dedlock (Ch. 56), the irascible Mr. Smallweed (Ch. 27), the scornful Judy (Ch. 21), the gentle Judy (Ch. 26), the triumphant Judy (Ch. 34), the interesting Judy (Ch. 47), the placid Vholes (Ch. 39), the equable Vholes (Ch. 39), the astounded Tony (Ch. 39), the careful Phil (Ch. 47)

The following are collocations which lack judgemental or emotional adjectives:

the late Mr. Krook's obstinacy (Ch. 33), the late Mr. Tulkinghorn (3 times) (Ch. 54), the present Lady Dedlock (Chs 7, 40), the present Sir Leicester Dedlock (Ch. 7), the superannuated Mr. and Mrs. Smallweed (Ch. 21)

All of the collocations of the type *'the* + adjective + personal name' quoted above, occur in the third-person non-dialogue. With respect to this type of collocation in Esther's non-dialogue, there are only three examples of the third type of collocation: *the elder Mr. Turveydrop* (Chs 23, 38) and *the identical Peepy* (Ch. 14) (Mr Guppy, Mr and Mrs Snagsby, Smallweed, Chadband, George and so on also appear in Esther's narrative but the collocational pattern *'the* + adjective + personal name' is not used). The collocation *the elder Mr. Turveydrop* is used for distinguishing Young Turveydrop from his father. On the other hand, regarding the type of collocation 'adjective + personal name' (which lacks the definite article), there are many instances in Esther's non-dialogue:

poor Peepy (Ch. 4), poor little Peepy (Ch. 14), poor Miss Jellyby (twice) (Ch. 14), poor Caddy (Chs 14, 23, 30, 50), little Miss Flite (Chs 24, 35, 60), poor Miss Flite (Ch. 24), poor little Miss Flite (Ch. 24), my poor, dear, sanguine Richard (Ch. 23), poor Mr. Jellyby (four times) (Chs 23, 30), poor Charley (Ch. 31), poor little Charley (Ch. 35), poor dear Richard (Chs 37, 67), poor Gridley (Ch. 47), poor

Jo (Ch. 57), our poor dear Richard (Ch. 67), poor crazed Miss Flite (Ch. 65)

The adjectives *poor*, *little* and *dear* in these collocations do not describe the characters' personalities, situations or temporal emotions, but rather reveal the narrator Esther's spontaneous emotions towards them.

One of the functions of the definite article is as a specific reference, which 'can be identified uniquely in the contextual or general knowledge shared by speaker and hearer' (Quirk et al. 1985: 265), but a proper name itself functions as a specific reference. In fact, the use of the definite article *the* is not absolutely necessary in order to add an adjective to the proper name. According to Quirk et al. (1985: 290), 'nonrestrictive premodifiers are limited to adjectives with emotive colouring, such as: *old* Mrs. Fletcher, *dear little* Eric, *poor* Charles, *beautiful* Spain, *historic* York, *sunny* July. In a more formal and rather stereotypical style, the adjective is placed between *the* and a personal name: the *beautiful* Princess Diana [Princess Diana, who is beautiful], the *inimitable* Henry Higgins [Henry Higgins, who is inimitable].' Therefore, the collocational pattern '*the* + adjective + personal name' in the third-person non-dialogue, which tends to convey a relatively long-term, stable aspect of character or situation, rather than a temporal emotion, reveals a more formal style as well as the omnipotent attitude of the narrator toward characterization.

What is striking in the collocations of the third-person non-dialogue are their multifunctional usages. Let us consider the following:

General burst of cousinly indignation. Volumnia thinks it is really high time, *you know*, for somebody in power to step in and do something strong. Debilitated cousin thinks – Country's going – Dayvle – steeple-chase pace. (Ch. 40)

In the second sentence above, *you know* functions as a marker of conversational discourse.

The following is more complex:

'How do you do, Mr. Tulkinghorn?' says Sir Leicester, giving him his hand.
Mr Tulkinghorn is *quite well*. Sir Leicester is *quite well*. My Lady is *quite well*. All highly satisfactory. The lawyer, with his hands behind him,

walks at Sir Leicester's side, along the terrace. My Lady walks upon the other side. (Ch. 12)

'Mr. Tulkinghorn is quite well' is Tulkinghorn's reply to Sir Leicester's greeting. 'Sir Leicester is quite well' is Sir Leicester's reply to the unnarrated or unwritten Tulkinghorn statement, 'How do you do, Sir Leicester?' and, 'My Lady is quite well' is Lady Dedlock's reply to Tulkinghorn's unnarrated statement, 'How do you do, My Lady?' The discourse marker of conversation *quite well* is repeated in the same sentence construction among three people. The repeated collocation *quite well* seemingly proves the third-person narrator's comment *all highly satisfactory*. However, the narrator's sequential description of the three characters' directions of walking, especially that of Lady Dedlock's walking 'upon the other side', suggests disagreement between them. This implication may be supported by the iconicity of the sentence structure. This passage has been elaborately controlled by the narrator. Consequently, the fixed conversational collocation *quite well*, functioning generally as a phatic communion ('speech communication as used to establish social relationships rather than to impart information'; *OED*) of everyday language, takes on a shade of ironical meaning.

Such an elaborate ironical tone seems to provide part of the underlying structure of the third-person non-dialogue. Let us consider the collocation of *the learned gentleman*:

(1) *The learned gentleman* who is always so tremendously indignant at the unprecedented outrage committed on the feelings of his client by the opposite party, that he never seems likely to recover it, is doing infinitely better than might be expected, in Switzerland. (2) *The learned gentleman* who does the withering business, and who blights all opponents with his gloomy sarcasm, is as merry as a grig at a French watering-place. (3) *The learned gentleman* who weeps by the pint on the smallest provocation, has not shed a tear these six weeks. (4) *The very learned gentleman* who has cooled the natural heat of his gingery complexion in pools and fountains of law, until he has become great in knotty arguments for term-time, when he poses the drowsy Bench with legal 'chaff', inexplicable to the uninitiated and to most of the initiated too, is roaming, with a characteristic delight in aridity and dust, about Constantinople. (Ch. 19)

This describes the learned gentleman at Chancery Lane, during a long vacation (the *OED* defines *learned* in this case as 'one "learned in the law"; hence applied by way of courtesy to any member of the legal profession'). We discover a repeated sentence structure (1), (2), (3) and (4) in the passage, as the following shows:

(1) The learned gentleman
   who is always so tremendously indignant at . . .
   is doing infinitely better than might be expected, in Switzerland.
(2) The learned gentleman
   who does the withering business, and who blights all opponents
      with his gloomy sarcasm,
   is as merry as a grig at a French watering-place.
(3) The learned gentleman
   who weeps by the pint on the smallest provocation,
   has not shed a tear these six weeks.
(4) The (very) learned gentleman
   who has cooled the natural heat of his gingery complexion . . .
   is roaming, with a characteristic delight . . .

Every sentence has the same structure (subject + who-clause + predicative part) and the same subject (*the learned gentleman*), though the intensive adverb *very* is added to the subject of sentence (4).

Further, the content of the predicate in the main clause is in a contrastive relation to that of the subordinate clause. In sentences (1) to (4), the subordinate 'who-clause' represents the condition of the learned gentleman during the court term, while the main clause is that of the learned gentleman during the court's long vacation. For instance, the learned gentleman in sentence (1) is *always so tremendously indignant* during court days, but during vacation he becomes *infinitely better*. To express this in a different way, during the long vacation he has a feeling of (+ pleasure) while he has a feeling of (– pleasure) during the opening of Chancery. The same thing can be applied to sentences (2), (3) and (4).

In addition, *learned* in *the learned gentleman* (which also means 'having profound knowledge gained by study') contains in it the semantic features (+ reason) and (+ prudence). However, the phrase *the learned gentleman* collocates with emotional words having the semantic features (– reason) and (+ feeling) as *indignant, gloomy, merry* and the like. These elaborate rhetorical devices of repetitive parallelism and collocative clash are responsible for creating the ironical meaning of the collocation *learned gentleman* and the narrator's satirical attitude toward *the learned gentleman*.

This repetition of words and phrases, that is, a co-occurrence of the same collocational structure in immediate contexts, is found more often in the third-person non-dialogue than in Esther's non-dialogue. Essentially, the third-person narrator takes an objective stance towards events and characters, but his descriptions are sometimes tinged with personal compassion or indignation, as if he were a first-person narrator. As an instance we can observe the description of Jo's death:

> The light is come upon the dark benighted way. Dead!
> *Dead, your Majesty. Dead, my lords and gentlemen. Dead, Right Reverends and Wrong Reverends of every order. Dead, men and women, born with Heavenly compassion in your hearts.* And dying thus around us every day. (Ch. 47)

What can be noted in the passage is that the narrator's grief is directly expressed by the repeated collocational structure 'dead + terms of address', minus subject and verb (that is, *he is*). The terms of address shift from upper-class characters such as *your Majesty* and *my lords and gentlemen* to the common, such as *men and women*. Finally, the narrator's vision broadens to include the narrator and reader, as seen by use of the word *us*. This seems to show that the narrator considers Jo's death as a typical tragedy of the poor, who are passing away every day, and at the same time he feels anger against all those who did practically nothing to help the poor, like Jo.

As the figures in parentheses given below show, however, the gradual distance of words from the first use of the word *dead* to its next repeated use, through to the last sentence (lacking the word *dead*) may lead the reader's awareness to the fact that the narrator's grief and anger cannot help but fall into resignation.

> Dead! (1) Dead . . . (3) Dead . . . (5) Dead . . . (9) Dead . . . (11) And dying thus around us every day.

The differences of usual collocations we have so far observed in Esther's and the third-person non-dialogues, demonstrate an obvious difference in their narrative attitudes. Esther's non-dialogue is written in her conversational and personal style; her moderate, self-denying attitude is ascribed to her style of understatement as a narrator. On the other hand, the third-person non-dialogue has a less conversational style; the narrator makes more elaborate rhetorical use of usual collocations, which contribute to his satirical and sympathetic tone – this is the underlying structure of the third-person non-dialogue.

5.3.6 Unusual collocations of Esther's narrative and the third-person narrative

A majority of critical readers of *Bleak House* have the impression that the third-person narrative is apparently more unusual or deviant than Esther's narrative in its use of language. For example, Norman Page (1990: 55–6) points out language differences between the two narratives as follows:

> Her [Esther's] language is for the most part simple and at times even banal, and her tone informal and confidential; the other narrative by contrast is rhetorical, linguistically experimental, and dramatic . . . Language and style apart, there are further differences between the two narratives. Esther's, for instance, is more consistently serious; most of the comedy in this novel (and there is a good deal) is found in the more imaginative and highly coloured third-person narrative.

W.J. Harvey (1969: 226) also mentions Esther's simple and invariable narrative:

> The contrasting styles of the two narratives, while they offer the reader relief and variety, also seem to me evidence of Dickens's control in making Esther what she is, even at the risk of insipidity and dullness. The omniscient style has all the liveliness, fantastication and poetic density of texture that we typically associate with Dickens. Esther's narrative is plain, matter-of-fact, conscientiously plodding.

The third-person narrative is described as linguistically experimental, dramatic, lively and possessing poetic density, while Esther's narrative is simple, banal, insipid and dull. Is this difference reflected in the collocations as well? What is it about Esther's narrative that leaves us unable to describe her language and style as linguistically experimental, dramatic, lively and so on? Keeping these issues in mind, I would like to consider some of the language differences between the third-person narrative and the first-person narrative in terms of unusual collocations. First, the results of an informant test of the relative degrees of unusuality of collocations in the two narratives will be discussed. Second, the unusual collocations will be divided into seven types in order to emphasize the differences between unusual collocations in the two narratives, according to the classifications of unusual collocations in Chapter 3. Third, a comparative study of unusual collocations in the two narratives will be presented (also based on the classifications of unusual collocations). The unusual collocations to be dealt with in this section are only those collected from Esther's non-dialogue and the third-person non-dialogue, and do not appear in any other dialogues. This is because the non-dialogues reflect each narrator's perspective, attitude and stance on the events and the characters, as discussed in 'Discourse structure' (Section 5.3.1).

An informant test: unusual collocations in Esther's and the third-person narratives

Aim The aim of this informant test has been to determine whether or not specific collocational differences between the two different narratives are comprehended by native speakers, although it is recognized that there may be some fundamental design problems with this type of information gathering. Whereas a native-informant test is quite effective in studies of contemporary English, it may be problematic regarding nineteenth-century English. Additionally, some informants may attempt to adjust the collocations to their assumed appropriate contexts, that is, peculiar or poetic environments. Nonetheless, as Greenbaum (1970) has pointed out, whether or not a collocation is usual is not necessarily decided by frequency only, but may also require a native speaker's intuition. Therefore, the result of this informant collocation test may help to provide useful information in determining collocational difference between the two distinct narratives in *Bleak House*.

Procedure For a 'usuality/unusuality' test, informants were first given instructions (detailed just below). Secondly, three example-types of collocation were given (for example *dark night* as a usual collocation, *raw afternoon* as an unfamiliar but not unusual collocation, and *old infant* as an unusual collocation). Twenty collocations were chosen at random from each narrative. The total number of test collocations included 40 examples. Each informant selected from five degrees of range, with 'usual collocation' on the left, ranging to 'unusual collocation' on the right. Informants were instructed to choose one degree out of the five degrees. A silent interval of six to seven seconds was given between each example – the total time given to tick off all the boxes was five minutes. Informants must select each example within seven seconds, so that they do not consciously create a context in which to adjust to an unfamiliar or unusual collocation. ('A silent interval of twenty seconds was allowed during which the sentence was to be written down' (Greenbaum 1970: 33).)

Directions (as spoken to informants) 'This is a short questionnaire which will ask you to determine how usual or unusual certain word-collocations are. There are five degrees of difference between a usual collocation and an unusual collocation. Choose one degree out of the five degrees for each collocation and tick off that box. Please look at these three examples: *dark night* is a usual collocation. *Raw afternoon* is an unfamiliar collocation but not an unusual collocation. *Old infant* is an unusual collocation. You will have five minutes to complete this questionnaire. I will check in with you once a minute. Are you ready? Please begin.'

Informants All the informants were native speakers of English, and undergraduates studying at Edinburgh University. The total number of informants for each group:

Group I: 13 informants: First or second-year students, wishing to specialize in cultural sciences such as psychology or anthropology; language or literature students are not included in this group.

Group II: 20 informants: First-year students wanting to specialize in English language or literature.

Group III: 37 informants: Second-year students specializing in English or literature.

Group IV: 8 informants: Third or fourth-year students specializing in English language or literature.

Sampling of examples Forty examples of Dickens' collocations were chosen at random out of over 700 examples. These examples were not used by other novelists in the eighteenth and nineteenth centuries, according to the *ECF* and the *NCF*. Twenty examples were collected from each of the two *Bleak House* narratives (excluding dialogues): the third-person narrative and Esther's narrative.

The syntactic construction of the collocations examined 'Adjective + noun'.

Evaluation Each example has five degrees. Therefore, if all examples from Esther's narrative are unusual, the points will total 100, as each

Table 5.7:   A questionnaire for an informant test of 'unusuality' in collocation

What is your native language?
What year of study are you in? Circle your year of study (1   2   3   4)
What subject do you specialize in?

Collocation	usual 1	2	3	4	unusual 5
e.g. *dark night*	X				
e.g. *raw afternoon*			X		
e.g. *old infant*					X
(1) admonitory finger					
(2) apologetic cough					
(3) bloodless quietude					
(4) bright week					
(5) captivating looseness					
(6) chilled people					
(7) colourless days					
(8) congenial shabbiness					
(9) disdainful hand					
(10) dismal grandeur					
(11) emaciated glare					
(12) exalted dullness					
(13) exhausted composure					
(14) friendly indignation					
(15) frosty fire					
(16) gentle seriousness					
(17) gloomy relief					
(18) good-natured vexation					
(19) harmonious impeachment					
(20) healthy shore					
(21) housekeeping key					
(22) implacable weather					
(23) leaden lunches					
(24) light-hearted conviction					
(25) loving anxiety					
(26) mad lips					
(27) massive simplicity					
(28) minor surprise					
(29) pertinacious oil lamps					
(30) ravenous pens					
(31) rigid secrecy					
(32) serene contempt					
(33) smiling country					
(34) stolid satisfaction					
(35) thoughtful baby					
(36) timid days					
(37) troubled hands					
(38) ugly report					
(39) well-remembered finger					
(40) wicked relief					

Table 5.8: General results

	Group I (13)	Group II (20)	Group III (37)	Group IV (8)	All groups
Third-person narrative	68.3	71.1	66.0	69.1	67.9
Esther's narrative	59.7	63.0	58.9	60.4	60.1
Difference	8.6	8.1	7.1	8.7	7.8

collocation has been given 5 points for 20 examples. If all examples from Esther's narrative are usual collocations, the total will be 20 points ($1 \times 20 = 20$).

Results of the informant test (Table 5.8) indicate that the third-person narrative accrued 67.9 points, while Esther's narrative accrued 60.1 points. The difference between the two narratives is 7.8 points. This small difference seems surprising, as it is generally considered that there is a distinctive contrast between the two narratives in the use of language. What is more striking is that Esther's narrative received more points than expected. Is it possible to guess which examples are from which narrative? It seems unlikely that the respective source of each collocation can be guessed correctly.

There do not seem to be any distinct differences in total numbers of points between the various groups. Group IV informants show the largest difference between the two narratives of unusual collocations (8.7 points), but Group I informants show a near-identical 8.6 point difference.

Table 5.9 looks at individual collocations.

The highly unusual collocations which scored four points or over are:

Third-person narrative: bloodless quietude (4.1), exalted dullness (4.0), frosty fire (4.6), harmonious impeachment (4.2), pertinacious oil lamps (4.3), ravenous pens (4.5)

Esther's narrative: captivating looseness (4.0), well-remembered finger (4.4)

In the third-person narrative, *frosty fire* and *harmonious impeachment* are oxymoronic collocations with a collocational clash of the literal meanings, while *bloodless quietude* and *exalted dullness* are oxymoronic collocations with a discrepancy of the connotative meanings (compare Section 3.3). *Pertinacious oil lamps* and *ravenous pens* are personified

Table 5.9: The points given to each collocation in Esther's narrative and the third-person narrative

Collocation (Esther's narrative)		Collocation (third-person narrative)	
bright week	2.5	admonitory finger	3.2
captivating looseness	4.0	apologetic cough	2.3
chilled people	2.5	bloodless quietude	4.1
colourless days	2.2	congenial shabbiness	3.4
friendly indignation	3.0	disdainful hand	2.4
gentle seriousness	2.6	dismal grandeur	3.3
good-natured vexation	3.6	emaciated glare	3.3
healthy shore	3.8	exalted dullness	4.0
housekeeping key	2.2	exhausted composure	3.1
loving anxiety	2.4	frosty fire	4.6
light-hearted conviction	2.9	gloomy relief	3.2
mad lips	3.4	harmonious impeachment	4.2
rigid secrecy	2.1	implacable weather	3.0
serene contempt	3.1	leaden lunch	3.8
smiling country	3.8	massive simplicity	3.4
thoughtful baby	2.8	minor surprise	1.6
timid days	3.7	pertinacious oil lamps	4.3
troubled hands	2.5	ravenous pens	4.5
ugly report	2.6	stolid satisfaction	3.3
well-remembered finger	4.4	wicked relief	2.9
Total	60.1	Total	67.9

collocations. In Esther's narrative, *captivating looseness* is an oxymoronic collocation with a discrepancy of the connotative meanings because *captivating* has the semantic feature (+ favourable) as the connotative meaning, while *looseness* has the semantic feature (– favourable) as the connotative meaning. *Well-remembered finger* is semantically incongruous. What is interesting concerning *well-remembered finger* is that *admonitory finger* shows lower unusuality (3.2 points), though *well-remembered finger* and *admonitory finger* seem to be of the same type of unusual collocation.

This informant test may not give as clear a result as Greenbaum achieved in his 'completion tests', but we can conclude, at least for collocations which are not used by any other novelists in the eighteenth and nineteenth centuries, that there are unusual collocations in Esther's narrative as well as the third-person narrative. The following sections will pursue the unusual collocations of Esther's narrative and the third-person narrative as linguistically experimental collocations.

5.3.7 Unusual collocations in Esther's non-dialogue and the third-person non-dialogue

Bleak House contains many unusual collocations which are not found in other eighteenth or nineteenth-century fiction (*ECF* and *NCF*). Of the more than 700 examples collected for this research, over 300 occur in Esther's narrative – almost the same number as occur in the third-person narrative. It appears that the unusual collocations of Esther's narrative are as linguistically experimental as those of the third-person narrative, although there seem to be certain differences, of both collocational type and semantic structures of unusual collocations, between Esther's narrative and the third-person narrative. In this section, these unusual collocations will be broken down into seven types, according to the classification given in Chapter 3, though some may belong to other types. Moreover, the differences of unusual collocations in Esther's narrative and the third-person narrative will be discussed within each type of unusual collocation. The unusual collocations treated in this section are those of the non-dialogues only, for the reason that a narrator's attitude and 'mind-style' that is, 'any distinctive linguistic presentation of an individual mental self' (Fowler 1977: 103) can be observed only through the presentation of a non-dialogue and not through characters' dialogues (as discussed in Section 5.3.1 above).

1. *Metaphorical collocations*

The first type of unusual collocation we will examine is metaphorical. A typical metaphorical collocation is personification, regarding which Leech (1969: 158) points out the following three categories: '[a] *The Concretive Metaphor*, which attributes concreteness or physical existence to an abstraction: "the *pain* of separation", "the *light* of learning", "a vicious *circle*", "*room* for negotiation". [b] *The Animistic Metaphor*, which attributes animate characteristics to the inanimate: "an *angry* sky", "graves *yawned*", "*killing* half-an-hour", "the *shoulder* of the hill". [c] *The Humanizing Metaphor*, which attributes characteristics of humanity to what is not human: "This *friendly* river", "*laughing* valleys", "his appearance and manner *speak eloquently* for him".' These categories seem to apply well to my current research, but as Leech admits, these three categories overlap and especially, the distinction between animistic metaphor and humanizing metaphor is not clear.

As observed in the scene of fog at the beginning of *Bleak House*, natural phenomena, such as *sunshine* and *moon*, are often given animate attributes and anthropomorphic characteristics, with the collocational pattern of 'noun + verb'. Such personifications are found in both narratives:

In Esther's non-dialogue
The purblind day was feebly struggling with the fog . . . (Ch. 4)
the light and shadow travelled swiftly (Ch. 18)
the night was very slowly stirring (Ch. 59)
The houses frowned at us, the dust rose at us, the smoke swooped at us, nothing made any compromise about itself, or wore a softened aspect (Ch. 51)
the morning faintly struggled in (Ch. 59)

In the third-person non-dialogue
The clear cold sunshine glances into the brittle woods, and approvingly beholds the sharp wind scattering the leaves and drying the moss (Ch. 12)
The moon has eyed Tom with a dull cold stare . . . (Ch. 46)
the long vacation saunters on towards term-time, like an idle river very leisurely strolling down a flat country to the sea (Ch. 20)
night pursues its leaden course (Ch. 33)

There are also personifications having the collocational pattern 'adjective + noun'. The following are a list of personified collocations in Esther's non-dialogue:

cheerful lodging (Ch. 13), cheerful town (Ch. 64), healthy shore (Ch. 35), hospitable jingle (Ch. 6), hungry garret (Ch. 23), inexpressive-looking books (Ch. 3), miserable corner (Ch. 37), over-ripe berry (Ch. 43), pleasant footpath (Ch. 18), ripening weather (Ch. 64), smiling country (Ch. 64), ungrown despair (Ch. 45)

In the above list of metaphorical collocations there are many adjectives expressive of sensory perception, such as *cheerful*, *healthy* and *hungry*.

Most of the metaphorical collocations work as a single metaphor but there are double-metaphorical collocations, as seen in the following:

In falling ill, I seemed to have crossed a dark lake, and to have left all my experiences, mingled together by the great distance, on the *healthy shore*. (Ch. 35)

After lying ill for several weeks, the real world looks strange to Esther, being different from the time she was healthy, as if she had crossed to the opposite shore of a lake. *Shore* compared to a life or life-circumstances is not naturally in mutual expectancy with *healthy*, but rather, is compared to her past: *healthy* thus symbolizes her past. The following double-metaphorical collocation is also striking:

> I look along the road before me, where the distance already shortens and the journey's end is growing visible; and, true and good above the dead sea of the Chancery suit, and all the *ashy fruit* it cast ashore, I think I see my darling. (Ch. 37)

The Chancery suit is likened to the Dead Sea, which ruins and kills the suitors. *Ashy* is symbolic of death and *fruit* is a metaphor expressing the result of the Chancery suit. *Fruit* connotes a good result in general but here it is used ironically.

Personified collocations in the third-person non-dialogue show only a slight difference from those of Esther's:

> argumentative backfall (Ch. 25), benighted England (Ch. 12), death-like hue (Ch. 58), discontented goose (Ch. 7), idle river (Ch. 20), inconsolable carriages (Ch. 53), invigorating pail (Ch. 34), penitential sofa-pillows (Ch. 66), pertinacious oil lamps (Ch. 58), ravenous (little) pens (Chs 33, 39), twinkle gaspingly (Ch. 58), upstart gas (Ch. 66), welcome light (Ch. 11), the night lags tardily (Ch. 58), perplexed and troublous valley of shadow of the law (Ch. 32), swanlike aristocracy (Ch. 39)

In these examples, *backfall* is used in the sense of 'A fall or throw on the back in wrestling. Often *fig*' (*OED* quotes from *Bleak House*); and *benighted* is used to mean '*fig.* Involved in intellectual or moral darkness' (*OED*).

In comparison to the personified collocations in Esther's non-dialogue, animistic metaphorical collocations 'which attribute animate characteristics to the inanimate' (Leech 1969: 158) are dominant in the third-person narrative. Esther also tends to use favourable or neutral words such as *cheerful* and *ripening* in the personified collocations *cheerful town* and *ripening weather*, while the third-person narrator uses not only favourable words but unfavourable or negative and judgemental words as well – *benighted, discontented, penitential, ravenous, perplexed* and *troublous*.

The following are visualized collocations which attribute an image to an abstraction or add a sharp image to concreteness or physical existence. The following occur in Esther's non-dialogue:

> *visualized collocations*: chivalrously polite (Ch. 9), colossal staircases (Ch. 35), colourless days (Ch. 51), fish-like manner (Ch. 45), flaming necklace (Ch. 35), full-blown girl (Ch. 43), musty rotting silence (Ch. 51)

In the third-person non-dialogue we find additional visualized collocations:

> *visualized collocations*: his biting screw of an eye (Ch. 32), buttoned-up half-audible voice (Ch. 39), clouds of cousins (Ch. 40), crooked knife of his mind (Ch. 46), dazed mind (Ch. 39), elephantine lizard (Ch. 1), feline mouth (Ch. 12), foggy glory (Ch. 1), frowning woods (Ch. 28), grim furniture (Ch. 28), icy stare (Ch. 54), iron bow (Ch. 48), leaden lunches (Ch. 40), reservoir of confidences (Ch. 10), nomadically drunk (Ch. 58), shadowy belief (Ch. 46), skeleton throats (Ch. 56), sparkling stranger (Ch. 49), swarm of misery (Ch. 16), swelling pride (Ch. 55), as hollow as a coffin (Ch. 39), unwholesome hand (that is the suit, Jarndyce and Jarndyce) (Ch. 1)

The third-person non-dialogue does not only have more visualized collocations but also a greater variety of visual images than Esther's. Additional metaphorical collocations are:

In Esther's non-dialogue
The examples of synecdoche: my guardian's delicacy had soon perceived this (Ch. 60), as if his natural generosity felt a pang of reproach (Ch. 37), her quickness anticipated what I might have said presently (Ch. 23)

Other interesting metaphorical collocations: calendars of distress (Ch. 5), crisp-looking gentleman (Ch. 13), dead glove (Ch. 45), divine sunshine (Ch. 35), gleam of welcome (Ch. 44), inheritance of shame (Ch. 44), ruin of youth (Ch. 60), summer joke (Ch. 9), my vanity should deceive me (Ch. 3)

In the third-person non-dialogue
The examples of synecdoche: her head concedes (Ch. 40), Mrs. Rouncewell's hands unquiet (Ch. 7)

Other interesting metaphorical collocations: deadened world (Ch. 2), deadly meaning (Ch. 48), forensic lunacy (Ch. 39), imperial luxury (Ch. 49), infernal stables (Ch. 45), maternal foot (Ch. 10), official cat (Ch. 39), unsavoury shelter (Ch. 16), imperturbable as Death (Ch. 34), imperturbable as the hearthstone (Ch. 39)

2. *Transferred collocations*

There are collocations which are not contradictory in literal meaning or connotative meaning, but are considered as transferred or dislocated collocations, in which an adjective or adverb grammatically qualifies a noun, adjective or verb while literally or semantically applying to a different word. Among transferred collocations, in both the non-dialogues, collocations of 'an adjective + a body part' are the ones most frequently found. These unusual collocations of body parts are divided into two types: (1) a transferred collocation referring to a temporary emotion of the possessor of a body part and (2) a transferred collocation referring to a relatively permanent character of the possessor of a body part. The following are transferred collocations of 'an adjective + a body part' in both the non-dialogues, which are not used in fiction before Dickens (*ECF; NCF*):

In Esther's non-dialogue (20 examples)
(1) a transferred collocation referring to a temporary emotion of the possessor of a body part: care-worn head (Ch. 15), darkened face (Ch. 3), disdainful face (Ch. 41), pleasant eyebrows (Ch. 49), quiet hands (Ch. 31), sudden eye (Ch. 9), surprised eyes (Ch. 13), too-eager eyes (Ch. 23), troubled hands (Ch. 38), warning feet (Ch. 36) (10 examples)
(2) a transferred collocation referring to a relatively long-term, stable aspect of character of the possessor of a body part: gracious hand (Jesus Christ's hand) (Ch. 7), quick face (Jarndyce's careful attention to people) (Ch. 6), resolute face (Esther's strong-willed aunt) (Ch. 44), trusting face (Ada) (Ch. 3), mad lips (Miss Flite) (Ch. 60), rustic faces (Ch. 18), sprightly eyes (Skimpole) (Ch. 43), sprightly forehead (Skimpole's Comedy daughter) (Ch. 43), sulky forehead (Prince Turveydrop's girl student) (Ch. 23), well-remembered finger (Inspector Bucket) (Ch. 62) (10 examples)

In the third-person non-dialogue (20 examples)
(1) a transferred collocation referring to a temporary emotion of the possessor of a body part: admonitory finger (Ch. 54), angry hands

(Ch. 26), anxious hand (Ch. 46), busy face (Ch. 46), cruel finger (Ch. 54), disdainful hand (Ch. 41), unconscious head (Ch. 41), wary hand (Ch. 47) (8 examples)

(2) a transferred collocation referring to a relatively long-term, stable aspect of character of the possessor of a body part: admonitory hand (Chadband, a hypocritical minister) (Ch. 19), calm hands (Mrs. Rouncewell) (Ch. 7), decent hand (Lady Dedlock) (Ch. 25), dreadful feet (Ch. 32), gracious head (Lady Dedlock) (Ch. 12), knowing eyes (Inspector Bucket) (Ch. 54), maternal foot (Ch. 10), murderous hand (Ch. 48), relentless head (Ch. 54), so-genteel fingers (Lady Dedlock) (Ch. 12), stately breast (Sir Leicester) (Ch. 12), venerable eye (young Smallweed) (Ch. 20), (12 examples)

These examples of transferred collocations are of nearly equal number and nearly equally used for both temporary emotions (for example, *angry hands*) and relatively long-term, stable aspects of character (for example, *decent hand*) in both the non-dialogues. What is different between them is that the persons to whom these transferred collocations of body parts are applied in Esther's non-dialogue are different from those of the non-dialogues (though exceptionally, Inspector Bucket's finger is described in both non-dialogues).

The transferred collocations of 'an adjective + a human behaviour' are also interesting:

In Esther's non-dialogue
attentive smile (Ch. 6), dejected bow (Ch. 9), dull thoughtfulness (Ch. 60), hopeless gesture (Ch. 45), observant smile (Ch. 14), sulky jerk (Ch. 57), sunburnt smiles (Ch. 52), triumphant rub (Ch. 62)

In the third-person non-dialogue
angry nods (Ch. 42), apologetic cough (Chs 11, 32, 42), comprehensive wave (Ch. 47), deferential cough (Chs 11, 12), emaciated glare (Ch. 46), explanatory cough (Ch. 10), fat smile (Ch. 19), gloomy yawn (Ch. 7), majestically interpose (Ch. 53), majestic sleep (Ch. 7), persuasive action (Ch. 53), sarcastic nods (Ch. 54), shrewd attention (Ch. 54), stately approval (Ch. 7), undisguisable yawns (Ch. 58)

The third-person non-dialogue shows a greater variety of adjectives and behaviours in this type of transferred collocation than Esther's non-dialogue.

Other transferred collocations are as follows:

In Esther's non-dialogue
affable dignity (Ch. 64), agreeable candour (Ch. 6), agreeable jocularity (Chs 37, 42), amiable importance (Ch. 35), bashful simplicity
(Ch. 13), captivating gaiety (Ch. 6), delightful confidence (Ch. 6),
delightful gaiety (Ch. 6), delightful weather (Ch. 18), deplorable
home (Ch. 30), dreary passage (Ch. 24), engaging candour (Ch. 6),
fearful wet (Ch. 59), gentle seriousness (Ch. 44), guileless candour
(Ch. 37), overweening assumptions (Ch. 8), painful belief (Ch. 31),
playful astonishment (Ch. 43), pleasant footpath (Ch. 18), pleasant
weeks (Ch. 23), serene composure (Ch. 4), surly stop (Ch. 57), timid
days (Ch. 44), thoughtful amazement (Ch. 5), timid tenderness
(Ch. 14), vivacious candour (Ch. 6)

In the third-person non-dialogue
angry reasons (Ch. 55), boastful misery (Ch. 20), disappointing knobs
(Ch. 66), grinning silence (Ch. 39), inconsolable carriages (Ch. 53),
melancholy trees (Ch. 2), restless pillow (Ch. 46), stately gloom (Ch.
28), stately liking (Ch. 2), uncomfortable tightness (Ch. 12), worn-
out heavens (Ch. 12)

Concerning other types of transferred collocations, we find more examples in Esther's non-dialogue. In addition, Esther tends to use transferred epithets with favourable adjectives such as *captivating* and
pleasant, while the third-person narrator shows a tendency to use adjectives more unfavourable in meaning, such as *boastful* and *uncomfortable*.

3. Oxymoronic collocations
Oxymoronic collocations are often used by both Esther and the third-
person narrator. In terms of semantic construction there are three types
of oxymoronic collocations, 'a word of favourable meaning + a word of
unfavourable meaning', 'a word of unfavourable meaning + a word of
favourable meaning' and 'others':

In Esther's non-dialogue (25 examples)
(1) *A word of favourable meaning + a word of unfavourable meaning*
    benignant shadow (Ch. 65), captivating looseness (Ch. 37), cheerful
    gravity (Ch. 13), curious indifference (Ch. 8), delightfully irregular
    (Ch. 6), friendly indignation (Ch. 52), good-humoured vexation (Ch.
    6), good-natured vexation (Ch. 6), loving anxiety (Ch. 50), modest

consciousness (Ch. 14), pleasant absurdity (Ch. 15), pleasantly
cheated (Ch. 6), pleasantly irregular (Ch. 6), professions of childish-
ness (Ch. 15), resolutely unconscious (Ch. 18), respectful wretchedness (Ch. 8), serene contempt (Ch. 50), smiling condescension
(Ch. 5) (18 examples)
(2) *A word of unfavourable meaning + a word of favourable meaning*
    absent endeavours (Ch. 6), haughty self-restraint (Ch. 36), mourn-
    ful glory (Ch. 61), old-faced mite (Ch. 50), plaintive smile (Ch. 13),
    rapacious benevolence (Ch. 8) (6 examples)
(3) *Others*
    thoughtful baby (one example)

In the third-person non-dialogue (24 examples)
(1) *A word of favourable meaning + a word of unfavourable meaning*
    affectionate distress (Ch. 55), affectionate lunacy (Ch. 55), exalted
    dullness (Ch. 56), harmonious impeachment (Ch. 49), magnificent
    displeasure (Ch. 28) (5 examples)
(2) *A word of unfavourable meaning + a word of favourable meaning*
    awful politeness (Ch. 40), cold sunshine (Ch. 12), dismal grandeur
    (Ch. 48), dull repose (Ch. 66), exhausted composure (Ch. 2), foggy
    glory (Ch. 1), frosty fire (Ch. 56), frowning smile (Ch. 54), gloomy
    enjoyment (Ch. 20), gloomy relief (Ch. 39), mechanically faithful
    (Ch. 36), stolid satisfaction (Ch. 49), stunned admiration (Ch. 25),
    wicked relief (Ch. 55), worn-out placidity (Ch. 2) (15 examples)
(3) *Others*
    boastful misery (Ch. 20), interminable brief (Ch. 1), official den
    (Ch. 39), waking doze (Ch. 58) (4 examples)

Of interest in the above list of oxymoronic collocations is that Esther's
non-dialogue surpasses the third-person non-dialogue quantitatively
(though a few more examples might be discovered in both the non-
dialogues). As Table 5.3 illustrates, each non-dialogue is almost the same
length (101,135 words in the third-person non-dialogue and 115,205
words in Esther's non-dialogue). What is even more striking is that with
respect to the semantic construction of oxymoronic collocations there
is a distinctive contrast between Esther's and the third-person non-
dialogue. That is to say, 'a word of favourable meaning + a word of
unfavourable meaning' is dominant in Esther's non-dialogue while 'a
word of unfavourable meaning + a word of favourable meaning' shows
an overwhelming majority in the third-person non-dialogue. Such a difference of a semantic word order of oxymoronic collocations seems to

be attributed to each narrator's difference of attitude towards the events and characters. To put it another way, Esther's oxymoronic collocations are used in a more generous, less judgemental manner than those of the third-person narrator.

4. *Disparate collocations*

Disparate collocations are incongruous combinations of two items taken from different semantic fields or registers, such as *a delicious hand*, rather than oxymoronic collocations, per se. 'Collocational clash' is caused by the contradiction of literal meanings or connotative meanings of the two conjunctive items. The following is a list of disparate collocations in Esther's non-dialogue:

cheap notoriety (Ch. 15), chilled people (Ch. 59), delicious sleep (Ch. 35), inheritance of shame (Ch. 44), kicking grief (Ch. 30), massively hushed (Ch. 37), playful impartiality (Ch. 61), solemn thunder (Ch. 18), transparent business (Ch. 37), tributary streams of tea (Ch. 21), unmeaning weakness (Ch. 18)

The third-person non-dialogue has the following examples:

bitterly knowing (Ch. 33), bloodless quietude (Ch. 39), homely filth (Ch. 47), homely parasites (Ch. 47), homely sores (Ch. 47), homely rags (Ch. 47), hot sleep (Ch. 19), legal cellar (Ch. 2), legendary hatreds (Ch. 1), native ignorance (Ch. 47), reservoir of confidences (Ch. 10), rusty legs (Ch. 39), the weather shut up (Ch. 58)

5. *Unconventional collocations*

The collocation *fixed sleep* is used for Tulkinghorn's death. *Eternal sleep* is a very common collocation but *fixed sleep* is a strange collocation. A collocation such as *fixed sleep* is dealt with as an unconventional collocation. This type of unusual collocation is not caused by semantic incompatibility between lexemes, as is found in the other four types of unusual collocations discussed so far. Therefore, component analysis (a linguistic method for explaining a semantic mismatch by pointing out the specific semantic features that activate collocational clashes) does not work well as an analytic method for this type of unusual collocation. Below are the unconventional collocations in Esther's non-dialogue and in the third-person non-dialogue. Collocations in parentheses are usual collocations, and are given for reference:

In Esther's non-dialogue
altered days (*different days*) (Ch. 44), bright week (*fine week*) (Ch. 37),
by ever fervent means (*by all possible means*) (Ch. 37), candid hilarity (*wild hilarity*) (Ch. 61), capital understanding (*full understanding*)
(Ch. 36), dreadful expense (*considerable expense*) (Ch. 13), dull
thoughtfulness (Ch. 60), enduring impression (Ch. 36), forcible composure (Ch. 8), hidden regret (Ch. 50), high-shouldered bow (Ch. 14),
housekeeping keys (Ch. 6), incessant smiling (Ch. 38), indignantly
sure (*completely sure*) (Ch. 52), infinite vehemence (Ch. 14), inky days
(*busy days*) (Ch. 50), light-hearted conviction (Ch. 61), moral Police-
man (Ch. 8), never-ending stairs (Ch. 35), quietly sorry (Ch. 35), rigid
secrecy (Ch. 36), rough salutation (Ch. 15), secret blow (Ch. 8),
speechless indignation (Ch. 14), thank him poorly (Ch. 44),
womanly bonnet and apron (Ch. 15)

In the third-person non-dialogue
business consideration (*health consideration*) (Ch. 41), business mind
(Ch. 41), fixed sleep (*eternal sleep*) (Ch. 53), hot buildings (*weathered
buildings*) (Ch. 42), implacable November weather (*miserable weather*)
(Ch. 1), raw afternoon (*rainy afternoon*) (Ch. 1), tight face (*sharp face*)
(Ch. 54), wild disturbance (*serious disturbance*) (Ch. 41), wintry roads
(*icy roads*) (Ch. 55), flung-back face (*up-turned face*) (Ch. 41), wet
hours (*wet day*) (Ch. 7)

6. *Modified idiomatic collocations*
Few modified idiomatic collocations are found in Esther's non-dialogue,
but the third-person narrator often seems to enjoy a form of word play
which involves changing or corrupting an idiom or a fixed expression
with the result that specific characters, as well as society in general, are
satirically criticized. The following is an example of modification via
substitution:

'Guppy,' says Mr. Jobling, 'I will not deny it. I was on the wrong side
of the post. But I trusted to things *coming round*.'
    That very popular trust in flat things *coming round*! Not in their
being *beaten round*, or *worked round*, but in their '*coming*' round! As
though a lunatic should trust in the world's '*coming*' triangular! (Ch.
20)

In this extract, Jobling uses the idiom *come round* to mean 'to veer
round, as the wind, to a more favourable quarter' (*OED*), that is, that

things get better. However, the narrator takes the collocational expression literally (on purpose) wilfully interpreting Jobling's *come round* to mean becoming round, as observed in the phrase *flat things coming round*. The narrator furthermore develops his word play on making flat things 'become round' by beating them (*beaten* round) or by working them (*worked* round) and the difficulty of flat things becoming round is expressed by the impossible idea of the world *'coming' triangular*. Satirical commentary produced by idiomatic collocational substitution is even more striking in the following:

> The light is come upon the dark benighted way. Dead! Dead, your Majesty. Dead, my lords and gentlemen. Dead, *Right Reverends and Wrong Reverends* of every order. Dead, men and women, born with heavenly compassion in your hearts. And dying thus around us every day. (Ch. 47)

This passage is the narrator's commentary on Jo's death, expressing grief, indignation and, finally, resignation. *Right Reverends* refers to bishops, according to the *OED*. The idiom *Right Reverends*, in the above passage, is followed by *Wrong Reverends*. So, the collocation *Wrong Reverends* is a pun made with the replacement of *right* by *wrong*. *Right* in the idiom *Right Reverends* does not have the meaning of 'whether things are true or wrong'. The narrator's pun of *Wrong Reverends* implies his strong indignation and bitter satire against reverends of every order who do not intend to do anything for poor people such as Jo, although they have their worthy name, *Right Reverends*.

The following modified idiomatic collocation is an example of expansion, where an element is added to the original quotation:

> From Mr. Chadband's being much given to describe himself, both verbally and in writing, as a *vessel*, he is occasionally mistaken by strangers for a gentleman connected with navigation; but, he is, as he expresses it, 'in the ministry.' (Ch. 19)

Chadband prefers to be described as a *vessel*, meaning 'he is in the ministry' because *vessel* can mean 'a person regarded as having the containing capacity or function of a vessel' (*OED*) in Biblical use. He shows his great capacity for receiving people even of the lowest class, such as Jo, in his sermon, as the meaning of the word *vessel* implies; but the narrator suggests a different kind of capacity by adding a modifier to *vessel*:

the best tea-service is set forth, and there is excellent provision made of dainty new bread, crusty twists, cool fresh butter, thin slices of ham, tongue, and German sausage, and delicate little rows of anchovies nestling in parsley; not to mention new-laid eggs, to be brought up warm in a napkin, and hot buttered toast. For, Chadband is rather *a consuming vessel* – the persecutors say *a gorging vessel*; and can wield such weapons of the flesh as a knife and fork, remarkably well. (Ch. 19)

The collocations *a consuming vessel* and *a gorging vessel* subvert Chadband's intended meaning. Grace, one of the heavenly virtues, which he must possess as a minister, is opposed to gluttony, one of the seven deadly sins, which he demonstrates here. By making fun of Chadband's *vessel* the narrator exposes the hypocrisy of the minister.

In the following example, a light word play is created by a 'blending' of two idioms:

'I take it,' he [Mr George] says, making just *as much and as little change in his position as will enable him to reach the glass to his lips*, with a round, full action, 'that I am the only man alive (or dead either), that gets the value of a pipe out of YOU?' (Ch. 21)

The narrator tried to describe the movement of Mr George's position by the phrase *just as much change in his position as will enable him to reach the glass to his lips*, but as Mr George's movement is slight, the narrator adds *and as little* to his description. This addition of *and as little* hardly seems to alter the cognitive meaning of the original, but creates an awkward expression because we cannot say *making just as little change in his position as will enable him to reach the glass to his lips*.

7. Relexicalized collocations

As discussed in Section 3.8, Dickens often implies a second meaning without modifying the form of usual collocations or well-known fixed expressions. This type of collocation was treated as a 'relexicalized' collocation, and is also found in Esther's non-dialogue, as observed in Esther's *sacred obligation*, meaning 'an obligation as a child who loves her mother'. There are a few examples of this type in the third-person non-dialogue. For example:

There are powdered heads from time to time in the little windows of the hall, looking out at *the untaxed powder* falling all day from the sky . . . (Ch. 58)

The collocation *untaxed powder*, being based on the historical fact that 'a tax was levied on hair powder by Pitt, who introduced it in order to help finance the war with France' (Shatto 1988: 285), is a common expression. However, this collocation is used for snow in the above quotation. In like manner, *familiar demon* refers to Inspector Bucket's forefinger as in the following:

> When Mr. Bucket has a matter of this pressing interest under his consideration, the fat forefinger seems to rise to the dignity of a *familiar demon*...Mr. Bucket makes a leg, and comes forward, passing *his familiar demon* over the region of his mouth. (Ch. 53)

The collocation *the ordinary home-made article* refers to Jo, an unfortunate victim who was produced in England:

> he is not a genuine foreign-grown savage; he is *the ordinary home-made article*. Dirty, ugly, disagreeable to all the senses, in body a common creature of the common streets, only in soul a heathen. (Ch. 47)

Other examples are shown below:

> ('to make occasional resurrections' means 'to visit')
> she [Volumnia] *makes occasional resurrections* in the country houses of her cousins. (Ch. 28)

> ('to be arrested' means 'to be grabbed')
> he [Smallweed] *is arrested* by Judy, and well shaken. (Ch. 27)

5.4 Conclusion

This chapter has offered an analysis of collocational characteristics in Esther's narrative and the third-person narrative both quantitatively and qualitatively and from two viewpoints: usual collocations and unusual collocations. With respect to usual collocations, we are able to discern various patterns of collocational difference in common words between the two narratives which are closely connected with the narrators' attitudes and emotional tones, that is, mind-styles. As far as new, unusual and creative collocations are concerned, *Bleak House* has a large number, which are likely to be overlooked, as they are not to be found in other eighteenth and nineteenth-century fiction. Esther's language or style in her narrative is generally said to be simple, plain, and matter-of-fact, but there are many unusual collocations in Esther's narrative and they are of various types (metaphorical, personified, oxymoronic, transferred and so on). Therefore, we can say, at the very least, that collocations in Esther's narrative are linguistically experimental and satisfactorily creative. Further, examining differences between Esther's narrative and the third-person narrative, qualitative differences relating to 'unusuality' or types of unusual collocations seem more apparent than differences relating to the quantity of particular collocations. In this regard, informant test results show that the degree of unusuality in the third-person non-dialogue is higher than that of Esther's non-dialogue (though the results are not as striking as expected). In addition, the third-person narrator tends to modify idiomatic collocations and give usual collocations a second, implied meaning but these types of modified idiomatic and relexicalized collocations are very rare in Esther's non-dialogue. Such differences between unusual collocations in the two non-dialogues leads us to an awareness that the third-person narrator is more deeply involved in, and in more direct control of, his narration than Esther is of her narration. Esther intends to narrate in an unobtrusive manner, as evidenced by her remark, 'I mean all the time to write about other people, and I try to think about myself as little as possible' (Ch. 9).

6
Collocations and Characters

An individual character in dialogue often repeats particular collocations. Such collocations are one of the linguistic features the character possesses, a 'literary idiolect' related to habits of speech. Brook (1970: 138) defines the term 'idiolect' as follows: 'the speech-habits of an individual, in contrast with a dialect, which describes the speech-habits of a group'. Such individual speech-habits are 'as unique (though not as unchangeable) as his fingerprints' (Page 1988: 97), and may be broadly classified under two headings: 'those indicating membership of some social or regional or other readily identifiable group, and those which are personal and idiosyncratic' (ibid.). This chapter will focus mainly on the latter; personal speech-habits, although some reference may be made to group speech-habits in some cases. Golding (1985: 8) also discusses idiolects, that is, speech features of the characters in Dickens' works, under 'four general headings: linguistic, typifying, rhetorical and rhythmic'. The speech-habits of individuals to be examined in this section fall under Golding's 'linguistic' heading, and will be discussed in terms of repeated collocations; collocational patterns for which characters have a predilection.

In addition to repeated collocations and collocational patterns peculiar to characters in dialogues, Esther and the third-person narrator also often use the same collocations or the same kind of collocational patterns for particular characters in their narratives (that is, non-dialogues). This section will discuss such repeated collocations and collocational patterns, as applied to particular characters in non-dialogues, first by being examined in their speech, and secondly in the narrators' narratives (that is, non-dialogues).

171

6.1 Collocations peculiar to characters in their speech

Among content words in *Bleak House* the highly-frequent word *friend* (292 times, Rank 69; Table 5.1) occurs 225 times in speech (138 times in the third-person dialogue, 87 times in Esther's dialogue). The word *friends* is also used primarily in speech and appears 81 times (55 times in the third-person dialogue, 26 times in Esther's dialogue), while *friends* is used 108 times throughout the text of *Bleak House*. Therefore, 77 per cent of the singular form *friend* (225 times out of 292) and 75 per cent of the plural form *friends* (81 times out of 108) appear in speeches. What is characteristic in the collocations of *friend* and *friends* in speech is the use of terms of address. With regard to the use of terms of address Page (1971: 16) states:

> The fictional usefulness of forms of address is twofold: in the first place, they may serve to define and emphasise the nature of a relationship, both in terms of social class and in terms of degrees of intimacy or formality; and secondly, the novelist is able to modify these forms in a manner which suggests, economically but often powerfully, a temporary or permanent shift in the relationship concerned.

This section, therefore, discusses Dickens' use of *friend* and *friends*. The collocations of *friend* and *friends* functioning as terms of address also show different collocational tendencies from character to character. For example, the term of address *my friends* will enable readers to remember Mr Chadband, a minister, who delivers a hypocritical sermon:

> '*My friends*,' says Mr. Chadband. 'Peace be on this house! On the master thereof, on the mistress thereof, on the young maidens, and on the young men! *My friends*, why do I wish for peace? What is peace? Is it war? No. Is it strife? No. Is it lovely, and gentle, and beautiful, and pleasant, and serene, and joyful? O yes! Therefore, *my friends*, I wish for peace, upon you and upon yours.' (Ch. 19)

In general, the form of address *my friends* is 'applied to a mere acquaintance, or to a stranger, as a mark of goodwill or kindly condescension on the part of the speaker' (*OED*). However, the repeated collocation *my friends*, in an immediate context, loses the main function of *my friend* working as a mark of goodwill or kindly condescension on the part of the speaker, and carries and reinforces an oratorical tone through the repeated use of rhetorical questions.

According to Biber et al. (1999: 1112), in present-day English 'vocatives occurring in final position are much more common than those in initial position. In addition, there is a noticeable difference between the length of units associated with a final vocative and an initial vocative. Initial vocatives tend to be associated with longer units, whereas final vocatives are associated with shorter units'. Chadband's use of the term *my friends* is very different from such a general tendency – his *my friends* shows the tendency of initial position (25 out of the 40 collocations of his *my friends*, throughout the work), in relatively short units in his speeches. Moreover, as Biber et al. (ibid.) state, 'an initial vocative combines an attention-getting function with the function of singling out the appropriate addressee(s)': Chadband's initial *my friends* expresses his eagerness to attract his audience's attention. His non-normative and frequent use of *my friends* loses the function of *my friend* working as a mark of goodwill or kindly condescension and, to the contrary, cumulatively conveys a patronizing and didactic tone.

My friends as a term of address occurs 42 times in *Bleak House*. Mr Chadband uses it 40 times; Mrs Pardiggle, a philanthropist, uses it once in the following context:

(Mrs Pardiggle visits a very poor brickmaker's house)
'Well, *my friends*,' said Mrs. Pardiggle; but her voice had not a friendly sound, I thought; it was much too business-like and systematic. (Ch. 8)

Mrs Pardiggle's *my friends*, does not carry the literal meaning and the intrinsic role of friendship, either. Therefore, we can conclude that *my friends* is not used as a mark of goodwill or kindly condescension and co-occurs with hypocritical characters.

Besides *my friends*, Chadband also uses the following terms of address: *my young friends* to 'the sparrows in Staple Inn' (that is, the students of law: three times), *my juvenile friends* to 'the sparrows in Staple Inn' (four times), and *my young friend* to Jo (12 times). Interestingly, these terms of address occur in Mr Chadband's speech only.

My dear friend is Grandfather Smallweed's favourite term of address. This collocation is used only by him in *Bleak House*. Smallweed calls George *my dear friend* 39 times and he calls Guppy it twice. He does not apply the term of address to any other characters. It is a specialized term used for a customer by a moneylender, and does not have a friendly function in a true sense.

Jobling, Guppy's friend has an interesting speech habit:

(Jobling dines with Guppy and Young Smallweed)
'Will you take any other vegetables? Grass? Peas? Summer cabbage?'
'Thank you, Guppy,' says Mr. Jobling. *'I really don't know but* what I
will take summer cabbage.' (Ch. 20)

Asked about vegetables, he first says *I really don't know but*, but immediately after, he orders his favourite. The speech-pattern continues;
when he is asked about dessert or another drink, he repeats *I (really)
don't know but*: 'Thank you, Guppy, *I don't know but* what I will take a
marrow pudding' and 'Thank you, Guppy, *I don't know but* what I will
take another glass, for old acquaintance sake'. While dining with Guppy
and Young Smallweed, Jobling uses this fixed expression five times. It
functions as a cushion, seemingly moderating the impoliteness of a
direct order, rather than carrying the literal meaning: that he does not
know what he should order.

There is another type of collocation peculiar to characters in speech.
For example, when John Jarndyce says 'the wind's in the east' it means
that he is in a bad humour. However, even when the collocation of *wind*
and *east* is used in other people's speech, it is always associated with
Jarndyce. In like manner the collocation *move on* is always associated
with Jo.

There are other collocations peculiar to or associated with particular
characters:

Mr Snagsby: *not to put too fine a point upon it* (15 times)
Grandfather Smallweed: *brimstone chatterer* (twice), *brimstone pig* (twice),
   *brimstone idiot, brimstone scorpion, brimstone poll-parrot, brimstone beast,
   brimstone baby, brimstone black-beetle, brimstone barker, brimstone
   magpie, brimstone tricks, your brimstone grandmother* (all the collocations of *brimstone* except *brimstone tricks* are used as words of abuse to
   his wife)
Mr Guppy: *there are chords in the human mind* (7 times)
Mr Guppy: *our mutual friend Smallweed* (4 times) (Mr Guppy applies this
   collocation to Young Smallweed)
Mr Bagnet: *Discipline must be maintained* (7 times)
Boythorn: *by my soul* (4 times)

6.2 Collocational patterns peculiar to characters in their speech

Following from the discussion of the use of the same collocations by particular characters, this section deals with collocational patterns peculiar to individual characters in their speech. First I would like to consider the case of Jarndyce. He often uses unusual collocations:

(1) ' "It's nothing, my dear," he said, "it's nothing. Rick and I have only had a *friendly difference*, which we must state to you, for you are the theme. Now you are afraid of what's coming".' (Ch. 24)

(2) ' "I don't mean literally a child," pursued Mr. Jarndyce; "not a child in years. He is grown up – he is at least as old as I am – but in simplicity, and freshness, and enthusiasm, and a *fine guileless inaptitude* for all worldly affairs, he is a perfect child".' (Ch. 6)

In (1) *friendly difference* is an oxymoronic collocation in terms of the semantic feature (favourable). In like manner *fine guileless inaptitude* in (2) is also an oxymoron. That is, *fine* and *guileless* are (+ favourable) words and *inaptitude* is (– favourable) in their semantic features.

Jarndyce also combines words used in different registers and creates uncommon collocations:

(3) ' "Mr. Vholes," said my guardian, eyeing his black figure, as if he were a bird of ill omen, "has brought an *ugly report* of our most unfortunate Rick".' (Ch. 45)

(4) ' "How much of this indecision of character," Mr. Jarndyce said to me, "is chargeable on that incomprehensible *heap of uncertainty* and procrastination on which he has been thrown from his birth, I don't pretend to say; but that Chancery, among its other sins, is responsible for some of it, I can plainly see".' (Ch. 13)

Ugly is a word relating to appearance and is not appropriate as a modifier for *report*. Typically, one would rather say *bad report*. The case of *heap of uncertainty* in (4) is a bit more complex. There is a collocational clash, a mismatch produced by the incompatibility between the semantic feature (+ concrete) for *heap* and the semantic feature (+ abstract) for *uncertainty*. Besides this unusual combination of words, *heap of uncertainty* also works as a metaphorical collocation for 'legal papers relating to Jarndyce and Jarndyce case'.

The following are transferred collocations in Jarndyce's speech:

(1) ' "Ha!" he returned thoughtfully, "that is a more *alarming person* than the clerk".' (Ch. 44)

(2) ' "Thank you, my dear. Do you give me a minute's *calm attention*, without looking at Rick".' (Ch. 24)

(3) ' "And as Rick and you are *happily good* friends, I should like to know," said my guardian, "what you think, my dear".' (Ch. 45)

(4) ' "It was her act, and she kept its motives in her *inflexible heart*".' (Ch. 43)

In (3) *happily* and *good* belong to the same semantic realm though *happily* does not modify the adjective *good*, and in (4) we can say *inflexible mind* but *inflexible heart* is not normal.

The following are other unusual collocations used only by Jarndyce: *clean blacksmith, dusty death* (from *Macbeth* V.v. 22), *exposed sound, infernal country-dance, stern prediction, trusty face* and *wicked heaps*. Jarndyce's unusual speech collocations as we have so far discussed are not used by other nineteenth century novelists (*NCF*). In this sense, Jarndyce may be said to be a creative speaker.

Jarndyce is also fond of using language-play with usual collocations. The first example is a pun:

> 'Now, little woman, little woman, this will never do. *Constant dropping will wear away a stone*, and *constant coaching will wear out a Dame Durden*.' (Ch. 50)

After Esther gets up in the early morning and finishes the housework, she goes to Caddy to take care of Caddy's baby. Then, Esther comes back to Bleak House where Jarndyce lives and he advises her not to work so hard. *Constant dropping wears away stone* is a familiar proverb. By parodying this proverb with the puns *wear away* and *wear out*, Jarndyce gives advice to Esther in a joking, soft tone (rather than a serious tone). He also imitates the rhythm of nursery rhymes in the opening sentence of his advice.

Another example of Jarndyce's language play:

> 'I went to school with this fellow, Lawrence Boythorn,' said Mr Jarndyce, tapping the letter as he laid it on the table, 'more than five-and-forty years ago. He was then *the most impetuous boy* in the world, and he is now *the most impetuous man*. He was then *the loudest boy* in the world, and he is now *the loudest man*. He was then *the*

heartiest and sturdiest boy in the world, and he is now *the heartiest and sturdiest man*. He is a tremendous fellow.' (Ch. 9)

In general, whenever a character is described in terms of the past and the present, we expect a contrastive change in the character's personality. Jarndyce's use of superlative degrees for the description of Boythorn's boyhood reinforces our expectancy of a drastic change in Boythorn's adult personality. However, our expectancy is deceived by the same use of superlative adjectives for his personality. The collocation *the most impetuous boy* is quite usual but the combination of *the most impetuous* and *man* in *the most impetuous man* may be slightly uncommon. In like manner, *the loudest boy* is very common but *the loudest man* may be a little strange. The reason why Jarndyce uses the superlative degree for the description of Boythorn in this passage is revealed in Jarndyce's later locution, 'His language is as sounding as his voice. He is always in extremes; perpetually in the superlative degree' (Ch. 9). Jarndyce is imitating Boythorn's habit of using the superlative degree. Jarndyce's creative use of collocations and his sense of humour is subtle and sometimes complex – a unique characteristic of his speech.

Such characteristic collocational patterns are found not only in Jarndyce's speech but also in that of others. Boythorn does indeed love using superlative expressions and exaggerated collocations:

> most abandoned ruffian (Ch. 9), most intolerable scoundrel (Ch. 9), most consummate villain (Ch. 9), most consummate vagabond (Ch. 9), least remorse (Ch. 9), slightest doubt (Ch. 9), worst-looking dog (Ch. 9), remotest summits (Ch. 9), most astonishing bird (Ch. 9), most wonderful creature (Ch. 9), greatest satisfaction (Ch. 9), proudest fellow (Ch. 9), most solemnly conceited and consummate blockheads (Ch. 9), most imperious and presumptuous coxcomb (Ch. 9), best years (Ch. 13), most infamous coach (Ch. 18), most flagrant example (Ch. 18), most profligate coachmen (Ch. 18), the most self-satisfied, and the shallowest, and the most coxcombical and utterly brainless ass (Ch. 18), deepest sympathy (Ch. 18)

Miss Flite's characteristic speech habit is a repeated collocational pattern. This pattern is divided into three types: (1) a formal repetition in which the earlier expression is repeated, (2) a repetition of meaning, that is, variation in which an alternative referring back to the same referent is used, and (3) a syntactic repetition in which a syntactic pattern is repeated, including the same word. Examples of the first type are as follows:

(1) ' "Shall I tell you what *I think*? *I think*".' (Ch. 14)
(2) ' "O *many, many, many* years, *my dear*. But I expect a judgement. Shortly" ' (Ch. 35)
(3) ' "And Fitz-Jarndyce lays the money out for me *to great advantage*. O, I assure you *to the greatest advantage!*" ' (Ch. 14)

In the second type of repeated collocation, Miss Flite partially substitutes the earlier expression with a slightly different word or with a word-variation, referring to the same referent:

(1) ' "*Ve-ry right!*" said Miss Flite, "*ve-ry correct. Truly!*" ' (Ch. 35)
(2) ' "*So sagacious*, our young friend," said she to me, in her mysterious way. "Diminutive. But *ve-ry sagacious!*" ' (Ch. 35)
(3) ' "*My dear physician* [Woodcourt]!" cries Miss Flite. "*My meritorious, distinguished, honourable officer!*" ' (Ch. 47)

Here are some examples of the third type of repetition in Miss Flite's collocational pattern:

(1) ' "*My father expected a Judgement*," said Miss Flite. "*My brother. My sister. They all expected a Judgement. The same that I expect*".' (Ch. 35)
(2) 'What could they [the Mace and Seal of Lord Chancellor] do, did she think? I mildly asked her.
    ' "*Draw*," returned Miss Flite, "*Draw people on*, my dear. *Draw peace out of them. Sense out of them. Good looks out of them. Good qualities out of them*".' (Ch. 35)

Miss Flite's repeated collocational patterns may foreshadow her future life, locked together with the miserable lives of the rest of her family, due to her involvement in the case of Jarndyce and Jarndyce.

There are other collocational patterns peculiar to particular characters. For example, Skimpole's frequent use of disparate and unconventional collocations such as *vulgar gratitude, imperfectly pleasant, inharmonious blacksmith, touchstone of responsibility* and *refreshingly responsible*.

The Honourable Bob Stables, a 'debilitated' cousin of Sir Leicester, as illustrated by his name Stables, implying 'a building where race-horses are trained', makes strange collocations by applying horse-training terms to Lady Dedlock: 'she is the best *groomed woman* in the whole stud'. (This remark appears three times in indirect speech.)

6.3 Collocations peculiar to characters in the non-dialogues

Just as a particular collocation in the dialogues is repeatedly used by a specific character, so there are also particular collocations used to describe specific characters in the non-dialogues. Such collocations are composed of two types: (1) the same collocation is repeated in reference to a specific character, or (2) collocations of the same word are used to refer to a specific character.

Let us examine the first case, the repetition of the same collocation. These tend to be used to delineate a character's appearance, behaviour or action.

Miss Volumnia, a cousin of Sir Leicester's utters a 'little scream'. The only character who ever gives a 'little scream' in *Bleak House* is Miss Volumnia; the collocation appears nine times:

> a *little* sharp *scream* (Ch. 28), another *little scream* (Ch. 28), a third *little scream* (Ch. 28), her favourite *little scream* (Ch. 40), her inno-cent *little scream* (Ch. 50), Volumnia's *little scream* (Ch. 53), Volum-nia's pet *little scream* (Ch. 56), her *little scream* (Ch. 58), her *little* withered *scream* (Ch. 40)

All of these collocations relating to Volumnia appear in the third-person non-dialogue. The following is a list of the same collocations for other specific characters (the number in parentheses indicates how often the collocation appears):

Jarndyce: *the protecting manner* (4)
Mr Chadband: *fat smile* (4). Variations include *oily smile* and *greasily meek smile*
the elder Turveydrop: *high-shouldered bow* (4)
George: *composedly smoking* (3)
Rosa: *village beauty* (3)
two gentlemen (that is, the public chroniclers): *ravenous pens* (3)
Sir Leicester: *particularly complacent* (2)
Tulkinghorn: *his rusty legs* (2)
Mrs Snagsby: *his little woman* (8), *spectacle* (*bass*) *voice* (2)
a street in Chesney Wold: *a street of dismal grandeur* (3)

These collocations are not used for other characters in *Bleak House*. Among them *fat smile, village beauty, ravenous pens, particularly complacent, rusty legs* and *dismal grandeur* may be judged to be Dickens' creative collocations, as other writers did not use these collocations, according to the *NCF* and the *ECF*.

There is yet another type of collocation particular to specific characters: that where same-word collocations are repeatedly used. For example, the aristocratic pride of Sir Dedlock, a mighty baronet, is reinforced through a repeated use of collocations with *magnificently* (for example, *magnificently disengaged, magnificently aggrieved* and *magnificently laying*) and with *stately* (for example, *stately gloom, stately protest, stately liking* and *stately breast*).

The collocations of Mr Snagsby's *cough* are more striking:

> (adjective + *cough*): admiring *cough* / apologetic *cough* / confirmatory *cough* / deferential *cough* / explanatory *cough* / forlornest *cough* / (*cough* + *of* + noun phrase): *cough of* consideration / *cough of* deference / *cough of* dismal resignation / *cough of* general application / *cough of* great perplexity and doubt / *cough of* general preparation for business / *cough of* general propitiation / *cough of* meekness / *cough of* mildness / *cough of* mild persuasion / *cough of* modesty / *cough of* submission / *cough of* sympathy / *cough of* trouble

These unusual collocations of *cough*, used to indicate Snagsby's state of mind, are not found in any other nineteenth-century writers. Moreover, all collocations of Snagsby's *cough* appear in the third-person non-dialogue – Esther does not mention Mr Snagsby's cough at all.

The following is a list of collocations of the same words for particular characters:

George: bolt *upright* / perfectly *upright* / stiffly *upright* / a broad-chested *upright* attitude / amazingly broad and *upright* / the quaint *upright* old-fashioned figure

Skimpole: *frankest* manner / *frankest* smile / *frankest* gaiety / *frankest* and most feeling manner

Vholes: *inward* manner of speaking / *inward* speaking / *inward* and dispassionate manner / *inward* voice

Vohles: *black glove* (3 times) / dead *glove* / *black-gloved*

Vohles and his daughters: his *buttoned up* half-audible voice / *buttoned up* in body and mind / his black *buttoned-up* unwholesome finger /

Mr. Vholes rose, gloved and *buttoned up* as usual / the three raw-visaged, lank, and *buttoned-up* maidens

Tukinghorn: the old gentleman is *rusty* to look at / his *rusty* clothes / his *rusty* small-clothes / this *rusty* lawyer / his old-fashioned *rusty* black / his smile is as dull and *rusty* as his pantaloons / that *rusty* old man / that dead old man of the *rusty* garb

Hortense: with many angry and *tight* nods of her head / with more *tight* and angry nods / her *tight* face / looking on with her lips very *tightly* set / with her lips *tightly* shut

Lady Dedlock: *languid* effort / *languid* resignation / *languid* unconcern

Richard: *light-hearted* boy / *light-hearted* manner (twice) / *light-hearted* conviction

The elder Turveydrop: *false* complexion / *false* teeth / *false* whiskers

Charley: a *womanly sort* of apron / a *womanly sort* of bonnet / a *womanly sort* of manner

Bucket: admonitory *finger* / well-remembered *finger*

Mrs Snagsby: another *tight* smile, and another *tight* shake of her head / a shake of the head from Mrs. Snagsby – very long and very *tight* / *tightly* shakes her head and *tightly* smiles

Fashionable people: *brilliant and distinguished* circle (8 times), *brilliant and distinguished* feat (twice), *brilliant and distinguished* meteors

6.4 Collocational patterns peculiar to specific characters in the non-dialogues

Next let us look into collocational patterns peculiar to specific characters in the non-dialogues. Lady Dedlock's characteristic collocational pattern involves oxymoronic collocations:

> My Lady Dedlock, having conquered her world, fell, not into the melting, but rather into the freezing mood. An *exhausted composure*, a *worn-out placidity*, an *equanimity of fatigue* not to be ruffled by interest or satisfaction, are the trophies of her victory. (Ch. 2)

The collocation *exhausted composure* is an incongruous combination, in terms of semantic feature (+ favourable). Similarly, *worn-out placidity* and *equanimity of fatigue* are also contradictory collocations. Such incompatible collocations used for Lady Dedlock are also found in other chapters:

(1) 'Mr. Tulkinghorn does so with deference, and holds it open while she passes out. She [Lady Dedlock] passes close to him, with her usual fatigued manner and *insolent grace*.' (Ch. 12)

(2) 'Lady Dedlock is always the same *exhausted deity,* surrounded by worshippers, and terribly liable to be bored to death, even while presiding at her own shrine.' (Ch. 12)

All these oxymoronic collocations except *equanimity of fatigue* take the semantic order of (– favourable) and (+ favourable). Similar examples are: *haughty self-restraint* (Ch. 36) and *enforced composure* (Ch. 36). It is interesting to note that in *Dombey and Son* (1846–48) Dickens uses *enforced composure* for Edith Dombey, characterized by 'the proud beauty of the daughter with her graceful figure and erect deportment' (Ch. 45). None of these oxymoronic collocations are used by other nineteenth-century fiction writers (*NCF*).

In contrast to the semantic order of (– favourable) and (+ favourable) of the oxymoronic collocations used for Lady Dedlock, the oxymoronic collocations applied to Jarndyce have the semantic order of (+ favourable) and (– favourable):

> 'Oh, dear me, what's this, what's this!' he [Jarndyce] said, rubbing his head and walking about with his *good-humoured vexation.* (Ch. 6)

Jarndyce's *good-humoured vexation* implies that his vexation does not make other people uncomfortable. However, if we replace this oxymoronic collocation, *good-humoured vexation* having the semantic order of (+ favourable) and (– favourable) with *vexing good-humour* or *vexed good-humour,* having the opposite semantic order, the changed collocation would also have a different or opposite meaning or connotation. *Good-humoured vexation* describes Jarndyce's vexation, but the modifier *good-humoured* not only tones down the impression of his vexation, but also adds a favourable or positive aspect to his character. Such an oxymoronic collocation having the semantic order of (+ favourable) and (– favourable) reveals Esther's delicate but favourable attitude towards Jarndyce. Esther uses other, similar oxymoronic collocations, with the same semantic order, for Jarndyce elsewhere:

(1) 'He [Jarndyce] had taken two or three undecided turns up and down while uttering these broken sentences, retaining the poker in one hand and rubbing his hair with the other, with a *good-natured vexation,* at once so whimsical and so lovable, that I am sure we were more delighted with him than we could possibly have expressed in any words.' (Ch. 6)

(2) 'My guardian [Jarndyce] . . . looked at him with a whimsical mixture of *amusement and indignation* in his face.' (Ch. 31)

(3) ' "Yes, Esther" said he [Jarndyce] with a *gentle seriousness*, "it is to be forgotten now, to be forgotten for a while. You are only to remember now, that nothing can change me as you know me. Can you feel quite assured of that, my dear?" ' (Ch. 44)

Next, we will turn to the case of Boythorn's collocational patterns. When Esther describes Boythorn, she uses adjectival superlatives:

> To hear him [Boythorn] say all this with unimaginable energy, one might have thought him the *angriest of mankind*. To see him, at the very same time, looking at the bird now perched upon his thumb, and softly smoothing its feathers with his forefinger, one might have thought him the *gentlest*. (Ch. 9)

Esther imitates the habitual collocational pattern (use of superlatives) of Boythorn's speech (cf. p. 177), as noted above.

7
Comparative Study of the Mind-Styles of First-Person Narrators in Terms of Collocations

Section 5.3 focused on the mind-styles of Esther, the first-person narrator and the third-person narrator in *Bleak House* from the viewpoint of collocations. In order to make the collocational characteristics of Esther's narration clearer, this chapter presents a comparative study of collocations used by Dickens' other first-person narrators: David in *David Copperfield* and Pip in *Great Expectations*.

As shown in the discussion of the discourse structure of *Bleak House* (Section 5.3.1), a novel has a narrator who is differentiated from the author. It follows that there are different narrators in different novels written by the same author, and this is particularly significant in those novels told by first-person narrators. Therefore, we can say that Esther, David and Pip, the three prominent first-person narrators in Dickens, have different mind-styles, that is, 'any distinctive linguistic presentation of an individual mental self' (Fowler 1977: 103).

Before examining some collocational examples from the three narrators, it may be useful to note the text size and word frequencies of each work. Table 7.1 indicates the text size and word frequencies of Esther's narrative in *Bleak House*, *David Copperfield* and *Great Expectations*:

It is interesting to note that, regarding the ratio of word tokens between non-dialogue and dialogue, the ratio of word-tokens in non-dialogue is lowest in Esther's narrative and highest in Pip's. In other words, Esther tends to make other people speak more, while Pip prefers speaking on his own. Table 7.2 provides a list of the word totals and ratios of different words in the dialogues and non-dialogues of the three narrators.

What is interesting in Table 7.2 is that in each text the ratio of different words per 10,000 is higher in the dialogues than in the non-dialogues. The ratio of different words per 10,000 words is highest in

Table 7.1:   The text size and word frequencies of Esther's narrative in *Bleak House*, *David Copperfield* and *Great Expectations*

Texts / Word	Esther's narrative*	David Copperfield	Great Expectations
Total number of word tokens of each text	192,476	358,272	186,649
Word tokens of non-dialogue	115,205	238,761	131,337
Word tokens of dialogue	77,271	119,511	55,312
Ratio between non-dialogue and dialogue	1.5 : 1	2.0 : 1	2.4 : 1

Note: * Esther's narrative does not imply the full text of *Bleak House*.

Table 7.2:   Word-totals and ratios of different words in Esther's narrative in *Bleak House*, *David Copperfield* and *Great Expectations*

Text / Word	Esther's narrative	David Copperfield	Great Expectations
Different words in dialogue	6,543	8,460	5,321
Different words per 10,000 in dialogue	847	708	962
Different words in non-dialogue	8,183	12,894	10,023
Different words per 10,000 in non-dialogue	710	540	763

Great Expectations' non-dialogue and dialogue. In general, the longer the text encountered, the lower the ratio of different words found. However, it is important to note that the 'different words' total in the non-dialogue of *Great Expectations* is more than that of Esther (although the word tokens in the non-dialogue of *Great Expectations* are greater than those of Esther). Similiarly, *David Copperfield* shows the lowest ratio of different words (per 10,000) in both its non-dialogue and dialogue. Therefore, David's phraseology may be more dependent upon repetition than that of Esther and Pip. Bearing these results in mind, we will discuss the collocations of the three different first-person narrators.

7.1 Collocations of *little, own* and *poor*

Monod (1968: 335) discusses language and style in *David Copperfield*, as follows:

> Dickens' use of language in *Copperfield* is characterized above all by the frequent recurrence of a number of words each of which corresponds to some aspect of his personality. In the first place, there are three adjectives whose significant repetition emphasizes the author's sentimentality: 'little', 'own', and 'old'.

He points out not only the high frequency of *little, own* and *old* but also of *poor* and *miserable*; the intensifiers *quite, great, indeed*; the phrase *a good deal* or *a great deal*; and the adverbs *ever* or *never*. This comment on language and style in *David Copperfield* is interesting, but we should deal with it carefully. For one thing Monod does not seem to distinguish between David as a narrator, David as a character and Dickens as author. Moreover, Monod does not differentiate between dialogue and non-dialogue when he discusses David's personality through his use of language. Neither are *little, own* and *old* in *David Copperfield* salient statistically when compared with Dickens' other works. Table 7.3 indicates the frequencies of *little, own, old* and *poor* in the three different texts.

Little and *poor* show the highest frequency (in words per 10,000) in *Bleak House*; the frequency of *own* per 10,000 words in *David Copperfield* is very close to that of *Great Expectations*. From this statistical breakdown, *David Copperfield* does not demonstrate an outstanding frequency of *little, own, old* and *poor*. More striking are the higher frequency of *little*

Table 7.3: The word-tokens of *little, own, old* and *poor* and ratios per 10,000 words

	David Copperfield (358,244 words)		Esther's narrative (192,476 words)		Great Expectations (186,628 words)	
	Word tokens	Per 10,000 words	Word tokens	Per 10,000 words	Word tokens	Per 10,000 words
little	1,092	30.5	732	38.0	371	19.9
own	401	11.2	161	8.4	191	10.2
old	637	17.6	332	17.2	312	16.7
poor	188	5.2	173	9.0	77	4.1

Table 7.4: The frequencies of *little*, *own* and *poor* in the non-dialogues and dialogues of the three texts

	David Copperfield		Esther's narrative*		Great Expectations	
	Non-dialogue	Dialogue	Non-dialogue	Dialogue	Non-dialogue	Dialogue
little	817 (75%)	275 (25%)	483 (66%)	249 (34%)	264 (71%)	107 (29%)
		1,092		732		371
own	260 (65%)	141 (35%)	96 (60%)	65 (40%)	116 (61%)	75 (39%)
		401		161		191
poor	75 (40%)	113 (60%)	91 (53%)	82 (47%)	27 (35%)	50 (65%)
		188		173		77

Note: * *Little* occurs 1152 times in *Bleak House* (420 times in the third-person narrative); *own* occurs 313 times in *Bleak House* (152 times in the third-person narrative); *poor* occurs 230 times in *Bleak House* (57 times in the third-person narrative).

and *poor* in *Bleak House* and the lower frequency of *little* and *poor* in *Great Expectations*. This section, therefore, will examine, among those words and phrases that Monod (1968: 337) characterizes as 'sentimental vocabulary', the collocations of *little*, *own* and *poor*.

Table 7.4 shows the frequencies of *little*, *own* and *poor* in the non-dialogues and the dialogues of the three texts.

Little occurs more often in the non-dialogues than in the dialogues of all three texts; the difference between its occurrence in non-dialogue and dialogue is greatest in *David Copperfield*. *Own* also occurs more often in the non-dialogues than the dialogues of the three texts; but there is hardly any difference in frequency ratios between them. Regarding the occurrence of *poor*, there are some textual differences. *Poor* appears more frequently in Esther's non-dialogue than in her dialogue, whereas the word occurs more frequently in the dialogues of the two other texts. It is noticeable that *poor* occurs less often in the non-dialogue of *Great Expectations*.

Table 7.5 gives the frequencies of *little*, *own* and *poor*, and the ratios of them per 10,000 words in the non-dialogues.

Little occurs 817 times (34.2 words per 10,000 words) in David's non-dialogue; in Pip's non-dialogue it occurs 264 times (20.1 words per 10,000 words); and in Esther's non-dialogue it occurs 483 times (41.9 words per 10,000 words). In terms of use per 10,000 words however, the

Table 7.5:   Frequency ratios of *little, own* and *poor*, per 10,000 words, in the three non-dialogues

	David's non-dialogue (238,913 words)		Esther's non-dialogue (115,205 words)		Pip's non-dialogue (131,337 words)	
	Word tokens	Per 10,000 words	Word tokens	Per 10,000 words	Word tokens	Per 10,000 words
little	817	34.2	483	41.9	264	20.1
own	260	10.9	96	8.3	116	8.8
poor	75	3.1	91	7.9	27	2.1

most frequent user of *little* is Esther. She uses *little* twice as many times as Pip. Esther also uses *poor* more often than the other narrators. David uses *own* slightly more often in his non-dialogue than the other narrators.

As we have seen so far, there are some differences in the usage of *little, own* and *poor* among the texts of the three different first-person narrators. However, more important and distinctive characteristics are revealed in collocations using these three words. The following are the lists of the top ten collocations of *little*.

David (817): little Em'ly (64: 7.8%), my little (25: 3.1%), very little (22: 2.7%), little room (18: 2.2%), little creature (15: 1.8%), pretty little (11: 1.3%), little Dora (10: 1.2%), little window (10: 1.2%), little way (9: 1.1%), little woman (8: 1.0%)

Pip (264): my little (12: 5%), very little (10: 4%), little while (10: 4%), little room (6: 2%), little garden (4: 2%), little girl (4: 2%), little Jane (4: 2%), little more (4: 2%), little girls (3: 1%), little window (3: 1%)

Esther (483): very little (17: 4%), little girl (12: 2%), my little (19: 4%), poor little (12: 2%), little old (11: 2%), little child (9: 2%), little creature (9: 2%), little lady (9: 2%), little more (8: 2%), little woman (8: 2%)

The distinctive characteristic in David's collocations of *little* is a collocation with *Em'ly*, that is, *little Em'ly*. The percentage of *little Em'ly*, if including *little Emily* (6 times), amounts to 8.7 per cent. It is important to note that in Chapter 30 (following the chapter in which Steerforth's secret love affair with Emily was implied), there is a co-existence of *little Em'ly* (the last example in the work) and *little Emily* (the first use in the work). In

Chapters 30 and 31, where David visits Peggotty to inquire after her husband, *little Emily* is used six times, but the collocation *little Em'ly* or *little Emily* does not appear again after Chapter 31. This collocational shift reveals David's subtle but significant change of mind toward Emily.

Approximately half the examples of David's *my little* (25 times) collocate with Dora (11 times) such as *my little Dora* and *my little wife*. On the other hand, *my little* (the top collocation of *little* in Pip) does not collocate with a person, but rather with concrete objects, such as *portmanteau* (5 times), *room* (3 times), *bedroom* (twice) and *window* (twice). Pip's tendency to collocate *little* with objects is also evidenced by the fact that seven types of collocations among the top ten collocations of *little* in his narrative do not modify human beings.

Esther's *little* shows different collocational patterns from those of Pip and David. Esther's *my little* is used for Charley (10 collocations out of the 19 examples), as in *my little maid* and *my little Charley*. For Esther, *little* tends to collocate with human beings. In Esther's non-dialogue, *poor little* and *little old* all modify people, such as *Charley* and *old woman*, and the top ten collocations of *little* (excepting *little more*) collocate with human beings.

Therefore, regarding the collocations of *little* among the three different narrators we can conclude, first, that Pip's *little* tends not to collocate with human beings and that *my little* exclusively modifies his belongings. Second, David's *little* overwhelmingly collocates with *Emily* and is used for a few specific people. Third, Esther's *little* tends to collocate dominantly with people, but does not modify one specific person.

Next we will turn to collocations of *poor*. The frequency of *poor* is lower than that of *little* in each narrator's non-dialogue, with the highest ratio per 10,000 words in Esther's non-dialogue. The following are the most frequent collocations of *poor* in the three different narrator's non-dialogues.

David (75): my poor (dear) mother (17: 23%), poor fellow (6: 8%), poor Traddle (5: 7%), poor Mr. Micawber (4: 5%), poor (harmless) Mr. Dick (2: 3%), poor little Dora (2: 3%), poor (old) women (2: 3%)

Pip (27): poor fellow (4: 15%), poor Biddy (2: 7%), poor (dear) Joe (2: 7%)

Esther (91): poor girl (11: 12%), poor child (5: 5%), poor Caddy (4: 4%), poor Mr. Jellyby (4: 4%), poor Richard (4: 4%), poor little Miss Flite (3: 3%), poor baby (3: 3%)

The attributive use of *poor* in collocations (for example, *poor Richard*) is overwhelmingly dominant while its descriptive use (for example, *Richard is poor*) is much less common: in David's non-dialogue, 53 of 58 examples are attributive, in Pip's non-dialogue 26 of 27 examples are attributive, and in Esther's non-dialogue 88 of 91 examples are attributive. This tendency of the attributive usage of *poor* is also true of the third-person non-dialogue in *Bleak House*: among the 17 examples of *poor*, 16 are attributive and one is descriptive. In its attributive use, *poor* almost always carries an emotional meaning, expressive of the narrator's sympathy.

David applies approximately 25% of the collocations of *poor* to his mother as *my poor mother*. He uses the emotive attributive for three other characters: *poor Traddle* (4 times), *poor Mr. Dick* (3 times) and *poor little Dora* (twice). Pip uses the emotive *poor* infrequently for specific people, twice for Biddy and twice for Joe. Esther's use of *poor* (applied to people) has a wider range than David or Pip. She feels sympathy for more people: girl, child, baby, man, Caddy (Miss Jellyby), Mr Jellyby, Richard, Miss Flite, Charley, Esther's godmother and Jo.

Lastly we will focus on the collocations of *own*. The word *own* is slightly more frequent in David than the two other narrators. The following are the top ten collocations of *own*:

David (260): my own (117), her own (64), his own (56), own (noble) heart (8), their own (8), own room (7), own mind (7), own hands (6), own (little tormenting) way (6), own old (5), own (old/bright, rosy) little (5)

Pip (116): my own (56), his own (28), her own (14), own (old/little) room (9), own mind (7), their own (8), our own (5), like (our/his/my) own (5), own eyes (3), own (old) little (3), own marsh (3)

Esther (96): my own (37), her own (22), his own (21), own room (11), their own (6), own heart (4), our own (4), own mind (3), own (old) face (2), own eyes (2), own (happy) thoughts (2)

There are no remarkable differences between the top ten collocations of *own* found among the three texts, in contradistinction to what was observed with collocations of *little* and *poor*. If forced to point out characteristics of collocations of *own*, we may say that *my own* is the highest-frequency collocation among the three texts and *own room* is a usual collocation among them. With respect to *my own*, the collocation amounts to 48 per cent of all the examples of *own* in David's narrative, 45 per cent in Pip's, and Esther's *my own* shows the lowest ratio (39 per cent) among the three texts. Quirk et al. (1985: 362) discuss the function of *own* as follows:

> The possessive cannot be accompanied by any modifiers or determiners, except for the 'emphatic determinative *own*'. Just as the emphatic reflective pronoun intensifies the meaning of a personal pronoun, so *own* intensifies the meaning of a possessive pronoun. For example, *my own* carries the force of 'mine and nobody else's' in: This book doesn't belong to the library – it's *my own copy*.

This intensifying function of *own* implies a narrator's subjective or emotional viewpoint, especially in the collocation of *my own*. The following are the collocates of *my own* used by the three narrators:

David: my own (117)
heart (7: 6%), room (6: 5%), mind (5: 4%), breast (4: 3%), age (3: 3%), old (3: 3%, my own old plate / my own old mug / my own old little knife), part (3: 3%), thoughts (3: 3%), bed (2: 2%), bread (2: 2%), breakfast (2: 2%), little (2: 2%, my own little cabin / my own old little knife)

Pip: my own (56)
little (3: 5%, my own (old) little room / my own little stool), age (2: 4%), eyes (2: 4%), mind (2: 4%), part (2: 4%), room (2: 4%), story (2: 4%)

Esther: my own (37)
room (9: 24%), heart (3: 8%), eyes (2: 5%), mind (2: 5%), mother (2: 5%), name (2: 5%)

In Esther, *my own* shows a high frequency of collocation with *room*. David's *my own* tends relatively often to collocate with *heart* and *room*. In Pip there are no distinctively frequent collocations of *my own*, but the collocation *my own* co-occurs with words having a negative meaning such as *my own ingratitude*, *my own fault*, *my own mistakes*, *my own ungracious breast* and *my own worthless conduct*. In the dialogue of *David Copperfield*, *my own* is used as a term of endearment between David and Dora 11 times (out of 44 examples); in *Great Expectations* there are no examples of this term of endearment; and in Esther's narrative the term of endearment *my own* is used three times.

7.2 Collocations of *my*

Table 7.6 indicates the frequencies of *my mind*, *my heart* and *my thoughts*. As Table 7.6 shows, there seem to be hardly any differences among the three texts in the ratio of each collocation per 10,000 words. However, concerning the ratios of these collocations functioning as the subject of the clause, Pip's non-dialogue is notable. This type of syntactic construction seems to reveal Pip's particular mind-style. The following is an example of *my mind* used as the subject in Pip's non-dialogue:

> *My mind* grew very uneasy on the subject of the pale young gentleman. (Ch. 12)

This may be called metonymy or synecdoche. Although *my mind* occupies the position of subject in the above passage, *I* may be used instead of *my mind*:

> *I* grew very uneasy on the subject of the pale young gentleman.

The cognitive meaning of the rewritten sentence is the same as that of the original. The difference between the original and the alternative is that *I* is considered as the superordinate of *my mind*, that is, a name for a more general class at a semantic level. The use of *my mind* as

Table 7.6: The frequencies of *my mind*, *my heart* and *my thoughts* in the three narratives

	David's non-dialogue (238,913 words)		Esther's non-dialogue (115,205 words)		Pip's non-dialogue (131,337 words)	
	Tokens	As subject	Tokens	As subject	Tokens	As subject
my mind	102 (4.3 words)	11 (11%)	35 (3.0 words)	3 (9%)	45 (3.4 words)	14 (31%)
my heart	64 (2.7 words)	10 (16%)	31 (2.7 words)	5 (16%)	29 (2.2 words)	6 (21%)
my thoughts	24 (1.0 word)	3 (13%)	9 (0.8 word)	2 (22%)	17 (1.3 words)	7 (41%)

Note: The parenthesis under 'tokens' indicates the ratio of each collocation per 10,000 words in each text. The parenthesis in the item 'as subject' shows the ratio of each collocation functioning as the subject of the clause in each text.

the hyponym of *I* may invite more careful attention to Pip's state of feeling than the case of *I*. Furthermore, the narrator's use of *my mind* seems to relieve Pip (the character) of much of the blame for his feeling toward the young gentleman. Some other examples are given below:

(1) '*my mind* was much troubled by these two circumstances taken together . . .' (Ch. 40)
(2) 'but *my mind* did not accuse him of having put it to its latest use.' (Ch. 16)
(3) '*My mind*, with inconceivable rapidity, followed out all the consequences of such a death.' (Ch. 53)
(4) 'Firstly, *my mind* was too preoccupied to be able to take in the subject clearly.' (Ch. 55)

Several similar examples modified by an adjective:

(5) '*My rapid mind* pursued him to the town, made a picture of the street with him in it, and contrasted its lights and life with the lonely marsh and the white vapour creeping over it, into which I should have dissolved.' (Ch. 53)
(6) 'and yet *my young mind* was in that disturbed and unthankful state, that I thought long after I laid me down, how common Estella would consider Joe, a mere blacksmith.' (Ch. 9)

In collocations such as (5) and (6) we cannot say that the original meaning is the same as that of the rewritten sentence with the replacement of *my rapid mind* or *my young mind* by *I*. These collocations of *my mind*, occupying the position of subject, are used for the description of Pip's state of mind as relating to dejectedness, fearfulness or irresoluteness.

Other collocations of *my* – *my heart, my conscience* and *my inner self* – as subject are also used.

(7) '*My heart* was deeply and most deservedly humbled as I mused over the fire for an hour or more.' (Ch. 52)
(8) 'that *my heart* should never be sickened with the hopeless task of attempting to establish one.' (Ch. 34)
(9) '*My conscience* was not by any means comfortable about Biddy.' (Ch. 34)
(10) '*my inner self* was not so easily composed.' (Ch. 6)

Here, it would be possible to use the first person *I* instead of *my heart*, *my conscience* and *my inner self*, and there would be no difference in cognitive meaning between the original sentences and the alternatives. However, their communicative value may be somewhat different in terms of 'thematic meaning', defined by Leech (1981: 19) as 'what is communicated by the way in which a speaker or writer organizes the message, in terms of ordering, focus, and emphasis'. In other words, *my heart* or *my conscience* or *my inner self* focuses our attention on a character who is fully aware of his own emotional responsiveness.

Also interesting are those cases where the use of *my mind* reveals a psychological distance between *my mind* and *I*. Here are some striking examples:

(11) 'While *my mind* was thus engaged, I thought of the beautiful young Estella, proud and refined . . .' (Ch. 32)

(12) 'nor did I vex *my mind* with them, for it was wholly set on Provis's safety.' (Ch. 54)

In (11) Pip's *mind* is occupied with thoughts of prison, crime, his childhood, his fortune and his advancement, but at the same time, he thinks of beautiful young Estella. To put it another way, *my mind* – 'the cognitive or intellectual powers, as distinguished from the will and emotions' (*OED*) – is contrasted with *I*, which represents the centre of crude emotions. A psychological distance which suggests that the narrator tries objectively to analyse the character Pip's inner experience is realized.

Similarly, (12) betrays the narrator's objective attitude toward the character's state of mind. Now, let us compare an alternative, which may be considered to be more normative on the level of cognitive meaning:

I was not vexed with them

As compared with the rewritten sentence, *my mind* in the original (which is separated from *I*), syntactically plays the role of *patient* (Fowler 1977: 15–16) or of *the affected participant* (Halliday 1970: 158). Such a syntactic structure, with which the narrator describes Pip's mentality, gives us the impression that there is a narrator who takes an objective view of *my mind* which is different from *I*. A few passages in which there is a coexistence of *I* and *my mind* are given below:

(13) 'In saying this, I relieved *my mind* of what had always been there, more or less, though no doubt most since yesterday.' (Ch. 30)

(14) 'for I was determined, and *my mind* firm made up.' (Ch. 39)
(15) 'I saw in everything the construction that *my mind* had come to, repeated and thrown back to me.' (Ch. 38)
(16) 'And now, because *my mind* was not confused enough before, I complicated its confusion fifty thousand-fold . . .' (Ch. 17)

A few examples of this coexistence of *I* and *my mind* or *my heart*, functioning as metonymy or synecdoche (that is, as the replacement of *I* or *me* in the same sentence), are also found in Esther's and David's non-dialogue:

(17) '*my mind* misgave *me* that he had found out about my darling Dora.' (DC 38)
(18) '*I* was greatly elated by these orders; but *my heart* smote *me* for my selfishness . . .' (DC 15)
(19) '*I* find *my mind* confused by the idea that they are singing . . .' (BH 5)
(20) 'But *my mind* dwelt so much upon the uncongenial scene in which *I* had left her . . .' (BH 51)

However, this type of collocation occurs much more frequently in Pip's non-dialogue than in either those of David or Esther, and reveals the narrator Pip's mind-style, the language of introspection or self-examination that the narrator uses to describe the character Pip's mind in the past.

7.3 Some different collocational types

As discussed in Section 5.3.5, there is a distinctive difference in the collocational pattern 'adjective + proper name', with or without the definite article *the*, between the different narratives of *Bleak House*. The collocational pattern 'the + adjective + proper name', such as *the eloquent Chadband*, is used in the third-person non-dialogue, but is not found in Esther's non-dialogue, while the collocational pattern 'adjective + proper name' (for example, *poor Caddy*) is used in Esther's non-dialogue, but not found in the third-person narrative. This difference of collocational pattern between the two different narrators is closely connected by a degree of formality in style as well as to the narrators' mind styles.

As far as Esther's non-dialogue is concerned, the collocational pattern 'adjective + proper name', without the definite article, shows that Esther's style is less formal, that is, more conversational. The nonrestrictive premodifiers such as *poor* and *dear* used for this collocational pattern reveal the narrator's sympathy or emotion, rather than any characteristics of the person under discussion. In other words, the meaning of *poor Caddy* is not 'Caddy is poor' but 'Esther feels pity for Caddy'. The reason why Esther does not use 'the + adjective + proper name' such as *the eloquent Chadband* in her narrative may be because she refrains from expressing her direct opinions or judgements concerning the people she meets. This difference in the collocational pattern 'adjective + proper name', with or without the definite article, is clearly evidenced in *Bleak House*. On the other hand, *Great Expectations* and *David Copperfield* are more delicate and complex in the difference of usage between '*the* + adjective + proper name' and 'adjective + proper name'; nevertheless, a consistent rhetorical choice between them is found in both Pip's and David's narratives.

When criticizing Pumblechook, Pip uses the collocational pattern 'the + adjective + proper name': *the servile Pumblechook* (twice), *the abject Pumblechook* and *the worldly-minded Pumblechook*. The more emotive demonstrative, *that*, 'implying censure, dislike, or scorn' (*OED*), is also used for Pumblechook: *that bullying old Pumblechook* and *that swindling Pumblechook*. This type of collocational pattern, with the definite article, is used for people about whom Pip has an unfavourable impression: *the invisible Barley*, *this blundering Drummle*, *the presiding Finch*, *the honourable Finch's* and *the terrible Provis*. On the other hand, Pip uses the collocational pattern 'adjective + proper name', without the definite article, for people he likes: *poor Joe*, *dear old Joe*, *dear good Joe*, *dear good faithful tender Joe*, *poor dear Joe*, *poor Biddy* and *pretty Clara*.

There are only three examples of the collocational pattern 'the + adjective + proper name' used for people towards whom Pip normally feels friendly: *the unconscious Joe*, *the wretched Joe* and *the unfortunate Wopsle*. In the contexts of these collocations Pip feels an unusual psychological distance from the other characters. For example, the collocation *the unconscious Joe* is used where Pip is forced to steal bread for Magwitch without being observed by his sister and Joe, but where Joe's good-natured companionship with Pip presents an obstacle:

> The effort of resolution necessary to the achievement of this purpose, I found to be quite awful. It was as if I had to make up my mind to leap from the top of a high house, or plunge into a great depth of water. And it was made the more difficult by *the unconscious Joe*. (Ch. 2)

In the case of *the wretched Joe*, Joe (normally a mild, good-natured, easy-going, sweet-tempered and dear fellow) cannot help beating Old Orlick soundly for Orlick's insult to Joe's wife. Pip senses a distance towards Joe, who is unlike his usual self. In the context in which Pip uses *the unfortunate Wopsle*, the narrator begins to have doubts concerning Wopsle's personality, as a strange gentleman raises several questions about the reliability of the newspaper Wopsle reads aloud:

> We were all deeply persuaded that *the unfortunate Wopsle* had gone too far, and had better stop in his reckless career while there was yet time. (Ch. 18)

However, it should be noted that the choice of the collocational pattern 'the + adjective + proper name' or 'adjective + proper name' may partly depend upon a syntactic structure and the type of adjective: we could not say *wretched Joe* without *the* instead of *the wretched Joe* or *the dear Joe* with *the* instead of *dear Joe*.

Regarding Pip's keen censure of Pumblechook, there is the collocational pattern 'noun phrase + proper name'. A typical example is *that abject hypocrite, Pumblechook*. This can be called 'apposition' and its effect is intensive. This collocational type, as recognized in *that abject hypocrite, Pumblechook* is accompanied by *that*. It is important to note that the use of the words *abject* and *hypocrite* is made by the adult narrator Pip, but does not represent the viewpoint of Pip as a child. The following are some similar examples: *that ass, Pumblechook, that fearful impostor, Pumblechook, that basest of swindlers, Pumblechook, the brazen impostor Pumblechook*.

In David's non-dialogue, there is also an obvious difference between 'the + adjective + proper name' and 'adjective + proper name'. David does not use the collocational pattern 'the + adjective + proper name' for Dora at all: he refers to her as *little Dora* (2), *dear tender little Dora* and *poor little Dora*. The possessive pronoun *my* functioning as an emotive intensifier is very often added: *my pretty Dora's, my pretty little Dora's, my little Dora* (2), *my dear Dora* (2), *my pretty Dora* (2), *my broken-hearted little Dora, my Dora* (2), *my darling Dora, my dear affectionate little Dora* and *my pretty, little, startled Dora*. In contrast, there is only one example of the collocational pattern 'adjective + proper name' for Agnes (*dear Agnes*). David does not add the possessive pronoun *my* to the name *Agnes* in his non-dialogue, though he frequently uses it in his dialogue. For example:

'*My dear Agnes*,' I began, 'if you mean Steerforth . . .'
'I do, Trotwood,' she returned.
'Then, Agnes, you wrong him very much. He my bad Agnes, or any one's! He, anything but a guide, a support, and a friend to me! *My dear Agnes!*' (Ch. 25)

The absence of an affectionate or emotional adjective such as *dear* for the name *Agnes* in David's non-dialogue reveals David's controlled expression of affection for Agnes, his second wife, in contrast to his emotional expression of love for Dora, his first wife. There are other examples of '(my) adjective + proper name' applied to people about whom David has a favourable impression: *pretty little Em'ly, little Em'ly* (64), *little Emily* (6), *little Emma, poor Mrs. Micawber, happy Miss Mills, poor harmless Mr. Dick, poor little Mowcher, dear old Peggotty, poor Peggotty, poor Traddles* (4), *my own peculiar Peggotty* and *my dear old Peggotty's.*

David uses the collocational pattern 'the + adjective + proper name' for people he doesn't like or of whom he has a low opinion: *the watchful Miss Murdstone, the otherwise immovable Miss Murdstone, the implacable Jorkins, the restraining demon Jorkins, the adamantine Jorkins, the respectable Littimer* (2), *the staid Littimer, the absent Littimer, the stricken Pidger* and *the dreaded Tungay*. The demonstrative (particularly *this* and *that*), implying censure, dislike or scorn is used instead of *the*: *this unfortunate Mrs. Gummidge, that grumbling Mrs. Gummidge, that miserable Mrs. Gummidge, this terrible Jorkins*, and *this destestable Rufus*. The adjective *worshipful* in *the worshipful Mr. Creakle*, the headmaster of Salem House where David is treated badly, is tinged with irony. Interestingly, David does not use this collocational pattern for people such as Murdstone and Heep, whom he despises utterly.

There are several examples of 'the + adjective + proper name' used for people towards whom David feels a psychological distance in some contexts, although he normally holds a more agreeable impression of them:

the good angel Spenlow [Dora's father], *the mild Mr. Chillip, the wretched Emily, the immovable Mr. Micawber, the wary Mowcher, the amazed Peggotty, the blushing and laughing Sophy, that sagacious Miss Mills*

8
New Compound Words as Collocations in *Bleak House*

Strictly speaking, compound words might not be a collocational matter. However, as shown in Section 4.3.3, more than 25 per cent (469 examples) of the 1779 lexical terms recorded as first-citations from Dickens in the *OED2* are compound words. This indicates Dickens' predilection for new combinations of two or more words and enables us to regard compound words newly created in *Bleak House* as a characteristic of his language use, or as one of Dickens' creative collocational types.

In this section, hyphenation will be used as the criterion for compound words, as it represents a clear objective indicator. However, the notation of hyphenation is often different among the various versions of *Bleak House*. Given this, we will follow the notation of *The Oxford Illustrated Dickens*.

In *Bleak House* there are more than 2000 compound words, of which 25 examples are recorded as first-citations in the *OED2*, while 27 examples are earlier than first-citations treated in the *OED2*. Moreover, 149 examples are not found in the *OED2* or in any other fiction in the eighteenth and nineteenth centuries (*ECF* and *NCF*). Table 8.1 gives the total number and the breakdown of Dickens' new compound words in *Bleak House*.

There are 201 compound words which can be considered to be used for the first time in *Bleak House*, and 75 per cent of them are not compiled in the *OED2*.

Table 8.2 gives the breakdown of parts of speech of new compound words in *Bleak House*.

There are four different parts of speech in these compound words, but in fact compound nouns and compound adjectives are dominant. Compound noun types are shown in Table 8.3.

Table 8.1:   Classification of Dickens' new compound words in *Bleak House*

Classification	Number of compound words
First-citations in the *OED*	25 (12.4%)
Earlier examples than the *OED*	27 (13.4%)
Dickens only	149 (74.1%)
Total (compound word)	201 (100.0%)

Table 8.2:   Classification of parts of speech of new compound words in *Bleak House*

Part of speech	Number of lexemes
Compound noun	124 (61.7%)
Compound adjective	72 (35.8%)
Compound verb	1 (0.5%)
Compound adverb	4 (2.0%)
Total	201 (100.0%)

As Table 8.3 shows, the type 'noun + noun' is dominant, and describes 70.4 per cent of the compound nouns. In the type of 'noun + noun', a hyphen may not always be necessary. The extracts below could be written without hyphens and the meaning would remain unchanged.

(1) 'The rain is ever falling, drip, drip, drip, by day and night, upon the broad flagged *terrace-pavement*, The Ghost's Walk.' (Ch. 7)
(2) 'It appeared to us that some of them must pass their whole lives in dealing out *subscription-cards* to the whole Post-office Directory – shilling cards, half-crown cards, half-sovereign cards, penny cards.' (Ch. 8)
(3) 'In the sequel, half-a-dozen are caught up in a cloud of *pipe-smoke* that pervades the parlour of the Sol's Arms.' (Ch. 9)
(4) 'He writes me that you and the ladies have promised him a short visit at his *bachelor-house* in Lincolnshire.' (Ch. 15)
(5) 'What connexion can there be, between the place in Lincolnshire, the house in town, the Mercury in powder, and the whereabout of

Table 8.3:   Classification of compound nouns

Type	Example	Number of lexemes
noun + noun	pipe-bowl[a], candle-ward[a]	87 (70.2%)
noun + verb-*ing*	wall-chalking[a], tomb-visiting	11 (8.9%)
adjective + noun	blue-jacket[b], sick-bedside	8 (6.5%)
verb-*ing* + noun	dancing-mistress[a], reading-glasses[a]	7 (5.6%)
noun + adjective	quidiron-full, bags-full	2 (1.6%)
adjective + verb-*ing*	counter-pattening[a], half-baptising	2 (1.6%)
ed-participle + noun	sprung-mine	1 (0.8%)
adverb + *ed*-participle	best-groomed[a]	1 (0.8%)
verb-*ing* + adv	putting-off[b]	1 (0.8%)
noun + adverb	mover-on	1 (0.8%)
verb[c] + noun	thaw-drop[a]	1 (0.8%)
noun + noun + noun	Chancery-folio-page	1 (0.8%)
word + *like*[d]	passage-like	1 (0.8%)
Total		124 (100.0%)

Notes: [a] Indicates a first-citation in the *OED 2*; [b] indicates an example earlier than the *OED*; [c] this means that the first element of the compound could be either a verb base or a noun; [d] as mentioned in Section 4.3.3 (p. 111), strictly speaking this kind of word might not be treated as a compound word but is near the boundary between affixation and compounding because the suffix *like* retains the meaning of *like* as a separate word.

The compound word *counter-pattening* is cited as the first example of the verb *patten* as meaning 'to walk or go about on pattens' from *Bleak House* in the *OED 2*.

Jo the outlaw with the broom, who had that distant ray of light upon him when he swept the *churchyard-step*? (Ch. 16)

(6) 'Now, if I had stayed at Badger's I should have been obliged to spend twelve pounds at a blow, for some heart-breaking *lecture-fees*.' (Ch. 18)

In cases where Dickens is able to convey the same meaning without using a hyphen, he would rather use a hyphen than not.

What is characteristic in the other types of compound nouns is a productive element of 'verb-*ing*'. Twenty of the 37 compound nouns (54 per cent) which are not of the type of 'noun + noun' are comprised of the element 'verb-*ing*'. All 20 examples are given below:

bell-jingling (Ch. 12), carving-fork (Ch. 9), coffee-bearing (Ch. 50), copying-office (Ch. 10), counter-pattening (Ch. 27), dancing-mistress (Ch. 14), flower-making (Ch. 21), folding-window (Ch. 57), girl-driving (Ch. 21), half-baptising (Ch. 11), law-writing (Ch. 10), oil-grinding (Ch. 54), quack-doctoring (Ch. 12), reading-glasses (Ch. 41), search-making (Ch. 54), sleeping-stuff (Ch. 59), street-crying (Ch. 41), sweeping-boy (Ch. 42), tomb-visiting (Ch. 12), wall-chalking (Ch. 41)

Table 8.4 gives a list of compound adjectives by classification. As Table 8.4 indicates, there are a wider variety of types of compound adjectives than of compound nouns where the 'noun + noun' type dominates (see Table 8.3). The most numerous type is 'adjective + *ed*-participle', representing one-third of the total. The most productive element in the compound adjectives is the *ed*-participle: there are 39

Table 8.4: Classification of compound adjectives

Type	Example	Number of lexemes
Adjective + *ed*-participle	weak-legged[a], green-hearted[a]	24 (33.3%)
Adjective + verb-*ing*	respectable-looking[a], fast-darkening[b]	7 (9.7%)
Adverb + verb-*ing*	worst-looking[a], never-lightening	6 (8.3%)
Adverb + *ed*-participle	now-extinguished,	6 (8.3%)
Noun + *ed*-participle	self-repressed[b], canvas-covered[b]	6 (8.3%)
Adverb + adjective	blandly-ferocious, half-thankful	6 (8.3%)
Noun + verb-*ing*	crisp-looking[b], soldier-looking	3 (4.2%)
Adjective + adjective	cold-black, swift-responsive	2 (2.8%)
Noun + adjective	brass-bound[b]	1 (1.4%)
Adjective + adverb	grave-enough	1 (1.4%)
Adjective + noun (attributive)	quick-march[a]	1 (1.4%)
ed-participle + verb-*ing*	blessed-looking	1 (1.4%)
Verb-*ing* + verb-*ing*	crossing-sweeping	1 (1.4%)
Noun + *and* + noun (attributive)	drum-and-fife	1 (1.4%)
adjective + *ed*-participle + verb-*ing*	good-natured-looking[b]	1 (1.4%)
adjective + adverb + *ed*-participle	good-enough-tempered	1 (1.4%)
noun + *and* + noun + *ed*-participle	sun-and-shadow-chequered	1 (1.4%)
word + *like* (attributive)	retainer-like	3 (4.2%)
Total		72 (100.0%)

Notes: [a] Indicates a first-citation in the *OED* 2; [b] indicates an earlier example than the *OED*.

examples (54 per cent), while the element 'verb-*ing*', which is the most productive in the compound nouns, is found in 19 (26 per cent) compound adjectives.
The characteristic lexical element in compound adjectives is *looking*.

> blessed-looking (Ch. 32), crisp-looking (Ch. 13), good-natured-looking (Ch. 15), inexpressive-looking (Ch. 3), public-looking (Ch. 57), responsible-looking (Ch. 28), soldier-looking (Ch. 52), sorrowful-looking (Ch. 59), worst-looking (Ch. 9)

These nine compound adjectives with *looking* are all used as attributive adjectives, and some of them make unique collocations, as illustrated by the following:

> a pink, fresh-faced, crisp-looking gentleman (Ch. 13), a blessed-looking candle (Ch. 32), at a public-looking place (Ch. 57), the inexpressive-looking books (Ch. 3)

Another lexical element used more than once is *half*: *half-quenched* (Ch. 27), *half-thankful* (Ch. 31) and *half-insensible* (Ch. 31). These lexical elements *looking* and *half* are Dickens' favourite terms, and more common compound adjectives with *looking* or *half* are frequently used not only in *Bleak House* but also in his other works.

The distinctive feature in the compound adjectives concerns their attributive use. Sixty-two of the 72 compound adjectives are attributive adjectives, 86 per cent of the total, and the other 10 are predicative adjectives. We may be able to say that Dickens' predilection for premodification produces new compound adjectives.

Concerning compound verbs and adverbs, there are only a few examples in *Bleak House*: one compound verb and four compound adverbs. The compound verb *cross-file* is used to mean 'to submit the opposite petition', as observed in the following sentence:

> We are always appearing, and disappearing, and swearing, and interrogating, and filing, and *cross-filing*, and arguing, and sealing, and motioning, and referring, and reporting, and revolving about the Lord Chancellor and all his satellites, and equitably waltzing ourselves off to dusty death, about costs. (Ch. 8)

The four compound adverbs are not found in other nineteenth-century authors' fiction, according to the *NCF*. Dickens uses them in the following contexts:

'And you're doing well, Mr George?' he says to the trooper, squarely standing *faced-about* towards him with his broadsword in his hand. (Ch. 26)

I happened to say to Ada, in his presence, *half-jestingly, half-seriously*, about the time of his going to Mr Kenge's, that he needed to have Fortunatus' purse, he made so light of money, which he answered in this way . . . (Ch. 18)

'I would like to kiss her!' exclaims Mademoiselle Hortense, panting *tigress-like*. (Ch. 54)

9
Conclusion

The first part of this book offered a rationale for the study of collocation in literary texts, particularly in Dickens, including a discussion
of proposed methodologies. There have been few satisfactory literary
collocational investigations to date, with the result that many research
approaches in the area of literary collocation have yet to be explored.

Part II examined both familiar and unusual collocations which may
be considered 'Dickensian', focusing particularly on unique creative
collocations used only by Dickens in the body of eighteenth and
nineteenth-century literature. Chapter 2 illustrated the usual collocations of some words showing strong tendencies toward particular collocates. For example, the tokens of *love* per million words in Dickens
were shown to be approximately half of that found in a nineteenth-
century corpus of fiction excluding Dickens' texts (NCFWD). On the
other hand, the tokens of the collocation *my love* per million words in
Dickens are two-and-a-half times that of the NCFWD. The co-occurrence
of *love* with *my* amounts to one-third of the 1932 examples of *love* in
Dickens. Therefore, this collocation could be said to be distinctive to
Dickens. In Dickens, *heartily* tends to collocate closely with *laughed* and
laughing – the ratio of the collocation of *heartily* with either *laughed* or
laughing amounts to three times that of the NCFWD. Above all, Dickens'
earlier texts show a predominant tendency of co-occurrence of *laughed*
or *laughing* with *heartily*. Such a discussion of usual collocations provides a new awareness and level of detail of Dickens' collocational patterns and his predilection for habitual and particular collocations, in
that the study of collocations of common words, the predilection of
individual writers for particular collocations and their avoidance of collocations that are frequent elsewhere, are the significant features of an
author's personal stylistics (compare Greenbaum, 1970: 81).

Chapter 3 discussed innovation or creativity in Dickens' collocations through the method of dividing unusual collocations into eight types, according to their structure: metaphorical (for example, *angelic rattlesnake*), transferred (for example, *cherubically added*), oxymoronic (for example, *wearily well*), disparate (for example, *delicious tears*), unconventional (for example, *raw afternoon*), modified idiomatic (for example, *by painful degrees*), parodied (for example, *all the queen's horses and all the queen's men*), and relexicalized (for example, *London particular*).

Part II concluded with an investigation into the relationship of collocations and neologisms in Dickens. Chapter 4 considered the significance of a first-citation in the *OED2*, pointing out several characteristics of Dickens as seen through an analysis of his first-citations, clarifying Dickens' activity as a linguistic innovator and discoverer by providing comprehensive data and analysis concerning the relationship between Dickens' collocations and neologisms. Evidence demonstrating that these neologisms have probably come about partly through Dickens' own collocational creativity was provided.

The focus of Part III extended beyond simple collocation. *Bleak House* was selected as a case study for a pragmatic examination of collocation in a sample literary text, demonstrating how collocation can be connected with literary themes, topics, contexts, characters and narrative. Among the several topics presented was the thesis that collocations in a first-person narrator (Esther Summerson's narrative) are linguistically experimental and satisfactorily creative, particularly in comparison with those of the third-person narrative, in contrast to a prevailing view that Esther's language or narrative style is simple, plain and matter-of-fact. Section 5.3 found many unusual collocations in Esther's narrative (including metaphorical, personified, oxymoronic, transferred collocations and so on), not found in other eighteenth and nineteenth-century fiction. This led to the conclusion that Esther's collocational usage is no less unique and creative than that of the third-person narrator.

When compared with those of other writers of English novels in the eighteenth and nineteenth centuries, Dickens' novels have collocational idiosyncrasies and a wide variety of different types of unusual collocations, as well as a richness of creative collocation. In particular, Dickens' use of both usual and creative collocations is closely related to idiolect, characterization, typification, satire, irony, voice and symbolization. In terms of creative collocations, at least, the present collocational study indicates that Dickens can be regarded as a novelist who, inheriting the language of eighteenth-century novels, brought a certain maturity and refinement to the style of English prose fiction.

More generally, it is hoped that this study has provided evidence of the potential rewards involved in corpora studies of literary texts, as this approach expands upon prior methods of linguistic analyses concerning authorial creativity. This corpus-based collocational analysis has hopefully illustrated that collocation is both significant and relevant to linguistic creativity – that usual collocations as well as creative collocations are worth investigating as important stylistic elements of a given author. Thus, corpus stylistics provides the benefits and strengths of comprehensive data, objective evidence and a more nuanced understanding of an author's use of language. Nonetheless, there are also pitfalls, particularly in the case of researchers who may automatically apply quantitative searches for distinctive linguistic features without reading literary works closely and sensitively.

Finally, I wish to conclude my treatise with some remarks on future possibilities for the study of collocation in literary texts. Sørensen (1984: 247) stated that 'the study of a writer's language may serve a twofold purpose: one aim is to identify the characteristics of his style and thus lay the foundations of a linguistics to form part of an assessment of his literary achievement . . . I suggest that such a study may also be a contribution to language history'. In order to identify the characteristics of Dickens' style, the language of *Bleak House* was used as a case-study focus, and the same comprehensive approach applied to Dickens' other texts should increase our awareness and understanding of novel collocations and collocational patterns, serving to open up new topics of study. A diachronic investigation of collocations in Dickens' entire oeuvre may offer objective and comprehensive proof of several grades of change and development of certain collocations. (For example, Yamamoto (2003: 447) states that 'Probably "line of business" represents the first grade of development, from which "line" has got detached as a sort of pregnant word and is fairly established idiomatically in the phrase "in the (potato) line" of which examples are most numerous.') A comparison of collocational style between Dickens' fiction and letters by using *The Letters of Charles Dickens on CD-ROM* (2002: this database contains the 11 published volumes (of a projected 12) of the letters of Charles Dickens, 1820 until 1867) may provide another interesting area within which to explore Dickens' linguistic creativity. Furthermore, it may be useful to compile a dictionary of usual and creative collocations which are considered Dickensian. A tentative title, such as *A Dictionary of Collocations in Dickens* might produce a detailed portrait of Dickens as a collocational innovator. By extension, a literary collocational analysis should represent a valid and novel way of approaching other authors.

As a contribution of the study of collocation to the history of English style we need to consider collocations within the context of the development of the language of fiction. Concerning Dickens' command of the comprehensive resources of literary style, such as 'word, phrase, rhymes and image', Leavis (1972: 274–5) asserts that 'there is surely no greater master of English except Shakespeare'. This statement may be confirmed by a collocational analysis. Therefore, the collocational approach, applied to literary texts, may inform us not only that collocation is an indispensable perspective for the study of the history of creative expressions in English, but also that one of the most important features in language creativity is a unique ability to combine words into collocations. It is hoped that collocational analysis, as a fundamental apparatus of linguistic description, will bring about a shift in research emphasis concerning the English language, whether in literary or non-literary contexts.

Appendix 1

The top row in the second column presents those collocates which an *-ly* manner adverb modifies. The middle row presents collocates which modify the *-ly* manner adverb and the third row presents those collocates of an *-ly* manner adverb which have no grammatical relationship of modification but do show distinctive characteristics.

Table A1.1: The usual collocations of the 35 highest-frequency *-ly* manner adverbs in the Dickens Corpus

-ly manner adverbs (occurrences)	*Collocates (occurrences) which the adverb modifies* *Collocates (occurrences) by which the adverb is modified* *Other characteristic collocates (occurrences)*
slowly (821)	walked (50), said (35), came (25), moved (23), went (19) so (6), very (71), more (18), too (1) down (45), up (38), head (17), up and down (15)
softly (466)	said (37), opened (20), went (14), walked (12), crept (10) so (14), very (25), more (2), quite (1) door (40), hand (16: softly laying her hand on his)
easily (459)	made (8), come (9), found (7) so (56), very (28), more (24), most (3), too (4), pretty (2), quite (2), less (1) could (45), have (40), might (36), may (26), can (21)
gradually (431)	became (16), fell (12) so (2), very (1) had (50), up (17), down (12), more and more (7)
quickly (424)	said (21), passed (14), returned (14) so (27), very (20), more (3), too (3), pretty (2), less (2)
hastily (400)	said (30), added (12) so (5), very (4), more (1)
gently (383)	said (28) so (7), very (15), more (3) hand (28), head (15), door (8)
quietly (361)	said (24), sat (9), went (7) so (17), very (20), more (3) face (7)
carefully (300)	put (18), closed (13) so (6), very (21), more (5), most (1), pretty (1) door (18), had (14), having (14)

209

Table A1.1: Continued

-ly manner adverbs (occurrences)	Collocates (occurrences) which the adverb modifies Collocates (occurrences) by which the adverb is modified Other characteristic collocates (occurrences)
heartily (250)	laughed (59), laughing (32) so (18), very (40), more (6), most (15), quite (2) hands (15)
steadily (215)	looked (40), looking (29), said (4), kept (5), look (4) so (7), very (6), more (4), less (4), pretty (1), quite (1) eyes (10), face (8)
frequently (193)	observed (5), repeated (6) so (11), very (6), more (7), most (1), less (6), too (3) have (20), had (13)
gravely (188)	said (24), shook (11), shaking (10) so (2), very (10), more (2) head (27)
earnestly (184)	said (25), looked (19), looking (18), talking (9) so (14), very (16), more (11), most (15) face (10)
thoughtfully (181)	said (32), looking (18), looked (13) very (1), more (3) fire (11), hand (5), head (7), face (5), eyes (4), hands (2)
hurriedly (173)	said (27), replied (4) so (2), very (1) had (10), man (6), hand (6), door (4)
eagerly (168)	said (25), looked (13), looking (13), cried (6), replied (4) so (9), very (1), too (1), less (1) face (8), no (7)
freely (160)	breathe (8), admit (6) so (15), very (5), more (21), most (2), pretty (7), too (4), less (1) own (5)
firmly (158)	said (14), set (7), believe (5) so (5), very (1), more (8), less (2), but (14), head (6), hand (4), hands (4)
happily (149)	married (9), lived (7), unconscious (7) so (14), very (4), most (3) had (7), have (6)
solemnly (149)	said (24), declare (9) very (1), more (1), most (4)
cheerfully (145)	said (28) so (3), very (1), more (6), most (1), quite (2)
sharply (143)	said (20), round (10), looking (9), turned (7), turning (6), retorted (5), asked (5) so (4), very (4), more (3), rather (6)

Table A1.1: Continued

-ly manner adverbs (occurrences)	Collocates (occurrences) which the adverb modifies Collocates (occurrences) by which the adverb is modified Other characteristic collocates (occurrences)
lightly (141)	said (4) so (19), very (1), more (3) hand (12), down (8), stairs (7)
anxiously (140)	looking (25), looked (14), said (8), asked (9), expected (7), glanced (6) so (7), very (1), most (1), quite (2) face (7)
silently (140)	looking (8), sat (8) so (4), very (3), more (1), most (0)
rapidly (136)	increasing (6), passed (5) so (11), very (4), more (3), pretty (1) down (6), up (7)
tenderly (135)	said (8) so (10), very (5), more (3), most (1), less (1), quite (2) hand (9)
impatiently (131)	said (33), cried (8), replied (6), returned (5) hand (5)
coolly (130)	said (19), replied (11), returned (8), looking (8), observed (6) so (4), very (11), quite (3)
attentively (128)	looked (24), listened (18), listening (11), looking (10), began (6) so (4), very (3), more (16), most (1), less (3) face (6), eyes (5)
seriously (125)	said (6), think (9), alarmed (5) so (3), very (14), more (2), most (1), quite (3) head (6)
angrily (121)	said (16), retorted (8), inquired (5), looking (5) so (2), very (1) round (6)
sternly (121)	said (24), looking (10), looked (8), demanded (7) so (1), very (2), more (3)
timidly (121)	said (21), glanced (6), replied (5) more (1) hand (9), child (5)

Notes: The occurrences of very and so as -ly manner adverb modifiers have been shown in order to compare their differing usages. Occurrences of more and most have also been counted. A blank in the third row shows that distinctive characteristics were not found concerning collocates that have no grammatical relation to the adverb.

Appendix 2

The following list gives examples of Dickens' first-citations which have been described as dialect in the *OED2*. The first item in quotation marks indicates the *OED2* description as a source, while the second represents quotations from Dickens' works. When there is any reference to an item in *The Concise Oxford Dictionary of Current English* (*COD*, 1995), its annotation is included. Any reference to the item in the *COD* means it is current in present-day English. The name of the character speaking the phrase is added in parentheses.

allus
: 'always' (BH 46) (Jo, the wretched little crossing sweeper in London) 'He wos allus willin fur to give me somethink he wos, though Mrs. Sangsby she was allus a chivying on me – like everybody everywheres.'

anyways
: 'in any case' (OMF II, 12) (Pleasant Riderhood, the daughter of Rogue Riderhood in London) ' "Anyways," said the damsel, "I am glad punishment followed, and I say so".' (*COD*) 'adverb. North America. colloquial or dialect. = anyway.'

fare
: 'to seem likely (with inf. it is often little more than a periphrasis for the finite vb.)' (DC 46) (Mr. Peggoty from Yarmouth) ' "How do you fare to feel about it Mas'r Davy?" he inquired at length.'

flick
: 'to strike lightly with something flexible' (NN 23) ' "Many and many is the circuit this pony has gone," said Mr. Crummles [the actor-manager of a touring theatrical company], flicking him skilfully on the eyelid for old acquaintance' sake.'

flummox
: 'to bring to confusion' (PP 33) (Tony Weller, Sam Weller's father in London) 'Sammy, that if your governor don't prove a alleyvim he'll be what the Italians call reg'larly flummoxed, and that's all about it.' (*COD*) 'transitive verb, colloquial, bewilder, confound, disconcert.'

ginger
: 'a light sandy colour' (OMF I, 2) 'mature young gentleman; with ... too much ginger in his whiskers'. (*COD*) 'of a ginger colour.'

heavens
: 'employed as an intensive adverb' (HW Xmas no. 21/1) 'A shy company though its raining Heavens hard.'

Ikey
: 'Familiar abbreviated form of the Jewish name Isaac' (SB Tales 10) ' "Let me alone," replied Ikey, "and I'll ha' vound up ... in five seconds".'

jolter-headedness
: 'cf. jolter-headed', (Letter 1852) 'the jolter-headedness of the conceited idiots who suppose that volumes are to be tossed off like pancakes.'

out-dacious	'corruption of audacious' (OT 17) (Mr Bumble) 'Mr. Bumble ... said, "They're all in one story, Mrs. Mann. That out-dacious Oliver has demoralized them all.'
pint	'point' (PP 23) (Tony Weller) 'Upon all little pints o' breedin', I know I may trust you as vell as if it was my own self.'
stand up	'to take shelter from rain' (SB Tales 11) 'Nobody thought of "standing up" under doorways or arches.'
surely	'in precise sense, or as a mere intensive' (PP 6) ' "Reg'lar good land that," interposed another fat man. "And so it is, sure-ly," said a third fat man.'
wanting	'mentally defective' (NN 34) (Squeers, the proprietor of Dotheboys Hall, a Yorkshire boarding school) ' "He wouldn't seem so old though to them as didn't know him, for he was a little wanting here," touching his forehead, "nobody at home you know, if you knocked ever so often".'
wax	'to burst into anger' (Haunted House 7) 'Nay, wench, dunna wax up so; whatten's done, is done.'
wimick	'verb, the sound of crying out, onomatopaeia' (DC 51) (Mr Peggotty) ' "Betwixt you and me, Mas'r Davy – and you, ma'am – wen Mrs. Gummidge takes to wimicking," – our old county word for crying – "she's liable to be considered to be ... peevish-like".' (Great Yarmouth, East Anglian dialect.)
work-a-day	'a work-day' (OCS 49) (Sampson Brass, an attorney and an legal adviser to Quilp from Bevis Marks in the city of London) ' "This is an occupation" said the lawyer, "which seems to bring him before my eyes like the Ghost of Hamlet's father, in the very clothes that he wore on work-a-days".'

Appendix 3

Additional information on slang expressions may be found in Eric Partridge's *A Dictionary of Slang and Unconventional English* (EP).

aggravator	'a greased lock of hair' (in *Bell's Life in London*).
balmy	'sleep' (OCS 8) (EP) 'Proberb, suggested by balmy slumbers (Shakespeare).'
bender	'a sixpence' (SB Scenes 12).
card	'applied to a person, with adj. (as knowing, old, queer, etc.) indicating some eccentricity or peculiarity' (SB Characters 11) (*COD*) 'colloquial a person, especially an odd or amusing one (what a card!; a knowing card).'
catch-em-alive-o	'name for a "fly-paper" for catching flies' (LD I, 16) (EP) 'Originally a fisherman's phrase, but by 1853, if not a year or two earlier, it had a tremendous vogue. Its intent was to raise a smile, its meaning almost null.'
a horse chaun	'one who sells horses fraudulently' (PP 42).
chaw up	'chiefly in US to chaw up: to demolish, "do for", "smash" ' (MC 21).
coffin-plate	'(orig. US), a cigarette (cf. nail n. 7 d); coffin-plate, a metal plate set in a coffin-lid, bearing the name of the deceased person, usually with dates of birth and death' (OT 5).
collegian	'an inmate of a prison.' (PP 44).
Conkey	'a nickname given to a person with a prominent nose' (OT 31) (EP) 'adjective, having a large nose. "Waterloo" Wellington was called Conkey at least a decade before 1815'.
crumb	'plumpness' (MC 29).
cut it too fat	'to "come it strong", overdo a thing' (SB Scenes 9).
damp	'a drink, a "wetting" ' (PP 27) (EP) 'not very general, elsewhere.'
do	'a cheat, fraud, swindle, imposture', SB Broker's Man (*COD*) 'British slang a swindle or hoax.'
drain	'a drink' (SB Scenes 22).
ginger	'a light sandy colour, resembling that of ginger' (OMF I, 2) (*COD*) 'of a ginger colour.'
gingerbread-trap	'the mouth' (OMF I, 2) (EP) 'jocular, colloquial.'
gonoph	'a pickpocket' (BH 19) (EP) 'cant, from about 1835, Ex. Hebres gannabh via jewish Dutch gannef.'
governor	'used as a vulgar form of address to a man' (MC 23) (*COD*) 'colloquial (as a form of address) sir.'

Greenland	'the country of greenhorns' (OT 8).
grinder	'See quot. 1837' (PP 31) 1837 Dickens (PP 31) 'Mr. Jackson . . . applying his left thumb to the tip of his nose, worked a visionary coffee mill with his right hand: thereby performing a very graceful piece of pantomine . . . which was familiarly denominated "taking a grinder".'
how goes the enemy	'what is the time?' (NN 19) (EP) 'about 19th century to earlier 20th century. A quotation from Frederic Reynolds, *The Will* (1797).'
I don't think	'used after an ironical statement, to indicate that the reverse is intended' (PP 38).
ikey	'familiar abbreviated form of the Jewish name Isaac' (SB Tales 10).
in one's socks	'as a condition of measurement of stature' (SB Tales 10).
Jack-in-the-box	'A game in which some article, of more or less value, is placed on the top of a stick standing in a hole, and thrown at with sticks. If the article be hit so as to fall clear of the hole, the thrower takes it' (Farmer Slang) (SB Scenes 12).
Jack-in-the-water	'an attendant at the watermen's stairs on the river and sea-port towns, who does not mind wetting his feet for a customer's convenience, in consideration of a douceur' (SB Tales 7).
jeff	'Circus slang. A rope' (HT I, 6).
leaving-shop	'an unlicensed pawnshop' (OMF II, 12) (EP) 'obsolescent *Morning Chronicle*, 21 December, 1857.'
lummy	'first-rate' (OT 43).
magpie	'a halfpenny' (OT 8).
make a hole in the water	'to make a hole in the water: to commit suicide by drowning' (BH 46).
mill	'shortened form of treadmill' (SB Characters 12).
mill	'to send to the treadmill; to send to prison' (OT 25).
nipper	'a boy, a lad. Also, a girl; a child of either sex; the smallest or youngest of a family' (DS 23) (*COD*) 'British colloquial a young child.'
ochre	'applied to money, in allusion to the colour of gold coin' (HT I, 6).
one-er, oner	'A person or thing of a unique or very remarkable kind; esp. a person preeminently addicted to or expert at something; a prime one' (OCS 58) (*COD*) 'a remarkable person or thing.'
over the left	'implying that the words to which it is appended express the reverse of what is really meant' (PP 42).
Polly	'Apollinaris' (BH 20) (*COD*) 'British colloquial a bottle or glass of Apollinaris water.'
prop	'A scarf-pin. Thieves' Cant' (Artful Touch in Repr. Pieces).

rasper	'A person or thing of sharp, harsh, or unpleasant character; also, anything remarkable or extraordinary in its own way' (NN 57).
roll	'a rolling gait or motion; a swagger. Esp. in phr. to have a roll on and varr.: to have a conceited bearing, to give oneself airs (Eng. Public School slang)' (SB Characters 7).
sawbones	'a surgeon' (PP 30) (*COD*) 'slang a doctor or surgeon.'
sew up	'To tire out, exhaust (a person); to nonplus, bring to a standstill; to put hors de combat; to outwit, cheat, swindle; also, to bring about the conviction of (a person)' (PP 39).
specimen	'Of persons as typical of certain qualities or of the human species. Also colloq. or slang with derogatory force, chiefly with defining adj., as a bright, poor' (PP 2).
spike park	'the grounds of a prison' (PP 42).
spoffish	'bustling, fussy, officious' (SB Tales 5).
stick it in	'to stick it in or on: to make extortionate charges' (MC 27) (*COD*) 'colloquial make high charges.'
stump up	'to pay down, "fork out" (money)' (SB Tales 10).
super	'very good or pleasant, first-rate, excellent, "smashing" ' (PP 41) (*COD*) 'colloquial exceptional; splendid.'
tall	'Large in amount, big. slang (orig. US) tall order, something expected to be hard to achieve or fulfil' (AN 14) (*Random House Dictionary* 2nd edn, 1987) 'large in amount or degree.'
timber doodle	'spirituous liquor' (AN 3).
time	'The duration of a term of imprisonment' (OT Ch. 18).
toke	'(A piece of) bread' (Letter 1843).
Tom Tiddler's ground	'any place where money or other consideration is "picked up" or acquired readily; also, a disputed or "debatable territory, a no man's land between two states" (Slang Dict.)' (DS 36).
U. P.	'the spelling pronunciation of up adv., = over, finished, beyond remedy' (OT 24).
wag	'To play truant' (DS 22) cf. (*COD*) 'noun British slang a truant.'
walk into	'To eat or drink heartily of, to "make a hole in" ' (PP 22).
waxy	'angry' (BH 24) (*COD*) 'British slang angry, quick-tempered.'
with	'in reference to liquor: mixed with sugar' (SB Characters 4).
without	'in reference to liquor: not mixed with sugar' (SB Scenes 10).
work off	'to put to death; to hang' (BR 63).

Appendix 4

Concerning items relating to commodities, several sources other than the *OED* were consulted, such as the *Encyclopaedia Britannica*. Listed here are only those lexical items which appear to have been in existence before or at the time of Dickens.

Abernethy	This is a kind of hard biscuit flavoured with caraway seeds, and was probably named after John Abernethy, surgeon (1764–1831) (SB Characters 10).
allotment-garden	small portion of land let out for cultivation to the poor (*All the Year Round*, 1 August 1863).
A1	Applied in Lloyd's Register to ships in first-class condition, as to hull and stores alike. 'The character A denotes New ships, or Ships Renewed or Restored. The Stores of Vessels are designated by the figures 1 and 2; 1 signifying that the Vessel is well and sufficiently found.' (Key to the Register). Added to the names of ships, as 'the fast-sailing ship "Seabreeze", A1 at Lloyd's', or used attributively, 'the splendid A1 clipper-built ship "Miranda"' Hence, fig. (familiar and savouring of commercial phraseology), A1, or in US 'A No. 1' is used adjectively for 'prime, first-class.'
	In the figurative sense of the word 'A1' Dickens is innovative although he is the first writer who used the 'A1' in either case: ' "He must be a first-rater," said Sam. "A1," replied Mr. Roker.' (PP 41).
Athenaeum	A bulletin of the Athenaeum Club, an institution for the promotion of literary or scientific learning which was founded in London by W. Scott and T. Moore. The weekly journal of literary criticism started in 1828 but the *OED* cited Dickens' letter of 11 November 1835 as the first example.
badger-drawing	badger tongs, tongs used to grasp the badger as it emerges from its hole, or to pull it out (OT 30).
bath-towel	a large towel (UT 29).
beer-bibber	'one who drinks frequently' (BR 13). However, the *OED* states this example as a first-citation but also contains the other example of this phrase in 1756 under the entry 'biber'.
beer-boy	'pot-boy' (OCS 34).
beer-chiller	'a funnel-shaped pot made of tin, used to warm, or "take off the chill" of beer over the fire' (SB Characters 5).
beer-pull	'the handle of a beer-engine' (OMF I, 6).
beer-shop	The *OED* cited an example of Kingsley in 1848 as a first one but the following example from Dickens' *Oliver Twist* in

	1839 is earlier: 'Field-lane . . . has its barber, its coffee-shop, its beer-shop, and its fried-fish warehouse' (Ch. 26).
birdseed	'canary-seed, hemp, millet, plantain, or other seeds given to caged birds' (OCS I, 13) (*COD*).
black cap	'spec. that worn by English judges when in full dress, and consequently put on by them when passing sentence of death upon a prisoner' (OT 52). I found an earlier example in Henry Fielding's Miscellanies (1743) than the *OED*: 'At the bottom of the Room were two Persons in close Conference, one with a square black Cap on his Head, and the other with a Robe embroidered with Flames of Fire. These I was informed, were a Judge long since dead, and an Inquisitor-General. I overheard them disputing with great Eagerness, whether the one had hanged, or the other burnt the most' (Bk 1, Ch. 4).
Blondin rope	'a tight-rope, a cable-way'. The name derives from the tightrope walker Blondin (1824–97) (UT 25).
boa	'a snake-like coil of fur worn by ladies as a wrapper for the throat' (SB Tales 5) (*COD*).
bowie-knife	'A large knife, with a blade from ten to fifteen inches long and above an inch broad, curved and double-edged near the point, carried as a weapon in the wilder parts of the United States.' This knife was made in 1836 for an American, James Bowie, after whom it was named (AN 3) (*COD*).
bowling saloon	'US, a building equipped with bowling-alleys' (AN 6).
bucellas	'a sort of Portuguese white wine'. This is named after a village near Lisbon (SB Tales 1).
butter-knife	'a blunt knife used for cutting butter at table' (DC 61) (*COD*).
cavatina	'a short song of simple character, properly one without a second strain and repeat; "frequently applied to a smooth melodious air, forming part of a grand scena or movement" (Grove)' (SB Tales 4). Originally an Italian musical term (*COD*).
clobber	'a black paste used by cobblers to fill up and conceal cracks in the leather of boots and shoes' (*Household Words* 19).
coffee-shop	'a shop where coffee is sold' (OT 26).
collier-brig	a two-masted vessel square-rigged on both masts for carrying coal (BH 1).
crush hat	'a soft hat which can be crushed flat; spec. a hat constructed with a spring so as to collapse and assume a flat shape; an opera-hat' (NN 19).
Cuba	'[The name of a large island in the W. Indies, also called Havana.] A cigar made of tobacco grown in Cuba' (PP 29).
devil-may-care	'wildly reckless; careless and rollicking. Hence as *n.*, a devil-may-care person, attitude, etc.' (*COD*).
draw-bench	'a machine in which wire or strips of metal are reduced in thickness or brought to gauge by drawing through gauged

apertures, also called drawing-bench'. We can know that this machine was already called 'draw-bench' among people at that time from the following citation of Dickens: 'a machine called a draw-bench where their thickness is perfectly equalised from end to end' (*All Year Round*, 2 July).

electric wire 'those of the electric telegraph' (HT I, 11). Electric wire was invented by Samuel F.B. Morse (1791–1872).

first floor 'the floor or storey of a building next above the ground floor' (OMF I, 4) (*COD*).

Greenwich time 'mean time for the meridian of Greenwich, adopted as the standard time by English astronomers' (GE 25).

Guinness 'the proprietary name of a brand of stout manufactured by the firm of Guinness; a bottle or glass of this' (SB Tales 1).

Newmarket 'a card-game in which the main object is to play the same cards as certain duplicates which are exhibited' (OCS 36) (*COD*).

saveloy 'a highly seasoned cooked and dried sausage' (PP 55) (*COD*).

square piano 'a piano of a rectangular form, now superseded by the upright or cottage piano' (BH 38). According to *Encyclopaedia Britannica* this type of piano was invented as a piano for domestic use in the middle of the eighteenth century. It was very popular around the 1760s and used until the 1860s in Europe while it was favoured until the 1880s in America (*COD*).

The following are items that appear to belong to the type of lexis relating to commodities existing before or at the time of Dickens.

air-cushion (SB Tales 1) / reading-glasses, 'a pair of spectacles for use when reading' (BH 41) / appointment book, 'an agreement or arrangement for a meeting' (OMF I, 8) / ballast-heaver (OT 48) / bed-winch (DS 59) / bell-lamp (SB) / bonnet-box (SB) / bonnet-cap (SB Scenes 12) / breakfast-stall (BH 47) / business hours (NN 40) / Captain's biscuit (MC 5) / cattle-market (OT 16) / coal-cellar (OT 2) / coal-whipper, 'one who raises coal out of a ship's hold by means of a pulley' (SB Tales 7) / door key (OT 26) / door-chain (SB Tales 6) / door-knocker (NN 15) / engine-pump (OT 48) / fish-basket (OT 21) / furniture-broker (AN 8) / German sausage (PP 31) / kidney-pie (SB Scenes 2) / milk-can (OT 45) / milk-shop (DS 21) / minuet dance (BR 4) / salad dressing (SB Scenes 18) (*COD*).

Bibliography

Collocation

Altenberg, Bengt (1991) 'Amplifier collocation in spoken English', in Stig Johansson and Stenstöm, AmmaßBrita (eds) *English Computer Corpora: Selected Papers and Research*, Berlin: Mouton de Gruyter, pp. 127–47.

Bäcklund, U. (1973) *The Collocation of Adverbs of Degree in English*, Uppsala: Uppsala University.

Baker, Mona, Gill Francis and Elena Tognini-Bonelli (eds) (1993) *Text and Technology: in Honour of John Sinclair*, Amsterdam: John Benjamins.

Bauer, Laurie (1983) 'An outline of English word-formation', in *English Word-formation*, Cambridge: Cambridge University Press.

Behre, Frank (1973) *Get, Come and Go: Some Aspects of Situational Grammar: a Study Based on a Corpus Drawn from Agatha Christie's Writings*, Stockholm: Almqvist and Wiksell.

Biber, Douglas, Susan Conrad and Randi Reppen (1998) *Corpus Linguistics: Investigating Language Structure and Use*, Cambridge: Cambridge University Press.

Biber, D., S. Johansson, G. Leech, S. Conrad and E. Finegan (1999) *Longman Grammar of Spoken and Written English*, London: Longman.

Brinton, J. and M. Akimoto (eds) (1999) *Collocational and Idiomatic Aspects of Composite Predicates in the History of English*, Amsterdam: John Benjamins.

Buren, P. van (1967) 'Preliminary aspects of mechanisation in lexis', *Cahiers de Lexicologie* Vol. 11, 89–111 and Vol. 12, 71–84.

Carter, Ronald (1998) 'Words and patterns', in *Vocabulary: Applied Linguistic Perspectives* (2nd edn), London: Routledge, pp. 50–78.

Cruse, D.A. (1986) *Lexical Semantics*, Cambridge: Cambridge University Press.

Daunt, M. (1966) 'Some modes of Anglo-Saxon meaning', in C. Bazell et al. (eds) *In Memory of J.R. Firth*, London: Longman, pp. 66–78.

Firth, J.R. (1957) 'Modes of meaning', in *Papers in Linguistics, 1934–51*, London: OUP, pp. 191–215.

Gerson, S. (1989) 'From . . . to . . . as an intensifying collocation', *English Studies*, Vol. 70, No. 4, 360–71.

Goatly, Andrew (1997) *The Language of Metaphors*, London: Routledge.

Greenbaum, Sidney (1969) *Studies in English Adverbial Usage*, London: Longman.

——(1970) *Verb-Intensifier Collocations in English: an Experimental Approach*, The Hague: Mouton.

——(1974) 'Some verb-intensifier collocations in American and British English', *American Speech*, Vol. 49, No. 1–2, 79–89.

Halliday, M.A.K. (1961) 'Categories of the theory of grammar', *Word*, Vol. 17, No. 3.

——(1966) 'Lexis as a linguistic level', in C. Bazell et al. (eds) *In Memory of J.R. Firth*, London: Longman, pp. 148–62.

Herbst, Thoms (1996) 'What are collocations: sandy beaches or false teeth?', *English Studies*, 4, 379–93.

Hoey, Michael (2001) 'A world beyond collocation: new perspectives on vocabulary teaching', in M. Lewis (ed.) *Teaching Collocation: Further Developments in the Lexical Approach*, Hove: Language Teaching Publications, pp. 224–43.

Hori, Masahiro (1993) 'Some collocations of the word "Eye" in Dickens: a preliminary sketch', in M. Ukaji et al. (eds) *Aspects of Modern English*, Tokyo: Eichosha, pp. 509–27.

——(1999) 'Collocational patterns of intensive adverbs in Dickens: a tentative approach', *English Corpus Studies*, No. 6, 51–65.

——(2002) 'Collocational patterns of *-ly* manner adverbs in Dickens', in T. Saito, J. Nakamura and S. Yamazaki (eds) *English Corpus Linguistics in Japan*, Amsterdam: Rodopi, pp. 149–63.

Hunston, Susan (1995) 'A corpus study of some English verbs of attribution', *Functions of Language*, 2, 2, 138–58.

——(2001) *Corpora in Applied Linguistics*, Cambridge: Cambridge University Press.

——(2001) 'Colligation, lexis, pattern, and text', in M. Scott and G. Thompson (eds) *Patterns of Text: in Honour of Michael Hoey*, Amsterdam: John Benjamins.

Hunston, Susan and Gill Francis (1999) *Pattern Grammar: a Corpus-Driven Approach to the Lexical Grammar of English*, Amsterdam: John Benjamins.

Hunston, Susan and Geoff Thompson (2000) *Evaluation in Text*, Oxford: Oxford University Press.

Ikeda, Yuko (1997) 'Fire in Dickens: with special reference to collocational cohesion', *KGU Journal of Language and Literature*, 4, 1, 39–61.

Ito, Hiroyuki (1993) 'Some collocations of adverbs in Richardson's *Clarissa Harlowe*', in M. Ukaji et al. (eds) *Aspects of Modern English*, Tokyo: Eichosha, pp. 528–47.

Joseph, John (2002) 'Rethinking linguistic creativity', in H. Davis and T.J. Taylor (eds) *Rethinking Linguistics*, London: RoutledgeCurzon, pp. 121–50.

Katsumata, Senkichiro (1958) *New Dictionary of English Collocations*, Tokyo: Kenkyusha.

Kjellmer, Göran (1994) *A Dictionary of English Collocations: Based on the Brown Corpus* (3 Vols), Oxford: Clarendon Press.

Leech, Geoffrey (1969) *A Linguistic Guide to English Poetry*, London: Longman.

Leech, Geoffrey, Paul Rayson and Andrew Wilson (2001) *Word Frequencies in Written and Spoken English*, London: Longman.

Leisi, Ernst (1985) 'Syntagmatische Semantik', in *Praxis der Englischen Semantik*, Heidelberg: Car Winter, pp. 196–224.

Lewis, Michael (ed.) (2001) *Teaching Collocation: Further Developments in the Lexical Approach*, Hove: Language Teaching Publications.

Louw, Bill (1993) 'Irony in the text or insincerity in the writer? The diagnostic potential of semantic prosodies', in M. Baker et al. (eds) *Text and Technology: in Honour of John Sinclair*, Amsterdam: John Benjamins, 157–76.

Mackin, Ronald (1978) 'On collocations: "Words shall be known by the company they keep"', in P. Strevens (ed.) *In Honour of A.S. Hornby*, Oxford: Oxford University Press, pp. 149–65.

Masui, Michio (1967) 'A mode of word-meaning in Chaucer's language of love', *Studies in English Literature*, English Number, The English Literary Society of Japan, 113–26.

McBride, Christopher (1998) 'A collocational approach to semantic change: the case of worship and honour in Malory and Spenser', *Language and Literature*, Vol. 7, 5–19.

McIntosh, Angus (1966) 'Patterns and ranges', in A. McIntosh and M.A.K. Halliday (eds) *Patterns of Language: Papers in General Descriptive and Applied Linguistics*, London: Longman, pp. 183–99.

Moon, Rosamund (1996) 'The analysis of fixed expression in text', in M. Coulthard (ed.) *Advances in Written Text Analysis*, London: Routledge, pp. 117–35.

—— (1998) *Fixed Expressions and Idioms in English: a Corpus-Based Approach*, Oxford: Clarendon Press.

Nakaoka, Hiroshi (1983) *A Concordance to Wuthering Heights*, Tokyo: Kaibunsha Publishing Co., Ltd.

Oizumi, Akio (1971) 'On collocated words in Chaucer's translation of "LeLivere de Mellibee et Prudence": a stylistic comparison of the English translation with the French version', *Studies in English Literature*, Vol. 48, No. 1, 95–108.

Osberg, Richard (1985) 'Collocation and theme in the Middle English lyric "Foweles in pe frith"', *Modern Language Quarterly*, Vol. 46, 115–27.

Partington, Alan (1993) 'Corpus evidence of language change: the case of the intensifier', in M. Baker et al. (eds) *Text and Technology: in Honour of John Sinclair*, Amsterdam: John Benjamins, pp. 177–92.

—— (1995) 'Kicking the habit: the exploitation of collocation in literature and humour', in J. Payne (ed.) *Linguistic Approaches to Literature: Papers in Literary Stylistics*, Birmingham: English Language Research, pp. 25–44.

—— (1998) *Patterns and Meanings: Using Corpora for English Language Research and Teaching*, Amsterdam: John Benjamins.

Renouf, Antoinette and J. Sinclair (1991) 'Collocational frameworks in English', in K. Aijmer and B. Altenberg (eds) *English Corpus Linguistics: Studies in Honour of Jan Svartvik*, London: Longman, pp. 129–43.

Shen, Yeshayahu (1987) 'On the structure and understanding of poetic oxymoron', *Poetics Today*, 8, 1, 105–22.

Simpson, Paul (1997) 'Words and meanings: an introduction to lexical semantics', in *Language through Literature: an Introduction*, London: Routledge, pp. 61–99.

Sinclair, John (1966) 'Beginning the study of lexis', in C. Bazell et al. (eds) *In Memory of J.R. Firth*, London: Longman, pp. 410–30.

—— (ed.) (1987) *Looking Up*, London: COBUILD.

—— (1991) *Corpus, Concordance, Collocation*, Oxford: Oxford University Press.

—— (1992) 'Trust the text', in M. Davies and L. Ravelli (eds) *Advances in Systemic Linguistics*, London: Pinter, pp. 5–19.

—— (1996) *J.M. Sinclair on Lexis and Lexicography*, (ed. by Joseph Foley), Singapore: Uni Press.

—— S. Jones and R. Daley (1970) *English Lexical Studies*, Report to OSTI on Project C/LP/08, Department of English, The University of Birmingham.

Singleton, David (2000) 'Lexical partnerships', in *Language and the Lexicon*, London: Arnold, pp. 47–62.

Sørensen, Knud (1980) 'From postmodification to premodification', *Stockholm Studies in English LII*, 77–84.

Spackman, I.J., W.R. Owens and P.N. Furbank (1987) *A KWIC Concordance to Daniel Defoe's Robinson Crusoe*, New York: Garland Publishing.

Stubbs, Michael (1995a) 'Collocations and semantic profiles: on the cause of the trouble with quantitative methods', *Functions of Language*, 2, 1, 23–55.

—— (1995b) 'Corpus evidence for norms of lexical collocation', in G. Cook and B. Seidlhofer (eds) *Principle and Practice in Applied Linguistics: Studies in Honour of H.G. Widdowson*, Oxford: Oxford University Press, pp. 243–56.

—— (1996) *Text and Corpus Analysis: Computer-Assisted Studies of Language and Culture*, Oxford: Blackwell.

—— (2001) *Words and Phrases: Corpus Studies of Lexical Semantics*, Oxford: Blackwell.

Takahashi, Hisashi (1957) 'Verb-adverb combination in Chaucer's *Canterbury Tales*', in Michio Masui et al. (eds) *Studies in English Language and Literature: in Honour of Dr. Tadao Yamamoto*, Tokyo: Kenkyuusha, pp. 241–52.

Varantola, Krista (1983) 'Premodification vs. postmodification and chain compound structure', *Stockholm Studies in English VIII*, 75–82.

Yamamoto, Tadao (1950) 'On collocated words in Shakespeare's plays', *Anglica*, Vol. 1, No. 1, 17–29.

The language and style of Dickens

Allingham, Philip (1987) 'The naming of names in *A Christmas Carol*', *Dickens Quarterly*, Vol. 1, No. 1, 15–20.

—— (1990) 'The names of Dickens's American originals in *Martin Chuzzlewit*', *Dickens Quarterly*, Vol. 7, No. 3, 329–37.

—— (1991) 'Theme, form and the naming of names in *Hard Times for These Times*', *The Dickensian*, Vol. 87, 19–31.

Axton, William (1966) 'Esther's nicknames: a study in relevance', *Dickensian*, Vol. 62, 158–63.

Brook, G.L. (1970) *The Language of Dickens*, London: Andre Deutsch.

Fowler, Roger (1989) 'Polyphony in *Hard Times*', in Ronald Carter and Paul Simpson (eds) *Language, Discourse and Literature: an Introductory Reader in Discourse Stylistics*, London: Unwin Hyman, pp. 77–94.

Furukawa, Yuko (1982) 'The language of Charles Dickens's *Bleak House*: with special reference to deviation', MA thesis, Kumamoto University (unpublished).

Gerson, Stanley (1965) 'Dickens's use of Malapropisms', *The Dickensian*, Vol. 61, 40–5.

Golding, Robert (1985) *Idiolects in Dickens*, London: Macmillan.

Hawes, Donald (1978) 'David Copperfield's names', *The Dickensian*, Vol. 74, 81–7.

Hollington, Michael (1992) 'Physiognomy in *Hard Times*', *Dickens Quarterly*, Vol. 9, No. 2, 58–66.

Hori, Masahiro (1993) 'Nursery rhymes in Dickens's language', *Kumamoto Studies in English Language and Literature*, No. 36, 68–86.

Ikeda, (Furukawa) Yuko (1982) 'The language of Charles Dickens's *Bleak House*: with special reference to deviation', MA thesis, Kumamoto University (unpublished).

—— (1986) *The Language of Charles Dickens's 'I'-Narrations*, MA thesis, Hokkaido University.

Imahayashi, Osamu (1998) 'Grammatical anomalies of American English in Dickens', *ERA*, Vol. 16, No. 2, 31–48.

Kaplan, Fred (1966) *The Development of Dickens' Style*, PhD, Columbia University, New York.

Koguchi, Keisuke (2001) *The Language of Charles Dickens's* A Tale of Two Cities *from a Cohesive Point of View*, Hiroshima: Research Institute for Language and Culture Yasuda Women's University.

Lodge, David (1966) 'The rhetoric of *Hard Times*', in *Language of Fiction*, London: Routledge & Kegan Paul.

Matchett, Willoughby (1908) 'The style of Dickens', *The Dickensian*, Vol. 4, No. 12, 320–2.

——(1917) 'Dickens as a Master of Words', *The Dickensian*, Vol. 13, Nos. 4 and 5.

Mcleod, Norman (1992) 'Lexicogrammar and the reader: three examples from Dickens', in M. Toolan (ed.) *Language, Text and Context: Essays in Stylistics*, London: Routledge, pp. 138–57.

——(2002) 'Which hand? Reading *Great Expectations* as a guessing game', *Dickens Studies Annual*, Vol. 31, New York: AMS Press, 127–57.

Page, Norman (1969) ' "A language fit for heroes": speech in *Oliver Twist* and *Our Mutual Friend*', *The Dickensian*, Vol. 65.

——(1971) 'Forms of address in Dickens', *The Dickensian*, Vol. 67, 16–20.

——(1988) *Speech in the English Novel* (2nd edn), Basingstoke: Macmillan.

Paroissien, David (1984) ' "What's in a name?" Some speculations about Fagin', *The Dickensian*, Vol. 80, 41–5.

Pound, Louise (1947) 'The American dialect of Charles Dickens', *American Speech*, Vol. 22, 124–30.

Quirk, Randolph (1959) *Charles Dickens and Appropriate Language*, Durham: University of Durham.

——(1961) 'Some observations on the language of Dickens', *A Review of English Literature*, Vol. 2, No. 3, 19–28.

——(1974) 'Charles Dickens, linguist', in *The Linguist and the English Language*, London: Edward Arnold, pp. 1–37.

Rosenberg, Brian (1982) *Character and Representation in Dickens*, PhD thesis, Columbia University, New York.

——(1985) 'Vision into language: the style of Dickens's characterization', *Dickens Quarterly*, Vol. 11, No. 4, 115–24.

——(1987) 'The language of doubt in *Oliver Twist*', *Dickens Quarterly*, Vol. 4, No. 2, 91–8.

Söderlind, Johannes (1976) 'A novel by Dickens linguistically analysed', *Poetics* (?), 60–73.

Sørensen, Knud (1954) 'Subjective narration in *Bleak House*,' *English Studies*, Vol. 40, 431–9.

——(1984) 'Charles Dickens: linguistic innovator', *English Studies*, Vol. 65, No. 3, 237–47.

——(1985) *Charles Dickens: Linguistic Innovator*, Aarhus: Arkona.

——(1989) 'Narrative and speech-rendering in Dickens', *Dickens Quarterly*, Vol. VI, No. 4, 131–41.

——(1989) 'Dickens on the use of English', *English Studies*, Vol. 70, No. 6, 551–9.

Stevenson, Lionel (1936) 'Names in *Pickwick*', *The Dickensian*, Vol. 32, 241–4.

Stone, H. (1959) 'Dickens and interior monologue', *Philological Quarterly*, XXXVIII, 52–65.

Tabata, Tomoji (1994) 'Dickens's narrative style: a statistical approach to chronological variation', *RISSH*, 30, 165–82.

——(1995) 'Narrative style and the frequencies of very common words: a corpus-based approach to Dickens's first-person and third-person narratives', *English Corpus Studies*, 2, 91–109.

——(2002) 'Investigating stylistic variation in Dickens through correspondence analysis of word-class distribution', in T. Saito, J. Nakamura and S. Yamazaki (eds) *English Corpus Linguistics in Japan*, Amsterdam: Rodopi, pp. 165–82.

Wales, Kathleen (1981) 'Dickens and interior monologue: the opening of *Edwin Drood* reconsidered', *Language and Style*, Vol. 17, 234–50.

Yamamoto, Tadao (2003) *Growth and System of the Language of Dickens* (3rd edn), Hiroshima: Keisuisha.

Young, R.T. (1906) 'Dickens's use of the word "Gentleman"', *The Dickensian*, Vol. 5, No. 6, 154–8.

Language and style

Adolph, Robert (1968) *The Rise of Modern Prose Style*, Cambridge, MA: MIT Press.

Arai, Yoichi (1998) 'Some applications of electronic dictionaries in English linguistics', in T. Saito et al. (eds) *English Corpus Linguistics*, Tokyo: Kenkyusha, pp. 211–32 (in Japanese).

Bailey, Richard (1996) *Nineteenth-Century English*, Ann Arbor: The University of Michigan Press.

Bakhtin, Mikhail (1981) *The Dialogic Imagination*, Austin: University of Texas Press.

Biber, D. and E. Finegan (1989) 'Drift and the evolution of English style: a history of three genres', *Language*, Vol. 65, 3, 487–517.

Birch, David and Michael O'Toole (1988) *Functions of Style*, London: Pinter Publishers.

Bonheim, Helmut (1982) *The Narrative Modes: Techniques of the Short Story*, Cambridge: D.S. Brewer.

Booth, Wayne (1961) *The Rhetoric of Fiction*, Chicago and London: The University of Chicago Press.

Brewer, C. (1993) 'The Second Edition of The Oxford English Dictionary', *The Review of English Studies*, 175, 313–42.

Burrows, John (1987) *Computation into Criticism: a Study of Jane Austen's Novels and an Experiment in Method*, Oxford: Clarendon Press.

Carter, Ronald (1998) *Vocabulary: Applied Linguistic Perspectives*, London: Routledge.

——(1997) *Investigating English Discourse: Language, Literacy and Literature*, London: Routledge.

Chatman, Raymond (1994) *Forms of Speech in Victorian Fiction*, London: Longman.

Chowdharay-Best, G. (1994) 'A reply to the review of the Second Edition of The Oxford English Dictionary', *The Review of English Studies*, 179, 397–8.

Cuddon, J.A. (1982) *A Dictionary of Literary Terms*, Harmondsworth: Penguin.

Crystal, D. and D. Davy (1969) *Investigating English Style*, London: Longman.

Emmott, Cathrine (1997) *Narrative Comprehension: a Discourse Perspective*, Oxford: Oxford University Press.

Firth, J.R. (1957) *Papers in Linguistics 1934–1951*, London: Oxford University Press.

Fowler, Roger (1977) *Linguistics and the Novel*, London: Routledge.
—— (1981) *Literature as Social Discourse*, London: Batsford Academic and Educational.
—— (1986) *Linguistic Criticism*, Oxford: Oxford University Press.
Gordon, Ian (1966) *The Movement of English Prose*, London: Longman.
Görlach, Manfred (1999) *English in Nineteenth Century England*, Cambridge: Cambridge University Press.
—— (2001) *Eighteenth-Century English*, Heidelberg: Universitätsverlag C. Winter.
Greenbaum, Sidney (1988) *Good English and the Grammarian*, London: Longman.
Halliday, M.A.K. (1970) 'Language structure and language function', in J. Lyons (ed.) *New Horizons in Linguistics*, Harmondsworth: Penguin.
—— (1973) *Explorations in the Functions of Language*, London: Edward Arnold.
—— (1981) 'Linguistic function and literary style: an inquiry into the language of William Golding's *The Inheritors*', in D. Freeman (ed.) *Essays in Modern Stylistics*, London: Methuen.
—— (1994) *An Introduction to Functional Grammar* (2nd edn), London: Edward Arnold.
—— and Ruqaiya Hasan (1976) *Cohesion in English*, London: Longman.
Hoover, David (1999) *Language and Style in 'The Inheritors'*, New York: University Press of America.
—— (2001) 'Statistical stylistics and authorship attribution: an empirical investigation', *Literary and Linguistic Computing*, Vol. 16, 421–44.
Hopper, Paul and Elizabeth Traugott (1993) *Grammaticalization*, Cambridge: Cambridge University Press.
Huddleston, Rodney and Geoffrey Pullum (2002) *The Cambridge Grammar of the English Language*, Cambridge: Cambridge University Press.
Ito, Hiroyuki (1980) *The Language of the Spectator: a Lexical and Stylistic Approach*, Tokyo: Shinozaki Shorin.
—— (1993) *Some Aspects of Eighteenth-Century English*, Tokyo: Eichosha.
Joseph, J.E., N. Love and T.J. Taylor (2001) *Landmarks in Linguistic Thought II*, London: Routledge.
Jucker, A. (1994) 'New dimensions in vocabulary studies: review article of The Oxford English Dictionary (2nd edition) on CD Rom', *Literary and Linguistic Computing*, Vol. 9, No. 2, 149–54.
Leech, Geoffrey (1971) *Meaning and the English Verb*, London: Longman.
—— (1981) *Semantics*, London: Penguin Books.
Leech, Geoffrey and Michael Short (1981) *Style in Fiction*, London: Longman.
Martin, Jim (1992) *English Text: System and Structure*, Amsterdam: John Benjamins.
Miles, J. (1968) 'A change in the language of literature', *Eighteenth Century Studies*, Vol. 2, No. 2, 35–44.
Milic, Louis (1991) 'Progress in stylistics: theory, statistics, computers', *Computers and the Humanities*, 25, 393–400.
Palmer, F. (1976) *Semantics: a New Outline*, Cambridge: Cambridge University Press.
Partridge, Eric (1933) *Slang Today and Yesterday*, London: George Routledge & Sons.
—— (1980) *Eric Partridge in his Own Words*, ed. David Crystal, London: Andre Deutsch.
—— (1983) *A Dictionary of Slang and Unconventional English* (8th edn), London: Routledge and Kegan Paul.

Payne, J. (ed.) (1995) *Linguistic Approaches to Literature: Papers in Literary Stylistics*, Birmingham: English Language Research.
Phillipps, K.C. (1984) *Language and Class in Victorian England*, Oxford: Andre Deutsch.
Quirk, R., S. Greenbaum, G. Leech and J. Svaitvik (1985) *A Comprehensive Grammar of the English Language*, London: Longman.
Schäfer, J. (1980) *Documentation in the OED*, Oxford: Oxford University Press.
Stubbs, Michael (1996) *Text and Corpus Analysis*, Oxford: Blackwell.
——(2001) *Words and Phrases: Corpus Studies of Lexical Semantics*, Oxford: Blackwell.
Uspensky, Boris (1973) *A Poetics of Composition*, University of California Press.

Literary study on Dickens

Allen, Walter (1958) *The English Novel*, Harmondsworth: Penguin.
Bentley, Nicolas, Michael Slater and Nina Burgis (1990) *The Dickens Index*, Oxford: Oxford University Press.
Bloom, Harold (ed.) (1987) *Charles Dickens's Bleak House*, New York: Chelsea House Publishers.
——(ed.) (1992) *David Copperfield*, New York: Chelsea House Publishers.
Collins, Philip (ed.) (1971) *Dickens: the Critical Heritage*, London: Routledge and Kegan Paul.
Connor, Steven (1985) *Charles Dickens*, Oxford: Basil Blackwell.
Dyson, A.E. (ed.) (1969) *Dickens: Bleak House*, London: Macmillan.
Ford, George and Lauriat Lane, Jr (eds) (1961) *The Dickens Critics*, Ithaca: Cornell University Press.
Fujino, Toshio (1987) *Mother Goose in English Literature*, Tokyo: Aratake (in Japanese).
Gager, Valerie (1996) *Shakespeare and Dickens*, Cambridge: Cambridge University Press.
Harvey, W.J. (1969), '*Bleak House*: the double narrative', in A.E. Dyson (ed.) *Dickens: Bleak House*, London: Macmillan Press.
Hawthorn, J. (1987) *Bleak House*, London: Macmillan.
Hayward, Arthur (1924) *The Dickens Encyclopaedia*, London: Routledge & Kegan Paul.
Ingham, Patricia (1992) *Dickens, Woman & Language*, New York: Harvester Wheatsheaf.
Jacobson, Wendy (1986) *The Companion to the Mystery of Edwin Drood*, London: Allen & Unwin.
Jaffe, Audrey (1991) *Vanishing Points: Dickens, Narrative, and the Subject of Omniscience*, Berkeley: University of California Press.
Kearns, M. (1984) '"But I cried very much": Esther Summerson as narrator', *Dickens Quarterly*, Vol. 1, No. 4, 121–9.
Kucich, John (1981) *Excess and Restraint in the Novels of Charles Dickens*, Athens: The University of Georgia Press.
Larson, Janet (1985) *Dickens and the Broken Scripture*, Athens: The University of Georgia Press.
Leavis, F.R. and Q.D. Leavis (1972) *Dickens the Novelist*, London: Peguin Books.

Metz, N. (1981) 'Narrative gesturing in *Bleak House*', *The Dickensian*, Vol. 77, 13–22.

Miller, J. (1971) 'Introduction', in N. Page (ed.) *Bleak House*, Harmondsworth: Penguin.

Miyakawa, Yoshihisa and Shigehiko Toyama (eds) (1985) *A Handbook of Nursery Rhymes: Volume I, Text, and Volume II, Concordance*, Tokyo: Kenkyusha.

Monod, Sylvère (1968) *Dickens the Novelist*, Norman: University of Oklahoma.

Opie, Iona and Peter Opie (1951) *The Oxford Dictionary of Nursery Rhymes*, Oxford: Oxford University Press.

Page, Norman (1990) *Bleak House: a Novel of Connections*, Boston: Twayne Publishers.

Partlow, Robert (1961) 'The moving I – a study of the point of view in *Great Expectations*', in Norman Page (ed.) *Hard Times, Great Expectations and Our Mutual Friend*, London: Macmillan.

Pascal, Roy (1977) 'Dickens and mimicry: *Bleak House*', in *The Dual Voice*, Manchester: Manchester University Press, pp. 67–76.

Sadrin, Anny (1988) *Great Expectations*, London: Unwin Hyman.

Schlicke, Paul (ed.) (1999) *Oxford Readers Companion to Dickens*, Oxford: Oxford University Press.

Sell, Roger (ed.) (1994) *Great Expectations*, London; Macmillan.

Shatto, Susan (1988) *The Companion to Bleak House*, London: Unwin Hyman.

Smith, Grahame (1974) *Charles Dickens: Bleak House*, London: Edward Arnold.

Sucksmith, Harvey (1970) *The Narrative Art of Charles Dickens: the Rhetoric of Sympathy and Irony in his Novels*, Oxford: Clarendon Press.

Tambling, Jeremy (ed.) (1998) *Bleak House: Charles Dickens*, London: Macmillan.

Wilson, Angus (1970) *The World of Charles Dickens*, London: Martin Secker & Warburg.

Zabel, Morton (1961) 'The undivided imagination', in George H. Ford and Lauriat Lane, Jr (eds) *The Dickens Critics*, Ithaca: Cornell University Press.

Zwerdling, A. (1973) 'Esther Summerson rehabilitated', *PMLA*, 429–39.

Electronic databases and software

Bank of English (2002) http://titania.cobuild.collins.co.uk/boe-info.html.

Dickens on Disk (1995) Illinois: Hall Design, Inc.

Like the Dickens (1994) New Jersey: Bureau of Electronic Publishing, Inc.

The Oxford English Dictionary on Compact Disc, 2nd edn, Macintosh Version (1993) Oxford: Clarendon Press.

Eighteenth Century Fiction on CD-ROM (1996) Cambridge: Chadwyck-Healey Ltd.

Nineteenth Century Fiction on CD-ROM (2000) Cambridge: Chadwyck-Healey Ltd.

COBUILD English Collocations on CD-ROM (1995) London: HarperCollins Publishers.

CONC Version 1.76 (1994) John Thomson and the Summer Institute of Linguistics, http://users.ox.ac.uk/~ctitext2/resguide/resources/c195.html.

Index of Names and Subjects

Index of Collocations in Dickens

tenderness: timid 163
tenements: dungeon-like 60
terrible: calmly 77; verb passive 71
thank: heartily 49; poorly 166
that sedate and clerical bird, the rook
92
the + adjective + proper name
145–6, 195–8
there are chords in the human mind:
Guppy 174
thickly: said 48
thinking: eyes 20
this is the way 93
thoughtful: amazement 163; baby
154, 156, 154, 156, 164
thoughtfully: face 51; fire 52; hand
51; head 51; looked 48; looking
48; said 47
thoughtfulness: dull 162, 166
three: gentlemen 39
throats: skeleton 160
thunder: solemn 165
tigerish: claws 62
tight: face 123, 166; Hortense 181;
Mrs Snagsby 181
tightness: uncomfortable 163
time: good 42; quick-march 123
timid: days 154, 156, 163;
tenderness 163
timidly: Florence 53; hand 51; said
47
tipstaff: white-headed 61, 105;
apple-faced 61, 105
to consist of 145
to go the extreme animal 90
to occur in 145
to refer to 145
to some extent: to a delightful extent
88; to a distracting extent 88; to
an insupportable extent 88; to an
unspeakable extent 88; to the last
extent 88
toga-like: simplicity 60
told: good-naturedly 76
too-eager: eyes 122, 161
too often 142
touchstone: responsibility 178
towers: extinguisher-topped 106
town: cheerful 158

transparent: business 165
trees: melancholy 163
triangular: coming 166
tributary: streams of tea 165
triumph: saw 67
triumphant: rub 162
triumphantly: completed 76
trouble: cough 180
troubled: eye 122; eyes 70; hand
70; hands 122, 154, 156, 161
true: eyes 22
trusting: eyes 20; face 161
trusty: face 123, 176
truth: love 41
tumbled up 86
turn: sailor-like 60
turned: eyes 40
twinkle: gaspingly 159
twinkling: eyes 23
two: gentlemen 39

ugly: charmingly 82; report 154,
156, 175
unaccustomed: foot 123
uncertainty: heap 175
uncomfortable: tightness 163
uncommon: eye 122
unconscious: head 123, 161;
resolutely 164
understanding: capital 166
undertaker-like: Cupid 60
undisguisable: yawns 162
unfeeling: bosom 71; eyes 71; hair
71
ungrown: despair 158
unhappy: head 72
unmeaning: weakness 165
unpensioning: country
unquiet: hands 160
unsavoury: shelter 161
un-swan-like: manner 60
untaxed powder 168
untidy: legs 123
unwholesome: hand 122, 160
up: blue 43; business 40; door 41;
eye 40; old 42
uphill and downhill and round
crooked corners 93
upright: George 180

womanly: bonnet and apron 166;
  Charley 181
wooden-featured: major 105
woods: frowning 160
workman-like: manner 60
world: deadened 161; link-lighted
  106
worn-out: heavens 163; placidity
  164
worn-out placidity: Lady Dedlock
  181
worried: head 68
wrathful: sunset 62

wretchedness: respectful 164
wrong: charmingly 76
wrong reverends 166
wroth: majestically 76

yard: prison-like 60; rat-infested
  106
yawn: gloomy 162; undisguisable
  162
you know 147
young: gentleman 39; gentlemen
  39
youth: ghost 83; ruin 160